DOMINION

AN ANTHOLOGY OF SPECULATIVE FICTION
FROM AFRICA AND THE AFRICAN DIASPORA

VOLUME ONE

**Dominion: An Anthology of Speculative Fiction
from Africa and the African Diaspora (Volume One)**
Collection ©2020 Zelda Knight (Limited)

www.aurelialeo.com

Previous Publications:
A Maji Maji Chronicle © Eugen Bacon [*Backstory Magazine* Volume 1, Issue 1 (Swinburne
University of Technology, 2016)]
The Unclean © Nuzo Onoh [*Unhallowed Graves* (Canaan-Star Publishing, 2015)]
Sleep Papa, Sleep © Suyi Davies Okungbowa [(*Lights Out: Resurrection* (The Naked
Convos, 2016)]

ISBN-13: 978-1-946024-88-6 (ebook)
ISBN-13: 978-1-946024-79-4 (paperback)
ISBN-13: 978-1-946024-89-3 (hardcover)
Library of Congress Control Number: 2020931970

Line Editing by Joshua Omenga
Editing by Zelda Knight & Ekpeki Oghenechovwe Donald
Book Design by Samuel Marzioli (www.marzioli.blogspot.com)
Cover Illustration © Henrique DLD (www.artstation.com/henriquedld)
Book Cover Design © Maria Spada (www.mariaspada.com)

Printed in the United States of America
First Edition: August 2020
10 9 8 7 6 5 4 3 2 1

CONTENTS

SHORT SYNOPSES

"Trickin'" © Nicole Givens Kurtz: An old god rises up each fall to test his subjects.

"Red_Bati" © Dilman Dila: Once an old woman's pet, a robot sent to mine an asteroid faces an existential crisis.

"A Maji Maji Chronicle" © Eugen Bacon: A magician and his son time-travel to Ngoni country and try to change the course of history.

"The Unclean" © Nuzo Onoh: A dead child returns to haunt his grieving mother with terrifying consequences.

"A Mastery of German" © Marian Denise Moore: Candace, an ambitious middle manager, is handed a project that will force her to confront the ethical ramifications of her company's latest project—the monetization of human memory.

"Convergence in Chorus Architecture" © Dare Segun Falowo: Osupa, a newborn village in pre-colonial Yorubaland populated by refugees of war, is recovering after a great storm when a young man and woman are struck by lightning, causing three priests to divine the coming intrusion of a titanic object from beyond the sky.

"To Say Nothing of Lost Figurines" © Rafeeat Aliyu: A magician teams up with a disgruntled civil servant to find his missing wand.

"Sleep Papa, Sleep" © Suyi Davies Okungbowa: A taboo error in a black market trade brings a man face-to-face with his deceased father—literally.

"Clanfall: Death of Kings" © Odida Nyabundi: The death of a King sets off a chain of events that ensnare a trickster, an insane killing machine, and a princess, threatening to upend their post-apocalyptic world.

PRAISE

"The sheer range of the stories in *Dominion* is a testament to the genius of Black authors working around the world today." — T.L. Huchu, Award-winning and Critically-acclaimed Author of *The Hairdresser of Harare*

"*Dominion* is worth picking up not just for the wealth it contains, but because it's an important anthology, one that will help shape this decade of reading." — Cat Rambo, Nebula Award-winning Author and former President of the Science Fiction and Fantasy Writers of America (SFWA)

"The *Dominion* Anthology contains an explosion of new voices and creativity from all across the diaspora. It's a feast of ideas that connects the old and the new, a song of new songs, and an exciting new collection of writers that I expect we'll see even greater things from in the near future." — Tobias S. Buckell, New York Times Bestselling, World Fantasy Award-winning, Hugo and Nebula Nominated Author

"*Dominion* is a massive achievement—the first new anthology with African editorship in some years. Established writers like Dilman Dila, Mame Bougouma Diene, Ekpeki Oghenechovwe, and Dare Segun Falowo join writers from Africa and the Diaspora. Each story is a coruscating world of its own." — Geoff Ryman, Award-winning and Critically-acclaimed Author of *Air*

"I love this anthology. New voices, new visions—science fiction would be much poorer without it." — Pat Cadigan, Hugo, Locus & Arthur C. Clarke Award-winning Author of *Synners* and Vice President of the British Science Fiction Association

"The *Dominion* Anthology is an excellent addition to the imaginative writing of authors of African/African Diasporan descent. The stories provide an exciting and thought-provoking journey. It's a mind-expanding book where the authors weave cultural details from their respective origins that are fascinating and enlightening. *Dominion* belongs in every speculative fiction anthology collection." — Milton J. Davis, Black Fantastic Author and Owner of MVmedia, LLC

"IF ONE IS LUCKY, A SOLITARY FANTASY CAN TOTALLY TRANSFORM ONE MILLION REALITIES."

—Maya Angelou

A SPECIAL THANKS TO ALL OF OUR KICKSTARTER BACKERS!

Anonymous
Rochell Rushlow
Søren Staugaard
Milton Davis
S. Qiouyi Lu
Steve Zisson
Sara Codair
Linda H. Codega
Selena E. L. Middleton
Cerece Rennie Murphy
Alexandra Fleming
Patrick Osbaldeston
IAN MARTIN
Vincent
Janito V. Ferreira Filho
Dagmar Baumann Phil
Balagtas
Debra Vigil
Kelly Prosen
Patrice Sarath
Keith Johnson
Bethany Sell
Peter J. King
Sara Lunsford
David VonAllmen
Paul F. Volpe
svovli
N.R. Lambert
Michael Sherman
Scott A Saxon
& Martin E Stein
Guthrie Taylor
Maria Haskins
Cynthia Huscroft
Kam Lukasz Przywoski
John Robinson IV
Bryce O'Connor
eSpec Books
Kora M. Sadler
Adam Fory-san Zalonis
William Franks
Andrew and Kate Barton
Kirsten Kowalewski
Rector
Crystal Weber
Christopher
Cody Black
Benjamin C. Kinney
Kevin Carey
Davery Bland
Eddy Webb
Meredith Peruzzi
Carvel Smith
Jaq Greenspon
Sharon Altmann
Matthew Abbott
Ronald H. Miller
David Lystlund
Melody Wolfe
Xander Powers
R. L. Dwyer
Ian J. Foster
Michael "Talthos" Willett
Swordsfall
Jenny L. Davis
Colin Anders Brodd
Jeffery "J.D." Duke
Anthony Jeremy Brett
Paul Cooke
Julian Purdy
Ofeibea Loveless
Dylan
Benito Melany
Arbelo
Chuck Clark
J. Williams
Parker & Malcolm Curtis
Patrick Riley
Andrew Lyons
James Sharpe
Elias Dennis
Matthew Bess
Brittany S.

Bogi Takács and R.B. Lemberg
Christopher J. Williams
Cat Rambo
Dedren Snead
Jon Rettie
James Lucas
Joey O
Michael Y
Bradford Elliott
Eric Hendrickson
Belinda Crawford
Bluegrass Geek
Thea Flurry
Terrie Hashimoto
Joanne Renaud
Aaron J
Michael the Horologist
Kelly Dwyer
Paige L. Christie
Merrie Haskell
Peter Thompson
Maya G
Julian Crosson-Hill
Silvia La Posta
Michelle M. Pessoa
Julie Ann Miller
Justina Robson
Margaret Fisk
David Azzageddi Farnell
Mary Fan
Brandon Crilly
Zoltán Velkei
Jamie Kramer
Krystal Windsor
Bob Huss
If This Goes On (Don't Panic)
Kimberly Wallace
Tania Clucas
Nathaniel Kunitsky
D. Simons
Pat Hayes
Ruth Coy
Josh Kanto
Cathin Yang
CJ Barberan
Jennifer Brozek
Cristina Alves
C Newhouse
Tim Whitworth
K.G. Orphanides
Sheryl R. Hayes
Mike Cassella
Ernesto Pavan
Brian Dysart
Olivia Montoya
John Kusters
Jonathan Leggo
Lutz Hofmann
Paige Kimble
Frances Rowat
Jordan Theyel
Jess Lanzillo
C.C. Finlay
Sarah Mott
Jenelle Clark
The Magus
Kevin James
Doug Hagler
Sammy Lev
Darren Lipman
Bridget McKinney
Demarest
Elsa Klingensmith
Nadia Hutton
D Franklin
Amanda Thomas
Andie Larson
Ruth Ann Orlansky
Nija Mashruwala
Jeremy Brett
Hog and Dice
Greg Berry & Janeka Rector
C. Harrison Fuller

Mike Martens
Markus Dirnberger
GC Rovario-Cole
Tracey & Tom Leroux
Matthew Egerton
Freddie van Os
Heiner Schulze
Scott Fitzgerald Gray
Ronda Searls
noarvara
Steve Scott
Gerry Saracco
Strange Worlds of Jason Kilgore
Kol Ceridwen
Carrie McClain
Alison Lam Brynn
Robin Hill
K. M. Leehan
Jack Shoulder
Deborah A. Flores
Luis Roncayolo
Erin Collins
Sib
Ben Madden
TH
A V Jones
Troy Liput
Madeleine Holly-Rosing
Melissa Manousos
Kelly Kleiser
Joelle Parrott
steven pirie-shepherd
Ari Marmell
Amanda Twigg
Travis Thomas
Susie Munro
Chris Pramas
Elliott Baye
AJ Fitzwater
Adam Hocum Stone
Sharon Scott Brooking
Jim DelRosso
Dawfydd Kelly
Catherine Oyiliagu
Wes Rist
B. Craig Stauber
Nightsky
David Mortman
Alison J. McKenzie
D Fasching
Susanna Chau
Judd Karlman
Jonathan Price
Beatriz Mingo
Gwenhael Le Moine
Alex Claman
S C Turnbull
Michael Gouker
Tom A.
Sarah G. Bolling
Ami Morrison
Phoebe Barton
Carsten Skansen
Thinking Ink Press
Tobias Sechelmann
Nathaniel Roberts
Robert Tienken
Pedro(Te)
Malissa White
Bryan Muensterman
Cathy Green
Cecilia Tan
Zac Searles
William A. Anderson
Brian Foster
Gav Thorpe
Melissa Shumake
Andrea Tatjana
Ariana Brady
Joshua Whitaker
Arnaud D'haijère

Shean,
Semeicha,
Sapphira, and
Corazon Mohammed
Kirsten and Aiyven Mbawa
Pete Smith
Serenity Dee
Kate Malloy
Ellie Russell
August Quinn
Constance Wilde
Erika Christie
John Appel
Nora
Cecil King
Ratchford Family
Sarah A Bates
Sasquatch
Scytrin dai Kinthra
Ojiki Augustine Jr.
Crystal Hall
Leedvermaak
PJ Nielson
Sasha De'ath
RaJaRak
Isaac Chappell
Katherine S
Pat Cadigan
GMarkC
Mathieu D'Ordine
Elizabeth Doherty
Dauchon Richard Sands
Maurice Gray
Christian Buggedei
Kynerae
Uriah J. Mach
Daniel M. Perez
R J Theodore
BookWol
Kiya Nicoll
Tracy Pinkelton
Nancy Blue Tice
Katlina Sommerberg
David Voderberg
Ben Nash
MyraD
Ira Grace
Zack O.
Laura B. & John C.
Dab of Darkness Reviews
Cheri Kannarr
Marco Cultrera
Robyn M
Wilhelm D Meriwether
Cathy Greytfriend
Kimberly Lucia
Fluker
Erik T Johnson
S. Kay Nash
Kae Petrin
Daniel Ironwood
Andrew Groen
Sharona Ginsberg
Adrian
Steven Peiper
Sam Nelson
Greg Stolze
Damien Brunetto
T. Kurt Bond
Damba Yansane
Kip Corriveau
Nija Mashruwala
Joseph Jones
Dominic
Nicholas George
Elizabeth Bonesteel
Steven B
Katherine Delzell
Victoria Baker
StLOrca (Ravenclaw or die!)
Elizabeth R. McClellan
A Grue
L. Grabenstetter

V. S. Holmes
Ruth EJ Booth
Faye Jeffries
Shaka Jamal
Matt & Camille Knepper
Elias Dennis
Jamal Joseph Crespo
yohanna baez
Hal Mangold
Arinn Dembo
RM Ambrose
Sambor Mika
CS Fitzgerald
Classicista
Whitney Chaka Barber
Violet Walker
Janet Tait
Paul Alex Gray
Jeremy D. Mohler
Edwin Okolo
Gabriel Gerni
Adri Joy
Sabrina Spruitenburg
Joyce Torme
Maur
Bruce Baugh
donnan33ly
J. Hill
Christoph Paul Aulbach
Kurtis Newell-Campbell
Katy Rex
Justin
Atthis Arts
Chanza
John M. Portley
Marie Irshad-Nordgren
RP Nausicaah
Fraser Ronald
Paul T. Davies
Cullen 'Towelman' Gilchrist
Tod McCoy
Chris Joseph
The Leaking Pen
Florian Rasche
Emma Bartholomew
Seymour Lavine
Elizabeth Buchan
Oliver Lauenstein
Seth W. Stauffer
Hasinah Koda El
Tiffany Peng
Forrest W
Marcus R. Jackson
Darrah Chavey
Robert Monroe, Jr.
Kevin Caler
Anne-Sophie Sicotte
David Proctor
Shawn Catanzarite
Gary D Henton
David Semmes
John Skinner Jr.
Heather Valentine
Cain Williams
Judith Tarr
James Kretsinger
Joe M McDermott
Victora Martin
Toni Saktiawan
David Bonner
Karl Moore
Matthew Cole
Zeb Berryman
Anna S
Jonathan Cohn
T.J. Franks
Jack Blastum
Michael Beck
Shay J
Derek Fletcher
Laurie Lamar
Bobbi Boyd
John Winkelman

FOREWORD

TANANARIVE DUE

My parents named me for an African city: the capital city of Madagascar, now called Antananarivo. When I had the opportunity to study for a Master's degree in English Literature at the University of Leeds, the course that most appealed to me was not in Victorian literature or American literature, but in Nigerian literature, where I first discovered works by Nobel laureate Wole Soyinka, Chinua Achebe, Buchi Emecheta, and Ben Okri. I felt shocked and betrayed that I had never been exposed to African writers during all of my years of schooling in the U.S. My world was forever expanded—and now, with the publication of *Dominion*, yours will be too. This electrifying anthology not only introduces readers to new voices in literature, but these writers all have embraced a component I never dreamed about as a student: it's all *speculative fiction* from African and African Diasporic writers.

The world has taken note of powerful speculative fiction rooted in African experiences because of superstars like Nigerian-American authors Nnedi Okorafor (Hugo and Nebula award-winner who coined the term "Africanfuturism"); and Tomi Adeyemi, author of the international YA bestseller *Children of Blood and Bone*. But they are only two examples of a growing number of Black writers who are finding platforms to tell their own stories of the fantastic and the future. And, beyond introducing additional voices rooted in Africa and the African Diaspora, this anthology also includes African-American voices—a revolutionary compilation that bridges the oceans between us.

I have always felt a deep desire to close the divide between Africans and African-Americans, which explains why my first book series that began with *My Soul to Keep* was centered around an immortal from Ethiopia. My protagonist, Dawit, fought in the famed 1896 Battle of Adwa, when Ethiopia repelled Italian troops...and *also* had experienced U.S. slavery, a hybrid of the Black Diasporic experience of both colonization and slavery, as if I were trying to knit together my desires to tell unknown African history *and* unknown

African-American history. I teach Afrofuturism in the Department of African-American Studies at UCLA, and while the definition coined by cultural observer Mark Dery in 1993 focused on African-American art and discourse, my focus in class is the speculative arts of the African Diaspora—literature, comics, music and film that embrace and repair history, celebrate myth and magic, and imagine technologies with Black people centered rather than sidelined or erased.

That's why this anthology, *Dominion*, had such an explosive effect on me.

Whether it's the reflection on existence and attachment in "Red_Bati" by Dilman Dima, the horror of curses and punishment in "The Unclean" by Nuzo Onoh, or the intersection of commerce and human memory in "A Mastery of German" by Marian Denise Moore, every story in this anthology brims in creativity and thoughtfulness as these authors confront the Old World and the New, the magical and futuristic planes, and the age-old question of what it truly means to be human. Every selection is strong, each voice distinct, and I've never read an anthology like it.

Sit back and enjoy these stories of myths and juju and robots and monsters.

In these stories, the curses are real. And the future is now.

TRICKIN'

NICOLE GIVENS KURTZ

The time had returned. Nestled beneath the rolling peaks from the mountain ranges, honeycombs of caves spread out in their gigantic girth, providing shelter from the weeping clouds. Raoul emerged from one of those caves. He scratched his scalp beneath his thick dreadlocked hair and squinted against the rain pouring across the lands.

The black, whispery rain fell, chasing everyone indoors and turning the roads further down the city to a glistening dark. Desperation clung to each drop, splattering on the unyielding surface. Once, a bustling metropolis existed, but now, only disappointment remained. A hushed quiet blanketed everything. Only the rain's soft drumming resonated throughout the valley, its melody rising up against the thick, humid hush.

"Great. Monsoon season." Raoul, a tall, but athletic man, shrugged against the cold rain pellets that bounced off the trees and splattered onto him. The bleak morning stretched onward, hovering in its gloominess. He adjusted his hood and flexed his feet inside his rain boots. Parts of him felt stiff and others felt foreign. The dark skin held hints of hair, tight black coils that sprung back to form after he tried to smooth them out. Different.

Yet, different didn't mean bad, only new. With it came an exhilaration to explore. Raoul jumped up and down on the balls of his feet before hunching back into his hood. Just inside the mouth of the cave, he peered out across the city's broken landscape of discarded storefronts, flooded and cracked sidewalks, and gloomy pedestrians. He couldn't see their faces from this distance, but their bodies spoke for them. Bent over, slow moving, they crept along the squall as if their spirits had been saturated with sadness and despair.

Despite the mournful mood around him, his spirit was glad. Today held special—no, *important*—meaning. After a long sleep, he'd awakened. He stepped out further, yanking on an old hoodie to protect his hair. With fluid familiarity, he slipped his dagger in its scabbard into the hoodie's front pocket. Who knew what or who he might run into on the path down or when he got to town? He'd travel light, risking the saturation he'd get in favor of being able to survive. He'd already missed far too much of the events, if the declining and decrepit structures could be believed.

With a deep breath, he could hear his momma's wisdom in his ear. Procrastination was the thief of time, and he'd wait no longer. The moment had come. With his hood pulled over his head, he set out into the downpour, eyes squinting against the rain, but his heart brimming with determination.

Today was Halloween.

Raoul made his way down the muddy slope, through the squall, and into a well-worn foot path that led into the city from the caves. The concrete buildings, tall but weak, pressed in against him. They spoke of another time, when they glistened with neon lights and dancing pumpkins. Now, they sat mournfully dark and glum.

As he peered out from his hood's shadow, he noticed how subdued and empty everywhere seemed. Once he reached Brower Avenue, he spied the tell-tale signs of life. Smoke swirls wafted up against the rain. The acidic whiff of hidden compost and hints of fire and food pervaded the air. As he slinked through the near-empty streets, his stomach rumbled, but he would wait. Treats would soon satisfy his gnawing cravings. Someone would venture out once the dark thickened, having forgotten the importance of this day. When they did, he'd be there to greet them with open arms, a raw hunger, and a sharp weapon.

Afterwards, he'd start on the door to door rounds, hoping to encounter those who recalled the importance of the day, the old ways, the *best* ways of which it appeared that some had forgotten. No orange and black parades or décor. No singing skeletons or black cats screeching. No witches, though Raoul doubted this. Witches had a way of blending in or hiding in plain sight. Most likely, there were still witches.

The abandoned streets of a once major metropolis unfolded in front of him. Already, nature had begun to reclaim what was hers. Thick, leafy vegetation crawled over defunct vehicles and concrete, sprouting and oozing over cracked sidewalks and curbs. Braving the rain, early morning critters scurried along the path; sleek and slick, they blended in with the shadows and rain. The only thing visible was a flash of teeth or a blink of swift movement.

He didn't know what happened to the others who had come before. When he woke, the memories had a haziness that left him disjointed and disconnected from the times before. He remembered the décor, but not much else beyond his present thought. Unreliable though his memory had become, he didn't know if that was how it had always been or how he *wanted* it to be.

Some spoke of a virus that each warring country deployed against the other in an effort to gain the upper hand in a battle already slippery from bloodshed.

Raoul's ancestors believed the countries had deserted their peoples, leaving them to fight in a debate that had long outlived its mouthpieces. Even his grandparents had been ancient to Raoul, and the older ones—the survivors—didn't know when the wars had ended. Only that at some point, no one spoke of it anymore.

No treaty was signed.

No declaration of peace was announced.

Just the eerie silence and burning stench of hundreds of thousands dead. Even within their semi-protected valley, many had perished.

Raoul shook his head to rouse himself from his musings. He tucked his chin into his hoodie against the rain. That rested in the past, out of his reach. Instead, he focused on the day, the one constant since his youth.

They celebrated on Halloween. He did remember that. All Hallows' Eve, the day to sacrifice to the darkness and all the powerful gods that governed humanity's souls. The ones who listened to their wretched crying and whining about their plight, instead of simply enjoying that they still drew breath. Raoul shook his head at the thought. Still, he stood straight and lifted his chin. These people would do so again. The ones who kept to the old ways and honored him would provide treats. They would be spared his wrath. No tricks for them.

Those that tried to deny him—well, he had something to give them. The cold smile on his face captured droplets of rainwater as it slid across his lips. The wind had picked up and now the rain fell at an angle, slanting and slapping into the buildings. It sounded like the clattering of dry rice. Must be growing colder, he thought, and it killed his grin. Colder weather meant folks would retreat into their homes, huddle against the fire, against each other. No, he needed them out in the streets, celebrating the return of Halloween!

He made a right turn and tumbled down into a residential street. An uneasy silence blanketed the neighborhood. He reached an abandoned single lane bridge. Already drenched, the cold rain made his hands numb. He flexed them to work out the creeping cold. All around him, the wet earth waited in hushed desperation. His gaze swept over the darkened doors, shut tight against the rain and the unknown. So much so he could feel it, a tangible need that crawled over his skin. He had to stop himself from digging into his flesh to make it stop. The last time he did that, he had needed stitches to seal up the wound. He'd nearly bled to death.

That *had* happened to him. He frowned. A haziness rose from where the memory should be. It blocked his access to the information as if it had been hacked. Only ragged bits of data escaped for him to access. He fingered the scars along his right wrist, but soon pushed the jagged memory away.

Quiet.

Only the hushed rain drumming against metallic shingles and tiled roofs. He walked past narrow, gloomy alleys and side streets, occupied by shadows and overflowing rain barrels.

There! The crunch of rainboots on gravel and loosened concrete. With his ears pricked in warning, he slowed down his movement. His muscles tensed as he inched back into the shadows crafted from the bridge's coverage. Would he get treats? His mouth salivated at the promise and prospect. Yummy goodness that would quiet his complaining stomach. With gritted teeth, he fingered his blade's scarred leather scabbard before taking it out. Small, but effective. A sigh—a short breath above the rain pattering on the pavement.

One pumpkin. Two pumpkins. Three pumpkins! He sprang from the gloom, white teeth and clean knife glaring, slicing through the dimness and tearing at the fiber of apathy and disdain.

"Trick or treat?!" He roared, his voice echoing off the bridge's underbelly.

A weathered old man stumbled backward, eyes wide, eyebrows drawn upward in terror and mouth agape in surprise at the sight of Raoul. His booted feet dragged the skinny, almost skeletal legs, the boots too heavy to move as quickly as their owner wanted. The rubber soles stumbled clumsily on the dry pavement beneath the bridge. "What?" The man's wiry and wrinkled arms shot up to protect his face. With his chin quivering, he seemed unable to form words. Strips of white hair lay plastered to his nearly bald head.

Pathetic.

"Trick or treat?" Raoul repeated. His belly rumbled in impatience.

But patient he had to be. To rush would be dishonorable.

"Uh, treat." The elderly man lowered his arms and drew a shallow breath. He reached into his rain-soaked pants pocket and removed a vial. He passed it to Raoul, his hands shaking so much that his rings clattered against the glass. Raoul snatched it and the elderly man yelped.

"Happy Halloween!" Raoul cajoled the elderly man, before cracking open the vial and dumping its contents into his wide, open mouth.

Some of the scarlet liquid smeared on his nose and cheeks. He shouldn't be so careless with the treats. With dirty nailed-fingers, he swiped the fluid from his nose and sucked his fingers. Blood-smeared and excited, he grinned at the man with a bemused expression.

But the old man had pushed on, not braving a single backward look. His boots slapped at the water puddles as he hurried away into the downpour.

Raoul gave a dismissive wave of his hands, unconcerned. No matter, he told himself.

Lips stained but stomach still rumbling, Raoul blinked back the fiery hunger. Now that he'd eaten something, his mental fog cleared. He wiped his mouth with the back of his hand, drawing a thin watery red streak across it. He was nowhere near sated. He sighed and his shoulders sagged. He had devoured the treat much too fast and didn't savor it. Licking his lips for the remnants of it, he searched his surroundings.

He would need more treats before tonight was over and he had to return to the caves, until next year. But there was no reason to panic. Not yet. Plenty of time left in the evening. A grin curled the corners of his blood-stained mouth.

Plenty of time.

The weather shifted, and the shower with it. Now, it had become more of a mist. Great. People would start to wander out of their little hidey-holes, thinking the rain had stopped, unaware it was only a small pause. The area stank. Desperation was a terrible aroma.

Raoul pushed on into the drizzle, veering away from the protection of the bridge's overpass. His dreadlocks felt heavy against his back, but he couldn't risk getting them wet. His power came from them, and tonight he needed all of his mojo. Sweat mixed with rain seeped into his eyes. He no longer felt cold. His body's heat had turned up in response to the fuel the treats provided.

He stalked down the vacant street. With the slap of his boots against the puddles, he made enough noise to send those who sought to avoid him scurrying. Not the best tactic, but as was the custom, he would go to their residences. His face distorted into a grin as giggles spilled out of the alleyway he'd just passed. A light, lyrical sound against the drab day.

Soon, a pair of lovebirds appeared at the alley's end. The woman, with kohl-smudged eyes, stopped short. She clutched a red umbrella in one hand and in the other, her lover's hand. He was a much larger male, with a dark hoodie and beady little eyes that peered out from underneath it. She wore a satchel style purse swung across her torso. Faded and tattered, it held all she had. The male stopped short but didn't carry anything.

Defenseless.

In this dark and dreary place? Foolish. Raoul's eyebrows rose as he looked closer, his eyes burning as he did so. Beneath the man's hoodie was a lithe and nimble body that spoke to a somewhat healthy diet and engagement with nature. Still, hollowness rimmed his eyes and his matted hair had not been cleaned, cut, or styled in years.

As she took him in, the petite woman swallowed hard and so loud that Raoul heard it and chuckled. Her eyes lingered around his face, over his wet skin, and the smirk on his lips. The woman appeared to have been pried out of bed and thrust into the wet, cold day. She lifted her chin in greeting.

"You on the prowl?" the man asked, forcing Raoul's attention back to him. "We don't have any food." His free hand rolled tight into a fist. With his other hand, he guided the woman behind him. "So get gone!"

Raoul nodded and removed his hands from his hoodie's front pocket. With a loud clearing of his throat, he asked, "Trick or treat?"

The man's eyebrows hunched down into a V, a furry caterpillar above his tiny, dark eyes. Raoul felt the man's scrutiny as he took him in. The man let go of his lover's hand and balled it too into a fist. He scrubbed his fist through his buzzed hair.

"Don't nobody get down with that crap anymore. Look around! We're drowning! The gods have abandoned us."

Raoul's vision burned as the man's words wormed their way into his ears, slithering into his mind, where they laid eggs that would hatch out raw anger. *Abandoned?* The word held little meaning for him, and he discarded it. Tonight was his, and he wouldn't let anyone sway his opportunity. He wouldn't stomach the insolence.

In the blink of an eye, the dagger appeared in his fist, and he leapt forward, screeching, "Then TRICK!"

He plunged the dagger deep into the man's chest, feeling the sharp blade glide through flesh, through weakened muscle, and then wedging itself into bone. A rib maybe?

The woman screamed, and backpedaled from the stabbing, from the violence, from the blistering truth of her situation. The man's blood sprayed Raoul's face and the upper sections of his hoodie in warm, scarlet streams. As he wrenched the weapon free, he chanted, "Trick or treat! Trick or treat!"

A crimson blur unfurled as Raoul and the man crashed to the drenched ground, Raoul stabbing him over and over again. Once spent, he pushed himself to his feet. The dagger's slippery handle had caused him to cut himself too. In the opened wound, a golden-orange light glowed. Raoul sucked his teeth. "Damn."

He wiped the warm blood from his face and licked it from his fingers. He even tongue-cleaned the dagger's surface, careful to avoid its sharp blade, but eager not to waste the treat.

A whimper interrupted the moment's enjoyment. He released an *ahhh*. His gaze flickered toward the woman, a scowl transforming his features. She stood tight-lipped and shuddering. Then she crouched on her knees, a jar in her trembling hands, the wet curtain of hair hiding her face. Her arms strained from the weight of her treat. The slick black coat shined from either blood or rain. Maybe both.

"What have we here?" Raoul tilted his head sideways as he turned fully to face her. Like a silly black cat, she'd been frozen to the spot, unable to flee when given a chance. He could unleash another trick on her, but no. That wouldn't be fair.

And yet she didn't flee even now. "You."

She swallowed again at his brusque tone, and hoisted the glass higher. "I offer my apologies! We—I—didn't recognize you in your new costume, Great One. Here is my treat!"

Raoul wiped a hand over his face. Beside her, the satchel's flap laid open. The jar contained a deep, red liquid. She shook so much that if the lid hadn't been screwed on tight, the treat would've sloshed all over her hands. Instead it jostled around the jar's interior. She stared at the ground, watching her lover's blood leak out and combine with the now misting rain and coupled on the pavement, pooling and congealing.

Wasteful.

It turned his stomach, the loss of deliciousness; but it hadn't been offered to him. So, despite the sweet anticipation that crawled into his mouth, making his lips salivate in longing, Raoul let out a frustrated breath. *Fresh.* He could tell by the vibrant color and its warmth that it had been sitting around. Tiny bubbles of condensation littered the jar's top closest to the lid that wasn't ruined by the sloshing.

The woman offered an ample treat indeed. He took it with long, blood-stained fingers, and brought it close to his nose. He inhaled deep and full, pulling the scent into his nostrils as if air to breathe. The coppery aroma tickled his sweet tooth.

His lips curved upward in a wide grin. This treat came from multiple donors, not just this one soul. The flavors mixed within the concoction. A true treat indeed! She'd been prepared, but had allowed her partner to die.

Yes! This will do.

He wouldn't have to perform a trick on the woman. They hadn't recognized his new costume. He leaned down closer to her face. She flinched, but only slightly. Now, so close, he could smell the mint on her breath and the fear lacing her tongue.

"Happy Day!" he shouted, stood up straight, and turned on his heel, the jar clutched in his fist. With a last warning look, he set about his journey, no longer fuming about the number of tricks he'd have to provide. He enjoyed the treats, not the rigmarole that came with delivering tricks. The male had become a time bomb, and he'd dispatched him.

As he started down the road, toward the central part of the once vibrant downtown, he heard the woman's sobs.

He left the neighborhood, heading instead to the western side of town. Raoul found a secluded spot between two buildings with a narrow space between them. With the flick of his wrist, the jar's lid came off and landed with a wet *smack* on the ground. Huddled beneath a tattered awning eaten away by mold, he took a long drag of the treat, feeling the lukewarm blood glide down his throat and into his belly.

When he paused, he looked around the wet brick, spied a few huddled people on the sidewalk, hidden by dark plastic tarps. He'd missed them, so intent on consuming his treat. Now he heard them scurrying beneath the weather-ravaged plastic like restless insects. Spaced out along the sidewalk like slugs, these people dared the rain and slept on the cold, wet pavement, sheltered inside their makeshift cocoons. When these people emerged from their internment, it wouldn't be as beautiful butterflies, but as ghosts, spirits leaving behind rail-thin husks of their former selves.

They had no treats to give and tricks had already been visited upon them by Fate. No, these people's treats had soured.

Raoul drained the rest of his treat, licking the jar's rim when he had depleted the contents. He burped; his mouth flooded with the strong taste of copper. Tense, he rolled his shoulders to ease the bunched muscles. Sighing, he set the jar down on the ground. He had to pace himself.

He had a long, fun night ahead.

Rain continued despite the arrival of night. Pitched in darkness, Raoul slithered along the homes and streets, ringing dilapidated doorbells and banging rusty door knockers. Thunder crashed overhead. No one hid in the dark recesses or nooks and crannies of the city. They'd hidden behind doors and cloaked themselves in a sense of security. Nevertheless, they gave him what he craved, or he gave them a trick. Trickin' wasn't easy, but damn, it could be fun.

Sated and sleepy, Raoul made his way to whence he had come. Skinned knuckles and weary limbs weighed him down as he made the trek up the muddy slope toward the caves. His heartbeat thrummed inside him as if humming out its joy. His boots stuck occasionally in the thick mud, and each step took the energy he no longer had. Raoul had worn this costume to its near end.

He sighed. Body singing with fatigue, he managed a small smile. Today had been glorious; he could not deny it. He licked his lips and tasted the faint flavor of the numerous treats he'd received, all given freely in the spirit of ancient times, in the long shadow of lore. Despite his initial concern, the people hadn't forgotten. A few here and there, but most of them still clung to the old ways, the nostalgia of when the town had been great and filled with festivals, trickin' and treatin' galore.

With a deep sigh of relief, he reached the threshold of the cave. He dropped to his knees, exhausted but satisfied. Raoul's lids grew heavy. With effort, he rolled over, putting his back against the slick rock. He tilted his head back, and at last, gave in to the exhaustion.

His eyelids lowered and did not open again.

Inside the cave, a black and smoky essence filled the space, funneling from Raoul's gaping mouth.

Only a few hours more.

The day after

"There! There he is!" Gina's hoarse voice coughed out as she climbed the muddy slope toward the shadow figure slumped against the cave's mouth.

She and Tyree had taken advantage of the slack in the rain to slip out into the morning mist. The light provided illumination to the usual morning dark. They had searched the cityand only brief comments and whispers about Raoul's strange and murderous behavior had been discussed, but not his whereabouts.

"Raoul! Raoul! Man, what the hell?" Tyree reached down and shook Raoul roughly on the shoulder. Raoul's head lolled to the left, his body drenched. Each squeeze produced a handful of rainwater. "He's soaked!"

"He's got blood all over his clothes. What the hell happened? Look!" Gina said, brushing the hoodie back from his face, as she cupped his cheek with her other hand. "He's breathing, so he's alive."

She tilted her chin to Tyree.

"Is he injured?" Tyree stood up and shoved his hands into his jeans pocket. "This ain't gonna be like that last time. Right? When he was in so much pain, he rolled up in a ball? He had that breakdown. I mean, he just freakin' melted..."

"No. This isn't like that. Ty, he's gotten cut, deeply. We've got to get this cleaned up before it festers..." Gina lifted the injured hand for Tyree to see. She pushed her braids out of her face and tossed them over her shoulder. Already soaked, the strands lead a swatch of water across her black jacket. Her jeans had been smeared with mud and flakes of garbage from their dumpster diving last night.

"Come on, Raoul." Tyree reached down and grabbed Raoul's injured hand. He then squeezed it as hard as he could in his own two large, strong hands.

"Ow! My hand!" Raoul exclaimed, rousing, his dark, unfocused eyes shifting from Gina to Tyree and back again as he wrenched his hand free. "What? W-w-where, where am I?"

He raised his hand, and turned it this way and that way, as if it didn't belong to him. He pulled it back and held it close to his chest. When he tried to sit up, he fell backward against the rock. Wincing in pain, he shut his eyes and groaned.

Gina crouched down beside him, her knees sinking into the soft earth. "You're at the mouth of the cave..."

"Last night was something," Tyree said, his eyes as flat as the tone of his voice. "You remember anything?"

"Are you bleeding anywhere else?" Gina touched his shoulder.

Raoul flinched and waved her off. "Bleeding? What? I dunno. It's all so damn hazy." He rubbed his temple with his fingertips. "I've just got one hell of a headache."

"Let's get you back home." Gina stood up and with Tyree's help, hoisted Raoul to his feet. They draped his arms round their shoulders, one each, and took a step.

"Hurry up. This place gives me the creeps." Tyree shifted Raoul's arm around his neck, allowing him to distribute the weight between himself and Gina. "Dark. Eerie. What the hell were you doing up here?"

"Wait. I'm gonna be sick!" Raoul tried to untangle himself from them as he scrambled to get clear. Tyree windmilled to keep himself upright, and Gina shouted at the rough treatment of her neck.

"Oh! Raoul!" Gina shouted, rubbing her neck. "You yanked my braids."

Raoul couldn't apologize even if he wanted. A short distance away, retching sounds and the *splat* of violent vomiting from Raoul sliced through the steady rain.

"Oh that's rank!" Tyree clasped his hand over his mouth. He shook his head and looked away. "Reminds me of that time we had too many treats..."

Gina silenced him with a look.

Raoul wiped his mouth with the back of his hand and got unsteadily to his feet. He wavered as he took a few steps back to his friends. Gina hurried to him and gestured to Tyree to join her.

"Come on, help! Damn it, Tyree! Help!" Gina implored, coughing to camouflage the chuckle at Tyree's queasiness, her anger gone.

The trio made their way back down the slope under the watchful eyes of the Great One. The gathering dark inside the cave rippled with laughter. Sated by treats, full and growing sleepy, they settled into the cave's shelter once more.

Next time, he would get a new costume.

RED_BATI

DILMAN DILA

Red_Bati's battery beeped. Granny flickered, and the forest around her vanished. She sighed in exaggerated disappointment. He never understood why she called it a forest, for it was just two rows of trees marking the boundary of her farm. When she was alive, she had walked in it every sunny day, listening to her feet crunching dead twigs, to her clothes rustling against the undergrowth, to the music of crickets, feeling the dampness and the bugs, sniffing at the rotten vegetation, which she thought smelled better than the flowers that Akili her grandson had planted around her house. Now, she liked to relive that experience. With his battery going down, he could not keep up a real life projection and, for the first time, she became transparent, like the blue ghost in the painting that had dominated a wall of her living room. Akili's mother had drawn it to illustrate one of their favorite stories.

Granny laughed at the memory. "That ghost!" she said. Her voice was no longer musical. It was full of static.

He could not recharge her. He had to save power, but he did not want to shut her down because he had no one else to talk to. He did not get lonely, not the way she had been: so lonely that she would hug him and her tears would drip onto his body, making him flinch at the thought of rust. She would hug him even though she complained that his body was too hard, not soft and warm like that of Akili. He did not get lonely like that, but Akili had written a code to make him want to talk to someone all the time, and he had not had a chance for a conversation since the accident, twelve hours ago.

He had resurrected her after her death, while he waited for a new owner. He used all recordings he had made of her during their ten years together to create a holographic imitation of her so he could have someone to talk to. It was not like walking with her in the mango forest, or sitting at her feet on the porch as she knitted a sweater and watched the sun go down. Technically, he was talking to himself; but it was the only chance he had for conversation.

"I would have enjoyed being an astronaut," she said, floating a few feet in front of him, her limbs kicking in slow motion the way humans moved in zero gravity. She was careful to keep behind the shelves, out of sight of the security camera. "This is the—"

She stopped talking abruptly when white-cell.sys beeped. A particle of ice was floating about like a predator shark. If it touched him, he would rust. He jerked, like a person awaking from a bad sleep, though the ice was ten meters away. Steel clamps pinned him onto a shelf. He could not get away.

The half-empty storage room looked like a silver blue honeycomb. They had dumped him in it after the accident ripped off his forearm. The Captain had evaluated his efficiency and, seeing it down to 80%, tagged him DISABLED. They could not fix his arm on the ship, so they shut him down and dumped him in storage until he got back to Earth. Entombed alive. Left to die a cold death.

"You won't die," Granny said, laughing. She sat on a fuel pod in a cell on the opposite shelf. "It's just a little ice. It's not even water."

He had lived all his life dreading rust, watching his step to avoid puddles, blow-drying his kennel every hour, turning on the heater all the way up to prevent dew from forming. He knew it was irrational, for his body, made of high-grade stainless Haya steel, was waterproof. He never understood his aquaphobia. Had Akili infected him with a program to ensure he stayed indoors on rainy days? Very likely. Granny liked playing in the rain as much as she liked walking in the mango forest. Yet every time she did, she got a fever, sometimes malaria. Akili might have written a code to force Red_Bati to stay indoors on rainy days, and so Granny, who used him as a walking aid and guide, stayed indoors too. Red_Bati could have searched for this code and rewritten it to rid himself of this stupid fear, but he did not. He loved it, for it made him feel human.

"I'm not worried about the ice," he said. "It's the temperature."

He was in Folder-5359, where temperatures stayed at a constant -250° C to preserve fuel pods. Technically, the cold would not kill him. He had a thermal skin that could withstand environments well below -400° C, but it needed power to function. Once his battery ran down, he would freeze and that would damage his e-m-data strips. Though these could be easily and cheaply replaced, he would lose all his data, all the codings that made him Red_Bati and not just another red basenji dog, all his records of Granny. He would die.

"That won't be a bad thing," Granny said, chuckling. "If you were a true dog, you'd be as old as I am and wishing for death."

He was not a dog. He was a human trapped in a pet robot.

Granny chuckled again, but did not say anything to mock him again. She watched the ice and tried to touch it, but it passed through her fingers and floated upwards. It would not touch Red_Bati, after all. He relaxed. If he had flesh and muscles, this would have been a visible reaction. Instead, white-cell.sys reverted to sleep mode, the red light in his eyes vanished and his pupils regained their brownish tint.

His battery beeped, now at 48% for white-cell.sys had used up a lot of power in just a few seconds. In sixteen hours and forty-three minutes, it would hit zero, and then he would die.

"You're not a human in a dog's body," Granny finally said, still watching the ice as it floated towards the ceiling.

"I am," Red_Bati said.

"Humans have spirits," Granny said. "You don't."

"I do," Red_Bati said.

"You can't," Granny said.

"Why not? I'm aware of myself."

"Doesn't mean you have it."

"Why not?"

"You're not a natural-born."

Red_Bati wanted to argue his point, to remind her of things that made him human, like agoraphobia; to remind her that he got consciousness from a chip and lines of code, just as humans did from their hearts, and brains. He was not supposed to be conscious, much less super intelligent; but Akili had wanted Granny to have more than just a pet, so he installed Z-Kwa and turned Red_Bati into a guide, a walking aid, a cook, a cleaner, a playmate, a personal assistant, a friend, a doctor, a gardener, a nurse, and even a lover if she had wanted. She could live her last years as she pleased rather than suffer in a nursing home.

After she died, Akili had put him up for sale along with all her property and memorabilia. For a moment, Red_Bati had feared that Akili would remove Z-Kwa and wipe his memory, but Akili contracted a cleaning firm to get rid of Granny's property and either forgot or did not care to tell them about the chip. Red_Bati was too smart to let them know he was more than just a pet. Nor did he show it off to the people who bought him, Nyota Energy, an asteroid mining company that, rather than buying miner-bots, found it cheaper to convert pets into miners. They gave him a new bios and software, a thermal coat, x-ray vision, and modified his limbs and tongue to dig rocks. They did not look into his ribcage cabin so they did not see Z-Kwa, otherwise they would have removed it. When they shut him down after his accident, Z-Kwa had turned him back on, aware that if his battery drained, he would die. He had self-preservation instincts, just like any other living thing with a spirit, and he wanted to tell her all these things, but she was draining his battery.

"Sorry," he said. "I have to conserve power."

"That's okay," she said.

He blinked, and she vanished. His battery life increased by two hours.

He examined the three clamps that pinned him to the cell. They had not expected him to awake, so they had not used electronic locks. With his tongue, he pushed the bolts on the clamps, and they snapped open. He could escape. The room had only one camera, at the front, to track crew who came in to pick up fuel pods. If it saw him, the ship would know he had awoken and service_bots would pounce on him and remove his battery. To hide from it, he needed the identity of another robot.

He checked the duty roster he had received before the accident. He did not expect the fuel roster to have changed since his accident only affected the cleaning roster. The next pickup was due in an hour, a karbull dragon-horse. It would not do. Six hours hence, it would be a tomcat, and then in thirteen hours, a robot that looked like him, a basenji dog. He wrote an identity-stealing app and hibernated.

He awoke ten minutes to time. His battery was down to 35% and would last for another ten hours. He slipped out of the cell, staying behind the shelves to hide from the camera. He floated to Shelf-4B and hid inside Cell-670, where he could see Cell-850, which had the fuel pod to be picked up next. He heard the outer door open and close. Then the inner door opened. The two doors ensured the temperature of Folder-5359 stayed at a constant -250° C, while the ship was a warm 16° C.

The basenji floated into view, riding a transporter tube. It saw Red_Bati but did not raise any alarms. It adhered strictly to its programming and ignored anything out of the ordinary, assuming the ship was in total control. Astral-mining companies stopped sending self-aware and self-learning robots many years ago after a ship had developed minor engine trouble and its crew, seeing their chance of returning safely to Earth had dropped to ninety-nine percent, landed on an asteroid and refused to move until rescue came. Fearing to incur such needless losses, the miners resolved to send only 'dumbots' incapable of making vital decisions without human input.

For a moment, Red_Bati wondered what had happened to the owner of this basenji. Its jaw was slightly open, its tongue stuck out to imitate panting, a design that little boys favored. He hoped its owner had only grown tired of it and had not died. He did not feel empathy the way Granny felt whenever she saw a dead ant; she felt so terrible that she would bury it. Granny had thought a dead child more horrible than a dead ant and Red_Bati wanted to feel as she might have felt.

He waited until the basenji turned its back to him as it positioned the tube to suck the pod out of the cell. He turned on his x-ray vision to see the basenji's central processor and the comm receptor chip, both located just below the backbone, and on which the basenji's serial number and LANIG address were respectively printed. Two seconds later, his app was ready.

It would take ninety seconds for the pod to enter the tube, and in that time, Red_Bati had to take over the basenji's identity. He aimed a laser beam at the other dog's left ear, which was its comm antennae, to disable it. He activated his comm receptor at the same moment that he fired the laser beam. There would be a delay of a thousand micro-seconds, between the basenji's going offline and

Red_Bati's assuming its identity, but the ship would not read that as strange.

Red_Bati went into hoover mode which consumed a lot of power but allowed him to move quicker. He tapped on the power button at the base of the basenji's tail, and the basenji shut down in three seconds. He grabbed it by the hind legs, guided it into an empty cell, and clamped it.

He raced back to the carrying tube and ten seconds later a beep came. The pod was inside the tube. He pushed it to the door. The tube had a temperature-conditioner that kept the pod chilled at -250° C to keep it from decaying. If a decayed pod ended up in a fuel tank, the engine's temperature would shoot from 80° C to a blistering 300° C within fifteen minutes. Fire would break out in the Ma-RXK section while there would be explosions in the Ma-TKP section. With eight engines, the ship would not stop if one was damaged, though its speed would drop. But fire in the engine made the ship vulnerable to hijacking.

Red_Bati turned a dial on the tube, turning off the temperature-conditioner. It would take two minutes to reach the fuel tank and by then, though the tube's temperature would have dropped by only two degrees, the pod would have decayed.

The ship was logged onto the tube, so the moment decay set in, the ship would be alerted and service_bots would not allow the pod into the fuel tank. Red_Bati had written an app to fool the ship into thinking the pod was still good. Hiding from the cameras, he had secretly fixed a finger into one of the tube's data rod to infect it with his app.

Stealing the ship, his calculations told him, was a very bad idea. The asteroid mining companies would not rest until they understood why a ship suddenly went dark. They would send probes to all corners of the solar system and Red_Bati would be running for the rest of his life. The other option, to hide until they reached Obares, an asteroid in the Kuiper belt rich in kelenite, did not seem possible. He could not hide his missing arm from the ship's cameras for the next two years of the journey. If he managed to, and got on the asteroid, he could sneak away with enough supplies, a tent, machines and spares, and he could use the sun to recharge; but that would mean growing old alone, with no one to talk to other than a holograph.

The ship was worth the risk. It had enough resources on board to sustain robot life for eternity, to create even a whole new world. It had VR printers that could give birth to new robots, who would be conscious like Red_Bati. Nyota Energy could have printed for him a new arm, but the cost was equal to buying another second-hand basenji, so they reserved VR printing to fix critical damages to the ship and to replace worn-out engine parts.

Once he had the ship under his control, he would take it somewhere far from human reach, maybe beyond Earth's solar system. He could hop from one asteroid to another, mining minerals to make fuel and VR cartridges, until he found a place big enough and rich enough to be a new home. The VR printers could give birth to new robots, to other VR printers, and even to new spaceships. He would not be lonely anymore.

Red_Bati kept his body close to the tube to hide the missing arm from the cameras and opened his mouth and stuck out his tongue to imitate the panting basenji. The storage section was on the lowest level and the engines were in the midsection at the back of the ship. He followed tunnel-like corridors and did not meet other robots until he neared the engines, and the three he passed did not notice him: their eyes were focused in the distance. If they were humans, he would have exchanged nods with them in greeting, maybe even a cheerful, "How's it going?"

He reached Engine 5 without raising any suspicion. The fuel tank was in the first room. Its floor looked like the swimming pool which Granny had in her backyard. Things that looked like purple ice cubes swirled in a mist in the pool, under a glass lid. Red_Bati placed the carrying tube on the edge of the glass and pressed a button. The tube opened, the glass parted, and the pod slipped into the pool. The moment it touched the mist, it broke apart and thousands of ice cubes floated about. They were not a deep shade of purple like the others: they looked desaturated, but the ship would not immediately pick this up because the steam swirling above the pool gave the cubes fluctuating shades. It relied entirely on the tube to alert it of a decayed rod.

Red_Bati hurried out of the engine, still shielding his body with the now empty tube. When he reached the Supplies Folder, he did not shelve the tube, for he needed it to hide his missing arm. He settled in a corner, and five minutes later got the first message from the ship, which had noticed that he was not going to Docking for his next assignment. The message had a yellow color code, indicating low level importance, inquiry only. If he were any other robot, he would have auto-responded by sending the ship an activity log and system status, and the ship would have analyzed it and notified the Captain to take action. Z-Kwa blocked his Comm_Sys from sending the auto-response. The ship sent another message two minutes later, with a blue color code and an attachment to auto-install a program to force a response, but Z-Kwa deleted the attachment. The ship waited another two minutes, and then sent a third message, in white color code. It had notified both the Captain and Nyota Energy on Earth about his strange behavior, and it had told them that two service_bots were on their way to take a physical look at him.

Before they could reach Supplies Folder, the ship sent a message in red color code to everybot: *A Red-Level event has occurred in Engine 5.* Red_Bati could not hear the explosions. The ship was silent, as though nothing was happening. The ship would know that decayed fuel was responsible and would associate Red_Bati's strange behavior to the crisis, but all service_bots would be needed in the engine to contain the disaster and none would come after Red_Bati.

The first sign that the ship had become vulnerable to hijacking came in the next red message, hardly ten minutes after Red_Bati got the yellow message. *Kwa-Nyota is going into sleep mode.* Once in hibernation, other engines would shut down, all non-essential programs would shut down, all auto functions would cease, and all robots, apart from the service_bots and the Captain, would go to sleep too. Seventy-five seconds after the message, the lights went out.

Red_Bati activated infrared vision and made his way to the heart of the ship, where the data servers glowed in the dark like the skyscrapers of Kampala. When he was sold to Nyota Energy, he had scanned the internet for everything about the company and its space crafts. He did not have any particular need for the information but was only responding to a very human instinct: *know your employer.* He had blueprints of the ship, a Punda Binguni model built by Atin Paco, a Gulu-based company that had pioneered low cost space travel. He had the source code of all its software and its operating system, Kwa-nyota. First, he went to the Comm Control Panel and flipped several switches to OFF, cutting communication with Earth. Now, Nyota Energy could not stop the hijack by sending the Captain direct instructions, nor could it track the ship.

The Captain would notice that it had lost communication with Earth, but would not send a service_bot to check, for all fifty service_bots were in Engine 5.

It took Red_Bati fifteen minutes to write a program to convince the ship to take instructions from him rather than from Nyota Energy. Then he used a jiko data cable to connect physically to the ship's mainframe, making him a part of the ship. It took him another ten minutes to deactivate the security programs and install the hijacker. When he unhooked the cable, he had control of the ship.

All that work had drained his battery down to eight percent. He had to wait for the service_bots to put out the fire before recharging. He went to sleep again. He stayed in the data room, for the rest of the ship froze during hibernation.

The Service_bots spent nearly an hour putting out the fire and stabilizing Engine 5. The ship came out of hibernation and so did Red_Bati. He checked the cameras and saw smoke billowing from the engine, though this was mostly from komaline fire-suppressing solution. Three service_bots were severely damaged and were on stretchers to Storage. It reminded Red_Bati of Granny after her last stroke, as medics took her to a waiting air-hearse. Like the Captain, the service_bots had humanoid structures, though their thermal coats gave them an alien skin, and as Red_Bati watched them leave Engine 5, he began to daydream about finally leaving his dog body.

He hurried to Docking where the robots were still asleep and sat on a charging chair. The other seven engines ignited, and in thirty minutes the journey resumed. The robots in Docking woke up. One of them was a humanoid in police uniform, a pet that girls loved. Red_Bati did not want to think about the little girl who had owned it. They had programmed it to be one of the ship's extra eyes. It noticed Red_Bati's missing arm and sent in a report. If Red_Bati had a face of flesh and skin, he would have smiled at this cop. Instead, he blinked rapidly and made a happy, whining sound. Granny would have known he was laughing at it. Red_Bati sent all robots a message, stripping the cop of his powers, and the cop stopped looking at him.

Once the ship was running again, the Captain checked its inbox for new instructions. It could not maintain speed, now that it had lost one engine. It could not reach Obareso on schedule. The ship needed a new schedule. Every bot needed a new schedule, otherwise their systems would hang up in confusion. The captain found only one new message which, when opened, auto-installed a program and changed its coding and instructions. The captain immediately changed course to another asteroid, Madib Y-5, a flat rock ten miles long, seven miles wide, right in the middle of the asteroid belt, with generous supplies of kunimbili, from which they could make enough fuel pods to take them beyond human reach.

Granny flashed on, no longer bothering to hide from the cameras. With his battery now at 60%, she looked real. Her smile was full of teeth. It surprised him because she never used to smile like that. She did not like false teeth and thought the few teeth in her gum made her ugly.

"Good job," she said.

He shrugged only in his mind, because his body was incapable of shrugging.

"I don't see the point," she added. "After you land on a bare piece of frozen rock, what will you do with your life?"

Nothing, he wanted to say. I'll be alive. I'll start a new world. Then he saw what she meant: robots sitting on frozen rocks, basking in the sun like lizards, looking out at the emptiness of space, enjoying the brightness of stars that shone around them like a giant Christmas tree. Just sitting there and not looking forward to anything. The VR printers would give birth to more of his kind, but they would not grow like human children. They would be fully functional adults at birth, with almost nothing new to learn because they would have all the knowledge that forebots had gathered.

Would exploring for new worlds and searching for new matter give their lives a meaning?

Humans needed a purpose to live. School. Job. Wedding. Children. Adventure. Invention. Something that would make them wake up the next day with a cheerful smile, though they knew there was no purpose to it all and that they would eventually die, and all their achievements would turn to dust. What life would his kind have? He could write coding to make them think like humans, to make them fall in love and get married and desire children, to make them have aspirations and build grand cities and spectacular spaceships and desire to travel deep into the galaxy. But they would be self-aware and self-learning and might then wipe off the code. Some might even decide to return to Earth.

He wanted to smile, to tell Granny that that was the beauty of it all. Like humans, they would live without knowing what tomorrow would bring.

"I want to rest in peace," Granny said.

"You are not a ghost," Red_Bati said.

"Am I not?" she said. "Look at me, look!" She walked as though the ship had gravity. She tried to touch things, but she was like smoke. "See? I'm a spirit."

"You are not," Red_Bati said.

"What do you think spirits are?"

He was quiet for a while, thinking of the painting her daughter had made. He could not be sure anymore if it was all code. Humans, after all, imagined spirits into existence.

"You'll be our goddess," he finally said.

She laughed. "That's a beautiful dream," she said. "But I want to rest in peace. I don't want to spend the rest of eternity talking to a metallic dog that thinks it's human."

Red_Bati imagined himself giving her a smile, the polite smile that a human would give a stranger in the streets. Then he shut her down and wondered what had gone wrong. She had never been mean to him. She had never called him a 'metallic dog' before.

Maybe he should write new code so he could have Granny again, the Granny who took him for long walks in the mango forest, not this grumpy spirit.

A MAJI MAJI CHRONICLE

EUGEN BACON

Maji! Maji! Myth or legend
Or a scheme of fads, ideas embedded
One battle, one struggle.
Freedom! Freedom!
Painted features, glistened spears.
Maji! Maji! Myth or legend?
Sanctified water skims no bullet.
Grave, the lone stream bleeds scarlet.

1905 AD

A copper-breasted sparrow circumvented the tree line. Flapping, he savoured the natural scents of Earth that lingered in the wind: coppice, flora, even rain beneath layers of clay and loam soil. Milk of woodland saplings blended with compound complexities of bodily secretions from nocturnal creatures marking territory or warding off peril.

The little bird surveyed the silence of twilight within a new smell of burning that explained a curl of black smoke in the horizon. He fluttered lime-mottled wings and landed on a branch tremulous from tepid wind. So this was Ngoni Village, the warm heart of German East Africa. He reined himself with the tips of his claws, leaned his body with a subtle shift of weight on the bough. His face twisted skyward, where an eagle soared in a battle dance overhead.

Broad wings slowed. Gleaming eyes angled at the limb of the thorn tree. The eagle swooped with power and a wild cry, talons outstretched with skill and focus.

Schwash!

The eagle and the tiny sparrow toppled in a downward shred of branch, twigs and leaves, and a curtain of red and lime-mottled fluff entangled in silver eagle feathers. The little bird floated out first. He preened himself and hopped two steps away in good recovery on firm ground.

"Surely, Papa!"

Papa was Zhorr, the grand magician of Diaspora. "I did not mean to loosen your feathers, younglin." He looked around, cleared his throat and said, "Well!" A gust of something burning swept into his nostrils. It grew stronger and wilder in the air, wild enough to push rain clouds away.

"This bird thing won't do," Pickle, his son, said. "Now what? Mmhh? What?"

"We go to the village."

"Like this? As birds?"

"And that troubles you, I see. Pretty much everything displeases you, ingrate lad."

"Having travelled back in time to build a picture of history, we'll be dinner in a human's pot before we catch up with that past. Imagine the possibilities: skinned or feathered, how will they eat us? Apprentice, guinea pig or bird, Papa, I do not goad fate."

"Relax. We won't be birds long. But we need to observe before we can morph and fit in."

"Fit? We could have fitted in better had we done the vortex. Churn, swirl, a blast of colour and *schwash!* Right into this world in our normal forms. Why come as birds?"

"No mess, no structural changes," said Zhorr. "The black hole causes atomic fusions and chemical transfigurations. Flying in was safe. Safer! I understand your frustration. You must appreciate that 3059 to 1905 AD is a hell lot of years."

"No kidding. So why birds again?"

"You make an awful sparrow." Zhorr regarded Pickle for a moment. He swirled. Monster wings flapped and a swell of rapid air slapped Pickle to the ground. "That better?"

Pickle lifted on two legs. He sniffed around, scratched his ear and landed back on fours— a reddish brown mouse. He scurried into clumps of grass, dragging his tail.

"No point sulking," the magician said, now transformed to a grey squirrel himself. He gnawed his forefeet and shaped his nails. He rubbed his whiskers and sat on a bushy tail.

Above them, the dazzling eyes of a shadowy owl picked bustle in the shrubbery.

"Either way, Papa," came Pickle's voice from the brushwood. "In all these shenanigans, you leave me silly and game. If humans don't gobble me, that darn owl up there will."

"I'll do something. Maybe. At dawn."

They veered north, eating miles away in bristle undergrowth on a forest walk. Shadows peeped in and out between leaves and soft moon glow. Zhorr and Pickle steered by thick smoke curling in the horizon. They found an open field dazzled by white stars. The meadow closed to unfenced farmland bulging with blonde ears of maize. Yellowing grass trembled and snapped at their chins. Pickle legged it out. But digging, scratching and sniffing at whim, he simply couldn't keep pace with Zhorr, who looked fine and strong.

Pickle struggled, out of breath, way out of legs and famished. This is some adventure, he thought. A sudden nostalgia for Diaspora overwhelmed him—its gold and rainbows and snow-capped crags. In this godforsaken past, the wind looped and whined with speed and ferocity. The trees murmured and loomed tall like mountains to Pickle's modest size. A whisper ran across the grass and nearly scared him out of his fur. A dried leaf raced near his cheek. Behind the leaf's rustle came a gasp from a rousted and irate cricket. It *zinged* past Pickle's muzzle.

Zhorr and Pickle travelled over a dirt road stippled with clumps of dung in various stages of drying. Hungry, they paused and nibbled sprouting maize shoots by the roadside. Further north, a golden carpet of millet and sorghum fields spread. Fallen stems by the roadside crumbled at their feet.

"I'm still hungry," said Pickle.

Zhorr shook ears of grain into his paws and they had another meal.

Finally, they came upon sporadic huts. Zhorr and Pickle moved along a cattle fence and into a forest of mango trees laden with fruits. A narrow footpath led to a mud hut with thatched roofing. Beside it, they ate their way into a food shed where they huddled in sound sleep on a golden bed of drying grain, malleable as a waterbed.

Zhorr awoke to the crow of a cockerel and transformed himself into an old man. Drums echoed in the distance. The staccato beats left Pickle's sleep of light snores unruffled. The grand magician appreciated his son's exhaustion from a flight across years. The great land of Diaspora stood eons away from a small African village invisible on the global map but only visible in a magic bowl with special effects.

He contemplated washing his face. He perused the compound and took note of a well that had seen better days. He prayed it held a trickle or three, else he'd have to cast a spell. A tin pail lay beside the well... all seemed hopeful. But before he could stir or rise, within minutes of the cock's crow, hinges of the hut's wooden door groaned. A boy with tight hair and bark loin came out. His lazy hands rubbed sleep from his eyes. He lifted the empty pail and took to his heels, swinging the handle, presumably on his way to the river for a day's ration of bath, drink and cooking water. That trampled the well's possibilities as a washing place for the magician.

Zhorr waited until the boy was out of sight and clapped his squirrel paws. Pickle woke up—a human boy. He was chocolate skinned and naked. He gazed in wonderment at his father's new form: a salt and pepper wise-man with ancient eyes.

"No need to look so pleased, younglin," he said. "I never thought you'd eagerly embrace childhood. Being human, of course, afflicts you with all their scourges."

"Such as?"

"Disease and incontinence." Zhorr pointed to a rickety shack gated with maize stalks. "Pit latrine right over there."

Zhorr applied a sprinkle of sorcery and fashioned garments for them: Pickle in bark loin and Zhorr in dried cattle skin and a single-shoulder robe. A clap from the magician, and they soared to a new home, their very own, wetness still clinging to its fresh mud walls.

Pickle eyed two beds of elephant weed and covered his face.

"Breakfast. If you'll excuse me—" Zhorr vanished and appeared seconds later with new-found knowledge and ingredients, having completed an observation tour of Ngoni Village. "Twigs. Fetch me twigs, younglin."

Twigs, three stones, a conjured pot and a wooden spoon—the magician stirred sweet potato powder into lukewarm water in the pot. He mixed it well and removed lumps. The concoction came to a boil. He pulled out twigs and lowered the heat, stirring the porridge all the while.

"Ah, bowls." He scratched his head.

Clap, and half-moon gourds appeared.

He served the porridge. Pickle made a face but, in the end, licked the inside belly of the gourd with relish.

Replete, Pickle had one question: "The villagers don't know us. How will we fit in?"

Zhorr clapped again. "They know us now."

Sure enough, they were warming chilled hands over a twig fire, burning morning breeze from stiff knuckles, when a rap came across the wooden door. Chief Ngosi— whose wives, huts and extended family Zhorr had perused earlier that morning in his three-second flight—stepped into the hut. He led a dozen reed-thin elders, their walk too slow, too careful for the limited amounts of greys on their heads.

"Greetings Zhorr," Chief Ngosi said in a dialect that Zhorr and Pickle seemed to fully understand.

"Greetings, good Chief."

"I trust you and the boy are well?" Chief Ngosi asked.

"As well as can be."

Zhorr nodded at Pickle, who rose and left his coveted spot beside the fire and leaned by the mud wall, as the elders huddled around the merry flames. They were wiry-haired men with blank faces that carried eyes as still as a swamp. One elder bore wrinkles as numerous as the tales of the dead. There was no doubt that, behind their retinas, those elders carried wealth of culture that seasoned them with much knowledge. But theirs was a wisdom merged with gloom.

Chief Ngosi drummed his lips with a finger to call for silence. He glanced at the elders, then at Zhorr, completely ignoring Pickle, and delved into the focus of their visit.

"Zhorr," he began. "We all know that you and medicine man Shona are the most powerful sorcerers of our land." He sat on the ground, his knees thrust upward. "You know what happened to the village of Tumbi."

"Toom-bee," Zhorr repeated, rolling the consonants. The elders watched him closely. He cleared his throat and nodded, having no inkling of Tambi or Tompei, or what had happened to it, although Ngosi's tone indicated something awful. He hoped someone would tell him the headlines or the whole village thing would become pig's ass for Pickle and him.

The chief pulled a small twig from the embers. "When Whiteman came from the sea, we welcomed him with a feast. We gave him our wives and daughters to warm his loins. What did he do? He brought more white men. Soon, we didn't have enough wives or daughters to go around. To add insult to injury, Whiteman spoke of a thing called cotton and how much better it would be in our farms. Cotton. Better than millet, maize or cassava, Whiteman said. When we refused Whiteman's request, his soldiers came with magic sticks that threw fire. So we grew cotton, only a little at a time, in small portions at the corners of our farms, to make peace."

The chief poked the twig on the ground and made small holes. "Now this cotton does not feed the stomach. Our children need grain. Instead of being satisfied, Whiteman wanted half our farms to grow sisal. Then he introduced coffee on the Mount where the gods live. Before we could cough, he called himself Imperial Commissioner and demanded land tax."

"Yes," said Zhorr, not much enlightened. "Yes, indeed." So what happened to Tongsey again?

"Whiteman took our young men," said Chief Ngosi. "He forced them to work in his plantations. We gritted our teeth and bore it, for the gods were unhappy with us and there was nothing we could do. Finally, unable to take it anymore, the people of Tumbi asked Shona for help. They wanted something stronger than spears to fight Whiteman's stick that vomited fire."

"And Shun..." the grand magician cleared his throat. "Shona helped them?"

"Why do you test my knowledge, Zhorr? Of course Shona helped them. He told them to mix millet seeds, water and castor oil, and he blessed the potion. He said the magic potion would turn the hot pellets in Whiteman's stick into water."

"If you ever heard a load of boloney—" began Pickle, leaning forward from the mud wall, arms folded. Zhorr silenced him with a look.

"Village warriors drank the potion," said Chief Ngosi. "They wore headbands and waved spears. *Maji! Maji!* they cried and burst into Whiteman's compound."

Zhorr nodded. "Whiteman's bullets did not turn into water."

Chief Ngosi spat. "They did not. The wails of the women," he spoke slowly, "the children's crying... My ears are still ringing."

Zhorr touched his arms. "What do you want me to do for you?"

"Trouble is brewing. White soldiers are moving through the country. They are burning millet and maize. Tumbi is no longer a village. It has been reduced to an orange blaze. The soldiers are moving inwards. In the village of Tana, they raped girls and mutilated men. Soon they will invade Ngoni. If we do not die of the Whiteman's stick that spits fire, we'll surely die of famine."

Desperation scorched his eyes. "I am a leader and a warrior. The bones and blood inside my body cannot stay silent. If I sat like a stone and did nothing for my people, I'd be alive but dead. No one would sing of my creation, my story, my journey. There'd be no fire, wind or kingfish song. Not even a frog song. No one would tell stories to my children and their children's children."

"And you think I can help you—how?"

"If Whiteman's medicine was more powerful than that of Shona, then only you can defeat him. This morning, we beat drums to summon young men. They have formed gangs to rip cotton off Whiteman's plantations, burn his cattle and capture his women. In order to fully succeed, we need your magic."

"But Papa, you cannot interfere!" said Pickle.

"Silence, boy."

Zhorr pondered. Finally, he spoke.

"If you promise not to harm the children or kill the women—they know nothing of your war—maybe I'll help you."

"We'll shed no child's blood or lay a finger on any woman. We'll banish them to the gaze of the sea where they came from."

"And if they can't swim?"

"We'll give them dhows and then banish them."

"Return to your huts and wait there until dusk. When the moon casts its light, summon your warriors. Meet me at the door of my hut and I will speak."

"Speak? Is that all you'll give us? Words?"

"I'll give you more than words, more than immunity to bullets with plain water. I will give you," he paused. "Magic."

After the last of the elders had shuffled out, Pickle rushed to his father. "You have not well thought through this. Surely you can't!"

"Primarily because?"

"You'll change history!"

"So it would seem." He scratched his head. "We shall see."

"But—"

"You'll know the outcome in due course." His mind slipped to a hidden place. Nothing Pickle said could reach him.

✦ ✦ ✦

"The first stir of twilight brings scores to our door," said Pickle.

Zhorr raised his brows.

"The entire village of Ngoni," said Pickle. "And gate crashers."

The chief's wives wore cowry shell bracelets and heavy gold anklets that clink-clanked with every stride. The rest of the women balanced, without finger support, fat clay pots on their heads. The men built a fire.

Everyone danced.

Ngoni Village had brought feast and dance to Zhorr's door.

Faces shone with body paint: ochre red streaked with white clay. Bellies distended with banana brew, roast goat, cassava and millet.

Seed rattles and bead-filled shakers tied to dancer's arms and legs chimed in tempo to the drum's *poom! palah! poom!* Necks swayed. A sky dance, a river dance, a new rites dance, a war dance. Expression, transition, choreography. Someone double looped through a ring of fire. Triple flip. Loop. Loop. It was more religious than anything else.

Pickle moved away from prancing feet in a ceaseless sequence of pace and loop, and walked towards Zhorr, who was seated in close vicinity to a banana leaf carpet piled high with food. In one hand, Zhorr clutched a gourd of mulled fruit.

Pickle touched his father's shoulder and knelt on the ground beside him. "I don't see how this will help my learning, Papa."

Zhorr took a swig of brew. "They rot fruit to pulp, crush it with feet, and ferment it to make this." He swirled it. "Clear water that boggles the mind."

"But Papa—"

"Look," Zhorr pointed.

Chief Ngosi stood fine-looking in ceremonial robe. Tails of peacock headdress fell to his shoulders. He stood tall in paraphernalia, leopard skin and gold anklets. A strong white moon in the shape of a plump woman's bosom caught the shine of dark skin rubbed with fresh sheep fat.

The chief raised an arm and waved his people silent. Zhorr unfolded from the ground and climbed to full height. All eyes turned towards the grand magician. The people observed him with curiosity. "Today is a day of reckoning," said Zhorr. "I will give you—" Animation danced in charcoal eyes. The crowd shuffled. "I will give you ghosts!"

Children heckled. Men and women looked at each other and howled. Elders shook their heads, scratched their cheeks, muttered under their breaths.

Even Pickle's jaw dropped.

One wave of the chief's arm, though he didn't look reassured, silenced the jostling crowd. The elders still hummed.

"Before you throw bananas at me," said Zhorr, "swallow the import of my words."

Pickle folded his arms.

"We're listening," said Chief Ngosi.

Zhorr scanned the chief's entourage. "To defeat the enemy, I'll make you," he paused, "vanish at will."

The first attack on the homesteads of the white men at the sleeve of the Mount came just before dawn. A servant later narrated what happened:

A burst of war cries trampled army fencing. Startled, white soldiers jumped from their beds in pyjama-striped bloomers and snatched their guns from the holsters on the walls. They sought with their eyes for the enemy and saw flying spears this way and that, catapulting from invisible energy fields. Four or five volleys of shots, and random bullets caught a few unseen targets who cried out. But, blind to their enemies, white soldiers lost their fight to stay upright. Ghosts slashed white men's throats open, knocked guns from their hands and fired back at them. At the end of the attack, women and children huddled in dreadful stillness inside cotton plantations.

Zhorr and Pickle saw all these events from the surface of still water inside a clay pot.

"Is this the initiation ritual you promised?" cried Pickle. "The one that would turn me into a 'made' magician? If this is it, I don't want it! I don't want to be part of this anymore."

"This is a lesson that supersedes spell recitals from *The Book of Magic* in the comfort of a floating castle in Diaspora. Now stop talking."

Pickle turned towards the grand magician. "You brought me half-way around the galaxies to witness men die? Your magic has created phantoms."

"Mouth all, youngling, I am not conflicted by it. If the Ngoni have become smitten phantoms, they are phantoms of choice."

A wall of soldiers stood on guard outside the courtyard. One appeared, from his headdress, to be in command. Zhorr approached him.

"I must see Chief Ngosi," he said.

"Who are you?" the guard said.

"May your gods take pity on you, for I shall grant you none when I am through answering that question."

The warrior stepped aside. "Chief Ngosi is with his first wife." He pointed towards a distant hut with brand new clay.

After a wait, Chief Ngosi emerged.

They sat under the shade of a banana tree whose leaves spread like an awning. Zhorr declined a gourd of millet wine. Chief Ngosi indulged. He wiped his lips with the back of his hand and suppressed a burp.

"What can I do for you, my friend?"

"I am concerned," said the grand magician.

Chief Ngosi regarded him.

"Since the massacre at the Mount, your warriors powered with invisibility potion, an ability to appear and disappear with the wind at will, continue to plunder Whiteman's farms and kill indiscriminately. They have forgotten anything about amnesty to women and children."

Chief Ngosi nodded. "I will ask them to show restraint. Is that all?"

"At this point, yes."

"Good. Perhaps you will join me for lunch. Fresh caterpillars from Yassa land."

A week later, Pickle pointed at the water gourd. "Look, Papa."

Zhorr observed Ngoni warriors on rampage outside the tribal frontiers.

"Kill! Kill! Kill! White is white!" they chanted. "Kill! Kill! Kill!"

They marched past the Great Lakes to the coastline and left in their wake vultures looping the air in hordes.

"Greetings, Chief Ngosi. I wonder—" Zhorr began in their next visit to the chief's palace.

Ngosi's face tightened. *"Emperor Ngosi,"* he corrected. "I'm a very busy man."

"So I see."

Emperor Ngosi would speak nothing of his warriors' actions. In a stab of whatever modest hospitality he had left, he showed Zhorr his newfound treasures. Inside one hut, metal boxes, each carrying 500 rounds or more of ammunition, stacked high. Another shed was a museum of gadgets from an Arab Sheikh: pistols, shot guns, machine guns, live ammunition and rifle silencers.

The Emperor cradled a laser sight rifle in his hands. "A rarity even in the western worlds, I hear. Isn't she a beauty?"

"Better than invisibility magic," Zhorr said through tight lips.

"This," the Emperor lifted another item, "is a bazooka."

In a third and desperate visit to the palace, Zhorr discovered that Emperor Ngosi was not so friendly anymore. He appeared out of mist and waved the magician silent. His court was now full of sorcerers whose powers he appeared to trust.

Emperor Ngosi locked his hands, his eyes dulled. "We are a master race," he said. He thinned into black fog where no one could see him. Invisible Ngoni soldiers lifted and tossed the grand magician and his son out of the palace.

Lust predated greed that predated power that predated altruism. The Emperor gathered a harem of one thousand wives whose shelter spread across three villages. Their feed took resources from twelve more villages now forced to pay 'protection' tax to the palace.

"You *do* understand the long-term outcome of this?" Pickle said to his father.

"Yes." Zhorr's smile was wistful. "What you witness is not genetic betrayal. It's not a modern phenomenon. It is simple quintessential greed. Recognisable as it is age old. Emperor Ngosi knows he can climb higher up the money cum power tree—that itch is powerful. He's obsessed in a rather clear way in a quest for continental supremacy that will only be a speck. In dramatic nuance, history will repeat itself, only with a new face."

"Yes," said Pickle. "A face called tragedy."

They regarded each other.

"The Emperor has grown more powerful," said Zhorr. "Guns are no longer to him magic sticks that spit fire. He understands the mechanics, complexities and gains of advanced weaponry. Soon, his troops will invade Europe, Asia, Australia and the rest of the world. He will destroy opponents with weapons of famine, disease and bombs. The release of weapons-grade material will change the Earth's ozone layer. A tidal wave will unleash a tsunami that will kill millions. Changes to the earth's epicenter will give rise to tectonic forces that will bend the earth's crust. Earthquakes and lava bombs will kill millions more. Survivors and generations after them will become crippled with incurable illnesses far worse than mutable forms of bird flu, COVID-19, HIV or Ebola."

"And my lesson?"

"Clearly it works," Zhorr said in uncompromising attitude. "My method works very well. Too well, in fact, for the scoop of emotions it uncovers in you. Did you want me to teach you about galaxies and how a sprinkle of magic could keep them efficient? Did you want me to clap my hands and say: *Look at this world. Isn't it beautiful?*" Zhorr pressed his hands together. "This, my son, concludes our history session."

One clap and Zhorr regained his true form. Silver ringlets of hair fell to his waist. Jewelled apparel full of shadows, melancholy and river song wrapped around him. Onyx eyes glittered and lit the hut. The grand magician of Diaspora towered two heads above his apprentice son.

He laid a gentle hand on Pickle's shoulder, crisp with starched livery in lace, lavender and cream. "Tell me. What have you learnt then? What have you really learnt?"

Pickle's face shone with clarity. "No matter how strong the urge or goodwill," he said, "never use magic to flirt with history."

"Unless—" said Zhorr with utmost professionalism, "you have a rule to cover it." He ruffled Pickle's copper head. "Well done, my boy. With that knowledge, you have earned a diploma. Now we must depart fast track and travel between worlds to where we belong."

"Fast track?"

"Straight to the year 3059 and I will die in peace."

"What about the *no mess, no structural changes* that favoured us flying as birds to the vortex? Atomic fusion, chemical transfiguration and what else, that's what you said."

"Pure gumbo." Zhorr toyed with tresses falling down his shoulder. He combed off tangle with a finger. "I always wanted to fly."

Pickle's brow creased. "But Papa—"

"Mmhh?"

"I am desperate to leave this world. My faith in you is restored. Partially restored, at least." He glared.

"Did you 'But Papa' me to fault my motive?"

"Can't we, must we not..."

"Must we not what?"

"Undo it?"

"Undo the lying bit or my dying in peace?"

"The damage. The course of history that you have altered."

"Ah, that. 'Course we can undo it. It's our obligation to do so. Yes, you must." Zhorr's strong fingers poked Pickle in the chest. "You," almost absent-mindedly. "Yes, you. Put your wizard hat on. Quick! Time leaks perilously."

Before Pickle could lift a finger, the door burst open.

Zhorr and Pickle barely transformed to prior form—just barely!—before Emperor Ngosi fell in.

"I don't want it anymore," he cried. "I don't want it!"

Zhorr scratched his salt and pepper wise-man hair and regarded the Emperor with ancient eyes. He took a step forward, laid a hand on Ngosi's shoulder, an action that appeared to carry calming effect.

"What is it you don't want, Emperor Ngosi?"

"The power. Take it. Take it!" He tossed down his staff. "It has made a monster of me. Oh, what have I done? My own people! Zhorr, I am a sick man. My forefathers groan in their graves. I see reason now. I don't want greater power."

"Do you speak from your heart?"

"All men are equal. There's no master race. Please remove your magic now."

"I am delighted you have found sense. I couldn't have enforced it without infringing your free will. Go home." Zhorr gave Ngosi an indulgent pat on the back. "We shall work some arrangement."

After Emperor Ngosi had left, shuffling his steps and carrying much weight, Zhorr and Pickle glanced at each other. Pickle spoke first.

"Your magic eyes didn't see that coming."

"N-no." He was back in his jewelled robe. "Time travel brings paradoxes and anomalies. That was an anomaly."

"Knowledge for the future. What happens now?"

"Ngosi has no need of us, really. Having seen light, his world will embrace him once more. The blood of a speckless rooster or three will appease the spirits of his forefathers. As for the powers of invisibility, he will no more use them for harm."

"Yet you hesitate, Papa."

"A small predicament really. Ngosi has no desire for greater power and he has already won the Maji Maji war. But, for the implications of changing history, although he is a reformed man, we must reverse the effects of my magic."

"Heaven forbid. Reversal will—"

"Different historical outcomes are not necessarily better that the ones that eventuated them. We cannot tamper with this world. Take us back to exactly one minute before Ngosi and the elders first entered this hut and sat around the fire." Fog touched his voice. It became hoarse, old as a museum. He glanced at his son with unwavering eyes. "You know what that means?"

Pickle nodded. "The calculation is simple." He turned away from his father. "A simple calamity, really." He stood still for a moment. "Ngoni warriors will use millet seeds and water to lose the war."

"I cannot stop it." Zhorr's museum voice trembled. "And neither can you."

"Yes." Pickle answered. "No one can."

In a flash, Pickle swished his gown. A glow of light on his forehead swelled in changing shape and size. It filled him with magical powers that lifted the grand magician's philter of invisibility on the Ngoni.

The cloak whirred again.

Zhorr and Pickle soared with outstretched hands into naked space.

Soft tips of Diaspora mist lifted and touched a cobalt line of hillocks. Crystal water gushed between pieces of boulder and cascaded downwards in a waterfall. A snow-crested mountain ridge climbed towards a floating fortress with an iron gateway. An array of white lights in every arched window blinked. The flying castle sighed in welcome exactly three nanoseconds before a timid rap on the wooden door of a mud hut somewhere in Ngoni country.

THE UNCLEAN

NUZO ONOH

"There is nothing the eyes will see that will cause them to shed blood-tears."
– Igbo Proverb

Ω

UKARI FOREST - 9 PM

My husband's corpse lies on the raffia mat, spread underneath the giant Iroko tree that towers over the thick vegetation of Ukari Forest. The Iroko tree is legendary in the ten clans of Ukari and even beyond. Its broad branches reach up to the skies, fighting for airspace with the eagles and the kites. Its circumference covers at least eight arms-length of marriage-age men. The other trees in the forest bow their leafy obeisance to the Iroko tree, paying homage to their great lord, just as the humans of Ukari village kneel to it.

All is still. Nothing breaks the grave-like silence of the vast forest. Apart from the occasional snake or lizard, no other creature stirs in the perennial gloom of this accursed forest. From my kneeling position by my late husband's body, I force my bloodied eyes to look upon his reviled face, coal-dusted by death and decay. His features, swarthy and harsh, have not yielded their cruelty to death. The white cloth shrouding his bloated body is stained with the death fluids seeping from his fast decomposing body.

In the two nights I've spent in the forest with my husband's corpse, I have been unable to keep my eyes from his face....and IT. I feel its malignancy, the threat in its unnatural turgidity. I live in terror of what IT would do to me should I take my gaze away from its terrible erectness.

I look away, return my gaze to his face. My body shudders yet again, expecting those swollen lids to lift, his cold eyes promising harsh retribution for sins I can never recollect. Yet, I cannot escape. I am rooted to my husband's side by limb-freezing terror. My heart leaps into my mouth, filling it with bile and panic each time the trees stir, the dry leaves *rustle or an owl hoots his midnight vigil from a distant tree. Had I slept, my dreams would have been dreams of escape, freedom, and peace. But I am forbidden that relief, chained as I am to my husband's corpse by the witch-doctors' powerful incantations and the customs of our land.*

I am a prisoner in a jail without bars. I am the condemned, convicted before her trial. I am the accused, facing her judgement at the one-man jury in the court of the great Iroko tree, known to the villagers as The Tree of Truth. The Tree of Truth is the final arbiter in every dispute in the village, the righteous judge and jury that condemns and sentences with ruthless efficiency. It is said that none who is guilty ever escapes its merciless justice. Its roots are swollen with the blood and cries of its victims, men, women and even children, accused of crimes ranging from witchcraft to night-flying. And I, Desdemona, first daughter of Ukah, wife of Agu of Onori Clan, have joined that wretched fraternity of The Tree. I am a condemned criminal awaiting my fate beneath the unforgiving leaves of The Tree of Truth.

As I prepare to endure my third and final night by the side of the putrid body of my late husband, I know with a feeling of total despair that my ordeal is far from over. Even if by some unbelievable stroke of fortune The Tree of Truth rejects my blood; if by some divine intervention my husband's vengeful spirit fails to strike me dead by dawn as is widely expected in our village, I could yet be dispatched to my own ancestors' hell by a myriad of foes, too strong, too powerful, for a mere widow to resist.

For, I am the most accursed of widows. I am a widow without offspring, cursed with the womb of a man, my belly filled with soured eggs that will never again yield the precious fruit of a child. Even worse, I am a widow without a son, left without protection like a day-old baby abandoned in the middle of an African thunderstorm, exposed to the flings and thumps of the merciless force of nature.

For my failure to provide my husband with an heir and name-protector; for my desperate and foolish attempts to produce that precious gift; for my own mad folly and ignorance, I will pay with my life when the cock crows in the dawn and his relatives come to extract the life from beneath my chest—my coward's heart, my foolish heart.

I married Agu a few months after I turned seventeen, just one year past the age of female wisdom. It was a time of great changes in our country, a time when people said the white men would give us back our land and return to their own. The calendar in our parlour had the year, 1953, stamped on it. It also had pictures of our new ruler, Queen Elizabeth II, on all its twelve pages. There used to be pictures of the king. But the king was dead, and the queen now owned our lands and calendars.

Agu arrived at our house one rainy day as we made to prepare Papa's lunch of *yam fufu* and bush-meat soup. I was in the smoke-clouded kitchen, attempting to keep the kerosene stove going, when the kitchen door flew open and my little brother, Ibe, rushed in, all excitement and glee, knocking over Mama's wooden stool in his haste.

"Desee, Papa wants you now," his eyes were wide with what seemed like awe, his voice pitched like a girl's. I wondered what had given the sudden animation to his customary indolent disposition. Ibe took his role as the only son very seriously. And both Papa and Mama made sure we, the daughters, recognised and respected his privileged status as "heir," regardless of our superiority in both age and intellect. I had already passed out of senior school with grades that were good enough to secure me a teaching apprenticeship at the village primary school. My sister, Gono, also seemed certain to follow in my footsteps.

But Ibe, despite the attention and praise lavished on him by our parents and family at large, never succeeded in producing a report card that could make any teacher or parent proud. Yet, Papa would insist on giving him the chair of honour in the family living room, right next to grandfather's stone grave, while Mama would chant her "hero song" whenever he sneezed, coughed or even farted, her face glowing with a mixture of pride, determination and a sad kind of martyrdom that left one won-dering why she'd even bothered giving birth to her precious son in the first place.

"Jealous people, leave my tiger alone, Envious people, look at my prize, Evil people, turn your eyes from my son, My hero, my solace, my king."

And well might she praise the little sod, since without his timely appearance, Papa would have replaced her with a second wife to produce the much-wanted heir and "name-protector." As Papa was fond of telling my sister and me, a woman has no name, no religion, no country, no custom and no honour except that given her by a man, a husband. Ibe's name said it all—clansmen, brothers! Ibe was the only one amongst us given an Igbo name, showing how valued he was. We, the girls, had been left to the mercy of poor Mama when it came time for name selection. She in turn had turned to her "learned" brother, uncle Silas, who had promptly lumbered us with the most high-faluting names imaginable, courtesy of one Mr. Shakespeare of England. Everyone knew me as Day-see-mona (Desee, for short), except my schoolteachers, who had struggled in my student years to read out *Desdemona* in the class register every morning. My younger sister was known as Gono to everyone, but diligently wrote her full name in her textbooks—*Goneril*.

"Desee, hurry up or Papa will get angry with you," Ibe was almost hopping by the open kitchen door. I heard a grunt and turned to look at Gono, who had stopped pounding the *yam fufu* in the wooden mortar as soon as Ibe made his announcement. Her brows dipped in a frown of displeasure. I was unsure who her anger was directed against—Ibe or Papa, both of whom she loathed with equal intensity.

"What does he want with Desee?" Gono barked at Ibe. "Can't he see we're busy preparing lunch for you two bigheads?" She shot Ibe a look that dripped with contempt, her body, wiry and small, as tense as a featherweight boxer's in a boxing ring.

Aggression emitted from every pore in her body as she stood clutching the long wooden pestle. She looked as if she intended to bash in someone's head with it.

Ibe looked at her and quickly averted his eyes. "I don't know," he mumbled, slinking out of the kitchen, but not before I caught a shifty look in his eyes that convinced me he was lying—as usual. That boy would lie to God Himself if he ever made it to St Peter's gates. Gono was the only one amongst us —Papa included—who inspired some form of fear in the lout. Gono's temper was notorious in the five clans and many had already predicted she would remain a spinster with her harridan's temperament—a fact that pleased rather than dismayed her. Even Papa avoided sending her on errands, at least, as much as he could without appearing weak. Gono was the only one of his children that never cried when he took the birch to her.

I entered the sitting room, hard on Ibe's heels, to see two strangers, both men, seated on the whitewashed wooden benches that circled our sitting room. Each of the strangers, including Papa, cradled a ceramic mug of palm-wine in their hands, while a brimming cup of the brew was placed atop my grandfather's raised grave positioned in the centre of the parlour. Papa never drank palm wine without offering some to my grandfather. I did a small curtesy to the seated strangers and a deeper one to my grandfather's grave.

"Aahh! Desee, come sit down my daughter," Papa patted the chair of honour, the seat next to his own and nearest to the elevated rectangular grave, Ibe's special chair! Papa's face beamed with a benevolence I'd only ever witnessed when he addressed Ibe. More worryingly, he had called me Desee, instead of his habitual "*Agbogho*"— girl. Something was clearly wrong. My heart was thudding as I took the proffered seat, ignoring Ibe's displeased frown as he settled for the little stool by the snuff table.

"These gentlemen are from Ukari," Papa said, with a nod at the strangers. I glanced up quickly and lowered my eyelids just as rapidly, to preserve my modesty. "They've come a long way indeed to see us, or should I say, to see you, my daughter." Papa chuckled in a manner that could have been interpreted as coy had he been a woman. I wanted to hide my face beneath the thin fabric of my yellow cotton dress; such was my discomfiture.

"Yes indeed. We have travelled a six-hour journey to come and view your famed beauty," I heard one of the men say, the old grey one. The oily quality to his voice repelled me. I felt the heat of embarrassment on my face, at the same time feeling a sudden prick of apprehension at the back of my neck.

"Our son here is Agu, son of Onori of the Onori clan," the old man continued. His hair was sprinkled with ash, as were his bushy brows and thick beard, giving him the look of a grey-dappled hyena. "Agu is a prosperous trader and travels as far as *Ugwu-Hausa*, the Muslim northern territories, to buy and sell various foodstuff," continued grey hyena, nodding at the young man next to him. "In fact, Agu owns the only storey building in our village and a Mercedes Benz, which you can see parked outside your father's compound," his voice was oiled with pride.

Instinctively, I glanced out of the open curtain-less window, as did Ibe, to see a white car—a large silver-wheeled car—getting washed by the pouring rain outside our compound. Papa feigned disinterest though I could read a gleam in his eyes that indicated otherwise to me. But he was a proud man and I guess he deserved his dignity. A bicycle, even an almost new British Raleigh that had cost him a handsome sum, could never compete with a Benz.

"As we were telling your good father before you came in, we'd heard of the famed beauty of the white chicken he housed beneath his roof. So, we decided to rush in and express our interest in purchasing that white chicken before others, less worthy, beat us to the market." The grey one smiled at me, a front tooth missing.

I quickly averted my gaze and glued my eyes to my hands, which had suddenly started trembling as if I'd been struck down with malaria.

"Your father has been very kind in indicating his willingness to sell us his precious chicken. So, we thought it was a good time for you to meet your future husband, Agu, before we begin formal negotiations for the marriage rites. After all, a girl must be allowed some choice in these matters even though the ultimate decision rests with her esteemed father—and rightly so." Grey Hyena gave a small chuckle, which was echoed by Papa and even the little idiot, Ibe.

I felt the racing of my heart. *Some choice indeed!* I felt the sting of tears in my eyes as my palms broke out in hot sweat. I wanted to get up and run out of that crowded room with the stuffy odour of strange bodies and palm-wine. But fear of Papa's wrath and a cramp of embarrassment kept me glued onto Ibe's special seat. I forced my eyes up and took my first proper look at my future husband, Agu.

What I saw was a man, short of stature and lacking in bulk. Age-wise, he was at the peak of his manhood, somewhere between thirty and forty years. It was difficult to tell his exact age because of his small size. He was dressed in an *Agbada*, a loose native garb covered in an assortment of animal prints. His hair was trimmed close to his skull, giving him an almost bald look. Sat next to his older relative on our wooden bench, his head barely reached Grey Hyena's shoulders. Yet, there was a carriage to his head, an arrogance of bearing that marked him as the leader despite his puny size. He was dark, very black-skinned, like the Enugu coal miners at the end of their work shift beneath the bowels of the earth. His eyes were small, closely set. There was an expression in them that reminded me of the eyes of the frozen fish heads we used in cooking Papa's chilli pepper-soup. Their black depths betrayed little emotion as they settled on my person; just the detached assessment of a trader inspecting some ware before making final purchase. Even when he smiled at me as our eyes briefly met for the first time, there was no gentling in his pupils or his lips—thin, fleshless lips—unusual in a native of our country. Something about him frightened me, placed a cold hand over my heart, a silent terror that didn't subside even after I got up and noticed how I towered over him by at least three fingers' length.

Instinctively, I hunched my shoulders, feeling ashamed of my tall slenderness, emphasised into giant proportions by his small stature. I caught the strangers' nod of satisfaction as I returned to Papa's side and knew with a tight feeling in my stomach that my fate was sealed.

Despite knowing—always having known—that my duty as a daughter was to reward Papa's sacrifices with a good bride price, it still rankled that I was denied the choice of deciding who should pay the price on my head. I had no doubt that I would fetch a handsome bride price as a result of my light skin and secondary school education. I was after all, the reincarnation of my great-grandmother, who had been famed in her lifetime for her amazing fairness and beauty.

My sister, Gono, on the other hand, with skin as dark as our father's, even if smoother to the touch and glossier to the sight, was not burdened with any such great expectations. Papa said that Gono's only hope of bagging a respectable bride price lay in acquiring an exceptional education, but only if her stubbornness allowed her to complete secondary school without getting expelled. But we knew we would be lucky if Gono deigned to give any man her hand in marriage for a bride price, respectable or otherwise. I pitied my sister because I feared she might never know the joys of marriage, as was the right of every woman as nature intended, a situation I suddenly found myself now facing without any feeling of joy.

Later that night, after our guests had gone, I cried as I had never cried in my seventeen years of growing up in Iburu village. I cried for the impending loss of my home, my family, my freedom, my career, my burgeoning affection for my fellow apprentice teacher, Chudi. In particular, I cried for the man, Agu, that cold stranger, who was soon to become my husband and my master.

✦ ✦ ✦

UKARI FOREST – 11:45 PM

The cold night wears on in the dreadful forest, as I feel the bile rise in my mouth for the umpteenth time. I turn away from my husband's corpse and retch into the wet grass, already stinking with my urine and vomit. The pain in my stomach is unbearable. It feels as if the imps of Satan have taken residence in my belly, wrenching my innards for their sport. The thirst burns my throat and my body shivers and trembles with cold and hunger. I cast my eyes, made blurry by tears and bruises, at the water jug that stands on the mat next to my husband's body. I stretch out a trembling hand in its direction. Then I stop, pull back my hand as if stung by a scorpion, as remembrance floods my memory, dulled by four days of starvation and sleep deprivation.

The water in the jug is corpse water, the water used in bathing the decomposing body of my husband; the water I had been forced to drink in the presence of all the clan as punishment for my crime. In the aftermath of Agu's death, I was held down by cruel hands, my nose squeezed shut, as endless cups of corpse water were forced into my open mouth in relentless succession.

I cannot begin to describe the taste of that hideous fluid, the sour salty tang, the cloying milkiness of pus, the lingering bitterness of decayed flesh. The more I retched the more I was fed the cloudy corpse water, with punches, slaps and curses to compound my humiliation. And now, even as I crouch beside my late husband's corpse, I can still feel the swelling on my face from the beatings. My ears still ring with the invectives heaped on—Murderer! Husband killer! Child murderer! Mermaid witch! Evil stranger! Wicked sorceress! Ogbanje! Man-woman!

And much more...much worse. And all because of my desperation, my bad Chi my foolishness, a desperate need that has now brought me to this wretched state.

As I listen to the painful growling of my stomach, I draw in my knees to keep within the salt-lined boundary set by the three witchdoctors on the hard soil of the forest, and turn my eyes to the dry-barked trunk of The Tree of Truth. The tree hulks over us, its branches stretching into black infinity. Its massive trunk is scarred with ridges of dry gum, flaky barks and aborted stumps of unborn branches...and blood; a red-wash of blood. There is an ancient power within its unfathomable depths that shrouds it with wisdom and terror. Within its all-knowing roots lies my salvation.

I bare my body and my soul to the towering guardian of justice. I plead for its vindication, its protection, its forgiveness. And when finally my wailing voice grows hoarse, whimpers into a whisper, I bury my head in my hands as I allow my mind to travel back into the terrible events that have led to my present sorry predicament and could yet lead to my ultimate demise.

From the day I entered Agu's house as his bride, I ceased expecting anything good, and as the weeks merged into months and the swollen moon brought in numerous years, I gradually became immune to the bad things that befell me in my matrimonial hell. As I observed the birth of each new moon, my heart felt like a bare bottom sat on a heaving anthill. Queen Ill-fortune rides the full moon as every child and adult knows. Together, they invoke evil, awake the dead and spread devastation along their route as they journey through mankind's lands and lives. Everyone cursed with a bad *chi* knows to dread the arrival of the full moon.

Married life had never been a life of songs and dances for me because I was a learned wife from a different village. However, things took a turn for the worse when four years went by and I failed to produce the desired heir for my husband. Despite Father O'Keefe's novenas on my behalf, nothing stirred in my womb. It remained as fruitless as a man's stomach.

One day, Agu's eldest and fattest sister, Uzo, took matters into her hands and dragged me to their witchdoctor to find a solution to my barrenness. The man was seated crossed-legged on a hard, cement floor with strange drawings and herbs strewn around him. Blood still dripped from the neck of a freshly butchered chicken hung above his head. The red fluid soaked his unshaven head, crawling around his face and neck like bloated worms. The sight caused my empty gut to heave. I forced my eyes to study the thin veins on my folded hands instead. I felt his eyes on me, burning, probing. My shoulders folded in, rolled forward in a hunched pose of shame, and my hands began to tremble. *What sinful thoughts would he read in my mind? Holy Mary! Please help me! What will he read in my future?*

Suddenly, the decrepit man-demon screamed, pointing a gnarled finger in my direction.

"Ogbanje! Water sorceress! Be gone!" he shrieked. Turning glaring eyes at my sister-in-law, he shouted, 'Why have you brought me this accursed daughter of the river Niger?" Still pointing that filthy forefinger at me, his thin arm weighted by multiple charmed amulets, he demanded, "Why do you bring upon my old head the wrath of the powerful mermaid? Go! Take her away! No one can help her. She belongs to the water, to *Mamiwata.* She's not your brother's wife. She's no mortal man's wife. Her womb will never yield fruit to your brother. Go! Depart from my presence and never return! Go!"

We scurried away, my heart pounding in terror. My sister-in-law abandoned me at the dust road, leaving me to make my own way back to the house. Within hours of Uzo's return, the entire village had heard of my stigma and my shame.

"We should have known she's an *Ogbanje* mermaid," the fat sisters snapped out the demon over their heads with outstretched arms as I walked past them. "Have you ever seen anyone so light-skinned unless they're albinos? Or with hair so long it stretches like a mermaid's? But this one is clearly not albino, just water-bleached by her real mother, the evil *Mamiwata* mermaid. Agu should have listened to us when we warned him of the perils of marrying an outsider. One can never tell the curses that follow such people. Oh! Our poor brother!"

By the time Agu returned to the house, a great crowd of relatives had gathered inside his parlour, waiting to fill his ears with the news of my curse. I was standing by my bed when he crashed into my room, the whites of his eyes red-streaked, his pupils as coal, burning with a hate that had hitherto been absent in the four years of our marriage. I barely had the time to mutter the obligatory *"onye-ishi,"* master, when he grabbed my hair, forcing my knees to the floor and dragging me into his room with a strength that defied his puny size and my considerable height. Once inside his room, he descended on my body with every arsenal at his disposal, venting his fury with his fists, his belt, his birch whips, his walking stick and even the twisted metal clothes-hanger that harboured his array of clothing.

My screams fell on deaf consciences. Everyone in that over-populated household heard my howls of pain but no one dared or even wanted to venture into the master's bedroom to halt my thrashing. I pled for mercy, seeking his forgiveness for my barrenness, for the bride-price money he had wasted on the defective good I had now become.

Agu's hands continued to descend on my head, pulling clumps off my scalp. His feet shot home countless goals on my body. Soon, my screams turned to whimpers and my voice grew hoarse in my throat. When eventually his arms grew weary and his breathing laboured from exhaustion, Agu dropped his belt on the floor and marched out of the room in the same death-silence with which he had carried out the prolonged attack on my person.

As for myself, I was at the gates of mental darkness and mortal hell, my vision hazy from dizziness and pain. Choking back the countless hiccups that threatened to kill my breathing, I crawled my way back to my room, bright blood stains marking the white linoleum floor of the corridor. I stumbled my way to the wall mirror, fearful, yet desperate to see the damage to my person.

The scream that escaped my lips at the image the mirror returned to me was louder than any I had made while the damage was wreaked on it. I shut my eyes tight, fighting to blank out the swellings, the open cuts, the blood dripping from every opening in my face. But I couldn't shut out the agonising throbbing in my body, the shame and the fury. Most of all, I couldn't shut out the sudden hate that burnt in my heart like a bush fire gone wild.

That night, and many more nights over the course of several months, Agu vented his fury and frustration on my body with his fists and everything he could lay his stumpy hands on. On numerous occasions, I was kept locked up in my room, guarded by the mammoth sisters and numerous house-helps. The only times they were let off their guard duty were on the nights my husband came to claim his conjugal rights on my body, a brutal ritual carried out in silence and darkness, leaving me with a feeling of defilement and shame.

Eventually, I could bear the abuse no longer. One day when Agu left for his monthly trade trips to the Muslim north, I made my escape back to my father's village. *Just wait till I tell Papa*, I thought over and over as the Mami-wagon rumbled its bumpy way to my village. *Just wait till I tell Papa*.

◆ ◆ ◆

I arrived at my father's village a few hours later and walked the short distance to his compound. As I walked through the low metal gate of our compound, my feet grew sudden wings as I raced the last few yards to our front door. I pulled my scarf from my head, wincing in pain as the cloth connected with my bruises, dislodging fresh scabs. I heard the sound of approaching footsteps and felt the sudden tears spill down my cheeks, tears of self-pity, relief, pain and anger all mixed into one loud bawl.

My sister, Gono, opened the door. She took one look at my battered, tear-streaked face and started howling. She just stood at the open door, her hands pressed tightly against her ears, staring at me with wide streaming eyes, her bare feet stamping on the floor like the frenzied dance of the *Adamma* masquerade. Except her dance wasn't one of joy or excitement, but rage and pain, a pain I knew was as biting as mine because of the great love she bore for me. Behind her, I saw my brother, Ibe, craning his neck and trying to see what the ruckus was all about. His eyes widened as he took in my bruises before hurrying away without a word to me. Mama rushed out, Ibe fast on her heels, his eyes gleaming with sly excitement.

"What's all this foolishness about? Don't you know your father is having his afternoon siesta?" Mama scolded, pushing Gono away from me. Then, just like Gono, her eyes widened as she too took in my battered face. She threw her arms wide into the air, her eyes raised to the low ceiling in an attitude of supplication. "Jesu!" she shouted, making a quick sign of the cross before leading me by the arm into Papa's presence, her breathing hard and fast.

"Papa Ibe! Papa Ibe, wake up," she shook Papa's shoulder with urgent hands. I felt the slight irritation of old stir in my heart at the usurpation of my right. I was the first born and prior to Ibe's arrival, Papa had been known as "Papa Desee" by everyone. But with Ibe's birth, him being a son and all, that coveted status was taken from me and given to the wretched sod.

As Papa slowly awakened, Mama went over to her armless chair, folding her arms over her bosom. She had the look of a guard dog awaiting the "attack" order from its master. It was a look that filled my heart with a warm glow. I felt like a child whose big brother was going to thrash the school bully for picking on him. Papa forced his eyes apart, his movements sluggish, confused. A look of annoyance clouded his face as he kissed his teeth in an angry hiss.

"Can't a man get any rest in his own house?" he grumbled, stretching his hand for his snuffbox by his side table. His mood didn't lighten any when his eyes settled on me. I could see the dark brown tobacco stain at the tip of his nostrils, just above his lips. Mama nodded at me to speak.

Once again, I could not hold back my tears as I told Papa my tale, showing him the wreck Agu had made of my body. I was angry, shouting my rage as I recounted the litany of abuse Agu and his people had inflicted on my person. It was as if my voice, long buried, had been given a new life; as if my pride, long murdered in Ukari, had been reanimated within the safety of my father's house.

I wanted vengeance. I wanted Papa to take the tough village boys to Ukari and trash the skin off that midget trader and his obese sisters. I wanted Agu and his family to cry as I had cried, to feel the burning of birch, the pounding of fists, the cutting of flesh, just as I had done. But most of all, I wanted my old room back; that small book-choked room I'd shared with my sister once upon a blissful time, before I was driven from its womb-like warmth to the cold soulless Hades of Agu's house.

Papa listened to me in total silence, his dark face inscrutable, unyielding. The hard blackness of his eyes told me that he would not save me from my matrimonial hell.

I was not mistaken. Papa looked at Ibe as if to say, "Take good heed of this

41

crucial lesson for when you have troublesome daughters of your own," before turning back to me. A deep frown creased his forehead as he piled his nostrils with yet more tobacco powder.

"You are your husband's chattel now," Papa said, fixing me with a fierce look that would brook no arguments. "Nobody can come between a man and his wife. Whatever food they dish out to you should be eaten with endurance and gratitude. It is bad enough that you have shamed this family with your barrenness without adding the dishonour of a divorce. Where do you expect me to find the money to refund him the dowry he paid on your head should you return, eh? Do you want me to sell my *Ogodo*, my precious loincloth, to raise money to refund your dowry? Go, return to your husband and cease your whinging and childish behaviour. Kindly remember that you're the *Ada*, my first daughter. Your sister looks to you to set a good example. Do not let her down."

My father waved me away from his presence. I cast a wild look at my mother, unable to comprehend, to accept what my ears had heard. Surely, Mama would not stand by and let this happen to me; surely, she would talk to my father, convince him that I must never return to Ukari under any circumstance...

But my mother shrugged and looked away. My mother would not meet my eyes. The guard-dog look left her face and instead, I saw her lips curl down in that familiar manner I remembered from childhood, that silent message that said, "Your father knows best. You have to do as he says". But this was no longer some petty quarrel between siblings, some childish ploy for attention. This was a matter of life and death...*my life, her daughter's death!* Surely, she would not fold her hands and watch me die. She had to do something, say something to change Papa's mind. She was my mother, *my mother!*

"Mama!" My cry bore the weight of my pain, my terror. It forced itself from the depths of my soul, insisting on being heard. But my mother remained silent, a silent partner in her husband's crime. For in my mind, what they were doing was criminal, heartless, even evil. How could two people who conceived and gave life to me calmly hand me over to my killer for thirty pieces of dowrysilver?' They were no better than Judas Iscariot.

With weary resignation, I turned away from both my parents and walked out of the parlour, setting my face into the stoic mask of the example-giver, calm, patient and forbearing, just like a pious nun. After all, as my father said, I was the first daughter and my sister expected me to set a good example.

Thankfully, my father was wrong. My sister, Gono, did not expect any such martyr-like example from me. She took one look at my set features and rushed over to me. Her tears re-awakened my own. She clasped my shuddering body in her arms as I poured out my despair to her ears, the only ears that truly heard my pain. My body shuddered with the force of my tears and anger.

"Bastards! Men are all bastards! Useless lumps of pig shit!" Gono raged. "I wish

I were a man. By God, I will reincarnate as a man in my next life and then we'll see who calls the shots. Look at that idiot, Ibe. Already he's a replica of Papa, an *akologholi,* a useless little jerk with no brain cells in his big head. He's not a child anymore, for Christ's sake. He's almost seventeen years now, the same age you were when you married that dwarf. If he were a real man, he would go to Ukari and trash the living daylight out of that short bastard that calls himself your husband. But don't worry sis, don't cry. Everything will be okay soon, you'll see."

I hugged my little sister tightly, unwilling to separate our bond. I was allowed to spend the night under my father's roof on the proviso that no one found out that I'd done so without my husband's permission and that I left before the crow of the rooster the next day.

It was with a weary heart that I dressed up at the crack of dawn to make my feet-dragging way back to my husband's house. Just before I got on the Mami-wagon taking me back to Ukari village, Mama ran out and pushed a piece of paper into my hand before rushing back into the house again, ever fearful of incurring my father's wrath for encouraging my perceived rebellion. The short note, written in the familiar dear hand of my sister, Gono, contained the address of a famed Spiritualist, Pastor Brother Ezekiel of an *Aladura* spiritualist church. My sister's bold calligraphy penned Mama's wishes for me to visit the powerful pastor without delay, as he was the key to my problems. It was an instruction I was happy to obey. I was at the end of my endurance and ready to dine with Lucifer himself if he would free me from my marital yoke.

Pastor Brother Ezekiel proved to be everything I had hoped for and more. He identified and broke all my ancestral curses, binding the demons of infertility with chicken and goat sacrifices, a full body wash in consecrated water, mixed with the blood of my monthly curse and a burnt offering of my shaved pubic hair, the pages of the book of Psalms and a newborn's umbilical cord. I sold my best *Ashoke* ceremonial gown to raise the money to buy the last item from a private midwife and it was worth every last *Naira* note in the end.

Pastor Brother Ezekiel was possessed with the spirit of Arch-angel Michael on the night of my spiritual cleansing at his *Aladura* church. He spoke in tongues, wondrous and mysterious holy words that sent my senses into righteous ecstasy. And when Arch-Angel Michael possessed my trembling body, filling my womb with the holy seeds of fertility, I knew that my sorrows were finally at an end. Queen Ill-fortune had finally met her match in the all-conquering angel of our omnipotent creator, the Arch-Angel Michael himself!

I gave birth to my son exactly nine months to the date of my holy cleansing and my husband aptly named him Chukwuebuka, meaning, "God is great!" Everyone called him Ebuka, the shortened version of his name. Ebuka's birth healed the pain of my childless marriage, four years of humiliation, abuse and contempt. My sisters-in-law, overnight, metamorphosed from Lucifer to St. Peter, guarding my well-being and that of my son with the same zeal with which St Peter guarded the gates of heaven. Gone were the harsh words, the accusations, the bitter recriminations, the beatings. Even my husband had not lifted a violent hand on my person since the birth of his heir.

As the months went by and Ebuka grew stronger, Agu became kinder to me. He began addressing me with the endearment, *Nkem*, meaning, "my own." I was treated with respect by the villagers and addressed by the proud title, *Mama Ebuka*. I was now a mother. I had fulfilled my calling as a woman, a daughter and a wife. I had finally earned my place in society and gained acceptance amongst my husband's people.

I soon grew fat on a diet of contentment and pride. As our people say, a beggar who never dreamt of becoming a king will drown himself in ivory amulets from his heels to his chest so that no one will be in doubt of his importance. I was as crass as that stupid beggar, boasting of the beauty, the strength, the cleverness of my son, Ebuka. My eyes were haughty with pride, my voice loud in confidence, my mien complacent in contentment.

Until the day Queen Ill-fortune paid me an unexpected and devastating visit, wreaking deadly vengeance on me for my contempt of her might; that fatal eve of the New Yam festival, when the house-maid brought in the small lifeless body of my son, Ebuka, his features swollen and distorted by the venom of the evil viper, Echieteka, whose fearsome name meant, "tomorrow is too far to live."

The clanswomen said that I would not let go of my son's lifeless body; that I clung to him like a bat to its cave, fighting all that tried to pry him from my arms with the strength of ten mad women. They said that even after I had finally been restrained by the men of the clan, my relentless keening had kept the inhabitants of the surrounding compounds awake for several nights. According to them, the mourning food cooked for me by the village women went uneaten, while my body withered and wasted with the speed of my mind's deterioration.

I remembered none of it. I remembered nothing beyond the cold, cold body of my beautiful son... and the callus laughter of Queen Ill-fortune ringing in my brain, day and night.

My son was dead. No one would ever again call me "*Mami*" in that sweet baby voice. Arch-Angel Michael had been roundly defeated by Queen Ill-fortune. I was soul-weary, tired of resisting my fate. Whatever evil I had done in my previous existence had to be paid for in full in my present life. I had now paid my dues. Ebuka was gone. I had lost everything. All I wanted was out, freedom to join my son in the dark, cold embrace of death. I knew there would be peace in the sandy warmth of the grave. At least in my next reincarnation, I would finally return with a good *Chi*.

By the time my mind found its way back to the land of the sane, it was too late for me to find my son. Search as I could, ask as I dared, no one would show me where the tiny corpse of my son lay. All I knew was that he was buried in *Ajọ-ọfia*, the bad bush, a barren and desolate stretch of landscape inhabited by the cursed bodies of the unclean, those who died a cursed death. Their bodies were discarded in the bad bush, unmourned and forgotten—suicides, murderers, witches and wizards, night-flyers, poisoners, victims of lightning, mothers who died giving birth, widows who died while in mourning, children who died before their parents and people who were judged and destroyed by the Tree of Truth.

Nothing grew in *Ajọ-ọfia* but giant anthills, housing massive termites bloated from gorging on the corpses of the damned. It was no place for my innocent beautiful son, a laughing and happy child once beloved and cherished by all. His little red shoes still lay hidden in my room, buried deep in my *Adu, a* weaved cloth basket that held my expensive wrappers. My Adu kept the tiny shoes safe from the evil and prying eyes of the clanswomen. They would burn those beautiful shoes with the same speed with which they'd burnt all his clothing, wipe out all traces of his existence with the same cold and ruthless efficiency they had cast away his tiny body in *Ajọ-ọfia*, his grave unmarked by stone or cross, ensuring his name would be forgotten by mankind for all eternity and his spirit would never find its way back to its home to reincarnate amongst its people.

And for what crime? For dying from a poisonous snake bite? For dying too young before his time, before his parents? What had my innocent baby done to deserve such evil from the entire clan and village? I wanted to find his grave, to visit that accursed bush where his body lay discarded like bat-eaten mangoes, rancid and worthless. But my cowardly woman's heart feared the vengeful ghosts of the accursed dead that shared the bad bush with my little son. No matter how many *Hail Marys* I chanted, how many bottles of holy water I drank, how many wooden and metal crucifixes I collected or how many *Jigida* charmed amulets I wore around my waist to ward off evil spirits, my courage refused to reside in my heart and I could never make the long and fearful journey to my child's last resting place and mark his unhallowed grave with a mother's loving touch.

UKARI FOREST – 2 AM

Agu's eyes, closed by death, suddenly fly apart, staring their bloody glare into my eyes, eyes stretched to my ears by heart-thumping terror. My limbs melt, my breathing stops, my heart falls to my stomach as I fight to retain my sanity in the midst of the latest horror that has descended upon me in this forest of the damned. As I struggle to revive my feet, to flee from the zombie ghoul on the raffia mat, his right arm, rotting with peeling flesh, shoots up and grabs my throat, squeezing out my life with a strength and malignancy that is beyond the realms of the living.

I scream—yell—as I struggle to escape from the vengeful decaying demon that had once been my husband. But my voice is silent, my cries swallowed by my terror. I see the stinking, bloated carcass slowly rise from the forest floor, the raffia mat clinging to its pus-seeping skin. The stench of decay and rank is overpowering, almost stealing the air from my lungs. That bristly and mottled organ is hard against my thighs, rough and painful. IT demands forceful entrance to my secret place, still bruised and hurting from all its previous assaults. The hands on my throat tighten their grip, squeezing, hurting, till I feel the darkness of death pounding in my brain, seeking entry.

Yet, even as death waits impatiently for my soul, even as I feel the deadly pressure on my throat, something in me refuses to give in, to give up without fighting for the one thing that still belongs to me—my life. As pathetic as it is, it's still my own to keep or destroy. I know that if I don't flee, find a way to break through the charmed salt boundary set around me by the witchdoctors, my soul will become entwined with Agu's for all eternity.

For that is the fate of all murderers. Their lives are destined to be taken by their victim's ghosts, to be joined to their victims in death, like co-joined twins, condemned to an eternity of vengeful justice at the hands of these earth-bound spirits. Blessed Virgin! *I do not want to become a restless dead amongst my other curses and for all eternity, denied the chance of a better reincarnation. I begin to struggle with a desperation born of mind-killing terror, kicking, scratching, screaming, shoving.*

My eyes fly awake and I rise to the sound of silence, a graveside stillness that makes me wish for the oblivion of death by its sheer soundless terror. My heart is thudding so loudly I fear I will faint and then truly be damned. With small whimpering cries, I scramble away on bruised knees from Agu's bloated corpse, pulling myself to the very edge of the salt ring that has me chained to The Tree of Truth, shoulders hunched, my arms clasped tightly around my raised knees.

I stare—peer intently into Agu's swollen face, searching, looking for any sign of the terrifying animation I'd witnessed in my nightmare. Do his eyes flicker? Do I see his nose twitch? Surely, I hear something that sounds as soft as dandelion pores, a pungent exhalation that blows a sudden chill on my exposed flesh!

I force my eyes to take a brave peep at the jutting monster between his naked thighs, still throbbing in its knobbled evil, the undead tentacle in the lump of fetid rottenness that was my husband. It pulsates with a living strength that defies the rancid body that houses it. Oh Mary Mother of God! Will IT never die? Will IT never wilt? Will IT ever let me go?

Pulling my hair, tangled in filthy clumps on my scalp, I feel like hammering a stoneinto my skull to punish my brain for its stupidity. How could I have allowed my guard to slip, to give in to sleep, allowing Agu's vengeful spirit to attempt the possession of my body and chain me to him in eternal servitude? God knows he has enough to be vengeful about. My stupidity and desperation had cost him among other things, his life.

If only I hadn't been so desperate, so frightened. But what mother can hear the pitiful cries of her child and turn a deaf ear? Everything would have been alright if only Ebuka hadn't died, if Enu hadn't come into our family, if I had stayed away from that demon, Ogbunigwe. If only I hadn't been so foolish, so...

Eight months after the death of my son, Agu took a second wife, Enu. Older than me by several years, she was young enough to provide the male child to replace my late son and ensure the perpetuity of our husband's bloodline. Enu also had the advantage of being a local woman, born in Ukari of Ukari parentage. I was considered a tall woman but Enu towered over me by several fingers. She was a woman of mammoth proportions. Seeing her together with our husband for the first time was a sight I would never forget. Agu could have easily been mistaken for her son but for that strutting walk of his, peculiar to all pocketsize dictators. I would have burst out in a maniac's laughter had my situation not been so dire.

As soon as the wretched woman swaggered her way into our house, Agu threw me out of my room and consigned me to the back quarters of the house, the section reserved for the domestic helps. Enu took over ownership of my room and all the privileges of the main wife, from the domestic helps to the shopping and food management. I couldn't tell which was worse—the scorn of my husband and his sisters or the indifferent pity and contempt of the house-servants, who soon sucked up their way into the new mistress' favour with tales of my anguish. I would see them gathered, sniggering, whispering into their new mistress's ears. I was her senior in rank, the first wife, but our husband had stripped me of my rank and the respect that went with it. At best, I was no higher than the house servants now.

◆ ◆ ◆

Less than a year into her marriage, Enu fulfilled expectations with the birth of a son, whose striking resemblance to our husband was confirmed in his name, Nwanna, his father's son. On the night of Nwanna's birth, Queen Ill-fortune's gleeful laughter rang so loudly in my head I feared I would lose my sanity. But I masked my face with celebratory smiles at the wondrous arrival of our husband's heir, Nwanna, even as I sensed the malice behind the smiles of the clanswomen, heard the velvet spite behind their solicitous enquiries about my well-being.

However, there was nothing I could do to shield the evidence of my pain, try as I could. My reddened eyes remained puffed with unfinished tears, ready to shed my agony at the slightest excuse. Once, I had known the bliss of holding a child in my arms, suckling his little head on my tender breasts, his skin soft, silky to the touch, his voice beautiful and sweet when he called me *"Mami."* I had nothing now, would never know the glory of motherhood again. The same villagers that had once treated me with respect, now scorned me with indifference. Every honour now went to Enu and her new son. Our husband had ceased to know me as a wife from the day my son died. Now he had another wife and son, I had become an outcast of both man and the gods.

One night, a year to the birth of Nwanna, I awoke to the sound of a child's cries outside my window. It was mournful and muted, yet at the same time, piercing and insistent. I sat up on my bed, its loose springs squeaking out in protest. The cries stopped—just for a few seconds—then resumed with louder intensity. It sounded like a *Bush-Baby,* that nocturnal primate with a child's fingers, which mimics the cries of a newborn baby. It is a cursed creature, sent by enemies to cast evil spells on unsuspecting people. When sent to a woman, it kills all affections the husband has for her, ensuring she'll never become pregnant and have a child. Tricking unwary women with their infant-like cries, these evil creatures assume the form of wicked goblins, raping the women and biting off their toes after the vile act so that people know what had taken place. Consequently, all future children born by the molested women must be killed and buried at the *Ajo-ofia* to ensure the *Bush-Baby* curse is destroyed.

I stumbled through the darkness to my window, to make sure the latch was firmly secured before returning to my bed, my heart thudding in unbridled terror. I *knew* who had sent me the Bush-Baby—Enu, my husband's second wife. Not content with taking my husband, my bedroom and my status, she now wished to inflict the vilest of all curses on me by having me molested by the goblin Bush-Baby. *Oh Holy Mary mother of God! Would my travails never end?* I spent the rest of the night in wakeful misery, listening to the incessant cries of that evil abomination till Agu's prize cockerel crowed in the dawn and the unholy cries finally ceased.

For three more nights, the accursed *Bush-Baby* outside my window tormented my sleep. On the fourth night, it entered my room.

I awoke to the familiar child-like wails, feeling a terror grip my heart beyond anything I've ever felt since the death of my son. The cries ceased as soon as I opened my eyes. *Something was wrong, very wrong; bad.* The unnatural stillness in my room was heavy with a waiting quality that made the darkness a solid malignant mass. Covered in cold sweat, I fumbled for the box of matches to light my kerosene lantern. In the thin light of the lamp, I picked out a sudden movement near my *Adu,* the high basket that contained my special clothes, reserved for weddings and Sunday service. Something scuttled to the back of the *Adu,* something the size of a dog, yet faster in motion than any dog I had ever seen.

Then it cried, a sound so piercing and terrible that my heart froze. *Bush-Baby! Oh Holy Maria! Jesus!* What to do? There was no escape through my door as the *Adu* stood behind the wooden door on the inside of my bedroom. My eyes darted wildly around the room, looking for something, anything, to defend myself. The gleaming silver of my crucifix on the small table beckoned like an angel's halo. I reached out my hand to it and felt a sudden chill cover my entire body in goosebumps.

Ebuka, my beautiful, sweet son, stood in front of me; Ebuka, naked as the day he was born, his skin caked in the dirty mud of his unhallowed grave! I wanted to scream...I think I screamed. Then my mind died.

◆ ◆ ◆

I awoke, drenched in cold water, surrounded by Enu, our husband, the fat sisters and the house-servants. Enu held an empty bucket in her hand. I figured she must have doused me in cold water to bring me out of my faint. For a few seconds, my shame dulled my memory, especially when I saw the fury in Agu's eyes. Then recollection returned with terrifying panic.

"Ebbbbbuka!" I stuttered, struggling to speak through the terror that still held my heart in its grip. I cast wild looks around my room as I struggled to my feet, my wet cloths clinging to my skin, bringing shivers to my entire body. "Ebuka... Where's Ebuka? He's here...he's back..."

"*Chei! Tufia!* Heaven forbid evil! The woman is crazy again!" Enu shouted, snapping her fingers to ward off being infected by my lunacy, a cold smirk on her face. "*Onye-ishi,* when are you going to get rid of this mad woman, eh? It's not fair that our peace is ruined by her. Your son, Nwanna, needs his sleep, which this crazy woman won't let him have. I think..."

Agu raised his hand, cutting off Enu's tirade with that single gesture. At the same time, he waved away his sisters and the wide-eyed house-helps, his cold eyes fixed on me all the while.

"Return to your room," he said to Enu without taking his eyes from me. I saw a look of rebellion flash across Enu's eyes as she hesitated. "Go! Now!" Agu barked. Enu didn't need a second warning. Despite her mammoth size, I've heard her loud yelps on a few occasions, as a result of Agu's fists. I'll say it for our husband, he was indiscriminate in his violence, even if I got the lion share.

As the door slammed behind her, Agu approached me, his steps silent, deliberate. I huddled closer to the bedpost, pulling my pillow close, anything to ward off the blows I knew were coming my way.

"So...your son returned to you, did he?" Agu's voice was soft, dangerous. "You dare mock me with a name that should never be mentioned in my house! You stupid, stupid woman."

My pillow was useless, as were my cries for mercy. Agu rained his fury on my body, my head, my face, leaving me a bloody, crumbled wreck on the floor when he was done.

The next night, when my son returned to me, I knew better than to scream or faint. I fought my terror and spoke to my son. By the time we were done talking, all my former fears had disappeared. The following night, I had a basin of clean water and new clothes waiting in my room, together with his tiny red shoes I had saved since his death.

I washed the grave-mud and death odour off him, oiled his body with palm-kernel oil, combed his thick hair and dressed him up with his new clothes and the red shoes, which still fitted perfectly. Then I carried him in my arms and rocked him till sleep came to me.

When I awoke the next morning, Ebuka was gone and his clothes and little red shoes lay abandoned on my bed. I felt the tears choke my throat at my new loss, a loss now magnified by the brief bliss of motherhood I had experienced in the night. Suddenly, the pain from Agu's brutality on my body returned with throbbing intensity. I had felt nothing since my son returned to me and his disappearance re-awakened all my dormant pains, both mental and physical. For the first time, I contemplated suicide. Surely, death was better than this earthly torment!

The next night when my son came back to me, naked, again caked in filthy mud from his unhallowed grave, with that foul smell of decay still clinging to him despite all my scrubbing and washing, I welcomed him into my arms with indescribable joy. I again carried out the loving chore of cleansing and dressing him, secure in the knowledge that he would be back the following night, till my love held him back for good and he lost the urge to go back to *Ajọ-ọfia*.

So began my second phase of motherhood. I nursed and loved my dead baby who neither ate nor stayed beyond the light of dawn. No matter what delicacies I offered him, Ebuka would never take a single bite nor drink a sip of water. His eyes remained open through the night and his cold little body would never soak the warmth from my cradling arms. But he was happy to be together with his loving *Mami* again.

And me? My steps grew lighter and my face glowed with ecstasy. I noticed the suspicious looks of the household, the whispers—*It's the madness... she's too far gone now for help!* What did I care? I had my son again. But I wasn't enough for Ebuka, though. He started asking me to bring him back for good. He was lonely and sad in *Ajo-ofia*. The cursed soil kept coughing up his corpse, rejecting his body as the humans had rejected it. It had taken him years to find his way back to our house, a miracle in itself, considering the remoteness of his gravesite. He missed me desperately and wanted to remain with me, but he could not return for good till he was reincarnated back to us. I knew Ebuka's only chance of reincarnation lay with me getting pregnant, enabling him to return through my new birth. But how could I make that happen when our husband no longer touched me as a wife?

I visited Ogbunigwe's hut at midnight of the next full moon. He would only see supplicants at that specific time. Ogbunigwe was as fierce-faced as his reputation, tall, marble-featured, coal-skinned and bloody of eyes. His body was knife-carved with intricate *Nsibidi* designs too mysterious for me to decipher. His voice when he spoke to me, was deep, yet raspy, full of authority and ancient knowledge. The aura of menace about him terrified me even more than the macabre place he lived, set deep in the forest and littered with numerous human skulls and animal carcasses. The metallic smell of blood was strong, overpowering, coupled with another strange odour I could not fathom. The great medicine man was dressed in nothing but a loin-cloth and multiple amulets and charms.

As I stepped through the low door of his hut, I noticed that the cement flooring of the room was polished with blood. Briefly, the thought flickered in my mind—*What will Father O'Keefe think of me if he knew where I was?* I couldn't believe that I, Desdemona, once an aspiring teacher and a devout Catholic, had now descended to this level of fetishness. I waved the thought away. *We are all what our Chi decides for us. Who can say what is right and what is wrong? After all, didn't King Saul himself visit the Witch of Endor in the Bible and spoke to God's prophet, Samuel?*

I bowed my head and fell to my knees before the great Juju-man. "Great One, please, hear the pleas of your handmaiden." I could neither control the tremor in my voice nor the quake in my body. "My husband no longer touches me as a wife, and I am a woman without a child. My childbearing years are shortening, and my departed son is now a restless dead. He cannot reincarnate back to his clan without a pregnancy in my belly. Help me, great and wise One. Give me the pregnancy I seek. Give me back my son. Chain my husband to my side, so that my belly may once more swell with the seeds of a child and the bloodline is preserved." My tears flowed unchecked as I beat my chest repeatedly with my fists.

Ogbunigwe was silent for several minutes, staring down at me from his great height, his face inscrutable, like the jagged rocks surrounding his abode.

"Are you prepared to pay the price?" His voice was low, deep, terrible. "I have saved enough money," I said, reaching to the lumpy knot at the edge of my wrapper, where my folded Naira notes were hidden.

"Foolish woman! Keep your money," his hand waved away my offering with disdain. "Listen with your ears and pay heed to my words. I repeat, are you prepared to pay the price?"

Then I knew. And yet I did not know. I suddenly recalled another saying of my people—*never dine with the devil without a very long spoon, in case you need to make a speedy escape.* A favour from the devil always came with a price in blood. *But whose blood? Whose death?* I could already sense the presence of Queen Ill-fortune at my side, mocking me, laughing at my dilemma.

Her glee decided me. I was done with being the plaything of the Queen of Misery.

"I am ready, Great One," my voice was resolute, with no signs of its earlier tremor. "I am ready to pay the price."

"On your head be it. Before the gods, I wash my hands of any guilt and blame. I am but a messenger of the spirits. Your contract is with them, not me. You have entered this agreement of your own free will and so shall it be. There is no turning back now. Give me your hand."

With a swift flicker, Ogbunigwe pierced the skin of my thumb with a blade, drawing the blood in a thick spurt. I saw the red drops hit the floor of his shrine with a hiss that had me almost bolting from the room. From nowhere, smoke suddenly filled the room, as if a thick fog had descended from the skies. The smell of blood was overpowering. My head was swimming, my eyes watering. My breath came out in short gasps. I saw movements in the fog, quick darting motions of figures I could not decipher. They seemed human, pale and ghastly, yet, too insubstantial to the sight. And surely, no human could move with such speed, even faster than hurricane. *What on Amadioha's earth were they?*

Ogbunigwe gave me a list of items I needed to bring to him for the preparation of the charms. When I heard the list, my blood almost froze in my veins. They included the hair from my dead child's skull, our husband's under-garment, a vial of my menstrual blood, the blood from a week-old baby boy and several other animal and human parts and herbs too numerous to recount. He also wanted hair from Nwanna's head—Nwanna, our husband's new son.

I felt my resolve falter at that last item. Why Nwanna's hair? Why not hair from any other child? I voiced my thoughts, but the great medicine-man hushed my words with a glare that put the terror in my heart. I wanted to flee from the skull-littered shrine, to hide away from the terrible visage of the witchdoctor. But I recalled his words, *"There is no turning back now."* I also remembered the melancholy face of my son, Ebuka and the arrogant swagger of Enu. I knew then what I had to do.

"It shall be done, Great One," I bowed my head again, stooping to kiss the ringed toes of Ogbunigwe's bare feet. "It shall be done."

Ogbunigwe's list was daunting and almost impossible to secure. But as our people say, *there is nothing the eyes will see that will cause them to shed blood-tears.* A desperate need will always find a miracle. My will to bring back my son was as strong as an elephant's charge. I found my miracle in my wonderful sister, Gono, who had gone ahead to become a successful headteacher at a top secondary school, one of the handful of female head-teachers from our country, rubbing shoulders with the white Irish nuns who ran our education institutions.

As my father had long dreaded, Gono had indeed refused to give him a befitting son-in-law and dowry, preferring to earn and keep her own money instead. She had become a very wealthy and respected woman who some people predicted would have a successful political career in the new political climate that had won us our independence from the Queen of England. Men were now seeing the hidden beauty in my sister which our father had failed to recognise on account of her dark skin. But Gono had my wretched marriage as a constant reminder of what that vile institution harboured for women. She vowed never to relinquish her freedom and wealth to any man.

Gono gave me the exorbitant sum I requested for the purchase of most of the items demanded by the medicine man, Ogbunigwe. She neither asked, nor did I volunteer the reason for my need. As always, she was happy in my happiness and I again thanked Our Virgin Mary for blessing me with such a loving sister, whose kindness I did not deserve.

Afterwards, for several days and nights, I agonised over the terrifying trip I had to make to *Ajọ-ọfia* to obtain a palmful of my dead child's hair. It was a trip which I had always lacked the courage to attempt, a journey I could not avoid, a visit that had been waiting to be made since the day they dumped my son's little body in the unhallowed grounds of *Ajọ-ọfia*. It was a trip now inevitable in order to bring my son back to life.

For three nights in a row, I attempted to cut the hair off Ebuka's head when he visited me. I used a small scissors to cut off a generous amount of his hair, which remained thick and lush despite the ravages of the grave. Yet, every morning when I awoke, the hair, just like my son, were gone, leaving me with nothing but the little red shoes that remained as new as the day I bought them. My son told me that I must go to *Ajọ-ọfia* to get his hair. He said he would lead me to his grave. He told me that his grave was a shallow grave, barely an arm-length in depth, as was the way with all unhallowed graves. Accursed corpses required no respect or protocol. I could easily dig open his grave with nothing more than my farming hoe. He said it was a job I could complete in the course of a single night.

Ebuka knew why I needed his hair and the knowledge made him happier than I'd ever seen since he returned to me. It was strange, the contradiction in his age and demeanour. In size, he had not aged a day beyond the three years he was when he died. Yet, his speech and reasoning were that of an *Ozo*, a wise and titled old peer of the clan. He calmly informed me that he would not come back to me until the day I became filled with the seeds of his reincarnation.

"But my son, how will you know when I get pregnant if you don't visit your poor *Mami*?" I asked, my eyes pleading, my voice cajoling.

"I will know, *Mami*," was all he said. "I will know."

On a moonlit night of still air and sleepless insects, I made my stealthy journey to *Ajọ-ọfia* accompanied only by my son and my farming hoe. I started off just after midnight. I soon developed the vision of the night bat and the agility of the forest monkey as the journey progressed. I engaged in lively conversation with my son to rein in my terror. Ebuka was as surefooted as the bush antelope as he navigated through wild vines and erosion gullies, leading me further away from Ukari village and deeper into the forest. The night seemed to go on forever till, suddenly, I found myself in a desert-like landscape populated with nothing but giant anthills and uncountable mounds that housed the corpses of the damned. Like a macabre farm, the mounds grew ghastly white masks, each fortified with charms and potions to chain in the evil dead within the confines of the bad bush. A foul smell pervaded the corpse-farm, an odour of badness and decay; a vile smell that I'd tried in vain to wash off from my son's body.

My heart froze. My speech ceased. My head began to swell and expand, and my breathing hung. All sounds stopped, vanished, as if cocked inside a sound-proof bottle. The noisy insects that had accompanied us through the night, the barking dogs, the hooting owls, all ceased their clamour. Even the very air seemed to succumb to the stillness of the desolate and chilling landscape. In the unnatural silence, I heard the thudding of my heart like the beating of the drums of the masquerade dancers. I heard the harshness of my breathing and the roaring in my ears.

Then I saw them...*oh Jesus, Mary Mother of God*...I saw them all, the soulless inhabitants of the accursed land, *Ajo-ofia,* the doomed outcasts of the gods and men, the unclean! Gathered in a silent, waiting crowd, hollowed eyes dripping blood as black as tar, each posed in the manner of their demise, they impaled me to the ground by their appalling visage.

A young mother with a rotten foetus dangling between her wide thighs; a large man with a rope tight against his impossibly-angled neck; an albino that glowed inhumanly white beneath the brightness of the moon, his body bloated and battered from the beating that caused his demise; a tiny baby wailing and writhing on the ground, his wide mouth exposing a full set of upper teeth—they were the abominations of nature and the rejects of men.

Amongst them was my son, my beautiful, sweet Ebuka, standing silently in the midst of the other small spectres, each doomed for dying before their parents or being born with abominations such as a set of teeth, an extra finger, a single testicle. One second, Ebuka was by my side, his tiny hand gripped firmly in my right hand. Then in a blink, he was gone, gone without a sound, without me seeing his departure, only to appear amongst the ghoulish gathering of the damned, the cursed inhabitants of the unhallowed grounds of *Ajo-ofia.*

The sound of my hoe hitting the ground resonated like a thousand footsteps in the awful silence of the burial ground. It also released the voices of the apparitions, who started to howl in an unearthly cacophony that chilled the marrow in my bones. My voice joined their discordance, terror and panic cloaking my screams. Prayers spilled from my lips, babbles, the distinct sounds of supreme lunacy. Inside my head, Queen Ill-fortune shrieked in glee, her cackle as manic as my screams. Above us, the moon grew fatter and brighter, revealing the ghoulish figures in all their undead horror.

I tried to run, turned to flee, feeling the hot piss of terror flood my thighs. I stumbled against a mask...*no*...the mask rose against my feet as if flung by an invisible hand. Then all the other white masks joined the attack like a sea of skulls, hurling themselves against my face, battering my body and my head till I fell onto a soft grave, feeling the mud cover my face and fill my screaming mouth. It was the same mud that clung to my son, the vile grave-mud of the unhallowed ground I'd tried in vain to wash off my son.

My fall stilled the masks. They fell to the ground with muffled thumps. From the corner of my eyes, I saw them scuttle away, countless white masks, like the crabs on the beach of River Niger, each returning to the grave-mound they guarded, their hollowed eyes watchful, dark and terrifying. In the sudden stillness, I heard another sound, a noise like the roar of the winds.

And suddenly, they were everywhere, the ghosts of the damned, in front of me, behind me, at my right side and left side. And when the light of the moon dimmed above us, I glanced up to see the flying ones, *Amosu*, witch night-flyers who had carried on their nefarious art even to the grave. I felt their hands on me; cold hands, clammy hands, pus-wet hands, peeling hands, skeletal hands. Reeking bodies swamped me, seeking the warmth of my blood, the light of my humanity, my very soul. I tried to push, to crawl to safety on hands and knees, to be free of the repulsive touch of the foul undead. But I was but a woman, a weak and foolish human who should have known better than to challenge the might of the queen of malignancy on her most potent night.

But desperation was never a person of caution or reason. Desperation would dare the gates of hell and the wrath of Queen Ill-fortune to fulfil its goals. Desperation gave me the voice to scream out my son's name, to call for his aid and his intercession. Desperation fuelled my garbled explanations, my pleas for their forgiveness, my supplications for their help in finding my son's grave amongst the hundreds of unmarked mounds that grew in that accursed farm of corpses.

Suddenly, I was free—free of hands, of bodies, of voices, of the pulsating hate that had engulfed me and left me cowering on the cold hard soil of *Ajọ-ọfia*. Once again, my son was by my side, his little hands filled with an impossible strength, raising me to my feet, his face sad, *oh Jesu*, so very sad.

I wanted to die and lie with him in that bad bush for eternity. *How can any mother bear to see her child abandoned in such a desolate and terrible place? How could I ever sleep in the warmth of my room when my only child wandered in the dark wilderness of these cursed grounds? How could I walk amongst the living when I knew that my son walked amongst the damned, the restless and angry souls of the accursed?* As if he read my thoughts, Ebuka pointed to a small grave barely the size of a yam-tuber mound in a flourishing farm. It was guarded by a repulsive white mask that resembled a leering goblin. I shuddered as my eyes encountered that accursed object, reluctant to bring my person within its malignant reach. My heart still quaked with the recent memory of the white masks' vicious attack on me.

My son motioned me to dig, his small hands holding up my discarded hoe. Once again, my resolve was re-ignited as I stumbled my way to the small mound and started to dig. Through that moonlit night, I dug till the sweat lay on my body like a bucketful of water, till my palms went raw and bloody, till my joints ached as one crushed by a palm-tree, till my eyes ceased to see anything but brown hard soil, till my breath rushed in staggered gasps through open mouth and nostrils clogged by dirt.

Till....till I finally struck the brittle bones of my poor, poor son, dumped in that terrible grave without the dignity of a coffin.

I began to howl.

I slumped on the dirt floor of the grave and wailed—keened—mourning my dead son all over again as if he had died anew. The pain was as raw as the day the evil viper, *Echieteka,* stole him from me. My heart burnt with anger and pain, fury at the callous way they had discarded my son's body and a hurting pain that threatened to steal what was left of my sanity.

I felt the presence of the ghosts, felt their compassion surround me as I tore the hair from my scalp, knocked my forehead on my hunched knees, beat the ground with clenched fists and bawled my pain into the cold dark grave of my son. I felt his little hands on my face, stroking my wet cheeks, his small cold body nestling against me, his thin arms around my neck. I held him close, so tight, I would have squeezed the life force from his body if there was any left to destroy.

"I'm so sorry, my son," I choked between sobs. "I'm so sorry. Forgive your poor *Mami* for not protecting you, for letting them do this to you."

"Don't cry, *Mami*," his voice was muffled against my chest. "Don't cry, please *Mami*. Look, my hair is still here, see?" Ebuka pointed to his tiny skeleton which indeed still harboured a long bush of hair. That was the day I realised that hair was immortal. And it finally made sense why Ogbunigwe had demanded that particular item. Only immortality could confer life. My son's immortal hair would reincarnate him back to life. Nwanna's living hair would link the bloodline, ensuring a successful reincarnation.

I did not need a pair of scissors. The hair left my son's skull in an easy clump, filling my hand with its kinky soft texture.

"You have to go now, *Mami,* before the sun rises or there will be no one to show you the way back to Ukari. We have to sleep when the morning dawns. Come, let me take you back now."

I allowed my son to lead me out of that terrible place, my eyes filled with tears, my heart breaking with sorrow at the tragic plight of those pathetic souls that haunted the grounds of *Ajọ-ọfia*. I knew some of them were guilty of the crimes that had consigned them to the bad-bush. But most of them were innocent, like my son, like those poor teethed babies. Yet, all of them were equally damned for eternity. *But not my son, not my sweet innocent baby. By Amadioha and all the gods, I'll free him from that terrible curse and return him to the loving fold of his family.*

I now had the final and most precious item demanded by Ogbunigwe, the great witchdoctor. Ebuka's hair would be the final piece in the charms that would secure the affections of our husband once again and germinate my womb with my son's reincarnated foetus.

When the door of my bedroom swung open a couple of weeks later and Agu stepped into my room, I knew that Ogbunigwe had lived up to his reputation. Even before he began stripping off his clothes, I knew from Agu's face that he had not come to inflict violence on my body. From the minute I covered my face with the foul-smelling oil given me by Ogbunigwe, I noticed a growing look of desire on Agu's face. And when he unexpectedly called me by the long-forgotten endearment, *"Nkem,"* I knew that he finally belonged to me, at least in body, if not soul. Already, a cup of palm-wine laced with the cloudy liquid the medicine man had given me to feed our husband stood by my bedside, a drink which also had to be spiked with the residue of his semen before he drank it.

Afterwards, when Agu had drunk the charmed wine and once again mounted me, I noticed a difference in his *Amu*. It looked and felt double its original size and remained solidly erect even after his release. I saw the look of baffled pleasure on Agu's face as he observed his enlarged and turgid organ. It was the look of a young boy discovering his first tuft of manly beard.

Over the following weeks, Agu continued to visit my room every night. His desire was insatiable, and my body soon grew weary of the incessant demands made on it, coupled with the fact that his visits were affecting my son's. Ebuka had not paid me a single visit from that terrible night he led me to his grave to collect his hair from the skeletal husk that lay beneath the shallow grave at *Ajo-ofia. Holy Mary! Jesus our Saviour!* I still shudder, still wake up in sweats, still glance behind me in unspeakable terror at the memory of that dreadful night.

As the weeks turned into months, Agu's nightly visits gradually increased to afternoon and evening visits. The intimate name, *Nkem,* never left his lips when he addressed me, even in front of strangers. Soon, malicious tongues began to wag, fuelled by Enu's spite. The words "Witch" and "Mami-water" cropped up once again in reference to me. They were tags I hadn't heard since my son's death gave birth to new names, *"Akula,"* Mad woman.

But this time, their insults left me cold. Despite the element of truth in their accusations, I felt none of the guilt and shame I'd felt in the days I was falsely accused. *What did I care about their feelings as long as I brought back my son to life?* The Holy Virgin knew I was paying my own heavy price, enduring the rough and incessant attentions of our husband to achieve my goal. My secret place was raw from the persistent demands made on it by our husband.

And yet, despite the passing months and the increased frequency of Agu's carnal visits, my belly refused to germinate with the seeds of fertility. Nothing grew inside my soured womb. But something began to grow on our husband.

◆ ◆ ◆

The first mole appeared on Agu's *Amu* on a Sunday afternoon. I know the precise time and date because I remember being dragged into my room as soon as I returned from Sunday Mass and mounted before I could even undo my *Enigogoro* head-scarf. After the act was over, I noticed Agu starring at his *Amu,* which as always, jutted up towards the low ceiling of my room, bloated with useless seeds that could not fertilize my womb. I instantly noticed the spot on his organ, a spot more like a giant mole than anything else I could imagine. It formed a solid round mass at the tip of his *Amu,* its reddish hue contrasting starkly with the blackness of that organ.

Chickenpox! That was my first thought; *Agu has chickenpox!* Trust the wretched man to do everything differently. Other people got the pox on their faces but not Agu. Oh no! He had to go get it on his blighted *Amu.* By the next day, four more moles appeared and within a week, the entire length of his *Amu* was covered with the unsightly red moles. It was about this time that I noticed a difference in his possession of me. It felt as if he performed the act for reasons other than desire, as if something else was driving his frenzied thrusts, an itch perhaps, an uncontrollable urge to scratch, relieve the irritation in his skin. But why use me? Why wouldn't he keep away from me till his pox or whatever it was ailing his organ was cured?

Because of Ogbunigwe's charms, you fool! The mocking voice in my head was as nasty as Queen Ill-fortune's laughter. I'd asked for our husband to be enslaved by desire and I had my wish. Something else told me those wretched charmed drinks I had fed him over the course of several weeks were equally responsible for the disgusting moles that were fast turning his *Amu* into a twisted grotesque appendage. Conjugal exercises had never been pleasant with our husband, even at the best of times. Now, they were just awful, terrible acts of torture that tore up the tender skin of my circumcised womanhood and left me dreading the simple act of weeing or washing. My days were now lived in terror of those hurried footsteps headed to my room, knowing that my objections would be quashed by violent hands and thrusting hips. He would not discuss the state of his *Amu* with me. In fact, he seemed determined to ignore the ghastly thing, despite the fact that other alien bits had joined the moles, long spiky hairs and worm-like welts.

I tried not to look at that monstrosity. Jesus knows just how much I tried to keep my eyes away from it. But the eye is the master of curiosity. It will look where it should not and seek where it is forbidden. So, my eyes followed the gradual distortion of that organ, observing the festering malignancy of that benighted appendage as crusted pus was replaced by fresh eruptions and I wished.... *dear Lord*...how I wished I could sever that evil with a sharp knife and free us both from our nightmare.

We were now the talk of the whole village. Agu no longer stepped out of the house, seeing as he could not wear anything save the loose wrapper he kept secured around his waist. His visit to his *Dibia* had not cured his ailment, neither had all the ointments and antibiotics prescribed by the doctors at Park Lane Hospital. Enu and the three fat sisters shouted to all who would listen that I had chained our husband with witchcraft, that he had lost his mind as I had lost mine. His business was failing, and his workers were running lawless. Enu was pregnant with yet another child and our husband ignored that fact and provided little for her comfort. The news of Enu's pregnancy almost drove me wild with jealousy. Why should she have all the luck, a living son and another easy pregnancy, when I had been going through months of torture to achieve the same fate without success? Clearly, the blasted woman was born under a very good *Chi* despite her meanness.

Except she wasn't after all.

On a dark rainy night, Nwanna got the runs. All night, I heard the sound of the housemaids rushing up and down the stairs as they emptied the child's potty. Enu burst into my room a couple of hours later, rousing our husband from his deep sleep in my bed.

"Your son is dying, and you lie here like an idiot," she shouted at Agu. Her eyes were red and puffy, her hair dishevelled.

"What's wrong with Nwanna? Can I help?" I asked. I felt a sudden pity for the woman. Despite everything, she was still a mother, experiencing a mother's hurt at her child's suffering.

"Keep away from my child, you witch," Enu snarled, dousing my goodwill with her spite. I shrugged and turned away, feigning disinterest. Agu dragged himself up from my bed, waving Enu away.

"I'll be with you soon," he said. "Send for the driver to take him to Park Lane hospital."

Enu stalked out of my room, slamming the door behind her.

"Nkem, I'll be back soon, ok?" Agu said, looking apologetic and guilty at the same time, as if he were committing a crime by attending to his sick son instead of spending time with me. *Ogbunigwe's charms had really done the works on* him, I thought with regret as I watched him hobble out of my room. I had not spiked his drinks in months, yet his *Amu* refused to heal and his slavish devotion to me refused to wan. If only I could convert that attachment to a pregnancy.

✦ ✦ ✦

Nwanna died that same night. Even the white doctors at Park Lane hospital could not perform their usual miracles. They said it was cholera, the deadly sickness of the intestines. Enu said it was witchcraft. I had finally killed her son with evil juju, as I had long intended since his birth. The accusation chilled my bones, filling my heart with terror. *Oh Holy Mary! Don't let Nwanna's death have anything to do with my visit to Ogbunigwe and that tiny quantity of hair I'd taken from Nwanna's comb!*

For several days following Nwanna's death I paced around my room, enduring sleepless night after sleepless night. *How could I live with myself if I had a hand in that innocent child's death? How could I possibly forgive myself if I had been instrumental in sending that poor child to join my son at Ajọ-ọfia, the dreadful corpse-farm of the doomed?* I derived no pleasure at the thought that Enu's child now shared the same fate as my son, having died of a deadly disease before his parents. *What mother would wish the same torture on a fellow mother?*

Enu's incessant wails and howls gave me no peace, just as my troubled thoughts gave me no sleep. The charm was not supposed to harm the child in any way and soon, I found my way to Ogbunigwe's hut for the final time. From the resigned look in his eyes when he saw me, I knew he had been expecting me.

"Nothing was supposed to happen to the child," I screamed at him, tears pouring down my cheeks. "You told me his hair was only needed to link my son's return to his bloodline."

"Foolish woman!" His voice was scornful, albeit I detected a hint of compassion in his bloodshot eyes. "I did warn you, didn't I? I am only a mouthpiece to the oracle and the gods never lie, not in my lifetime, nor in the lifetimes of my grandfather and great grandfather. I come from a long line of shrine-keepers and our juju have never failed."

"Then why am I not pregnant? Why has my son not returned to me yet?" My voice was shrill in the dead silence of the night.

"A life for a life, a son for a son. Fear not; the bloodline is not broken. The oracle never lies. Return to your home, woman, and disturb me no more. My patience with you now wears thin."

The witchdoctor waved me away with a casual flick of his hand, as if I were no more than a troublesome gnat, as if he hadn't just destroyed my life with his words, as if the death of an innocent child by his actions was no more than a splash of water on a Sunday gown. I stumbled out of his hut and into the warm blackness of the night. My body was shivering uncontrollably. My heart was pounding painfully, and a loud voice kept screaming, *no! no! no!* inside my head. *What have I done? Oh dear Jesus, what have I done?*

Following Nwanna's death, Enu and the three fat sisters called several meetings of the clan to air their suspicions and vent their rage. The clansmen consulted several witchdoctors, who all pointed their fingers at me. They said that the curse of Queen Ill-fortune had been brought upon the family by my actions when my son died. They claimed that I had an unholy union with some powerful deities which defied their own powers. The house of Agu, son of Onori, was a doomed one. The only way to break the curse was to sever my link to the family.

The elders reached a decision that I was to be sent back to my father's house without delay. I read the fear and repulsion in their averted eyes as they told me my fate. The only eyes that held no fear was Enu's. If hatred alone could kill, I would have been struck dead in seconds. Her eyes were the only gaze I could not hold in that large gathering of clansmen and clanswomen.

Our husband vetoed their ruling, telling them in no uncertain terms that I was his wife of no regrets, as he put it. He said that if anyone was to leave his house, it was Enu, not I. I heard Enu's sudden gasp, echoed by the rest of the family at Agu's words. His unusual stance confirmed all their suspicions but there was little they could do but wait, scheme, bide their time.

Until the day Agu finally succumbed to the infection that had journeyed from his deformed *Amu* to his veins, poisoning his blood and stealing his breath. He died in my bedroom, right on my bed, still trying to mount me even as death pulled him to its black door. The last words I heard from his lips were "*Nkem,*" repeated over and over till his speech was silenced by eternity.

And I suddenly found myself at the mercy of all the enemies I had made in that accursed village, Ukari, helpless, childless and with no-one to protect me from their collective hate. I had no one to speak for me, plead my cause and spare me from the nightmare of my ordeal in the accursed forest of Ukari and the terrifying judgement of the *Tree of Truth*.

✦ ✦ ✦

UKARI FOREST – 5:15 AM

Above me, heaven suddenly opens its mouth and spews down a thunderstorm on mankind. God's eyes flash His wrath across the skies and His anger roars over the world. In seconds, I am drenched, the rain washing the matted filth and blood from my body. I raise my face to the skies. My mouth is open as I drink in God's holy water of my salvation; real water at last, not the corpse water I've endured for days. The water rejuvenates me. It also rejuvenates the world of the living and of the dead.

I see them. Suddenly, I see them in the deep gloom of the forest. They are everywhere; soulless spectres, the restless spirits of all the victims of The Tree of Truth. They crowd around the tree, howling, pleading their case, begging forgiveness for past crimes, cursing, laughing—the pitiful laughter of the insane. They fly against the tree, through the tree, around the tree. They're drawn to the tree like moth to flame, powerless to leave the scene of their demise or the towering judge that sentenced them to sleepless eternity.

I recognise some of their faces; Ugomma the witch, Adaku the husband poisoner, one-eyed Chiadi, the child-napper and Ijeoma the night-flyer. The great tree had judged them all guilty, just as it might yet find me guilty. It seems to have a peculiar penchant for the evil souls of women. I do not want to be judged by The Tree of Truth. I fear I may not survive its wrath. I pray I do not become an unclean. Ajọ-ọfia is no place for eternal rest.

I see my son, Ebuka, hovering beyond the ring of salt. He is murky, coated in dirt and a strange darkness that renders him almost indistinct. My heart swells with delight then shrivels with terror at the look in his eyes. They blaze with hate, with rejection. He points at me, an accusing finger and I hear his voice, louder than the thunder that had heralded the storm.

"You lied to me," he screams. "You lied! You cannot bring me back because I don't belong to Agu's Obi, his ancestral compound. His blood does not flow in my veins so I can never be reborn to his bloodline. I can never return anywhere. Only Nwanna can go back. His bloodline is intact. His mother is pregnant. You have doomed me to Ajọ-ọfia for eternity. I hate you, Mami, I hate you."

I am wailing as I see my son fade into the night, the night that has suddenly turned as bright as day, lit up by the engorged moon.

Then, I see Nwanna. He flies like all the other spectres, hovering in the clearing, laughing, his voice tingling like little bells, his child's eyes happy, innocent. They bear me no malice, no hatred for my deeds. He glows with a dazzling brightness that is almost blinding in its intensity. Then he winks out, just like a star. And I am all alone with my guilt and my shame. The rain pounds down on me, relentless, merciless.

It has all been for nothing...nothing. After everything, all my suffering, all my hopes, my plans, everything. In the end, it has all been for nothing. If only I had gone back to Pastor Brother Ezekiel rather than that accursed witchdoctor, Ogbunigwe. If only I'd been born under a brighter Chi.

I hear a rustle. My head swivels. I see the waifs melt into the Tree of Truth, disappear into the massive trunk. The bark turns a sickly grey colour and the roots begin to heave. Oh Holy Mary! The Tree is alive! It moves! My husband's corpse stirs, sluggishly, blindly, its arms lifting, slowly. A bloated hand gropes its way to its Amu. It clasps the erect vileness and starts to yank in a grotesque act of masturbation. I gag, my stomach heaving, my muscles contracting, aching, hurting.

The head turns, silently, heavily, towards me, where I cower at the edge of the salt ring. I begin to shudder. My entire body is one continuous rattle, my teeth, my bones. Oh Holy Mary, sweet mother of God, don't let him open his eyes, please... Keep his eyes shut...

The lids lift and I see those eyes—bloody, black. They stare at me, fix me with their dead glare. I shut my lids and cover my head with my arms. The heavens continue to pour, and I hear my moans, whimpers that sound like Agu's dog when it is whipped for misbehaving. I hear another sound, a croak, like a strangled man's dying gurgle. Then I hear the words, repeated over and over and over and over...

"Nkem...Nkem...Nkem..."

I jump to my feet and scream. I remember too late the salt ring, the charmed circle made by the powerful witchdoctors to keep me trapped under the Tree of Truth. I hit an invisible wall. Bright lights explode inside my head as I stumble back, falling, falling, right atop the rotten carcass of my randy husband. I feel arms encircle me, strong arms, skin slimy against mine, sleeked by decay and death.

The stench is overpowering and just as in my nightmare, I feel the hard thrust of that rotting, jutting deformity against my thighs, feel the touch of those putrid hands pushing, prising my thighs apart with a strength not of the living. The pain is excruciating, unbearable. I hear that awful gurgling sound repeat the accursed name, "Nkem" into my ears. My soul is pulled, dragged from my being by a malignant force beyond the realm of the living.

And I am screaming, shrieking. Queen Ill-fortune is cackling, crowing with unholy glee. The fat moon smiles down benignly at my unholy ravishment and impending death. God is thundering, roaring, helpless as He's always been in the face of mankind's tragedy. Our husband is grunting, panting. The spectres gather closer, their ashen faces greedy for my dying soul, eager to welcome me into their foul and restless fold.

From a distance, I hear the sound of the approaching villagers, murder in their voices. A small smile twists my bruised lips. They will be too late. I can already sense my soul fleeing, fighting for release from my dying body. I am happy to give it its freedom. I am ready to be judged, to end this accursed cycle and heaven willing, begin a better one. If nothing else, I shall share the same unhallowed grounds with my son and be with him for as long as the gods wish. It is a better fate than one of eternal sexual servitude to our husband, who is still panting his pleasure on my immobile, dying body. I feel nothing now, not the rain, not the pain, not even the fear.

I cast my dimming eyes at The Tree of Truth, awaiting its final judgement. But the Tree of Truth... The Tree of Truth is silent. And in its silence, I hear my judgement, my salvation. Gono's voice, my sister's raging voice rising above the din of the villagers, ordering the police to arrest my abusers, handcuff the lot. My heart soars, my tears flow. I feel arms around me, different arms, warmer, firmer arms, loving arms.

"It's okay; it's alright, my sister. You're safe now. You're coming home with me, you hear me?" Gono's voice is urgent in my ears, her voice trembled by fury and pain.

I hear her. I also hear them; their unholy shrieks, their angry howls as they retreat into The Tree of Truth, disappear into the approaching dawn, The Unclean, the accursed ghouls. They will not have my soul after all, not this time... not yet. My blood will not fertilize the roots of The Great Tree; my soul will not be chained in eternal enslavement to my husband. The Tree of Truth has rendered its judgement and has deemed me worthy in the end. I am free...free...free...

I look up to the greying skies. The moon is a fading round shadow, weak, powerless. I listen for that cackle, that terrible screech of doom. But for the first time in a very long time, I hear nothing. Queen Ill-Fortune is finally still, as silent as the Tree of Truth.

Ω

A MASTERY OF GERMAN

MARIAN DENISE MOORE

Somewhere in the world, there is a man, seventy-years-old, a native New Orleanian who has never left the city except for the occasional Category 5 hurricane. He has a sixth-grade education but has always held some type of paying job. However, if you ask him a question in German, he will answer you without hesitation in an accent reminiscent of the region around Heidelberg. I still remember watching one of our Belgium-born board member's eyes widen in shock as Victor—that's his name—responded to a question in German. The executive immediately asked Victor where he had served in the army. No, he did not serve in Germany, or anywhere else for that matter, for as I said, he had rarely left the city and has never actually left the state.

Victor Johnston was sixty-five then and secure in his position as an elder, so he laughed in the manager's face. If asked, Victor could have also told the manager what it felt like to be an eleven-year-old girl and how it felt to have your period start thirty minutes before you left for school. But the executive did not ask those questions. Their conversation was brief, so the manager didn't notice that Victor's vocabulary was stuck at the level of an eighteen-year-old girl, my age when my family returned to the U.S. after my father's third tour of duty. He turned to our second trial subject and missed the problem and the promise of Engram's newest spotlight project. That was exactly what I planned.

◆ ◆ ◆

"We need a win, Candace," Lloyd said. He pulled his hand through his sandy hair, got up from his desk and checked the door to his office which I had already snicked closed. The move disguised his need to pace. I had struggled when describing him to my father. He was tall, but with too much nervous energy to be a golfer. I had decided on a retired track star who had graduated to the coaching ranks. He stood beside the desk now, too high-strung to sit down. Despite the chill of the room, his jacket was slung over the back of his chair.

We need a win. Translation: "I need a win." No difference. Lloyd was my supervisor. If he won, I won.

"I thought you wanted me to hang back and shadow Helene?" I said.

"Yes, well. About that," Lloyd sat on the edge of his desk. "I need you to take over one of Helene's projects. She's taking leave early."

"Before June? Before the bonuses are calculated? Isn't one of her projects on the spotlight list?"

I watched the flicker of annoyance cross Lloyd's face. Poor Lloyd. Saddled with two women to mentor—even if one of them did bring him plenty of reflected glory. I was willing to become a second star in his constellation. I had moved to New Orleans because of the opportunities presented by a new and hungry company.

"Doctor's orders," Lloyd said. "Nevertheless, she says that she will be checking in occasionally. That should be enough to keep her from losing out on a bonus because her baby decided to raise her blood pressure." He took another nervous pace to the door and back.

"I want you to take the Engram project," he said. "It's not on the company bonus timeline. But I need you to either kill it or bring it to some sort of conclusion. The technical lead is giving Helene the run-around."

"I've never heard of an R&D project named Engram," I said uncertainly.

"Because it is more research than development, I suspect," Lloyd said, frowning. "You need to talk to the lead. I think that he told Helene that he'd gotten approval on human trials."

Lloyd hailed his computer and directed it to send me the project plan. I felt the phone in my pocket vibrate as the new task jostled itself into my short list of responsibilities. Kill it or bring it to conclusion sounded like an execution order.

I should tell you what type of company Engram was at that time. For one thing, Engram wasn't the name. The name of the company was QND, named after Quinton Nathanael Delahousse, a MacArthur-recognized geneticist from LSU. QND was renamed Engram when it became the most successful product. When Lloyd handed me the Engram project, QND was five years old and still a startup as far as the tax laws of Louisiana were concerned. Some of the founding staff wagged that QND stood for "quick and dirty" because most of the projects were out the door faster than any other pharmaceutical company. During the first five years, most of our products were generics of existing drugs. None of them was the fame-making formulations that the Delahousse name seemed to promise. The spotlight projects were the high-risk, high-yield portfolios that QND hoped would support them after the state tax credits expired. Helene's spotlight had been underway since the company's founding and was finally coming to a close.

I weaved my way through the alleys of cubicles on my way back to my desk. Pausing, I poked my head around one of the seven-foot walls of textured fabric. Helene looked as busy as I anticipated. She was on the phone, firmly rehearsing the steps of some procedure or another. Her voice was level, but I could see the lines around her mouth deepen as she became more annoyed. The desk was full of folders, no doubt one for me. Helene was famous for killing trees. She'd had one presentation crash and burn because of a hard drive failure one day before an implementation review.

Glancing up at me, Helene nodded and tapped a cream folder on the top of the stack. "Yours," she mouthed.

I took the folder and retreated to my own austerer desk. I dropped Helene's folder into an almost empty desk drawer where it could rattle around with the one pencil and a cheap ad pen. I promised myself to check it for notes in Helene's handwriting before I shredded it.

I tapped the keyboard embedded in my desk and brought up the project timeline that Lloyd had already sent me. Within ten minutes, I kicked my chair away and stood over the wavering image of the project plan. Pages of bullet points were followed by empty spaces. Months of deadlines blinked in red because the dates had passed with no input. Pushing the display back into the desk surface, I leaned over it and silently cursed Lloyd, Helene and the entire board structure of QND.

I was still standing when a triple raps came on the metal frame of my cubicle wall. I looked up from my angry notes to see Helene. She pulled my rolling armchair toward her and lowered herself into the padded seat. Helene was 'all baby' as my elderly aunts would say. Her arms and legs were toned and model thin from years of yoga—she was always inviting me—and her face was the polished nectarine of a southern aristocrat framed by frosted blonde hair. The baby had concentrated all of its gravitas to her middle and she sat solidly in my desk chair with one hand perched protectively on the beach ball protrusion above her lap. Do I sound jealous? Maybe I was. It didn't matter that it had taken four years for her to become the yardstick by which I was now judging myself.

"What do you think?" she asked, pointing through me to the display on the desk. "I suggested that Lloyd give you this project," she added before I could answer.

"There are a lot of empty spaces in this plan," I said carefully.

"Yes, I know." Helene's eyes seared the surface of my desk pointedly. "There's more in the folder that I gave you. Desmond's not fond of filling out status reports. I have to drag information out of him every week. Maybe he will respond better to you."

I felt my back tense, but I retained my casual posture. And why would he respond better to me?

"When is your last day?" I asked instead. "Lloyd said that you will brief me on the project. Why is it so open-ended? That isn't QND's standard procedure."

Helene flipped her wrist over and examined her watch. "My schedule won't allow that," she said. "Desmond is in the downtown office to da y. Yo u sh ould introduce yourself. Ask him to brief you." She flipped an errant strand of blond hair away from her face and I saw the sheen of sweat.

Leaning over, I thumbed down the heated fan that sat beneath my desk. Immediately, the chill of the air conditioning rushed into my cozy enclave. When I checked the caged thermostat that morning, someone had managed to set the temperature to sixty-five degrees. I wasn't the only one on the floor w earing a sweater, but Helene was not one of us.

"Tell me about the team lead then," I said. "You said that his name was Desmond?" I wanted to sit down, but I didn't want to sit in the lower visitor chair. "The team lead isn't a geneticist?"

Helene looked at her watch again. "Desmond is Dr. Desmond Walker," she said. "I've known him since—" she shrugged. "Before QND. He and my brother were at Jesuit together. Delahousse was impressed with his research work at Hebei University in Shijiazhuag." Her tongue stumbled over the Chinese names. "I believe that his medical degree came from MeHarry in Tennessee. Have you heard of MeHarry?"

Only one of the best medical schools in the HBCU universe, I thought, but I only nodded.

"I have never heard of it," Helene said. "Dr. Delahousse was very effusive. I say this only so you understand—Desmond is a favorite. He has had results; I've seen the animal trials. Give me your phone?"

Helene fiddled with the calendar function and announced finally. "Desmond has an opening in two hours. I will add you to his schedule and you can get your questions answered. This should be easy. Let Desmond continue his research while you fill in the paperwork to appease Lloyd. I would have done more, but—" she patted her burgeoning belly "—this afternoon I have to review the press conference release. And then, there's the review of the drug insert that we negotiated with the FDA." She began to rise.

"You'll come with me for the initial meeting," I said quickly.

"You can do this," she said frowning. "All you have to do—"

"I would rather if he doesn't know that I'm his new PM immediately," I said. "You didn't include that in the meeting invitation, I hope?"

"You should not ambush Dr. Walker."

Oh, he's Dr. Walker now, I thought. "I don't plan to," I said. "I want him to explain the project without the expectation that I know anything. I'll read your notes." I pulled the slim folder from the desk drawer and slid it over the recessed keyboard. "But I don't want the type of canned rosy explanation that is created for a new boss. I want to really understand."

Helene sighed, but I knew that she was conceding. "We'll both be working through lunch in that case," she said. "Pass by my office in two hours and I'll take you down and introduce you."

Desmond Walker's office was a surprising modern emulation of Victorian clutter. Almost every surface was covered with personal effects. An electronic frame displayed a selection of cruise photos of his wife and two young sons at some Caribbean-looking location. There was one tall bookshelf on which some books were neatly arranged, and others lay on their sides, titles obscured and edges stained from use. Framed awards lined the walls, their lettering too small to read from my chair. Instead of focusing on them, I kept my hands in my lap as Helene ran through a brief introduction. Keeping her promise, she informed Dr. Walker that I was being introduced to all of the technical leads in Lloyd's division.

And why had that never actually happened? I wondered as I watched Desmond Walker's gaze shift from Helene to me with some wariness. He was tall, barrel-chested, and—as I had surmised from his choice of college—black. He was darker than I expected and probably in his late forties; but I was constantly fighting my expectation that all elite Black New Orleanians—the ones who could afford private schools like Jesuit—were Creole and the expectation that all Creoles were light-skinned. His hair was cropped as short as my father's, even though he had grown up in an era when dreadlocks were the cultural standard. But one could hardly carry dreadlocks into one's forties, I told myself.

"You've been here six months," Dr. Walker said slowly. "Have you worked in biotech before?"

Meaning, I thought, *You're young to be in management. What experience do you have?*

"No," I said. "I worked four years at BASF in Germany—two years at Exelon in Chicago and two years at Tenet in Dallas. When I interned at BASF, I realized that I was more interested in the process of seeing a project to completion. I found the political juggling for resources exciting; most people find it infuriating." I gazed firmly into his eyes, silently willing him to be impressed.

Out of the corner of my eye, I could see Helene frowning at her buzzing wrist. *Oh really*, I thought. *Did you arrange for a phone call just to get out of this meeting?* Then my phone rang.

"Sorry," I said and turned the sound off without checking the screen. Five minutes later, one of the framed paintings on Dr. Walker's wall faded to grey and lights began to chase around the frame's edge. Dr. Walker glanced at Helene and tapped the answer button on his desk.

"Walker!" Lloyd's voice barked from the pewter surface. "Is Helene there? Her intern thought she was meeting with you. I haven't been able to catch up with her."

"It's on speaker," Dr. Walker said sotto voce and nodded to Helene.

"I'm here," Helene called out. "Sorry, Lloyd. I was introducing Candace—"

"Have you seen outside?" Lloyd said. "Walker, turn your screen on. I'm sending you a feed."

The leaden display changed to a confused video of figures clad in jeans and pullovers shouting at men and women in business suits. The targets wore lanyards; each was zigzagging around the protesters, badging the lock quickly, and slipping through the office doors. Occasionally a member of the office staff had to throw up an arm to deter some demonstrators from following.

"That's right outside," I blurted.

"What is this?" Helene asked.

"They say that they're here for your press conference," Lloyd said.

"The press conference isn't scheduled until the end of the week," Helene said. Knowing her habits, I was certain that the notes for the event were probably printed and filed at her desk. "I haven't announced it yet."

"And yet, there they are. To oppose the Nil-facim project, I suppose."

"Who the hell protests a cure for malaria?" Helene grumbled, her voice roiling off the walls of Dr. Walker's office.

The video feed did not include sound. I watched the protesters organize themselves into a chorale that shouted at the glass doors of our office. I assumed that there must be a news team outside of the view of the cameras. Curious tourists were pausing, folding their arms and listening to the newly organized demonstration.

"Obviously, some people find it fun to protest a cure for malaria," Lloyd said, his voice tight. "Do you have someone to send down to them?"

I felt Helene's gaze land on me for a minute, but I didn't turn to meet her face. I kept my eyes on Dr Walker and the camera feed.

"No," Helene said finally. "I'll go down."

"You don't need that type of stress now," I interjected without turning. "You might...you might invite some of them up to the office. One of the protesters and one of the newsmen, preferably one with a science background. A meteorologist?"

Walker snorted behind his desk, but I saw Helene's initial smirk morph into something more thoughtful.

"It might be useful to separate the leaders from the followers," Helen said, rising. "You should stay, Candace. Desmond, could you run through your project parameters with her? It would be better if she got it directly from you. Is Lloyd still on the line?"

Dr. Walker looked at the indicator on his desk and shook his head. "He must have dropped off after you said that you'd go down."

With a curt goodbye, she was gone. Desmond Walker looked at the organized chaos displayed outside for a moment longer and then returned the screen to an indefinite southern landscape of oak trees dressed in Spanish moss.

He hummed thoughtfully, leaned back in his chair and asked, "What do you want to know about Engram?"

"All I know is that it is some type of research on memory enhancement or memory retrieval. I looked online but the closest that I could find were some studies done around 2010. Some researchers taught rats how to run a maze and then found that their descendants were able to run the same maze without training."

"Did you find anything else?"

I grimaced. "Five years later, some researchers were saying that the experience of American slavery was passed on to the descendants of the enslaved via the same process."

"Yes," Dr. Walker said. "That's one of the few follow-ups to the research at Emory University."

He swung his chair around, pulled a book off the shelf and thumbed through it. "There hasn't been much research on that angle since 2015."

"Does your research indicate that the effects of slavery can be edited out?"

"The people downstairs are protesting our plan to edit one mosquito genus to remove its ability to carry malaria," Dr. Walker said wryly. "What do you think they would say if I proposed to edit human genes to remove anything, let alone edit African-American genes? Tuskegee is always at the back of everyone's mind."

He tossed the book back on the shelf and stood, stretching. "At any rate, QND is willing to do diverse hiring, but they are not looking to solve problems unique to African-Americans."

"I'm not a diverse hire," I said.

"I didn't say that you were." He considered me silently for a moment. "You have memories and talents that are unique, no doubt. Your time in Germany, for example. You speak German?"

"Of course."

"Suppose I had a client who needed to transfer to Germany in a month. No time to study the language. Your knowledge would be priceless."

"A knowledge of anything? What if I needed to know how to waltz for a Mardi Gras ball?" I countered.

"No. Dancing is mainly a physical ability. A waltz or a foxtrot has defined steps; physical coordination is critical. Language is a better fit, though I think that it would be difficult to transfer the knowledge of a language like Xhosa to someone accustomed to a romance language like Spanish." He frowned as if the thought had brought up an avenue for consideration which he had overlooked. Leaning over the desk, he tapped notes into his desk surface.

"How are you going to get my knowledge of German into someone else's head?" Candace asked. "Write it on a chip?"

"Injecting silicone into people has an atrocious history," Dr. Walker said. "No, I am looking at a biological emulation of a human neural network." He glanced down at me from his six-foot height. "Despite what I said about editing human genes, I am proposing editing in, not editing out. I would be giving you explicit access to memories you have already inherited."

"I could give German to my children, but not to anyone else?"

"Not yet," he said. "Was that a sufficient explanation of Engram?"

"Yes." I looked at my phone and pretended to find something on my schedule. "And I do have another tech lead to meet, even if Helene isn't around to make formal introductions. Thank you."

Dr. Walker nodded, tapping on his desk again. He had already half-forgotten me. I edged out of the office. *Get a resolution or kill it,* Lloyd had said. Engram with its limited application certainly seemed ripe for killing.

"Hey, baby girl!" a gravely male voice bugled from my phone. I quickly squelched the phone to private mode.

I had the project plan and a spreadsheet open on my desk trying to find any pathway for Engram to be profitable. I was working on the scantiest of input from either Helene or Dr. Walker. Sooner or later, I would have to contact Walker.

"Hi, Dad. You know I'm at work, don't you?"

"Yeah—but I was wondering if you wanted to do dinner tonight?"

"Are you in town?" I asked. "You come to New Orleans and didn't tell me?"

My computer was insisting that I needed to take a break. I locked the machine and headed for the staircase. I was ten floors from the lobby. The staircase was private and a good way to burn off some of my aggravation.

"Nah," my father said. "I'm in San Antonio. I have this wall sized screen in my hotel room. I figured that I'd order in. You order in at home. We share a table virtually." I could hear the humor in his voice. "You can invite Brad-slash-Juan-slash-Phillipe-slash-Tryone to the meal if you like. Introduce me to your latest beau."

"You're crazy," I said.

One floor down, a door opened and someone pushed past me in a hurry to reach the next floor. I moved closer to the cinderblock wall to give the rushing worker room. "Are you still working off Mom's script?" My mother had died two years earlier after a long illness. I inherited my organization abilities from her, according to my father.

"Yeah," he said. "I still have the script with a few changes. Should I ask about a girlfriend? Want to invite Zawadi instead?"

"Not gay either, Dad."

"Not married, either," he retorted. "We left you all of those great genes, when are you going to spread them?"

"That was actually on her list?"

"Yes. First: ask her about work," he recited. "So, how is work?"

"Challenging," I said as I reached the next landing. "They haven't figured out what to do with me."

"Neither have I," he said. "Second: ask her about her relationship status," he continued. "And you said none. Surprising. Troubling. But I've checked that off. Third: are you happy?"

"I don't remember that question," I said.

"I usually let you vent about work," he responded. "That could go on for hours, especially while you were in Chicago. I'm glad you got out of there."

"So am I," I said.

"So dinner? You can tell me if you're happy over dinner."

"I have piles of data to read, Dad. And a decision to make."

"That sounds ominous." His voice was a pleasant baritone saxophone.

"As they say, that's why they pay me the big bucks."

"So—no dinner? You're not taking a break at all?"

"Dad, why are you in San Antonio? What are you chasing in Texas?"

"Your great, great," I imagined him counting out relations on his fingers, "great, great, grandfather. The census says he was a stonemason."

"In San Antonio?" I paused on another landing. "Do we have people there?"

"No," he said. "Wouldn't that have been something? I was stationed here for years after we got back to the States. It would have been nice to have family here to show us the ropes."

"Dad—why this sudden interest in history? You always taught me that it's easier to run forward than backwards."

"Dinner," he said. "That's a dinner discussion."

I sighed.

"Make your decision tomorrow," he continued. "Does it need to be today?"

"No, I guess not."

"Good, we're in the same time zone for once. So, eight o'clock. Please don't bring pizza again. I expect to see a real meal on the table in front of you."

He broke the connection and I trudged back up to the tenth floor. There was little sense in putting off the revelatory call to Desmond Walker any longer.

"Dr. Walker?"

There was a burble of voices on the other side of the line. Like most people at QND, Dr. Walker had disabled the built-in camera of his computer—which is why Lloyd had had to ask whether Helene was present earlier. It's a team meeting, I realized. Of course, there's an Engram team. If I closed down the project, I would have to consider what to do with the team. QND employees would have to be reassigned. If there were contractors, their agreements might require re-negotiation.

"Ms. Toil?" I heard Walker's baritone voice ring over the cacophony. "Did you have additional questions from this afternoon?"

"Yes," I said, "but I see you're in a meeting. We can talk tomorrow."

"Tomorrow I will be in the lab. In fact, I'm leaving for the lab shortly. If there is something quick..."

"This will take some time. I'm going over Helene's notes and the project plan. I am trying to reconcile the numbers for Lloyd."

"You should talk to Helene," he interjected.

"I will. However, you know that she's taking an early leave, don't you?"

"For the baby, yes, of course," Dr. Walker said in a level voice. "But she will be back. There is no need for you to worry over the details of this project. I know you want to understand everything—"

"Dr. Walker, Lloyd has asked me to take over management of the Engram project." I could hear the chatter die on the other side of the line. "I am the new project manager," I said, realizing that I was emphasizing the news for an unseen group. I needed to be as clear as possible. "I want to start going over the project plan when you're available."

The line was silent. "Dr. Walker?"

"You should come to the lab tonight," he said finally.

"Actually, I have a dinner engagement tonight."

"The lab is on the Westbank—on the other side of the river. I am messaging you the address now." I heard a murmur over the phone line. "I'll be certain to update the system so that it'll let you in." The connection broke.

Well, shit, I thought. I should just let him sit there and wait for me. But on the other hand, I was considering shutting down the man's team. I should give him the chance to make his case. If I got there early, maybe I could still pick up a decent meal somewhere and be home by eight for dinner with my dad.

QND's lab was an odd pair of buildings on the west bank of the Mississippi River, still within New Orleans city limits. I parked, carded myself in and paused to wonder in which of the two buildings was Desmond Walker's office. He had sent 201 as his office number, but both buildings had a second floor. I parked myself in front of the elevator in the first building, punched a button and listened as the antique mechanism inside woke up.

The first floor was dark, but I could hear voices. I soon spied a pair of figures, one pushing a mop bucket, both deep in conversation. The lights of the hallway connecting the diatomic buildings activated, flickering on and off, creating a virtual spotlight as the two walked. The elevator car arrived at the same time they did. Both men were vaguely Hispanic. The first nodded to me; the other ignored me, ranting instead about some local sports figure.

"I'm looking for Dr. Desmond Walker," I said. "He's supposed to be in room 201 but he didn't mention that there were two buildings."

"You're in the right place," the darker man said. He was the one who had acknowledged my presence earlier. "No one's in building two."

The two men trailed me into the elevator and punched the button above my second-floor selection.

"I'm sorry if I'm keeping you here late," I remarked, noting the skipped floor.

"Dr. Walker always works late," the second man said. "Him, he has his own man to clean that floor."

I noted the severe look that passed from the first man to the second. The second fell silent and stared at the elevator console.

"You not the reason we still here," the first man countered. "It's a big office—two buildings and all." The elevator shuddered to a stop.

"201's at the end of the hall," the second janitor continued. "Ignore the other doors. It's all one big room, but Professor Walker will be closer to the last door."

"Thank you," I said, stepping out. Both men avoided my face as the door clanged shut and I turned to the brightly lit hall. Despite the '60's exterior, the interior had obviously been gutted and redesigned. I was met with a gleaning hallway of glossy white tile, banded by polished steel and glass. As the janitor had mentioned, there were doors on my left leading into the work room; the only door that was open lay at the end of the hall. I could hear the muffled sound of jazz music from the local favorite station, WWOZ, echo off the hard ceramic walls.

Desmond Walker had altered his office attire slightly to match his current environment. A white coat replaced the suit jacket that hung on a nearby clothes tree. The tie had been loosened. He didn't rise to meet me but twisted around from his perch on a lab stool to watch me enter. Unlike his work office, this workspace was spare, the stark image of efficiency. The worktables held only computer interfaces and electronic equipment that I assumed were microscopes.

"Maybe you want to start by telling me why you didn't mention that you were the new PM this afternoon," he said.

"I've worked on projects where every morning the PL sent a smiley face to the PM as a status report," I said, ignoring his lecturing tone. "That's not what I wanted." I pulled a nearby stool closer to me and gritted my teeth at the grinding sound of its metal legs on the tile floor. "Was there anything you would've preferred to say?"

"I might have given you more time," Dr. Walker said.

"Lloyd gave me the project two hours before I spoke to you. I tried to read what I could before our meeting so that I could ask semi-intelligent questions, but..." I shrugged. "The project plan was skimpy to say the least. Helene's notes don't mention epigenetics at all." I looked across at his stern face. "Did Helene never ask? Or did she not care?" I didn't voice my more unwelcome fear—that he had spent QND money on his own dream project without consulting anyone.

Maybe my fear showed in my voice because he leaned over the worktable, thumbed a virtual keyboard to life and began pounding the keys with fury.

"I am forwarding you the research papers I've published," he said. "They go back to 2020."

"Wait—QND has only been in existence since 2037," I said.

"My research is why Delahousse brought me in," Dr. Walker said tartly. "Didn't Helene tell you that?"

"No—wait—yes—maybe. In her own way." I peered over the images of papers on the embedded screen. "I will need someone to explain this to me. My degree was in chemical engineering, not biology and certainly not genetics."

"Why should I waste the time of one of my team to explain genetics to you?"

"Because Helene may have been indulgent, but she reports to Lloyd just like I do," I answered. "His directive was to bring this project to conclusion or kill it. Neither of which means that you get to run a pure research project that has no commercial application."

He started to protest but I raised a hand. "Yes, I know—I could pass my knowledge of German down to my kids. There are cheaper ways to accomplish the same thing. I can't see QND continuing to pay for this unless you have something more." I paused. "Not unless you tell me that you have Delahousse on speed dial and can bring him in. Everyone gives me the impression that he started QND and then disappeared except for the annual board meeting."

Dr Walker was shaking his head.

"No? There's a story there, I'm sure. Listen, I'm willing to go to bat for you with Lloyd, but you have to give me something!"

Dr Walker was silent for moment and then brought up another file. "Sit down, I'm going to give you a genetics lesson."

I groaned. "I don't have time. I have dinner tonight with my father." I was immediately angry at myself for being so specific. Walker didn't need to know anything about my personal life. I needn't have worried, for he ignored my outburst and continued talking.

"Do you know what a haplogroup is?" he asked. I shook my head.

"No?" he continued. "You've never taken a DNA test?"

"That's my father's thing," I said. "I think that he had me do one of those cotton swab tests. He has the results."

"Well, a haplogroup is just a name of the group of genes that you inherited from your parents. Your father can show you your results. Over dinner." So he had heard after all. "Since the 2000s most people do DNA tests to find out where their family originated." He displayed a chart. "You know that homo sapiens originated in Africa. Therefore, every human on Earth descended from one woman in Africa."

The chart was shaped like a tree with a trunk labeled L0-Eve.

"If she's Eve," I interjected, "why is she L0? Not A0? Or even B0? Is it L0 because of Lucy?"

"Lucy was not in the homo sapiens species," he said. "The labels were assigned in the order that the homo sapiens gene groups were discovered." He clicked on the trunk of the displayed tree and highlighted two branches.

"Then let me guess. They started in Europe. And then, oops! Discovered that L0 was actually the oldest."

I think he chuckled even though he hid it well. "No, but it doesn't matter. L is a letter as good as any other. As my last paper indicates, I can give the memories of anyone on this line, say the L1b mutation to another person with that same mutation."

"Helene said that you were ready for human trials," I said.

"That paper was written two years ago," he said. "Those trials have been done."

I sat back down on a nearby stool and stared at him. "So when you said that you could give my knowledge of German to my kids, you meant now. Not, maybe after additional study."

"Yes, now."

"Then what are you working on now?"

There was a clatter in one of the darkened areas of the lab. I watched lights spring to life at the far end. Dr. Walker waved briefly. "That would be Victor. He cleans this floor."

"One of the janitors said that you had your own man for this floor," I said.

"Yes, well," he paused. "It's better when the team is deep in development that they aren't disturbed by the cleaning staff." He looked back at the screen. "You asked what I was working on now."

I nodded even as I noted his odd sidestep about requesting one particular person to clean his floor.

"You're African-American. Your primary haplogroup is probably one of the first branches of the L0 group." He expanded one of the tree branches on the display. "If it were L1b, I could certainly give your memory to another one with that haplogroup. Right now, the team is verifying that it is true for every mutation down the line: L1b1a, L1b1a1'4, L1b1a4 and so on."

"Why?"

"Excuse me?"

"Why is that important?"

"Because you're right. Passing your knowledge of German down to your descendants is not commercial. But everyone on Earth is a descendent of L0. If I could give your knowledge of German to anyone that would be commercial."

I felt cold and suddenly sick. "Does QND have a company ethicist?"

"What?"

"Ever since Henrietta Lacks, I thought that every pharmaceutical company had some type of ethicist or lawyer or someone to vet their work."

"QND was not set up like a normal pharmaceutical company, but I'm certain that we have lawyers. However, I don't see the problem."

"Shit." I rubbed my temples, remembered my makeup belatedly, stared at the traces of mahogany foundation on my fingers, then looked up at him.

"Can you separate my memory of learning to drive, or German, or walking into this building this evening from anything else I know?"

"Not as yet," he said cautiously.

"I didn't think so. And if I agreed to sell you my German, how much are you going to pay for the other stuffs? Learning to drive, the memory of my mother's death, My first sexual experience? Because I sure as hell am not going to give you those for free!" I kept my voice low, aware of the figure moving around at the other end of the long room. "My memories are me after all. You're proposing to sell me."

Desmond Walker's jaw was tight as he turned and closed down the screen display. "So you will close down the project," he said.

"No." I shook my head. "I'm going home to have dinner with my Dad over a video screen." I stood up. "I'll even ask him my haplogroup as you suggested. I need to think what to do."

"...And all of that history was sand. Easy to sweep away and ignore by the next generation."

"What?" I looked up from my plate where, deep in thought, I had been pushing a meatball around the swirls of red sauce.

"Oh, so you are still with me," my father said. "I wondered if you had rigged up a video loop like one of those crime capers that your mother loved."

I stared up at him. Thanks to my new video screen, it looked as if I had punched a hole in the kitchen wall into a neighbor's opulent bedroom. My father was centered in the window, but behind him hung a tapestry of an improbable frieze of two women in flamenco outfits standing in a plaza surrounded by market vegetables. It had taken two years, but he could finally mention my mother without his normally rich voice wavering like a mourning blues melody. He stood out from his lavish surrounding, a slim dark man with grey hair cut as short as it had been during his army days. He was dressed in a black polo shirt and khakis.

"Are you still mulling over that decision that you needed to make at work?" he asked.

Smiling, I touched two fingers over my mouth.

"Yes, I know you can't talk about work. But I saw something about your company on the news this evening. QND is GMO-ing mosquitoes. That isn't your project, I hope?"

"No, but—" I decided to give into my curiosity. "What did they say?"

"Depends on who you listen to. Some say QND is releasing a genetic menace;

some say that the company is a social justice warrior promoting a project that benefits Africans more than Americans."

I shook my head as I pushed my plate away. "There will be a formal press conference later; but no, that's not my project. I did hear most of what you said earlier. You found Josiah Toil. You talked about the buildings that he probably worked on. You said that you had reached a dead end. What does that have to do with history written on sand?"

A smile split his face and he laughed. "My multi-tasking daughter!"

Joining his smile, I got up and tossed the remains of my take-out dinner. The meal had been a little too good. I would have to hit the gym the next day. "Well?" I asked.

"Josiah had three daughters and two sons. The oldest son died in a Jim Crow prison." My father frowned. "The girls just disappeared after adulthood. Do me a favor and don't change your name when you get married." I ignored the prompt and he continued. "You women are hard to find after marriage. I wish that Elene had insisted that we hyphenate our surnames. She had no brothers. So as far as I know, you're the last of the Tolliver line."

"Is that why you asked me to do the DNA test?" I leaned against the granite counter and poured myself a shot of sparkling water.

"Part of the reason. The gene company tries to find matches for you. The Toil genes passed to you from me and the Tolliver genes passed to you along the matriarchal line."

"And all the way back to Eve," I mused aloud.

Dad raised an eyebrow that the video caught perfectly, and I grinned.

"One of my coworkers tried to give me a genetics lesson today. He said that some genes go back to the first human woman, Eve." I bowed elaborately. "Where do the Tollivers hail from? My coworker said that DNA tests tell you what country you originate from."

"Oh, you are old, Candace," my father said. Reaching behind himself, he pulled a laptop from beneath papers and flyers stacked on the bed. "Haplogroup L1c"

My hands tightened on the glass. I had not expected to get my question answered so easily.

"From central Africa around Chad, the Congo, or Rwanda. Home of the original humans." He looked up. "Sorry, that's still a wide area. That's where your shortness comes from. You were right to blame your mother's genes for that. I can send you the results if you want."

"Send it on." My own laptop was still in my briefcase. "And the sands of history?"

"Candace, I was just trying to wake you out of your funk," he protested. I watched him pour a sliver of bourbon into a shot glass. I insisted on an answer.

He looked away, sipped his drink once, twice and then looked back at me. "I hit a wall; this always happens. Josiah Toil was just a Black laborer, so his work wasn't recorded. Every generation," he paused, "like Black Wall Street, like all of the Black towns after the Civil War, like the Black miners at Matewan."

"We know all of that," I said quietly.

"No, we rediscovered all of that. It gets wiped away and then two generations later people say 'we were kings and queens in Africa'. Well, sure. But we were city planners, architects, engineers, bricklayers, and professors here in America."

"And Army officers," I said.

He chuckled. I was glad to hear real laughter after his bitter tirade.

"You can help me with a puzzle at work," I added. "Why would someone insist on his own cleaning staff for a lab? He says he's afraid the normal staff would disturb his team."

"And you don't think that that's enough? Is he afraid that his work would be stolen?"

"The guys that I met worship the ground he walks on."

"Does QND have a policy against hiring relatives?"

"Sort of. They don't want spouses or relatives to have to do performance reviews on each other. But I think the cleaning staff are contractors."

"You can ask, you know."

"I doubt the guy who runs the lab—"

"No, the janitor. I doubt that your guy thought to swear his janitor to secrecy. He's probably proud of the job. Ask him."

Lifting my glass, I toasted my father.

"What's a *parian*?" I ask tossing myself into a chair in Desmond Walker's office two days later. Not for the first time I wondered why a project leader had an office with a door that closed while I had a cubicle. Open door policy, Lloyd had said.

Desmond Walker made an elaborate point of putting his keyboard to bed and turned to me. "I think you know that it means godfather. Victor called me after you talked to him. He was worried that he'd done something wrong."

"Did you ask the contract company to hire him?" I asked.

"He works for QND," Walker said simply. "Contract companies lay their staff off whenever there's a downturn."

As I sat back in the visitor chair, I considered how to approach the real reason I had come down to Walker's office.

"You're not going to tell me that that is an infraction. Victor isn't related to me," he protested.

"No, Victor Johnston was only a puzzle that I wanted to solve. However," I leaned forward. "I'm willing to bet that you know his haplogroup." Walker stiffened and I smiled. "Humor me, Doctor Walker."

"L1c," he said, and I felt relief spread through me like a wave. "Why does it matter? You gave me the impression that you were going to close the project."

"I really don't want to. Lloyd needs a dog and pony show. We," I emphasized the pronoun, "need to give him a reason to continue your funding." I sat back. "I'm still going to insist on an ethicist to help us draw up conditions of use. I'd like to see families have access to their memories before they are exported and sold to others." *Especially Black families*, I thought, and shivered at the thought of accessing the memory of Josiah Toil seeing his son vanish into a prison that reproduced the slavery that he himself had escaped from.

"You are the one who pointed out that the ability to share a memory along one haplogroup was not commercial."

"I'm certain that every haplogroup would pay for their ancestral memories," I said. "Everybody imagines themselves the descendants of kings and queens. Every magnate wants to pass his genius directly on to his children."

I stood up full of nervous energy. Suddenly aware that I was patterning myself on Lloyd, I stopped and gripped the back of the visitor chair. "I'm not asking you to stop your research. Eventually, it will occur to them that if you could share across one close genetic group, you should be able to do so with others more distantly related. They will remember that we are one human family." I took a breath. "When that happens, I want standards in place for such sharing. And remuneration for the memory donor."

"It sounds like you have a donor in mind."

"I considered asking you. Or Victor. But your memories belong to your children. I'm proposing that you give my memory—my ability to speak German—to Victor. He would be the more dramatic demo for Lloyd."

I saw a wave of anger mixed with—what? guilt?—cross Desmond Walker's face. "You're asking me to experiment on my family?"

"Victor and I are in the same haplogroup: L1c," I said. Releasing my grip on the chair, I seated myself again. "You said that your human trials have been done. I suggested Mr. Johnston because he's such a strong character. He would charm the board with his stories in English; he would certainly do so in German. But, if you have another subject I will accept that. Mind you, I want to meet the person that you propose to give my memories to before you do that. There are other options." I paused and ticked them off for him.

"Second: if you tell me that you are ready now or even next week to transfer a L1c haplogroup memory to an IJ haplogroup subject, I would jump at that." I saw his surprise at my naming one of the European haplogroups. Yes, Doctor Walker, I did my homework, I told him silently. "Third: if you want me to go to Lloyd and tell him to give us two years and we will have that same demo for him, I'll do that."

"You don't think that he'd wait," Dr Walker said.

"No, I don't," I said.

"When do you want a decision?"

"By the end of the week," I said. "That will give me time to float the idea with a lawyer and discuss what type of protection we can offer the initial subject." I saw the word 'protection' enter Walker's consciousness and wondered what machinations had been needed to have QND hire Victor Johnston directly.

I didn't ask. Four weeks later, I watched with others in the lab building as Victor Johnston regaled that board member with his memories second-lining with his krewe on Mardi Gras morning. His German was as colloquial as a native teenager. Standing in the back of the meeting room, I clutched the legal documents that would guarantee Victor a position until he retired and a pension afterwards. As the memory donor, I had only insisted that the memories attached to my genes be given to no other person. I have frozen that moment in my mind: Victor regaling the board members after the formal test was completed, Lloyd smiling and nodding his head at my success, and Desmond Walker carefully defining the current commercial opportunities of his work and emphasizing the future possibilities.

I don't know where Victor Johnston is now. Eventually, he tired of being a guinea pig; he tired of having that "bougie Black girl", as he called me, in his head. No use explaining that I could not be extracted. He disappeared and Dr. Walker would not tell me where his godfather had moved. I could have queried human resources and found out where his checks were directed but I respected his wishes. I moved on; I listened to my father and started to date again. The Toil and Toliver family chart is waiting for another entry. I may be the last generation to pass down my story the old-fashioned way.

CONVERGENCE IN CHORUS ARCHITECTURE
DARE SEGUN FALOWO

ONE

I

STRUCK

In escape from sword and fire of war, Osupa was born.

Osupa was the sixty-something members of various tribes that had escaped from war in the city of Ile-Ife. Osupa was the land on which they survived and thrived. Osupa was the perfect rectangle on which stood fourteen circular huts made of solid sunbaked mud, all roofed with dense layers of dried banana leaves.

At the center of Osupa was a shrine—a large box of mud with a roof of thatch, supported inside with the trunks of many young trees. This was where the Awo Meta (Fatona, Fagbeja and Awojobi) lived. The mud walls of the square hut were covered in chalk drawings of the moon and three orisha: Esu, Orunmila and Obatala, each bearing in their arm the object depicting their role in the machine of the oracle of Ifa. The oracle itself was not depicted, because you would meet it if you walked into the shrine.

They had found the smooth hard land of Osupa hidden behind a wall of trees and bushes full of thorns in which babies cried under the glare of a full moon, the bombs and fires kissing the sky behind them. It was Ifa who led them to Osupa. It was Ifa who spoke guttural through the throats and saw through the eyes of the Awo Meta. The people followed their calls and the sway of their white garb and pointed staves through the night and into the teeth of the forest until they found the flatland which seemed to have been prepared, waiting for them. The Awo Meta stuck their staffs into the earth at the center of the space and called it Osupa, the moon.

As a sacrifice, the people of Osupa dug out a square for the shrine of Ifa that night before they all went to sleep, but the Awo Meta stayed awake, enchanting and drawing a ring of aabo (protective light) around the land that they had claimed. This made them invisible to the eyes of the demons, mercenaries and blood-drunk soldiers who would wander out of Ife in search of slaves and fresh kills.

In the morning, the Awo Meta showed the men—whose numbers were half that of the women—the breadth of the land, where the farm should lay and where the kitchen shed should stand. The men got to work cutting down branches and thatch to begin building. Outside the ring of light was a lake abundant with mud and from this lake the women collected mud in the large open gourds that once held their clothes and other personal objects.

While the people worked on their new houses, they forgot to mourn their dead; but after they had finished building their houses and the shrines, there was a loud weeping across Osupa by wives who had lost husbands and husbands who had lost wives and mothers who had lost children and children who had lost innocence.

The Awo Meta began to call meetings inside the shrine every seven days, teaching the people of Osupa songs of farewell to the dead, songs of healing and songs for the moon. And when the people sang these songs, the great sound of their hearts rose out of their mouths and travelled through the black night, seeming to touch the starry firmament above.

Osupa grew into its rhythm with the passage of three full moons. The widows found new husbands and sisters, and the widowers found new wives and brothers. The children were adopted by those who fell in love with them. There was bush rat and corn and yam and pepper and salt, and it wasn't rare to see the entire settlement of Osupa gather around fires to feast and dance and offer praise to Ifa and Olodumare for their survival. The aabo held strong and the war became like a bad dream that faded under the warm touch of a lover. Everything was going well. The people were in peace. The oracle and the three babalawos were joyous with their home and shrine.

Until Fagbeja threw cowries that flashed purple and filled the shrine with black smoke.

Until the storm came.

The Awo Meta did not tell the people of Osupa about the coming tempest. Instead, they told them that Olodumare was coming to visit. They made the people wear white and smear the blood of wild duck across their foreheads and thresholds, and then they made the people sing to Olodumare, the Fount and Cradle of All.

The Awo Meta partially believed their own lie and guessed the tempest to be the coming of a lesser orisha to cleanse their land through rain and flood. That night, enormous bulbous clouds rose black in the west, bleeding purple lightning and cold winds that made the forest howl. The people of Osupa curled up in their huts and prayed to Olodumare as the rain began.

The storm quieted just as dawn broke. Everything was heavy and wet. The water had risen to their knees and broken into their huts, lifting clothes and baskets of food and foundering the roof of the kitchen shed. Some huts, uprooted by the storm, lay half crumbled a distance from the line in which the other huts stood.

The people of Osupa began to fish for their belongings in the water. The shrine was unperturbed. Awojobi, the oldest of the babalawos—tall, with long hair plaited all back to his neck, and eyes laced with venom and kohl—called all the youth together and charged them to go check the damage to the farm. The older men set about rebuilding the broken huts. The Awo Meta prepared to cast a new aabo, the old one having been broken by the storm.

The clouds that had brought the storm remained heavy in the sky, casting their shadows over Osupa.

There were about twenty young men and women in Osupa. Most of them were orphans who had found new parents.

The quietest of these orphans was a young man named Akanbi. Wherever he went, he always wore on his head a gold and green abeti aja given to him by his father. It was woven with a rare heavy thread that made it stand firm.

Akanbi led the party of youth towards the edge of Osupa where the farm lay. Immediately behind him, walking side by side, were Gbolahan and Gbemisola Olohun, the twins with voices like heavenly trumpets. The rest of the youth were a distance behind, carrying baskets and hoes. But for those bonded by shared loss, no one spoke to each other. The only thing that brought them all together were the nights of praise when crop was abundant.

Akanbi stopped at the edge of the farm. The farmland by the slope was submerged by the lake which had burst its banks, so that only the tips of ripe corn poked above the still water like lumps of tangled light.

"Olodumare is angry at us for escaping our fate in the war." Gbolahan Olohun was melancholic in a way that only one possessed of so much beauty could be.

"We are lucky nobody died," his twin sister said. "I think what the Awo told us to do helped. The duck's blood...we are safe. Thank our Fathers and Mothers Past."

The remainder of the party arrived and gasped at the sight before them. Some swore under their breath against the orisha and Olodumare.

"Bring me baskets," Akanbi said. "And any one of you who can swim follow me, please." His voice was surprisingly deep for one so small and shy-eyed. He was ridiculously polite and told great stories about orisha and elemi, the spiritseen, punctuating the most fantastical and horrid episodes with a coy smile and a twinkle in his eye, swearing he knew because he came from a family with an ancestral braid that led back to Orunmila.

Akanbi took the basket and walked into the farm, slipping under the water with a silent splash, the basket trailing the surface like a ritual boat. Three other swimmers followed after him. Gbemisola could swim. Gbolahan could not and harbored the secret thought that his death would be by drowning. He stood at the edge of the farm with the others. Beside him, two girls spoke excitedly about the rage of the storm and the power of orisha.

It began to sprinkle light rain. The swimmers broke the surface near the middle of a row of cornstalks.

The storm clouds drifted, growing and stuttering, all lightning with no thunder.

The baskets slowly filled with wet cobs of corn and big red peppers. The swimmers drifted languorously through the submerged farm, rising to take breaths before sinking back into the underworld of water and wavering green stalk. Above, the morning light from the side of the sky not shaded by the storm clouds was milky, and nearly non-existent beneath the surface, but it was clear enough to see and pluck the softened harvest.

The storm clouds leaned into the morning even more and rumbled with new thunder. The boys and girls on shore began to call to the swimmers to return, feeling the drizzle was about to intensify.

The light grew dim and the air became cold again like it did the night before. The four swimmers began to approach the shore with three full baskets between them, kicking their legs and supporting the baskets with one arm while paddling with the other. The storm continued to roil, eating up the rest of the dawn without letting loose.

Lightning flashed and for a moment, everything seemed made from white stone. The returning thunder caused the earth to tremble and made most of them duck against their will. Gbolahan Olohun called on his sister to be faster. They still had to walk up the slippery underwater slope to set the baskets down before they could come out completely.

Two of the swimmers, tall brothers who lived close to the River Osun before the war, came out first. Akanbi and Gbemisola waited in the water to support the baskets from sinking. The brothers stood on solid ground just as the patter of light rain stopped. The remaining light took on an electric texture and the youth on the shore of the drowned farm wondered if their skins were glowing in the night that the clouds had brought.

A fork of lightning fell onto Osupa from above, pure and effervescent. The reporting thunder shook the earth deeper and all those standing fell to the ground, shivering from the sound. The baskets and the swimmers holding them slid back to the bottom of the farm.

Witnesses say they saw slow lightning touch the heads of Akanbi and Gbemisola Olohun with small bright hands.

They carried the lightning-struck and the dripping harvest to the village, running without a sound to conserve energy. Gbemisola's and Akanbi's bodies were limp and their eyes were rolled back to reveal only the white. The swimmer brothers and Gbolahan carried them into the shrine before the Awo Meta who were deep in a singular act of divination. The flat wooden tray before the babalawo was covered in fine white sand in which single or twin marks that told of many futures lay in vertical rows. They sat at its angles with their bodies held erect and eyes lowered.

Gbolahan was the first to shout for help, and his voice was so keen in its terror that Fagbeja and Fatona fell out of concentration. Awojobi rose to his feet in one sleek motion and was beside the tangle of bodies in a blink, asking questions. The brothers lowered the bodies of Gbemisola and Akanbi to the ground and stood back. Gbolahan shivered as he threw himself across his sister, caught between sobbing and silence.

"What happened?" Awojobi asked. Fatona and Fagbeja had recovered and were standing by his side. The three of them looked indestructible as a unit, as they had looked ever since the day they found Osupa together. Their eyes were hard as they stared at the situation before them.

"Lightning!" Gbolahan shouted to Fagbeja. "Lightning struck them while they were in the water. Aaaaah! Please help." Fagbeja, a small but mighty man with white hair everywhere, pulled Gbolahan off Gbemisola and give him several small slaps on his wet cheek. He wiped Gbolahan's tears with his pure white wrapper and told him to toughen up. *S'ara giri!*

Gbolahan swallowed the coming waves and yelled with panic, "Don't let her die, Baba!"

Awojobi was already in a crouch, laying his long-fingered right hand across the heart and temples of the fallen ones. Fatona was just as tall as Awojobi but had no single hair on his head. He pulled the swimmer brothers aside and asked more questions about the quality of the light and the air before the incident. When they responded, his mouth dropped in bewilderment. He turned to Awojobi, who nodded in confirmation.

The rest of Osupa was already gathered around the entrances to the shrine, some peeping in and others speculating.

Their work done, the stormclouds dissolved to let the late morning sun burn away the rain that had soaked into everything.

Akanbi's guardian, the old woman who he had clung to and helped as he ran away from the war, wormed her way into the shrine and limped towards where he lay. She put her hand to her mouth and stood as she watched Fagbeja send the people away from the entrances to pull down the white sheets of cloth that served as doors.

"What happened Baba Awojobi?" she asked quietly as she watched Fatona and Fagbeja layer mats and old cloth on the floor to make beds.

"Nothing, Iya Akanbi," Awojobi said, as he chewed a bitter root and his mouth turned dark green. "The children have just been called to see. They're dreaming vivid." The two babalawos lifted the limp bodies of Akanbi and Gbemisola and placed them on the two lengths of cloth.

"Dreaming?" Iya Akanbi asked.

"You won't understand yet, Iya." He put his hand on her shoulder and guided her towards the billowing door, where Gbolahan stood riveted, eyes on the prone body of his sister.

"Iya, tell the boys to bring us any dry firewood and oil and leaves that they can find." She nodded, still confused, and then walked through the cloth door. Gbolahan stayed. Fatona and Fagbeja had begun to lay out strange powders in lines around the beds they had made for his sister and Akanbi.

"Go and help them find dry wood, Gbolahan." Awojobi spat the bitterness from his mouth to the floor. "You cannot be here."

In one of the futures that the Awo Meta saw for Osupa, there was an exodus. In another, there was an expansion. They never saw the birth of two elemi, stripped of their skin by lightning, then called into the mind of Olodumare to see.

The three men, weary with worry over the fate of Akanbi and Gbemisola, walked around the fire that they had built near the heads of the dreaming ones. They had not slept all day and now the night was here. They could see the lanterns of the people of Osupa parading outside their shrine. They could hear people greet and console Gbolahan who had stayed outside since he and the boys returned with some dry thatch and wet wood.

The moon was a sliver of silver in the night above.

Fagbeja, an expert alchemist and brewer of potions, was boiling a broth, sweet and acrid, in a black pot on the fire whose warmth had managed to stop the random shivers of Akanbi and Gbemisola.

Awojobi and Fatona were undressing. They took off strings of charms and singular object-potencies from their waists and underarms, washed their mouths, armpits and faces with saltwater and wrapped their bodies in spotless white wrappers. They completed their armor by wrapping their heads and shoulders in shawls of knitted white aso-oke.

Fagbeja was already prepared and draped, his face covered completely in a mask of liquid chalk as he stirred his distillate of dream. Awojobi painted a circle around his left eye. Fatona drew twin lines from the center of his head to his jaw, slipping two fingers over his nose. They both stood by Fagbeja who put his hand into the red coals, picked up the pot and placed it gently on the floor.

"This is the strongest one I've made yet," Fagbeja said. "One large gulp and the spirit will forever be trapped outside the body, suspended in many dreams. We must take only six drops each. Enough to get us to them and not too much that we all can't return home to our bodies."

Awojobi, the oldest, was the weaver of light and the one who lived in constant trance already. He went first and lay on the bare ground opposite the fire, put his hands atop one another on his stomach and shut his eyes. He opened his mouth and Fagbeja placed six drops on his tongue. The distillate was terrible in its bitterness and the old priest's face crumpled as the liquid seemed to turn his tongue and throat black and sticky, then his face relaxed. His stomach filled with warmth and his tongue began to leak spittle sweeter than honey. He drifted to sleep.

Fatona, the healer whose body was sensitive as spider's web, lay down to the right of Awojobi and took the drops on his tongue. Bitterness darkened his insides, and in his sleep, sweetness bloomed.

Fagbeja went last, lying down and placing the pot next to his waist before taking the six drops onto his own tongue. His chalk-whitened face wrinkled, and he too went to sleep at the taste of sweetness.

Midnight crept by on long hushed toes. In the shrine, five bodies lay prone. The boy and the girl, covered in lengths of warm adire, lay to the right, three days asleep. Next to them, coals burned in a shallow pit, casting a glow of tender sunset across the dreaming bodies. The babalawos lay to the left of the pit, stiff as three logs on the bare earth.

Everyone in Osupa was asleep as if by some transference. Even Gbolahan Olohun slept beside the door where he had stood all day waiting for his sister to awaken.

In the sky above, three owls circled under the smile of a new moon.

II
IN EXHUMED NIGHTMARE

Awojobi, who went to sleep first, woke in the shared dream last. He found himself and his brother-babalawo standing on an endless plain of lustrous grass that seemed to flow in perfectly timed waves away from a mass that towered in the sky up ahead, at the focal center of the dream. Light sparkled around them, seeming to fall like dust from the cloudless blue sky above. No birds called and no wind blew.

Fatona was already walking up ahead towards the thing at the center. It was an immense blight, black and slick, blotting out the bright fabric of the dream, throwing thrashing shadows. It grew from deep in the earth, spreading as it made its way up towards the heavens. Right at its mouth stood Akanbi and Gbemisola Olohun, dwarfed into insignificance.

Fagbeja was close behind Fatona, an owl on his shoulder. They all wore fine heavy agbadas of white aso-oke shot through with silver thread. Awojobi followed his brothers, swaying through the grass towards where the two dreaming Akanbi and Gbemisola stood like ants before the black thing writhing and splitting reality. He tried to remember if he had ever seen anything like it in his sixty years of trance but could not.

Fatona followed the waves of the plain, his owl-eye gleaming as the blight grew in size, polluting the blue above. As healer, he could sense that it was both wound and womb, a doorway from a distant place. Something began to push against the chaos of the blight. Its body flashed violet as it sluggishly began to distend the membrane of the dream through the blight.

Awojobi leapt and flew above the dream. He had gotten the wings of the owl. They flapped at their normal size a few breaths above the back of his agbada and helped him soar ahead of Fatona and Fagbeja to land behind Akanbi and Gbemisola.

Akanbi and Gbemisola's heads were turned towards the blight, their necks bolted in place. Their toes were sunken into the soil and from the bones of their legs sprouted buds and leaves. Their eyes were black as pools of ink. Awojobi moved to touch them.

The membrane broke and a titanic object floated out, twisted, burnt black and heavy as old bone. The sparkling light and the lush green fields disappeared in its shadow. The broken membrane sizzled like fat in fire and from the point of the blight, the entire sky boiled into starless night.

Awojobi went blind. Fagbeja stopped moving; the owl on his shoulder was simply a tether and advisor on how things were on the other side, where they lay in Osupa. Fatona saw clear as day with his owl eye, but he was still too far from where the two dreamers stood. He began to run.

Akanbi and Gbemisola opened their mouths at the same time. Akanbi began to speak incantations he didn't know and Gbemisola sang wordless from the bottom of her gut. Their voices reverberated, dissonant, through the air of the dream.

Turning his neck to follow the drift of the boneship, Fatona saw with his owl eye a living language, crawling and burning violet in the void of the night it had made.

Awojobi followed the sounds of Akanbi and Gbemisola to reach them, then he held onto their shoulders to keep them still till Fagbeja and the tether arrived. Awojobi immediately began to ululate and call to the boneship in an unknown tongue.

As the babalawos ran towards their patients and the boneship drifted imperceptibly to the center of the dream, camouflaged against the darkened sky, night against night, a guttural screaming began, random as birdsong, echoing from spots distant and near. Each voice allowed a scream to finish before the next rose with hair-raising pitch. They seemed to be screaming against the boneship, yelling as if they were each about to be devoured in the slimy jaws of a great beast.

Fagbeja ran faster, the prayers whispered under his breath carving open a path through the grass. The owl on his shoulder now flew low before his face, revealing the way to Awojobi.

The first snatch occurred. A scream was cut short by a blaze of violet fire, as the screaming body exploded into the air, burning a trail thin as thread from the distant plain into the gut of the boneship. The next scream was cut off as well, and nearer where the babalawo ran, a body ripped out of the earth, burning up as it shot into the boneship.

As Fatona and Fagbeja ran, aided by the earth beneath their feet, the black sky in which the boneship now hung static exploded with violet missiles. Bodies that seemed buried deep in the earth of the dream screamed and went mute as they were ripped out of the soil into the sky.

Fatona reached where Awojobi, Akanbi and Gbemisola stood making strange rippling sounds with their tongues, eyes blind and riveted to the boneship. With his owl-eye, he saw violet streams rushing out of their lips up towards the boneship, along with the burning missiles of the stolen bodies. They were reading the living language.

He pulled a lodestone out of his agbada. It was a perfect cube of white rock.

Fagbeja and the tethering owl arrived. He nodded to Fatona and Fatona threw the cube up and placed a hand on Awojobi's shoulder. The lodestone burst into white light and hung still as sun but flashed as though it was full of shadows of rippling water. Fagbeja put one hand on Fatona's back and the other around the owl's feet.

The tether flew, lifting them up as if they were dry leaves. It took them out of the dream into the lodestone.

In their absence, the nightmare continued, and the earth was pillaged for her bounty of soul.

The cube of the lodestone opened up inside the shrine at Osupa. Serpentine forms, aglow with shifting light, slipped out of the blinding brightness of the lodestone, casting shadows against the walls as they moved about weightlessly, swimming through the air and slipping into the mouths of the five sleepers.

The lodestone collapsed into a sparkling point of light so bright it lasted in the air for the several breaths that Gbolahan Olohun took as he woke up. He peeped into the shrine and watched the babalawos as they woke up, each vigorously rubbing their eyes and back and ears as if to remove impurities. The sparkle vanished. A white owl flew out of the shrine.

Gbemisola Olohun and Akanbi stirred and moaned as they returned into the heaviness of their bodies. When they opened their eyes, their pupils were clouded silver with sleep, and when they opened their mouths, nothing came out.

III
HERALD THE MASONS

Three days passed before Gbemisola and Akanbi could stand up and walk around inside the shrine. They remained speechless. The Awo Meta consulted and divined every waking moment, taking turns at tossing opele on their oval boards and drawing lines in a circle of white sand. Ifa showed nothing, said nothing; but they continued to persist with the oracle and tend to their mute patients.

Awojobi knew what was going to happen: a breach into Ile-Aye, by something from another world, something powerful and hungry and beyond human understanding. He had touched Akanbi and Gbemisola's shoulder in the dreamscape and seen and heard through their senses. But he couldn't remember speaking as they did. The burning violet language was a message to open—a call, a courier.

In all his life as a babalawo jumping through space-time and seeing realms above and below, Awojobi had never witnessed anything so strange. Awojobi also knew that Ifa was not speaking to the three of them, for the two voices he had selected for his use were currently muted.

Fatona and Fagbeja continued to work around Gbemisola and Akanbi until they tottered back to lie on the ground—Fagbeja with his herbal tinctures and dense aromatic submergence and Fatona with his cool hands and silent tears. Awojobi, draped in white shawls, sat in the corner and stared into the firepit at the center of the shrine, seeing violet.

Gbolahan snuck into the shrine on the morning following the night through which the three Babalawos had watched over Gbemisola and Akanbi, trying to get them to explain what they had seen in the shared dream.

Was the boneship coming for the settlement of Osupa alone or the entirety of the world? Was it the war and bloodshed of Ile-Ife that would draw this hungry thing into this world?

Gbemisola only stared at them with the eyes of a newborn, a strange amused smile on her face. Akanbi returned to his bed and slept soundly, curled into a fetal position.

By sunrise, the Awo Meta were also asleep around the firepit in the center of the shrine. Gbemisola was wide awake but unable to speak. She tried to shout or say something, but all that came out was a hushed whisper. Her pupils dilated in her effort to speak.

Gbolahan woke at the first crowing of the cock and saw that the Awo Meta had drifted to sleep, leaving only Gbemisola awake. He was so overjoyed at seeing his sister alive that the babalawo had barely begun to snore before he ran into the shrine and threw his arms around her. Gbemisola was still for a while, and then she struggled out of his arms. They stood apart and stared into each other's eyes: Gbemisola's full of terror and Gbolahan's loving and tired.

"Gbemi! I was...so afraid. I thought you would never come back."

She turned away, arms wrapped around her chest. She looked at him over her shoulder. He walked over to her and tried to place a hand on her shoulder but she moved before he could touch her.

"Gbemisola? We are here and alive. Speak to me!"

She walked even deeper into the hut, closer to where her bed lay beside Akanbi, and where the Awo Meta were knocked out, catching their first sleep in days. Gbolahan stopped moving towards her and she stopped walking backwards.

Gbemisola pointed to sky through the roof of the shrine. She began to walk in a circle, then she stopped for Gbolahan, hoping that Gbolahan understood her. Gbolahan did not understand, but did what he always did when they had a fight and struggled to communicate: he kept his voice low and let a song spill out of his lips, pleading and embracing in deep warm tones.

Sister.
Tell. Where did you go?
What did you touch?
Did you see the gods all lined up
in a circle in the sky, welcoming you
into the chaos of their forever?
Sing, sister. Tell.

Gbemisola watched and listened as Gbolahan sang, modulating his voice to avoid waking the sleeping ones. Two of the sleepers stirred but continued in their sleep. Gbemisola's eyes widened as memories flooded her mind. Their first language had been song. She turned and ran towards the billowing curtain door that led to the back of the shrine. As children, whenever they sang and it was her time to respond, she always found a way to run, to lead Gbolahan out of his safety into a space where she could shine.

The center of Osupa was full of people in morning rhythms of cooking, gossiping, cleaning, kissing and eating. A hush fell over them as Gbemisola Olohun ran out of the shrine into morning light. Roasted yam fell back into palm oil and teeth-cleansing herbs fell out of mouths. Gbemisola looked at the people around her, dressed roughly in morning wrappers, their cheeks marked, their noses bold and their eyes expectant. She held them in anticipation as she looked around, finding herself in a place both familiar and alien. She wanted most to see Ma'ami, but none of the women here was her.

Gbemisola looked up, her twin's song still echoing in her ears and down into her heart. The sky was clear with trails of thin white cloud whose tips glowed with the pink of a rising sun. The black boneship hung high, small as a hawk, and cast no shadow because none could see it but her.

She opened her mouth and sang—

To the door, to the door was where they birthed us.
Two without skin: one the clarion, the other the salve.
Obatala and the other, coming thief
Held us between each other and waited
Till the thief began to reap us out of our ancient home.
Where the harvest goes, it will know no peace,
Only din, only monument, only sand, only—

Her throat went hoarse and she began to choke.

Gbolahan ran towards her and she ceased coughing and started speaking in a hoarse tongue that caused her eyes to roll back and her listeners to desire silence instead. They covered their ears. Gbolahan staggered back, covering his ears also. As she continued speaking, the earth beneath her feet began to swell and relax, like the belly of a sleeping man, lifting her up gently and setting her back down. Her blank eyes were set on the thing in the sky which only she could see. Her neck was clutched in her hands as if she wanted to stop the sound from pouring out of her.

An object-potency came flying from the direction of the shrine, shaped like a rabbit. It struck her in the shoulder and she went still and stiff. Gbolahan caught her before she hit the ground.

The Awo Meta walked towards the twins, eyes heavy with sleep. They collected the girl and carried her back into the hut, where Akanbi was still sleeping the sleep of the dead.

High up in the sky above, no one saw a blight the size of an eye close.

✦ ✦ ✦

After the incident, Gbemisola and Akanbi slept for seven days without water or food. The Awo Meta were reluctant to go into their dream again on a rescue mission. They tried with all their power, casting spells and laying hands and slipping bittersweet potions between the teeth of the sleepers, but the sleepers only jerked their limbs and mumbled. Once, still asleep, Akanbi sat up and said, "I can't dig myself in any deeper."

The Awo Meta switched their approach and decided that protection would be the next step to take, until their dream bond was broken. They cast a second line of aabo around the shrine, warding off all unwanted spirits, human beings and creatures. Even Gbolahan Olohun found it hard to stand inside the shroud of circling mist that surrounded the lower-half of the shrine.

The people of Osupa were grateful that there were no more rains, so that their clothes and huts and crops became dry. The Awo Meta stayed close by while the two sleepers continued deeper in their sleep. Gbolahan spent his time alone in the branches of trees, pondering the lyrics of the song Gbemisola had sung to him, which had scared him at the time.

The Awo Meta, who only heard the tail-end of Gbemisola's song, wondered again what they had seen in the dream they shared with Gbemisola and Akanbi. Although they were used to experiencing strange realms and objects and skies, this one made them feel uneasy, specifically when the bodies were ripped out of the earth to disappear into the boneship.

They did not speak about it among themselves, though they knew from her symptoms when she awoke that Gbemisola was a herald. Usually, heralds preceded orisha and other beings from the realms above prior to their arrival on earth. Heralds didn't have to sleep for so long; they simply fell into trances of song or dance, and sometimes intricate handwork. They didn't make the ground beneath their feet beat and swell when they spoke in other tongues. Nor was their sleep filled with repeated cycles of a singular nightmare.

The Awo Meta continued to ponder the boneship and Gbemisola's song as they sat sleepless around the two sleepers. They also began to worry for the future, anxiety filling their chests in slow, gradual spikes.

Awojobi was full of guilt and regret for leading his brothers into establishing Osupa and bringing the people he had thought he was saving into a conundrum that could soon be worse than war. He contemplated the best way to escape being sucked into the corruption in the sky.

Fagbeja thought of his inability to adapt to new spiritual spaces without first breaking out into a mental rash and experiencing bouts of raw madness. He hated coming that close to chaos within and so he began to keep a pod of poison in the folds of his cloth, ready to burst it in his cheek if the real sky above his head broke open as it did in the dream.

Fatona wondered what the owner of the boneship wanted. Was it Olodumare in disguise, testing their settlement of refugees before gifting them a better future if they passed said test? No. Not after all they had seen in the shared dream. Olodumare would never corrupt his creation to pass a message or bestow a gift. The girl was right: it was a thief coming.

The third babalawo decided he would wait, to see what would happen.

The thief came at the witching hour.

Gbemisola Olohun awoke, her eyes flying open. She began to cry, calling with every three breaths in elongated tones to all who could hear. *They have come.*

The sky above Osupa surged with faint violet light. Awojobi and Fagbeja woke after Gbemisola. They moved towards where she seemed riveted to the mat, screaming on her back, her body stiff as wood. *They have come,* she announced continually. Awojobi, covered neck to toe in dust-stained white, his head bowed to the ground, went outside to ascertain her announcement. When he looked up and saw a shapeless hole rippling with violet light, growing across the sky, he turned his heel and walked out of Osupa. *They have come.* He was never seen again.

Fagbeja was able to move Gbemisola Olohun to stand on her feet. He didn't know what else to do. Another object-potency striking her flesh might do her permanent damage. She stood but did not stop crying at the top of her lungs between moments of utter calm. *They have come.* Fatona stirred at her cry and woke up. Her eyes were wide open, staring hard at the air before her, blind to Fagbeja's presence. *They have come.*

Fagbeja walked outside to see the people of Osupa sleepwalk out of their huts. Behind him, Gbemisola's clarion call became louder. Up in the sky where he looked, he saw as in the shared dream, a blackness staining the night, the emergence of a void in the flesh of reality. *They have come.* The violet light radiating from the core of the void intensified. Fagbeja could finally hear what was wrong. The night was quiet as a stone; no insect or frog or bird made a peep. *They have come.* He turned and walked to the lake, out of Osupa, his head and heart beginning to boil over with the always unfamiliar static of madness. He put the pod of poison in his teeth and crushed it, swallowing as he walked into the lake, to sleep beneath pale waters the color of corn cream. *They have come.*

Fatona watched as Gbemisola walked out of the shrine, her head locked into her shoulders. She did not seem to be losing any steam or power and her voice showed no signs of cracking or fraying, instead it seemed to grow stronger, resonating down the length of her body and out into the air around her. *They have come.* Fatona shuddered. The time had come. There was only so much he could do.

He turned to Akanbi, who remained rock asleep, and checked with his fingers if he was still breathing. He was, but was strangely exhaling once for every six breaths which Fatona himself let out. Fatona covered him with a piece of white cloth and followed Gbemisola, who was making her way slowly out of the shrine, through the billowing doors of cloth into the night. *They have come.*

Fatona stepped out of the shrine behind Gbemisola and beheld the people of

Osupa, standing and waiting, sleeping on their feet. *They have come.* Awojobi and Fagbeja were nowhere to be found. He turned back into the shrine to be sure he was seeing right. Yes, his brothers were gone.

"Wake up!" he said as he ran into the midst of the sleepwalkers, panic settling into him. He clapped his hands and shook the shoulders of Gbolahan Olohun, and slapped the faces of the swimmer brothers who had brought Gbemisola and Akanbi to the shrine on the day that they were struck. *They have come.* Nothing happened.

"Wake up!" Fatona screamed again, and Gbemisola, whose voice had become an essential part of the tone of the air, shut up.

Fatona looked at her. Her face was turned upwards to the widening void in the sky. The brightness of the violet light was now rippling off the earth and the huts and the bodies of the people of Osupa, like midnight sun rippling off water. Fatona watched as all the sleepwalkers around him lifted their heads to look at the sky, their eyes shut.

The prow of the boneship, dark as raw charcoal, broke the surface of the void in the sky. Just as in the dream, it sailed out, titanic and weightless, graceful and deformed. Every inch of its surface was engraved in the language that he had seen in the shared dream. The symbols of this language burned and sparked with violet fire in rapid winks and flashes. It made no sound, even the burning of its symbols was soundless. Fatona was wide-awake. The void through which the boneship had sailed out continued to shimmer with violet light even as the language engraved on the body of the ship glinted and flashed rapidly.

The people of Osupa screamed when they opened their sleeping eyes to behold the behemoth. Gbemisola Olohun was the first to catch on lilac fire and shoot into the belly of the boneship. She did not scream like the others who, looking at the ship, were trapped and unable to move their bodies or shut their eyes. She sailed up silently. Once she entered the ship, all the symbols on its body exploded in unison and sent a wave of light across the sky before dying down into nothing. The ship was now black as a cold coal.

A single symbol lit up and another person screamed as they were ripped out of their world into the guts of the ship. The symbols began to flash haphazardly, as people caught fire and flew up into the boneship. Some of the people of Osupa combusted with the beautiful fire and turned into ash without flying to the ship.

Fatona watched as they all went up into the gut of the boneship trailing threads of faintest light. Everyone stood and looked bored, insensate, until the moment. The moment a single wail left their mouths just as their bodies caught on fire and they ascended into the black body of the ship. The boneship swallowed all without discrimination: women who had escaped war and men who had refused it and children who did not know its scars until later in their lives.

Fatona staggered backwards away from the harvest, his mind deciding too late that he should have done as his brothers and escaped the moment he realized what was happening. Awojobi had always said his heart was too soft to belong to a babalawo. There were three of them left behind—Akanbi's guardian, an orphan girl who loved to mold clay heads and talk to them, and him. He watched as the girl screamed loud enough to cause his ears to ring, then her body caught on the hungry fire that was white inside and purple outside. She rose into the air and vanished into the boneship. Iya Akanbi raised her hands up in praise. She screamed as the fire engulfed and pulled her up.

Fatona looked around at Osupa. It was empty. Sadness filled him. He was afraid. He did not look up but only spun around in a circle, riveted to the earth. The boneship remained silent above him.

He remembered Akanbi and moved towards the shrine doors, which were motionless in the stillness of this arcane robbery.

A waterfire that was both cold and hot bloomed in his stomach and flowed up to his heart before it surged out, sank into his skin and wrapped around his long white toga. He threw his head back and screamed in ecstatic agony till his throat seemed to tear.

He went numb, and in his blindness, he became nothing.

TWO

I

SLEEPLESS

Akanbi's eyes flew open.

He rolled over on the bed of layered cloth and saw that he was alone. The firepit burnt low, the coals going to sleep under a blanket of ash. The air was completely still. Akanbi heard his breath as it slid in and out of his body.

He tried to remember what had awakened him. He last remembered the black bone in the sky eating more and more bodies. Gbemisola had left him alone in the flat green place. He had continued to look and call alone, even as the dream cycled back to the bright spotless plain again, and the big man in white stood in the sky and looked at him with pity in his eyes, his cloth bright as a sun. When the big man disappeared, the winds began to ripple and the blackness of the void started to stain the fabric of the dream.

Gbemisola returned one more time, but there was no more song on her lips; instead she wept as she saw the bodies burn on their way up to the boneship. She disappeared in a blink as the nightmare reached the point where the black bone returned into the wound and the wound closed up. Akanbi had noticed her vanish but he couldn't turn his head until the bone was gone.

Akanbi sat in the shrine and every bone in his back cracked in a chorus. Sharp pains shot through his stomach and enveloped his head. He groaned and remembered. The big man had finally spoken to him, his deep voice circling the flat sky and plain in reverberating echoes. "Wake up, Akanbi! You must follow your people immediately."

He stood up with great difficulty. His head swam with a migraine that nearly sent him back to the floor. He leaned forward and retched. The white wrapper that Fatona had placed on his body remained on his shoulders. Akanbi began to sob, the discomfort in his body unbearable. The earth rumbled loud and brief, as if a herd of elephants had suddenly run through Osupa with the speed of a bush rat. He stood up, forgetting all pains. It was still dark outside. He walked forward over Gbemisola's bed, tottering and swaying, fatigued.

Akanbi knew that Osupa was already empty, but feeling it in reality made him want to go back to sleep. The night outside yawned with uncertainty and this, this new trembling outside. He walked across the shrine, one unstable step after the other.

The shrine was hung with various strips of white cloth, horns and teeth in strings. Bundles of object-potencies made from wood, limestone and mud swung in pouches from the roof. He walked past the altar which sat at the center of the shrine—three different statues of pale gold, black and dark red wood stood in a triangle on a layer of wood-shavings. Around their knees stood more object-potencies, a golden pyramid and several cubes of white marble. The statues were carved bluntly, exaggerating the features of their owners. Beside the statues was a gourd of chalkwater. Behind the altar, a white cloth hung covered completely in cowries. Akanbi's pointed cap was beside the altar. He bent and picked it up. The cowries rattled in the breeze that was now blowing through the shrine. It smelled sweet, of unwashed body, rotten fish and soil after rain.

Akanbi tottered past the altar and towards the billowing door of cloth. He stopped just before it. The cloth blew around his body as his heart beat hard in his chest. He wondered if the big orisha in white was protecting him. He prayed for strength, shut his eyes and walked forward into the night.

When he opened his eyes again, Osupa was empty as he expected. The huts in a circle around the shrine were hollow and void of firelight and the chatter of people. Looking closer, he saw that there was something different in the low light of the waning moon above. Akanbi saw what had caused the brief rumble of the earth. There was a pit in the ground which looked like an open mouth, red and black and slippery inside. Something heavy began to rise up out of the mouth. *Thud. Thud. Thud. Thud.*

The last thud of her small feet brought the ofiliganga out of the gut of the earth where she and her sisters lived. Akanbi took three steps backward as she walked onto the land of Osupa properly. She was five times as tall as Akanbi, and thick as a full-grown tree. Soggy skin the color of overripe oranges hung in fatty layers around her wide body. She was naked as a worm. Every inch of her body jiggled gently as she finally heaved her bulk to a stop. Her head was bald. Eyes and full thick lips took up either half of her face and her nose was a small nib in between.

Akanbi didn't know what to say. They both stared at each other for what seemed like forever, so much that Akanbi could now tell that dawn was on its way. Her eyes were clear pools of shifting black glass. They unnerved Akanbi. He held on tighter to his cap as new waves of hunger surged through him. The ofiliganga lifted her arms and spread them out on either side of her body, still looking towards where Akanbi stood. She brought them together with a clap! The air shuddered. Akanbi's bones seemed like sand and he fell to his knees.

"Boy. Nla Nla calls you." Akanbi stood up to his feet and bent over. His stomach was going to eat him before he understood anything that was happening to him.

"Do you hear me boy? Come down now." Her voice was deep and husky and made him feel suddenly surrounded by smoke.

Akanbi nodded. She turned back towards the slick red mouth in the ground, swinging buttocks each the size of a boulder over Akanbi's head.

"Follow me." Her voice echoed into the pit and she thudded down inside.

Akanbi followed, sliding his abeti aja over his head. He looked back at the empty land of Osupa before he slid down, following the ofiliganga into the sticky warmth within the belly of the earth.

II
BONESHIP

The stolen bodies from Osupa numbered a total of fifty-five. They each lay fetal, entombed in clear eggs that hung in the void of the belly of the boneship. Each egg was streaked with veins that glowed like trapped lightning. All the veins led into the throats and circled the heads of the catatonic human beings, pulsing as it nourished or fed on them. The clothes on their bodies were disintegrating slowly, dissolving into clouds of color.

The people of Osupa neither slept nor dreamt as the boneship streaked through an endlessness of stars, planets and moons and swirling eyes made of stardust. It shuddered as it broke through wave and portal, a grain of sand in an ocean of process and disorder, chance and order. It rode currents made by the sinuous bodies of suneaters and passed beneath wars flashing silent in systems beyond.

Eventually it started to move so fast that it seem to have stopped moving altogether. The black coal of its body began to burn, heating up to an unimaginable degree in the span of three breaths. It vibrated white hot in a standstill spot, although it was now moving at the speed of light. Then it disappeared, or rather it moved forward from the speed of light into that of thought and all of the cosmos stopped and the path of the flight of the boneship ceased to be linear. It spun with dizzying speed, carving circles of white fire in the void of the cosmos. Its motions became more ragged and haphazard as it swam through the body of the universe, traversing the breadth of twenty galaxies in mere blinks.

After a while, the boneship winked out of existence into the unknown.

III
AKANBI IN THE NEST OF THE OFILIGANGA

The ofiliganga thundered down the throat inside the earth. The air became more humid and dense with powerful smells as Akanbi slipped and slid after the running giantess. The earth beneath his feet was red and wet with mud. The ofiliganga reached the end of the tunnel and jumped. Akanbi's mouth fell open as he slid down the slope after her just in time to watch her fold into a ball as she fell down inside a vast well that made her large bulk seem inconsequential. He followed, slipping off the edge like an object flung, falling into nothingness.

Akanbi wanted to scream but did not. The feeling of falling into a hole in the earth made his belly feel hollow and cold, scraped of all its soft warmth. He held on to the abeti aja on his head as he fell head down, his heart beat slowing, the sickening cold in his belly growing. He heard a thud that reverberated through what he realized by the echo that widened forever, to be a cavern. The ofiliganga had landed on solid ground. Akanbi tried to turn around or twist his body, but the speed of his fall was immense and afforded him no extra motions, except to put his hand on his head. After falling for another eternal moment, Akanbi suddenly felt the ground rushing up to meet his face; it was the head rising off it that made him know. He started to scream, loud and unstable; but he barely got any sound out before he collided with a mound of softness that shut him up.

The mound drew him slowly into what felt like a pool of deep, warm dough, softer than fresh mud. Akanbi was plastered on all sides by it, but still kept sinking slowly, not yet done falling. Then his fall stopped abruptly. The thick warmth still covered him on all sides. He heard a familiar sound begin to surround him. *dim.dim. dim.dim. dim.dim.* Heartbeats. As the mound ceased to yield, causing him to rise back up to its surface, Akanbi realized he was surrounded by skin and sunken into the flesh of a great body. He struggled to sit up, but it was no use. The body was too soft, and his legs gave before he could even kneel properly.

A hand pulled at his waist and he was lifted through the air and placed on hard solid ground again. Akanbi wobbled and then stood still. His eyes adjusted to the lightless pit into which he had fallen, and he saw a host of very dim fires burning inside the sleeping bodies all around him. They beat: *dim, dim, dim, dim*. A nest of ofiliganga. Their massive voluptuous bodies rose in furrowed hills and valleys and layers dark and fair around him.

"Boy, come." The ofiliganga that brought him was standing right in front of him. He could barely see her apart from the mass of bodies lying around. Her voice was even deeper down here inside the earth.

"Boy, don't make any sound or the sisters wake and you no like that."

Akanbi nodded.

"Boy, look where you put your feet."

He checked for the wholeness of his body, which was already adjusting to the warmth of the bodies around. His abeti aja was in place and the white wrapper under whose cover he had woken in Osupa was still around his neck and shoulders.

"We no see toy in longest time," she said as she began to walk forward, swinging her body like a cat down the path that the bodies of the sleeping ofiliganga created. Her footsteps were completely silent.

Akanbi followed. The bodies rose around as he made his way through a maze of rippling flesh. There were hundreds and hundreds of them. To the one who brought him it was a normal situation but to him it was like walking through a dense forest made of limbs and buttocks, a house of sleeping skin.

After a while, Akanbi could feel the motion of their warmth rushing past him like an invisible river, could see little details and tell if he was looking at fingers or toes or shut eyes. And he could see bellies moving and hear breaths hissing.

The ofiliganga stopped moving. They had passed through the long winding path made by the bodies in the nest and entered a clearing. In this circle, the arrangements of the giantess' bodies had become even more ordered and clean. There was an orange fire going dim.dim, dim.dim, being passed among a gang of five ofiliganga who sat right in the center of the clearing, all with skin black as coal. The giantesses were hugging and kissing the fire that they held in their hands as if it was a bouquet of flame lilies, then handing it over to the next in circle. They were twice the size of the ofiliganga that Akanbi had followed, and their bodies seemed to be firmer and softer at the same time. Their skin didn't pucker or freckle or crease; it was just perfectly smooth and hairless. The ofiliganga that brought Akanbi walked into the center.

"What you need, small sister? You know better than to break a circle during Warmth," one of the assembled ofiliganga asked.

"I have bring boy, from up."

"Where is he?"

The younger ofiliganga pushed Akanbi to the center of the clearing where the skin of the giantesses gleamed as they continued to pass around the fire.

"Come closer."

He moved closer until he could see the fire in their eyes.

"Sleeping boy," said the elderly ofiligiganga, examining Akanbi. "Your father waits inside the earth. Go in and seek him. Use our body." The fire vanished between lips; the sound of biting and moaning passed around: the ofiligangas were eating fire.

Akanbi moved forward, pulled by something he couldn't see, until he was between two hips, tall as huts. A small cave of blackness opened where they leaned against each other. Akanbi knelt down and crawled into the emptiness.

The ofiliganga continued to eat their fire. And Akanbi fell into a hole.

IV
THE MUTE THIEF

The black boneship slipped out of thoughtspeed into an infinite ocean. The ocean was still and white as purest sap. The boneship ceased to move with any precision and began to drift and spin slowly. Nothing moved in the whiteness. There was no sound.

At the center of the white ocean hung a circle of eleven bodies made of rough serrated bones that ended in crowns where the heads should be, like dead trees ending abruptly without branches. They had no faces. Instead, they wore beneath their crowns hemispheres crafted from long spikes. Inside these hemispheres pulsed bright violet light. Small blinding suns sat where their chests should be, their light also of ultraviolet hue. Their arms and legs dangled uselessly, covered in big bony plates and a proliferation of spikes and scales.

These were the Mute Thieves and the white ocean was their mindscape.

The boneship drifted for eternity before it finally got pulled into the only motion under the ocean, a spiral that circled the Thieves. It swam around the thorny towers of the Thieves' bodies, an eighth the size of their heads, before it slipped into their center where the eye of the ocean rested. It was suddenly riveted and became still as an image.

The vertical hemispheres of the Thieves' faces began to flash rapidly, each Thief creating its own pattern of blips and longs flashes. They were speaking to themselves and to the boneship. The boneship's skin freckled with glowing symbols and glinted in response to its owners' queries.

The faces of the Thieves stopped flashing and the boneship broke into eleven pieces. The eggs in which the human beings of Osupa rested in catatonia slipped into the milk of the ocean. The pieces of the boneship drifted off in eleven directions, each slipping where a mouth should be in a Thief's face.

In the ocean, the fifty-one eggs gathered around themselves, sticking one to the other like magnets to metal, forming a cluster. The Mute Thieves began flashing their faces again and thin beams of pure light shot out of their chests and covered the eggs in a final fire.

The eggs broke open. The human beings slipped out, still in a cluster, floating boneless and naked as newborns. Their eyes remained shut. Gbemisola Olohun drifted out of the human cluster towards one of the suns that burned at the hearts of the Thieves. She grew smaller and smaller as she drifted closer to the sun, until she was but a grain, and then she disappeared, swallowed in the ultraviolet.

Gbemisola Olohun sat on a cube that floated in a blue sky. There was nothing below, just aquamarine all around. She remained naked, but she cared very little about that. Her eyes were fixed on the flow of an approaching cloud. It was a thin, long cloud that seemed to dance like a snake as it approached. Every time she blinked it was closer, until finally it was before her and its clean mist was washing over her being. She shut her eyes and felt every cell and nerve in her body sing with bliss. When she opened her eyes, it was as though she was staring into a mirror.

"Where do you think you are?" Gbemisola asked herself. Her voice was quiet and her gaze serene. Gbemisola knew she looked more tired and older than she saw. "Last I remember I was dreaming. Then I woke up and the sky opened and ate me. Is this another dream?"

"You are in Canetis Nix," a voice said to her. "We are Canetix Nix. We require use of your bodies and that is why we have brought you here."

"What does that mean? Brought you here? Is this not a dream?"

"You are far from home, youngling," the voice answered. "We require your throats for what you call sound, for we are unable to create this sound ourselves."

"Let me go," Gbemisola said. She tried to move her body but could not. "I need to understand what is happening please."

"Much has happened before now and much will happen after. We chose you for the power of your song. We tried to get you to see, through a dreamstate, what we required you to do, but we were obstructed by the presence of a radiant entity indigenous to your world."

"Akanbi?" Gbemisola realized she could still remember the dream that had kept her hostage for all those days. She could remember the boy she shared them with. Things started to get blurry when she attempted to cast her mind back to what had happened before, she began dreaming. A place called Osupa. Had she always been dreaming? How did she even come to be in a body?

She watched the mouth of the Canetis Nix move again in the sky where there was no sun but the light was clear as day.

"He is of that entity, yes. The entity chose to make physical contact with him at the very moment we attempted to do the same with you."

"Why?"

"Voices. We require your voices. We have found a peculiar world, perfect to store our menagerie. But it is formless and full of only dust. Only this sound can make it find form again."

"Voices?"

"Other members of your species are present. We require more than one tone to reshape this world."

"If we help you, will we ever return home? Or are we your slaves now?"

"What a strange word. Canetis Nix do not operate under such laws. Think of your work as that of an organ borrowed. You will be returned when said work is done."

"So you have taken us against our will and desire to use us as you please."

"We have taken you because you are a leader in convergence, and where your voice goes the rest will follow."

Gbemisola Olohun felt a knot of emotions tangle up in her chest. Her face remained placid as that of the thing before her, mirroring her. They both sat with legs hanging off the edge of the cube, hands covering breasts placed on hearts. Their backs were stiff and their eyes wide; one with confusion, the other with cold intelligence.

"Please, let us go. We do not want to be here. Please—"

"How do you know where you want to be? You haven't seen it yet. You haven't felt the power in this sound of yours. We are giving your young species a chance at purpose beyond the dreams of your creators. We are creating with you and your fellow human beings, a new form of architect."

The reflected Gbemisola Olohun stood on her cube.

The voice said, "Come with us and know glory." The Canetis Nix fell backwards and took the blue of the sky with her.

V
THE ORISA'S GIFT

Akanbi crawled down a cold, mud-sticky tunnel which he opened with his hands. In the lightlessness, his fingertips were numb as they sank into the tenderness of the subterranean ground and ripped it apart. He could see the perfectly fat ofiliganga talking his destiny over his head as they passed around the flame, their round cheeks announcing that he had to save the people taken from Osupa. They told him to go deeper into the earth's belly if he wanted to survive, if he wanted to begin the rescue mission. They laughed mischievously after they talked about the impossibility of humans ever doing anything right.

He stopped, out of breath. His lower body was covered in the sokoto which he had been wearing the night of the storm at Osupa. His abeti aja was gone. He found himself dozing yet digging, dozing, digging, and soon he was breathing in rhythm.

Akanbi fell out of the tunnel into a large white room that had always been there since Olodumare made Ile Aye, the walls covered in bleached spines from various species of men and animals in a serpentine pattern that fooled the eye with motion. A purple mat swirling with nebulae sat at the center of the room. There was a mountain of stiff white cloth burning with holy fire. Holy fire is blue like water.

Akanbi jumped out of his nap when his skull hit the white sand that flowed across the lower part of the room in clean waves. He rose to his feet. From beneath a covering of clotted soil, cold shivers tore into his spine and belly. He took three steps towards the radiance and collapsed to the floor. A shadow swung about the room, like an arm in a single wave, and the radiance opened. Something moved inside the burning cloth, and through slats in the stiff cloth, forms passed—a sliver of black flesh, an eye, blue and gold with god, a hand trailing cloud.

"Akanbi," a voice whispered. The fiery cloth pulsed with the deep rumble. "Wake up, Akanbi. Stand up. We have work to do." Though low and deeper than lion's cry, the voice remained warm.

Akanbi opened his eyes and stood again. The shivers returned. He could feel his every breath struggling to stay in his lungs. The room swirled and the spines slithered.

"Take palmwine."

Akanbi saw Obatala's eye and followed it to where a fizzing horn hung black in the air before the orisha. Panting, he pulled himself up to the horn and then he placed his lips on the rim and pulled till a hollow rang in the white room inside the earth.

"See." The orisha was standing behind him. He turned to look as the palmwine surged warm as love up and down his insides.

Obatala's hand came down and touched Akanbi's cheek. Akanbi looked into the orisha's face and saw himself. He saw himself on a coal-black eshinemi, galloping across a sky full of stars, streaking the air gold.

"You are to ride Ronke to the white place of our thieves. There you might break the chains of your kind."

Akanbi nodded furiously. The orisha's fingers on his cheek had put him into a stillness that unmoored him. He felt himself possible again. Maybe the fires of Ife had brought him here, into the presence of an aspect of Olodumare whose hand was grazing his cheek and filling him with emotions that had no sound. Akanbi asked about Ronke.

"The eshinemi? She is a being beyond your understanding. Ride her well and don't run when she starts talking."

"Why me?"

Obatala's hand left his cheek and the white room with the spines and the mat and the radiance were gone. Akanbi stood in a tunnel tall enough to hold an iroko. In his palm, a statue of white stone rested, and in the far distance, fields of fire burned.

THREE

I

SONGSTRESS

Flown out of the ocean of thought in which the Mute Thieves dwelled, back into the black glitter of emptiness and stars, the fifty-one human beings from Osupa floated out of the boneship that took them from Ile Aye into the atmosphere of Canetis Nix.

They all stood dazed and naked on a circular bone that spun slowly as it descended. Around their heads grew translucent membranes, bulbs with a rainbow sheen, to help them breathe and amplify their voices.

Light on Canetis Nix was alive. The rippling mists that filled the atmosphere seemed to be sheets of pure light that drifted in circles. The bone dais stopped one foot above the ground. There on the floor, it was like being on the shores of an endless white beach that was attached to an ocean of even whiter sand. A silence pervaded the air. This silence seemed to also control the wind, for no breath moved down on the ground, though in the upper stratosphere there had been some cool and distant roaring like a wave crashing forever without ebbing.

Gbemisola Olohun alighted from the bone dais first, her body plump and her skin smooth as skinned bark. On her back, where her shoulder bones met, something like a spiked crustacean made of finest limestone was fused into her spine. Twenty-four long segmented appendages followed the flow of her ribs and hipbones, slipping stingers half an inch beneath the skin where they stopped, in a pointed oval that started at the throat and ended inside the groin. Two of the appendages pinched above the collarbone, just beneath the voice box.

As Gbemisola walked onto the powders of Canetis Nix, her feet sinking to the ankle with every step, wondering as she had since the lightning struck if all was dream, the *olorin* on her back tightened its grip across her body. Gbemisola staggered and held her midriff. Something was trickling into her, building inside her; the poisons that burned at the tips of the stingers inside her body were releasing their toxins.

The trickle poured out of the *olorin* into her bloodstream and Gbemisola felt it flow through her, the tingles in her skin and then her bones. The collecting of that ache into a point tried to escape, to draw across all space a new thing. The toxins crested in her chest with a flush of euphoria that resonated across all her skin.

She began to sing of bliss, and the upper atmosphere of Canetis Nix was resonant.

It responded to Gbemisola's clear, loud voice and the way she pulled at the song from inside her belly instead of her throat. In the air around her body, vibrations began to collect, and when Gbemisola reached the tonal nadir of her song, the vibrations opened into the air and the remaining fifty-four people of Osupa could see tendrils of fine sand began to swirl around her, showing the outlines of the sonic sphere in which she stood, ten times taller and wider than her. The powdered white around her feet sank, forming a circle wide as the bone dais that brought them.

Rising out of the low note, Gbemisola flew to the higher reaches of her register, like a bird approaching death. The particles of sand followed the hum and sound of her voice, clinging and rippling and twisting like muscles around the vibrations of the song. Gbemisola finished the song and walked forwards, back to stand before her people. It continued to echo for what seemed like an eternity. Behind her stood a spherical structure, like a hollow ball made of strings and thick muscle.

The architect remained standing. She turned and looked at the structure. The bliss in her blood made her smile, even though looking at the sphere from which she had just stepped out, she had a strong sense of being outside of herself.

The fifty-four people all understood as they watched. Sound and the matter of this place were like magnet and iron, hand and mud. The *olorin* in their backs squirmed and poison-ecstasy filled their bellies. They alighted from the bone dias, and it slipped away into the atmosphere with the speed of air. They walked over to Gbemisola Olohun, who was standing staring at the structure, reading of herself in the sculpted sand.

The circle formed around the convergent and the first chorus began.

II

RONKE

By the grace of the palm wine he had shared with Obatala, the fields of blue fire that led to the center of the earth did not scorch Akanbi, but he still walked through them fearfully, placing his feet on the shattered coals that covered the ground as if they would burn him. All around him the fire roared. There was nothing for miles but fire like grass, rising out of hard, black rock. Above, there was no sky or cloud, only the returned glow of the fields below. The fire gave off no smoke.

Akanbi reached a river of molten lava and the statue in his hand buzzed. He began to follow the flow of the river, past rows and rows of hot tongues licking, seemingly planted. The river ended in a lake of fire that split off into a rash of smaller and larger pools up ahead. The lake was placid, like a spill of yellow and red soup. The earth around it was dead black, with no smolder.

This was how Akanbi saw Ronke, staring from the shore, her hooves submerged. She stood two times his height, white as fresh coconut, with one pair of snake eyes high on either side of her head. Beneath the snake eyes were two moons, sunken into the long skull. But Akanbi was riveted to what shone at the center of her head like a diamond sparkling.

Akanbi moved closer to her and she walked up from the lake and bowed her head till he could touch it. He pulled the statue out of his sokoto and placed it on her tongue. She began to crunch it as if it was sugar.

"Hop on my back," her voice came into his head unannounced. "Let me take you to the whiteness. I can see your friends. They are building cages."

Akanbi walked over to her middle and found that his head only reached her belly. She lay down flat, her white belly over black rock, and he climbed onto her back. She stood and Akanbi had a vantage of the fields of fire and the pools in the distance.

"Grab my neck," the voice said.

Akanbi slid forward and grabbed as much of her long neck as he could. She was cold like a fish, with flat scales like calcified feathers across her body. Akanbi shut his eyes. He had nothing to think of or wish. He was only following instructions in which the only thing needed was his faith. As the eshimemi began to gallop into the air, flying over the night above the fields of fire, he found that he had a desire to be told of as a story.

III
CHORUS ARCHITECTURE

In the millions of seconds that the fifty-five people of Osupa sang, they raised over five thousand of their indestructible spheres. The spheres peppered the surface of Canetis Nix like nests from an invasive species, all varying in size and pattern but remaining within the form of the sonic sphere that drifted around them every time they sang the structures up.

The olorin were growing deeper into their bodies and their bliss was getting stronger. They usually needed screams and shouts and roars to make the structures bigger. The olorin made sure they felt strong enough to break their throats.

Soon, the Mute Thieves themselves appeared, distant in the always-day skies of Canetis Nix like halved samurai. The bodies of Gbemisola Olohun and the fifty-four now spotted breastplates the color of olorin and throats like hard red stone. Their symbiosis with the euphoric was almost complete. It reached into their bones and turned them into hyper-vibrating elements, and made their ribcages into colossal echo chambers and their throats into weapons.

They knew how it worked. They wandered the powders of Canetis Nix looking for points of convergence. Only Gbemisola knew these points, where air and sky and sand found equilibrium enough to be shaped with song. Once found, they stood as symbol. Circle and dot. Chorus and convergent. Then the olorin flooded their blood with bliss and their wordless songs rose, followed after by the powders of Canetis Nix. The sands rose like smoke into the air and became steel at the end of sound.

To make the sandflow ornate, they used melisma; for flair, they roared like beasts; soprano brought finesse; bass-built foundation; and pitch increased density. They were a machine by now, their olorin growing tentacles that linked their mind, body and voice. They wandered Canetis Nix, building with voice, soaring, lost yet found.

After they built their last structure, the Mute Thieves appeared, sending thousands of boneships of varying sizes. Out of these ships came a zoo—smaller versions of the Mute Thieves with the same spiked bone armor and violet auras, leading and lifting and carrying abominations stranger than the eyes of the Convergent could believe. They put the creatures in some of the cages that the fifty-five had built and then afterwards, with a sting from the *olorin* and brief passages of voice, the cages were sealed.

Then, the Mute Thieves left the fifty-five alone on Canetis Nix, not to die but never to be let go, because they too were creatures acquired.

IV
RESONANCE

Ronke and Akanbi galloped up, with a sound like a shot, out of the darkness under the crust, onto the glazed deserts of Canetis Nix. As far as the eye could see, there rose spherical sculptures, layered and built like nests. Ronke zipped through this odd farm; Akanbi still gripping her neck, squinted through his eyes to see. He snapped up when Ronke stopped as if hit by a wall.

Twenty man-sized eggs lay in a depression on the ground of Canetis Nix. They pulsed and a fleshy redness squirmed behind their translucence.

"We are too late," Ronke said inside his head. "They are in metamorphosis."

Ronke knew too much. Akanbi suspected she was just Obatala in another form. He climbed down her cool body onto the heat of Canetis Nix and moved closer to the pod of eggs.

"How?" Akanbi asked.

"The time it took to get here might have seemed like a few days to you, but it was nearly a decade to them. They must have merged with the thieves and entered into this state."

The eggs were arranged in a spiral. The large thorny spheres that covered the surface of the white desert around them seemed immovable. Akanbi was unaware of all the cosmic life contained in them: hungry, thrashing, sleeping and calling to lost homes.

Akanbi stood by the eggs feeling futile. He could tell that his people, the people of Osupa were there. He could feel their hearts beating and smell a bitter sweetness in their blood. There were faces behind the sticky rainbowsheen of the eggshells. Gbolahan. The twins. Fatona.

He knew no one among them even though they had been recovering from their shared trauma as a collective. All his life he had been alone. He had failed those who sent him and now he was lost on another world. The discomfort of the situation hit him and Akanbi turned away from the eggs towards Ronke. He wanted to disappear completely.

"Ronke, can you take me anywhere I desire?"

"No. We are here to take these people home. We have to wait for them to wake up. Come, rest on my belly. You're doing good. Obatala will see you again after this."

Akanbi saw that the eshimemi was lying on the heat of the desert, joyous. He went over and lay on its soft cold belly and waited.

After an eternity of dreamless anticipation, the eggs opened.

V
CONVERGENCE

The olorin and the human being have fused into one being against the predictions of the Mute Thieves. They emerge from their pods, new soldiers of tone, their backs serrated and their eyes pools of nothingness in which sound can be seen. Their tender throats have become split red things, like sliced fruit, and their heads are covered in plates of a porous tomato-red shell, as are their chests and thighs. They are beautiful, fleshless beneath these shells. No more human.

Akanbi staggers back as they slip out of the dripping eggs into the heat. They lay and dry in the permanent sun, while the largest egg seems to wait. Ronke says nothing. Akanbi looks from behind her head. The eshimemi sits on her side and watches the birthing.

The newborns begin to sing, a sound strangely human, like a memory of human song. They circle Gbemisola, the convergent, unborn queen. Her egg splits and she spills out. No shell, no spikes.

Akanbi thinks he is looking at a placenta or yolk when the queen unfurls into the air, a mucosal serpent of white noise. Her motions set off melodies which the air sings to itself. She stretches tall towards the sun, her every atom blooming with harmony, long fins cycling above the ground.

Ronke stands up in respect. The chorus of nineteen, all turned male, look to their queen. She in turn looks beyond Canetis Nix, letting out a sound, like birdsong unraveled.

In the sky, a circle appears. Point of convergence, here to nowhere. Here to everywhere. The queen sails into the sky, towards the Convergence, gentle as smoke.

Her chorus follows.

EMILY

MARIAN DENISE MOORE

In antebellum New Orleans, John Henderson advertised in the *Daily Picayune*
for the return of a presumed runaway, a seven-year-old enslaved girl.

You are frozen there
Emily
one foot on the muddy gate to the American city
one foot raised over brick laced into concrete
between buildings higher than you've ever seen.
On foggy March mornings, women wearing starched cotton dresses stride
by you into work you would recognize.
If I keep you poised there, I don't have to imagine what happened:
the cotton dealer who misplaced his child's favorite playmate;
the brothel owner that thought you a charming whimsy for his parlor;
the errand that crushed you beneath a carriage's wheels;
the race along the levee that ended with a tumble into the river.
You can see that I am kin
I can think of so many horrors.
Therefore—a gift—I'll imagine one more possibility:
the man that recognized you,
hid you beneath his cloak,
and took you to live among the maroons in the swamp across the river.
Stay there Emily,
a moment longer
I only live ten miles and two hundred years away.
Your father is coming for you.

TO SAY NOTHING OF LOST FIGURINES

RAFEEAT ALIYU

Odun tore open a portal and it was as easy as brewing a cup of tea. He was eager to leave behind the dark wetness of the cave he stood in, and not just because it was cold in there. Within him, the voice of his stolen ngunja murmured and though Odun could not quite make out what they were saying, he took it as a good sign. The rip he made was a gaping hole that exuded colour and warmth. Odun stepped into it and had to blink at the brilliant purples, yellows and oranges that swirled in constant motion around him. The portal closed behind him and in the space between dimensions, he started opening a new one in the direction of Kur when he heard commotion.

"Hold it right there!"

The words came before a slight figure materialised in front of him. Odun gritted his teeth. The newly enforced inter-portal patrol only worked between universes that were hostile towards outsiders. He had been so excited at the thought of reuniting with his figurine that he had not bothered reading up on the laws of Kur.

"Greetings to you and to those you hold in your possession," the agent said in a deep, raspy voice.

"Greetings to you and those you hold in your possession," Odun replied.

Covered from head to toe in a flowing robe of pitch black, the border agent's identity was hidden. Yet the greeting signalled that the agent was someone like Odun, someone selected to control the variety of staffs, wands and figurines that made up the corpus of the ngunja. There was a pause as the agent seemed to study Odun who had no choice but to tap his foot, impatiently waiting for the formalities to be over. His right ear felt itchy, and as he reached up to pull at it, he heard his stolen ngunja again. It was a whisper that felt like a cold wind travelling up his back and leaving goose pimples in its trail.

"Finally."

On Tuntun Atlantic where Odun came from, no one was brave enough to touch a mage's ngunja, let alone steal one. A brief moment of carelessness months ago had left him without one of his most critical abilities. The worst of it all was that Jooh was initially so quiet that Odun couldn't even track down his own ngunja. Jooh formed part of the five nguja that were handed to Odun by his mentor before her death.

But this had to be the longest reading Odun had ever been subjected to. He could do the same—make use of his golden eye to reveal things that even that billowing cloak could not hide—but Odun was not as interested in the border agent as the agent was in him.

"Odun Kiamesa of Tuntun Atlantic," the agent droned as though precious minutes were not wasted since their initial greeting. "Possessor of time, shapeshifting, resurrection, psychosomatic and terrakinesis abilities. I'm only sensing four..."

"Actually, that's why I'm heading to Kur," Odun said. "My fifth ngunja is there."

There was a pause before the agent said, "There are no records of you having entered..."

"It was stolen and I'm in the process of retrieving it." Odun said. He thought: *If only the bureaucracy stepped out of the way now, there was really no need to waste any more time.*

"Oh, that will be a problem," the agent said. "Humans aren't allowed into Kur. You're an esteemed mage and can be granted entry but you'll have to emerge as you are."

"Returning with my ngunja will be returning as I am," Odun replied. "While we're on the topic of rules, you must know that harbouring a stolen ngunja within your borders is an offence that can be escalated to the A.J.E."

Even though he couldn't see the agent's face, he sensed a change in the air. Any mention of The Assembly of Justice and Enchantment—the supreme gathering of mages across portals and dimensions—tended to have that effect. It seemed his words had hit home. "Consult with whomever you have to," Odun said.

A few more minutes passed before Odun heard the confirmation he'd been waiting for.

"The authorities at Kur will make an exception just this once. You are free to enter and retrieve your item under the supervision of a Kurian official. You will be expected to leave within 46 small hours. I trust a mage of your calibre can do what needs to be done in that time."

By the time Odun emerged from the other side of the portal, it felt like hours had passed since he set out. Inter-dimensional travel was supposed to be quicker than the time it took a Pxyr to flap its wings and launch into the air. Odun's head swam as he adjusted to the new environment, and the heavy stench of something akin to rotting trees that permeated the air did not help. He tripped on something and landed on the ground with a splash. Wetness immediately soaked through the layers of his clothes. Odun wryly recalled the adage that "the best way to kill one who possesses ngunja is to meet them at the other side of the portal."

✦ ✦ ✦

When the notification came in, Aule thought it was a fluke. After five years as the sole government representative at the border town of Oeg, she was finally getting a job. Aule leaned forward to read the messages floating on her screen once more.

Task assigned: 20786876. Human mage at north-eastern border coordinates 10.1.13.

Banished to the far reaches of Kur, the only reason Aule knew the specifics of that code was because she had enough time to read the official handbook from top to bottom. She had once heard fellow mates at the training centre say that if one were to transfer all the data from the handbook to paper, it would occupy all 428 stories of the central government building.

Aule jumped when her transmission device beeped. Her device never beeped before, so she pressed *accept* hesitantly. It took a moment to recognise her immediate superior. The last time Aule saw Assistant Director Yon was five years ago after she passed her civil service exams on the sixth try. Yon looked at her, his distaste towards Aule obvious on his skin. On a normal day, it was mostly black outside the orange patches under his chin and around his wrists and ankles. The orange was now a bright red.

"Greetings sir." Aule resisted the urge to clear her throat. She had been around Kurians all her life and knew to guard her emotions.

"I trust you've received the missive," Yon said, opting not to reply to her greeting. "A human Esteemed Mage is at the north-eastern border. He has lost his ngunja. You are to escort him to pick it up and then see him out. No detours or unnecessary distractions."

Yon ended the call abruptly. Used to this kind of attitude, Aule leapt to her feet and stepped out of the shack that was her office. In Nwo and other big cities, government offices were shiny buildings that reached into the stratosphere. Here in Oeg, it was a neo-wooden shack that stood on stilts surrounded by the swamp. Aule slipped into her watercraft through the latch on the roof and ignited it with her bracelet-key. She really should be more excited. While this was not her first time meeting a human, this would be the first time she would be meeting one after her toying with the idea of leaving Kur. She already knew that it would be impossible; she would never get the appropriate approval, but a human-Kurian hybrid could dream.

As Aule glided over the brackish water of the mangrove, one of many that cover the surface of Kur, she passed by the citizens she represented. The inhabitants of the northern mangroves did not have limbs and moved by slithering on the ground or in the water. They were as intelligent as the other races in Kur, yet they were looked down upon. Perhaps it was this shared discrimination that created a tenuous bond between Aule and them. Here, when she waved in greeting as she passed by them and they saw her through the large windscreen, they waved their tails or heads slowly in reply.

When she reached the coordinates given in the message, Aule found the Esteemed Mage slunk against one of the giant roots of the red mangrove tree. The human sat in the low water—filled with mud as always—and was partly shielded by the green spiny leaves of the palm shrubs at the base of the tree. If there was a metaphor for how humans had come to be regarded in Kur, this was it.

Years ago, before inter-portal relations shut down, humans entering Kur did so at the western border which was a breathtakingly beautiful building laid in gold and emeralds. Now they entered in mud. Aule parked her vehicle as close to the mage as she could without hurting him and lifted herself out through the roof. There was a loud splash as she landed in the water, but the water easily slid off her skin and clothes. She squatted, resting on her haunches before the mage and reached out to shake him, gently because no one knew what these mages were capable of.

"Welcome to Kur," she said when the mage's eyes flickered open. At first, the mage looked around the surroundings, not quite seeing her. When he finally looked at her, he shot up to his feet, causing Aule to topple off balance.

"I'm so sorry!" the mage exclaimed as he stretched a hand to help Aule up. Aule ignored this and rose to her feet herself.

The mage looked down at his clothes: they were wet and muddy and yet he still attempted dusting down the front with his hands. "Wouldn't it be great if we had ngunja to change our clothes at will?" he asked.

From the perplexed look on Aule's face, the mage could tell that his joke did not translate well. Odun looked down at his clothes, they were wet and muddy and yet he still attempted dusting down the front with his hands. "Wouldn't it be great if we had ngunja to change our clothes at will?" he asked.

From the perplexed look on the Kurian official's face, he could tell that his joke did not translate well.

"Greetings. I am Odun, from Rin Atlantic," the Mage bowed in greeting as is his custom.

"Yes, greetings. I am Aule, your official escort and I was told that you're in a hurry." Aule replied.

"Indeed, I am," Odun said.

"This way please." Aule pointed him towards her watercraft. She frowned at his wet clothes and then at the smooth leather interior of her vehicle. "If you wouldn't mind, let me."

She touched his clothes tentatively with her right hand, first the knee length shirt, then the trousers, and in the process absorbed all the wetness. Her father was much more skilled in his sponge-like abilities. After she had absorbed the mage's wetness, there were still brown spots where the mud stained the indigo of the mage's clothes, but at least the inside of her craft would be mostly clean.

Inside, she guided him to the passengers' seat placed behind her and the control board. It still offered a view of the wet landscape through the large windscreen. As Aule started the machine, she was painfully aware that she had not been given any details about this visitor. He seemed to be collected and not at all surprised by her appearance or her vehicle, so she assumed he must be wide-travelled.

"Do you also possess the ngunja?" Odun asked, breaking the ice.

"Not at all," Aule replied. "The ngunja isn't magic and that is what we here in Kur can do. Where do I take you?"

"What, you mean there's no more bureaucracy here?" Odun laughed.

"Well, we could go to the government house to discuss the details, but I was told that you were in a hurry."

"Efficiency is good," Odun mused. "Give me a minute then."

Aule watched Odun as he closed his eyes and retreated within himself, his head cocked to one side as though he was waiting to hear something. Then suddenly, his eyes popped open and a huge grin spread across his face.

"Just wanted verification," he explained. "There's a house in your capital with the following symbols emblazoned on two columns near the entrance. That's where my stolen ngunja is."

Aule frowned as Odun sketched the symbols in the air. "Are you sure that's it?"

Odun nodded in affirmation. Still frowning, Aule entered the symbols into the navigation system and a number of results popped up. Seeing the confirmation of her initial concern, Aule gulped.

"Is anything the problem?" Odun rose and looked over Aule's shoulder at the screen.

"This is the Interior Minister's house," Aule replied.

"Well," Odun attempted to sound diplomatic. "I don't mean to accuse your government of theft. Perhaps the Minister or one of his family members bought the staff in error. But it won't be a problem for them to return it to its rightful owner."

Craning her neck, Aule looked up at Odun. "You really don't know anything about Kur, do you?"

She sighed and recalled Assistant Director Yon's words on distractions. This was undoubtedly going to be a mess, but it would also be the most exciting thing to happen to Aule in years, perhaps since her father passed away.

"Let's head towards Nwo then," Aule shrugged.

One part of Odun was seated in the watercraft, staring out the window at the changing landscape as they approached Nwo. Odun observed that Kur seemed to be a rolling green of trees with exposed gnarled roots that reached above the brown water. The air here was probably the freshest he had inhaled in his life. The other part of him—that inner corner of himself that was intimately linked with all the five ngunja he earned as part of his profession—was engaged in a deep conversation. Aware that he was closer to Jooh than he had ever been in the past two months, Odun could not help but smile, knowing that his abilities would be returned to him soon.

In the upcoming landscape-creating competition back home, the ever expanding Tuntun Atlantic would need that particular ability Jooh enabled. Tuntun Atlantic was always expanding and it was the job of Esteemed Mages like Odun, aided by his ngunja, to create new land for incoming colonists. The thought of not being able to participate had left Odun restless and unable to sleep for months. He had been the winning champion ever since he emerged from his mentor's shadow a decade ago. This year was particularly crucial: it would mark Odun's sixth win, qualifying him for a promotion and hopefully an all-expense paid move to another frontier town where he could push the limits of his ngunja and terrakinesis abilities.

Being so far away from Jooh had taken its toll on Odun. It felt as though a part of him was missing; as though he had been moving on stilted breath for months. It was hard to believe that he once walked about without being connected to and being in the care of his possessions. This craft could not be moving any faster, and where he came from, the fastest moving things were the pelorovis-drawn carriages. What Odun really wanted to do was sort things out himself and get back Jooh on his own, but rules were rules and the worst thing a mage could do was break them. So his mentor had drilled into him and what he had experienced at the border was just a slight taste of the bureaucracy that was slowly blanketing all dimensions and planes.

"You're sure your ngunja is at the Interior Minister's?" his guide asked, her voice jarring his thoughts.

Odun shifted in his chair, surprised that she had broken the silence but as he was now in a good mood, he was happy to indulge any questions.

"Of course," he replied. "We're in constant communication with our ngunja. At least the good mages are. It was stupid for anyone to steal it. You can't possess its power just because you possess the figurine."

"What does that mean?"

"It just means that there has to be some alignment between us and our ngunja for there to be magic. Not everyone has that ability."

"We don't know much about the ngunja and the mages here," Aule said. "What's it like in territories solely populated by humans?"

There was a certain flavour to her question, a desperation that Odun could easily detect even though she seemed to hide it well. He shifted in his leather chair and chose to ignore it, closing his eyes in concentration. There were many reasons a civil servant might seek escape but those were not Odun's concern when he could feel that Jooh was somewhere close by.

As Aule navigated past the mangroves, she struggled to keep her excitement in check. This was her first assignment, yes; but she was here with someone who could tell her more about the human world scattered across dimensions. She prodded gently with her questions, but the mage seemed occupied with what Aule could only suppose was some form of meditation. Nwo was a metropolis of closely packed houses, varying in size but all larger than anything they had passed on the way. The waters of the swamp led here, although they were hidden by elevated reinforcements that formed the foundation of most of the buildings in Nwo. The entrance to the Interior Minister's palace was guarded by four guards. They stood between the stone columns on folded hind legs with their long arms almost reaching the ground, their blue skins covered in warts and their poses ready to attack.

The building itself was made of the same stone as the columns, and though it rose two storeys high and looked imposing, it was nothing compared to the buildings in the central government area which they had passed by on the way. Aule parked a few paces ahead of the entrance but kept her vehicle running.

"I'll be right back," Aule said to Odun before heading out. She had barely taken a step when one of the guards pounced, launching himself in one great leap from the far distance to stand in front of Aule. The artificial earth trembled from the force and Aule geared herself up for a confrontation.

"We were not informed of any human visitors," the guard grunted.

"I am from the Oeg border," Aule explained, tapping her suit in search of her ID. "I am escorting an Esteemed Mage under the orders of Assistant Director Yon. He wishes to see the Interior Minister."

The guard was already hissing at her. Aule's skin shifted tones and grew lighter brown, indicating her growing irritation.

"Assistant Director Yon sent me," she hissed each word.

"I heard that part," the guard replied. "And I say, the Minister isn't expecting anyone."

"Look," Aule said, "the first human to step foot in Kur in years is behind me." Finding her ID, she presented it to the guard. Training at the academy must have worsened because the guards saw her movement as a threat, so that the other guards at the column leapt forward and surrounded her. Aule was immune to the poisons emanating from their glistening skins, so she stood her ground and glared at each of them. A few tense seconds passed before the guards stepped down.

"You can send the Esteemed Mage in," one of them said. "Only the mage."

Aule watched them retreat to their positions at the entrance before whirling to find Odun.

"You can enter, past those gates," she pointed behind her. "I will be waiting for you right here."

"Sure," Odun replied.

Aule watched him make his way towards the columns and the guards. Slowly despair set in. Aule kicked the ground in frustration. She hated this place.

Whatever challenge his guide surmounted back there, Odun was glad to be inside the Interior Minister's house. It was tastefully designed with art from across portals. Odun stood in the hallway waiting to be received, and in that moment understood how his ngunja could have reached here. Jooh was a brass figurine that featured a couple kneeling side by side; everything from the couple's elongated heads to the curve of their lips was realistic. He tilted his head in concentration, listening for Jooh's voice. Just then, one of the huge doors to his right opened and from it emerged a squat Kurian with red skin and large eyes completely black.

"It has been a while since we welcomed a human to Kur," the Kurian said, straight to the point. "To what do we owe this pleasure?"

"Good day, Minister," Odun replied, resisting the urge to crouch so that he was eye-level with the Kurian.

Odun considered the most diplomatic way to address the issue of his stolen ngunja. In that moment, his enthusiasm at finding Jooh had cooled off enough for him to realise the wisdom in travelling with someone who knew local customs. *Why had Aule not accompanied him*? *And what was the commotion with the guards*? He hadn't bothered to ask and now it was too late.

His host skipped over a reply and said instead, "I am the Minister's assistant. Surely you don't presume our Interior Minister will have time to attend to you."

"I'm looking for something." Odun said.

"And what would that be?" the Kurian asked.

"I'm a Mage from Tuntun Republic and my ngunja was stolen about nine weeks ago. I have reason to believe that it is here."

"That's impossible," the Kurian's skin turned a deeper red. It might have been embarrassment or anger but Odun took a careful step back. "Are you accusing the Interior Minister of theft?"

"You must know we are constantly connected to our ngunjas," Odun said, his voice rising. "I know it is here."

Odun did not have the time to engage in this kind of game. In that moment, he did something that he would not do under any other circumstance: he lifted his hand-channelling Wak, one of the ngunja he left at home. Anticipating his move, the sac under the Kurian's skin bulged till it was almost twice its owner's size. A sharp acidic scent suffused the air and as soon as it reached Odun's nostrils, his arm fell to the side useless.

"We do not tolerate any form of human violence here," the Kurian said. "Especially from humans. Your guide will escort you back to the border."

Some time had passed and Aule remained upset and embarrassed that the guards had not let her do her job. After centuries of trying to mimic human behaviours and manners, the Kurians had done a complete turnaround and made a concerted effort to exile humans and ban contact with them. Aule was an aberration, born from a liaison between her nomadic Kurian father and a human just when the ruling mages decided they had enough of human dealings. She had heard that her father had created her mostly from her mother's genetic material. He was the one who carried her in his back and hatched her. He was the only parent she knew, and his death meant an end to the shield that had protected her from Kurian discrimination.

She had a lot in common with other Kurians: living on water and land and breathing mostly through skin and hair. Yet Aule could do even more; she could camouflage better than other Kurians and possessed the ability to break bones when necessary. She would have been a star in any other era, but in this one she was just a freak that no one wanted to see or deal with.

There was a hard rap on the side of her watercraft. Aule pushed open the latch to see one of the guards carrying the unconscious Odun. The guard did not say a word before tossing Odun into the vehicle, and Odun's head barely missed the edge of the passenger's seat. Aule looked down at Odun where he lay slumped. She knelt down and touched his skin. She could taste the paralysing poison that he had inhaled. Aule tried to absorb as much of it as she could before driving away.

It would take about an hour before Odun regained consciousness. When he did, Aule's skin glowed in relief.

"This is unnecessarily difficult," Odun groaned, clearing his throat.

"If you don't mind, I'd like to propose a solution," Aule said. The time she had spent alone gave her the confidence to share this.

"What do you suggest?"

"I can go into that house, get your ngunja and no one will know. In return you can take me to Tuntun Atlantic."

The frustration Odun felt when he was unable to move his limbs while remaining slightly conscious of what was going on around him had faded only slightly. His muddled mind did not even consider Aule's suggestion.

"That will be against the law!" Odun proclaimed, shaking his head. Running through his mind were the dozen laws, both Kurian, Tuntun Atlantic and inter-portal, that they would be breaking.

"Do you want your ngunja or not?" Aule asked. "Kurians are diurnal and this is our chance."

It was his first time here and Odun was so consumed with the thought of his ngunja that he did not take the time to study Aule. She did not possess the long forearms, webbed digits, or powerful hind legs that the guards possessed. She looked human enough, but on closer inspection, he saw that her nose was small enough to resemble slits and that the black of her skin had an obsidian quality.

"Have you taken on this form for my benefit?" Odun asked.

"I have some human in me," Aule answered. "That's why I want to leave this place. You may have noticed how hostile Kurians are to humans. It's worse for someone like me. I can't do anything I like. Everywhere I turn I face alienation."

"Humans are most likely going to act the same way towards you," Odun tried to reason with her.

"The Kurian government has clamped down on everything," Aule pressed on. "There's no free movement outside this territory. Share those coordinates with me."

"That will be impossible," Odun said, eyeing Aule from the corner of his eyes. "You of all people know that Kur is strictly regimented and guarded. I've never had a personal escort follow me on any of my travels."

"Do you want your staff or not?" Aule repeated. "It is your choice. We have a few hours before your status becomes illegal."

Odun allowed himself to brood. The sun was setting outside, and he could not tell where they were, yet he was close enough to Jooh to hear it humming strongly. An Esteemed Mage was welcome across portals but in Kur, his stolen ngunja was hidden from him. Odun considered his options: he could somehow combine all five of his ngunjas to summon an earthquake and effectively ruin this place...then face the rest of his life outlawed by the A.J.E. Maybe he could even lose his ngunjas for good.

Jooh was now talking loud enough for Odun to decipher the message it was trying to send. It was going to change hands soon.

"Let's do this your way," Odun said.

For most of her life, Aule retained the ability to remain awake after sunset. Being reduced to inactivity after nightfall was a major weakness that technology still had not saved the Kurians from. Her father had often said it was the human part of her that made her an evolved Kurian. For Aule, the loneliest times were at night.

"Tell me what to expect," Aule said, and Odun described how Jooh looked and details of the room in which it was kept.

Her comms pad beeped; it was Assistant Director Yon again. The sun was quickly disappearing for the day and undoubtedly, he wanted to ensure that Odun was out of Kur by then. Aule ignored the incoming transmission.

Armed with the necessary knowledge, Aule exited her watercraft and dove into the brackish water. She had parked close enough to the Interior Minister's house that it was a short swim. Aule cut through the waters and when she emerged, she waited for her camouflage to kick in. She made a rude gesture as she snuck past the guards who were already powered down and dozing in their combative stances. Aule slipped undetected into the house through an open window on the ground floor. On any other day, she would have stopped to stare in awe at how large the building was, but now she walked towards the second floor.

According to Odun, his ngunja was placed in a room that looked out to the columns. She would have to make her way into each of the north-facing rooms. And when she entered the right one and found the ngunja for Odun, Aule would be one step closer to getting out of here. She struck wood in the third room on the left of the grand staircase. Odun's ngunja was stunning and Aule felt a muted energy buzzing from it as she picked it up. A blaring alarm went off. Aule froze, uncertain what to expect. Though the guards were sleeping outside, Aule knew that the Kurians just did not function in this time of the day.

"Someone's here," a deep voice grunted languidly. "Come out!"

She rushed out of the room and saw the guards falling over themselves as they leapt here and there looking for the intruder. The sluggish movements of the guards, unused to such disturbance, made Aule chuckle. She dropped her guard and took great pleasure revealing herself to the guards. Their movements were slow, as though they were moving through gel, and it did not take much for Aule to immobilise them with her own poison. That was what they got for underestimating her. Her father had created her well.

Odun was startled by Aule's sudden appearance. She kickstarted her craft and tossed Jooh at him with a slight apology.

"Things have changed," she said in a rush. "I was seen, and we need to leave right now. Your ngunja is beautiful by the way."

"What? Thank you..."

"Can you tear a portal here?" she asked as they started moving.

"It's illegal to..." Odun began, then paused as he recalled the unpleasant border official and the rules he'd broken already.

"It's a long way back to Oeg," Aule crooned. "Kurian jails are horrible."

"You've said enough," Odun groaned. He grasped Jooh and tore a portal, destination: Tuntun Atlantic.

SLEEP PAPA, SLEEP

SUYI OKUNGBOWA DAVIES

Max Aniekwu stands in the shadows of an abandoned danfo under the bridge at Otedola, where he always meets his buyers. Grime lines his wrist and tucks under his fingernails, making his increasingly sweaty palms greasy. Dark clouds splotch over a sky as gray as TV static, announcing an impending thunderstorm; yet Max sweats and juggles the Ziploc bag from one slimy palm to another in search of some friction. He shifts from foot to foot and wipes his gleaming forehead with the back of his free hand, leaving dark stains.

Max knows something is different this time. Beside the fact that the buyer is late, something in his chest simply doesn't sit right. He should never have taken this job, not from Chidi of all people. Max wipes sweat from his brow again, now rethinking it all. Chidi, whose tips and contacts have twice gone bad and landed three colleagues in the police net. Chidi, who every trader worth his salt in the black market has blacklisted.

He should turn around right now, dump the bag inside the abandoned danfo and leave. But that'll ruin his cred on the market. Rule number one: never stand up your buyer. He'll struggle with finding another buyer for sure, and God knows how he'll eat then. *Remember, Maximus. Remember why you gats to do this shit in the first place.*

There's a couple peals of thunder, and a mild drizzle begins to bathe the bridge overhead. Max, unable to shake off the spiders marching up the nape of his neck, considers a break for it. Worst case, he'd ask Chidi to call the buyer, apologize, and set another delivery time and date. He's tired from all the digging, anyway.

He's still thinking this when a shadow falls upon all other shadows around him.

Max looks up, into the scraggly face of a gangly dark man. The man wears a long, gray kaftan that cloaks a sheathed curved dagger clamped to his belt. He's draped in an equally gray shawl over his head, hiding most of his features, but Max can still see two lines of vertical tribal marks etched into each cheek, right below piercing eyes.

"Ne Maximus?" he asks. His accent is heavily northern.

Max swears under his breath, his anger flaring. Not only did Chidi tell the buyer his full name—you never tell a buyer your name because you never know what they're going to do with it—Chidi the idiot also brought him a northerner.

Was he not clear enough about his preferred client types or was Chidi just stupid? Even after Max made him repeat it like a mantra: get only middlemen who buy and smuggle to storage centers in Cotonou and Yaounde for shipping to boutique museums that do live exhibitions in China, Mexico and Poland, Chidi still defied his instruction. He knows that anyone else is a big risk with the police, especially these northern guys who everyone says only buy to eat, even though no one has ever been able to prove that, which makes it even more of a problem. *Knowledge is power, and the lack of it, danger*, his father used to say. Truest word, that.

Max looks the man up and down from shawl to sandaled feet. Twilight looms, and with the street lights yet to come up, there is nothing before him but a tall, gray ghost.

"Your order?" Max inquires.

There's a moment of hesitation, then the man says, "Yatsun, hakora, da kunnuwa."

Max nods. Having lived in Kaduna for a couple years, he knows what those Hausa words mean.

Toes, teeth, ears.

Max opens up the Ziploc bag and shows him its contents. The man stretches a bony index finger and pokes about in the bag, inspecting the five dead toes in the plastic, poking at both ears and making a squishy sound. The bloody teeth are wrapped in clear cellophane, and for a minute, Max thinks he's going to open it up and inspect that too, but the man seems satisfied after the ears. He reaches into his robe and produces a black polythene bag. He pulls out a bundle of dog-eared one-thousand naira notes and begins to count. Max counts along silently and re-zips the package. The man stops at fifty and hands it over.

Max hands him the Ziploc, grabs the money and shoves it into his jeans pocket, keeping his hands there. He turns and heads up to the bridge in the rain, jumps into the next yellow danfo down to Berger, climbs out and hops into another to Isheri, his hands tight in his pocket the whole time. The bus snakes its way into the heart of the maze that is Lagos. He drops off at Ishola Bello and walks the remaining couple of miles in the rain, down to his miniflat at the end of the close. At no point does he look back.

◆ ◆ ◆

The dead of night prods Max awake. Electricity is still out from the week before, and the rain from dusk has mixed with the bottled air in the cramped miniflat, producing humidity that is thick to the touch.

Max slogs through the living, out front to the verandah and powers on the

650VA gen. A couple yellow bulbs blink into life, except the living room's, which has burnt out. He turns on the TV for light and flicks through a couple of DSTV channels. Most channels are out of subscription, so he settles on EWTN, the Catholic station. He doesn't know why he still watches it. Maybe because his father, Mazi Aniekwu, made him watch it when he was growing up. *The Catholic way*, as he'd say. His father's been dead for years now, but Max has found rhythm and solace in the routines, the chants, the incense. It's his go-to for post-harvest downtime.

Max leaves the background noise on and, in the kitchenette, pours water into a bowl, squirts in liquid soap, and washes his hands for the sixth time since returning from the bridge. He turns out the water, squirts another dose of soap and starts again. *After the digging,* his father always said, *you have to wash death off you.* He was wrong, though, Max knows. You can never wash off death. Never.

He mixes three hits of fruit bitters and a hit of schnapps in a mug and gulps it down. It traces a familiar burning dryness from his throat to his chest and settles in a squirm of wet warmth at the pit of his stomach. He pours another slush and takes the mug to the living, just as the priest begins the Liturgy of the Eucharist.

There are mud tracks on the floor tiles that he didn't notice before. They run from the door, but don't end at Max's feet at the entrance to the kitchenette. The TV's light is insufficient, so Max squints to follow the tracks, which he notices are odd because while one is a complete footprint, the opposite foot has most of the sole with no trace of toes.

The footprints end at the couch where a man sits with his back to Max.

The mug slips from Max's hand and crashes on the floor. The man on the couch doesn't stir or flinch at the sound; Max is devoid of all movements but for the flickers of television images over his head. Cautiously, Max steps around the broken ceramic to the front of the couch.

The man's eyes are open and stare at nothing. There are only tunnel mouths where his ears should be, and Max discovers the cause of the odd footprints: one of his feet has five stumps instead of five toes. If Max could see into his mouth, he'd see that the teeth were gone too.

But Max is frozen with shock at the face.

The face is that of Mazi Aniekwu.

Later, Max can only remember little of how the next few hours of this night went.

First, Max fights a persistent urge to swoon. The TV lights blur, and he no longer hears the priest's invocations. Then he hiccups, dashes into the restroom and hurls the schnapps and Mummy Isheri's jollof rice and Coke into the sink. He wants to turn on the tap to rinse the waste, but his hands shake so much that he pulls off the faucet head.

After some time, Max rises but does not return to the living room. Instead, he locks the bedroom door, and without putting out the light, gets into the bed and throws the blankets over his head.

An hour passes, maybe two. Max's eyes are wide open and bloodshot, his tongue tasting of ethanol, bile and dread. Sleep is a faraway phenomenon incomprehensible to his restive mind, but he persists, counting the seconds with his heavy heartbeats, asking questions and answering them himself.

The second rule: never dig up the grave of your own relations. *Never.*

The second rule that's supposed only to be a myth, a story to scare wannabe harvesters who think grave robberies are for kids. The second rule he has now broken, and that has now come home to roost—literally.

The generator groans from low petrol once, twice, then shuts down.

Oh God, fuck it.

Another hour passes before Max dares to rise and grope his way across to open the bedroom door. Armed with smartphone torchlight, he focuses the beam on the floor.

There are no footprints where the first beams land. Hope and relief start from the bottom of his stomach and swell as the beams pass from tile square to tile square, showing nothing. Nothing. Nothing.

The next tile has a footprint, but without toes. The tile after that has only a footprint also. And so the one after, and the one following that.

The thing that used to be Mazi is still seated in the couch when Max lifts the beam from the floor. It sits frozen, but the *blink blink* of its dilated pupils are directed at Max.

Max spins, speeds into the bedroom and slams the door.

Max stays holed up in the bedroom for half a day before any manner of sense returns and he realizes he cannot retain his sanity if he spends another night with Mazi's ghost in the house. If it does not return to the depths from which it came, he will have to take it back himself.

Dread piles in his chest at the thought of touching it. He hasn't touched his father since... when? The day he packed up and left the man alone with his big dreams of grooming his son into taking over the family's funeral parlor. That was no life for Max; he didn't want to be a pawn in Mazi's fantasies.

But Kaduna was hard for a twenty-something year old man with no university degree, and after several failed efforts to find some steady way to build his life, Max decided that life as an undertaker was better than surviving on hope alone. So he packed his bags once again and headed back to Lagos.

Except, by then, Mazi and everything he built was gone. No trace, no extended family, no will, nothing. The most credible story came from word on the streets, that it was Mazi's apprentices, a group of three known harvesters, who murdered him and ran off with everything he owned. There were stories that said they'd cut him up and sold his parts in the black market. *Na im make him body lost,* they said. Others said he'd been buried somewhere remote, but no one could point Max in the direction.

Max knows it's his fault. If only he'd stayed then, he'd at least have known where his father was buried and avoided it completely.

He did eventually stay, but only after it was too late. Nwanso, the biggest name in the undertaking and harvesting business and friend to his father, had taken a good look at his hands and said, "Come work for me." He wormed his way into the market under her tutelage, met her nephew Chidi on an early run and took a weird bonding to the guy despite that Chidi was, and still is, pretty shit at his job.

Maybe Chidi reminds him of what he would've been had Mazi remained alive: a young man stuck in the family's grim business. Maybe Max is living his father's dream vicariously through Chidi. Or maybe he is saving Chidi—or thinks he is—to keep the shadow of guilt at bay. Over time, the lines have blurred and Max no longer remembers why he does it: because it's work with little risk and few consequences that puts food on the table; or worse yet, because it keeps him close to his father.

Handle this thing, Maximus. Handle it.

Max grits his teeth and tiptoes out of the bedroom with his eyes shut. To look upon it will be acceptance of its existence, and Max refuses to look and tries to un-know what he thinks he knows. He gropes, breathing heavily, his teeth clenched. He reaches out, retracts his hand, reaches out again and yelps when his fingers touch something sticky.

The thing sits as he left it. *Blink blink.* Max lifts a leg, the one with toes still complete. The body slides off the couch as one unbendable unit and thumps on the ground like an ounce of hardened bread. Its skin cracks when it lands. As he pulls it, more cracks appear and travel upward, upward. Max retches but does not stop dragging. Across the tiles, to the kitchenette, where he shoves it under the shelves with his leg and shuts the door. He retches again, but there is nothing left to vomit. He shuts and opens his eyes, shuts and opens them again, blinking away the ghostly caricatures that form on the edges of his vision.

Finally, he fetches his only two neckties and binds the hands and feet of the thing, a hankie over his nose the whole time. Max does not look it in the face, choosing instead to look at the stumped toes and remind himself that this is not Mazi. The hankie soaks a couple trickles of tears from his watery eyes. Max tells himself it's because of the smell.

He has to borrow a car. Chidi's hearse, maybe. The bastard was dumb enough to make this mistake so he has no choice but to help in getting Max out of it.

It's drizzling under an early gray sky when Max catches a danfo to the funeral parlor at Ojodu. It's a stall squeezed between a coffin maker and a provisions store, only long enough to house a casket and a corpse table. Chidi sits on a stool under the canopy outside, for the lack of a corpse to attend to, running his fingers over a phone screen in a way Max knows he can only be playing Candy Crush. Before he hails Max's arrival, Max grabs him by the singlet and shoves him into the back room of the parlor. There's an office the size of a toilet cubicle in the back, too small to have a desk, but with a desk in it anyway. Max shuts the door and puts Chidi up against the wall, his heavy wide palm on Chidi's chest.

"Maxy, wait, wait," Chidi pleads. He's thin and haggard, and has nothing on Max, who has spent too much time with crude weights fabricated by a roadside welder.

"Don't be calling me that name, are you mad?" He hates it. *Maxy.* Sounds too much like Mazi.

"I no tell you about the northerner guy because you for no do," Chidi says, "but I need that money die, I swear." He touches the tip of his tongue with his index finger and points to the sky.

"You stupid idiot," Max snarls. "Which kain grave you arrange for me?"

Chidi frowns.

"Answer!" Max pushes against his chest. "Who dey inside that grave?"

"I no know na. I no check before I mark am."

"Eh?" Max slaps him across the cheek, hard. Chidi yelps. His eyes water and sweat pools in the curve of his singlet. Finger marks start to materialize on his cheek.

"Wetin be the first thing I tell you when we start this business?" Max asks, his hard stare boring holes in Chidi's face. Chidi breathes and breathes and says nothing.

"You gats to check the fucking register for every single harvest!" Max says. "You gats to check! You don' forget wetin Nwanso talk? You don' forget?"

Chidi mumbles a no.

"And even if you forget, you no get eyes? You no see wetin happen to Nwanso? You no see say na everlasting fuckup to—"

"Harvest your own people, I know," Chidi says. "But no be your person we harv—"

"Fuck you!" Max screams, fighting a choke in his throat. He releases Chidi and pounds the desk and kicks a chair. "You for check this grave, Chidi! You for check this fucking grave!"

He turns his back on Chidi and hides his anger in his elbow. *Why, why?* He wanted to see his father again; yes, but the real one, the one who taught him to watch EWTN. Not this, not *this.*

Chidi shuffles on his feet and watches Max, unsure. After a silence punctuated by Max's sniffles, he asks, "You dey cry?"

"Shut the fuck up." Max wipes his eyes and turns to him. "Wey the wagon?"

Chidi coughs. His breath smells of tobacco. "Why, wassup?"

"Are you mad? You dey still ask stupid questions?"

Chidi frowns. "Ah? Na my car now. I gats to ask—"

Max's grip on Chidi's throat is strong enough to cut him off.

"Get me the fucking keys."

◆ ◆ ◆

Max returns to the miniflat at Ishola Bello after the fall of darkness. There are dull throbs in his joints from digging twice in two days, and the drive back from Jafojo Cemetery was especially jarring because the hearse is a rusty old container. The only thing he can think of is sleep.

He strips and takes a freezing bath, then proceeds to wash his hands in the wash basin. He does it six times, seven times, but it does not stop him from replaying the *blink blink* of the Mazi-thing's eyes once he put that first shovel of humus into its face. Taking another freezing long bath does not drown out the sight of its gap-toothed mouth, the stumped foot as the earth closed it up. Even sleep and two sweaters cannot melt the iciness in his chest.

Max wakes after midnight, swamped in a cocoon of wool and sweat. He pulls off the sweaters and heads to the kitchenette for a bitters-and-gin mix.

There are footprints from the door, thicker, muddier than the last time. There's a man in his couch.

◆ ◆ ◆

Heavy pounds rattle his front door by morning. Max opens the door a peep and finds himself staring into Chidi's face. He sidles out and shoves Chidi backward.

"You this boy, you no dey hear word? We agreed no visit."

Chidi puts his hands up. "I know, I know. But I get work today, so I need the wagon."

"Ugh." Max shoves his hands into his trousers and tosses him the keys. "Oya go. Leave me alone."

Chidi lifts a finger. "Wait first. Another thing."

Max rolls his eyes. Chidi pretends not to notice.

"I go Jafojo this morning, go check the register." He blinks, zones out for a second, as if trying to disbelieve what he saw. "The name whey I see there, the name no make sense."

Max already knows. "Just go to work. We go yan later."

"Na your Popsie name dey there, Maxy. Na Mazi Aniekwu dey the register."

Max holds Chidi's eyes. "Go to work." He turns to leave.

"They say the body dey since like four, five years," Chidi continues, oblivious of Max's efforts to deflect him. "Nobody know, because na one mass burial like that, different people from different hospitals with no relatives for mortuary." He sighs. "Bro, I swear, I no know—"

Max puts up a hand. "Just go."

Chidi sighs again and heads for the car. Max goes back in, shuts the door and listens to the grunting sounds of the hearse until they're out of earshot before he opens the kitchenette.

The thing is still there, where he'd bound it with the neckties and stowed away under the shelves once again. Max, blinking, studies it and worries about his own safety. Imagine what the police will think about having your father's mutilated body in your kitchenette. How many years in prison does one even serve for something like this?

Max runs a hand over his head. This was how Nwanso's madness started, first with the simple panic that leads to denial. Then came the slow descent into dementia, so much so that she had to be driven out, to sea. He feels it already, the onset of his own promised madness. What is this exactly, juju or what? He's never really believed in all that rubbish, but then what happened to Nwanso happened, and now there's a dead-but-not-dead father in his kitchenette. He isn't going to sit around asking stupid questions.

Nwanso's shanty is six two-by-four timbers dug into the sand of Oniru beach, with tarpaulin wrapped over and around them, situated only as far from the shore as the waves go at the highest tide. The woman herself is as ragged as the tarp and as old as the sea, her skin as pockmarked as the stabs of footprints in the sand around her shanty: stray dogs, seagulls, crabs left behind by rushing tide. Max notices his are the only human footprints beside hers.

They sit opposite each other on little stools outside the shanty, the breeze snatching her words. She peers into Max's face through cataract-ridden eyes, her hair wild and separated, like seaweed.

"I told you, you don't touch your people," she says.

"I know, I know. It was a stupid mistake."

"You don't touch your people," she repeats, "because if you've kept them alive enough in your chest, they will come back. Then you will think you can let them stay, you will think you can't lose them again. And that's how you become mad, old, rotten." She shakes her head "That's how you become *them*."

Max has known the hidden dangers of harvesting all along. Difficult to recognize a loved one who has bloated, shrunk and then decomposed, and sawing off body parts in pitch darkness didn't help. You had to fail to know, and by the time you did, you'd already awoken something you couldn't send back to sleep.

"You're saying I can't take it back?" Max asks.

She gazes at him, blank. "You don't touch your people. It is known."

"Biko, Nwanso," he says, leaning in against the breeze. "There has to be a way at least."

She shakes her head again, mumbles to herself. Max watches solemnly, remembering the once vibrant woman from her days as senior mortician at LASUTH, when she still topped the harvesting charts on the market. Not the crackled and remiss caricature that sits before him now, the ash dust of morning after a night of glowing embers.

She stops mumbling, then says something. The breeze swats it aside.

Max leans in. "You said what?"

"You need to destroy it," she screams back.

Max lifts his eyebrows. "Like, burn the body?"

She laughs, shakes her head. "You're foolish. You think I haven't tried that?" She casts a quick glance behind her, at the shanty's opening. "Burning only worsens the smell when they come back."

"I don't get."

"You still have something that keeps bringing it back that you need to destroy."

Max thinks, then it strikes him. "I've sold them already."

"Destroy it," she says, looking past him at something distant, beyond the shore.

A thrill runs up Max's calves. "You mean I have to go and get it back?"

Her eyes shift to him.

"Destroy it," she repeats.

Max swears under his breath, then to Nwanso, "So there's no other way?"

She shrugs.

"Did you destroy yours?" he asks. When she frowns, he adds, "Your sister."

Her face stays expressionless for seconds, blinking.

"You're still here," Max says. "You must've found a way."

She studies him for a beat, then slowly, pitifully, she shakes her head from side to side, and glances back at the opening to the shut-off shanty. Max follows her eyes and notices two sets of footprints there. One leads out to where Nwanso sits. The other meanders about the opening, but never goes past it.

Max knows he must go back to the buyer. Or else.

Chidi pulls the hearse off the Ketu-Oworonshoki expressway and eases down the windy path to Chinese Village. The arch-and-turret simulation of the Great Wall that passes for the entrance into the village looms above. Max thinks the "China Commercial City" written in logograms bears a dismal look. It frowns down at them, caught the wrong way by the setting sun.

It is quiet inside the village, which is wrong in many ways, for it once possessed the vibe of the commercial hub it's meant to be, until the customs authority raided it in 2006. So now, the shop windows have lace fabric, flower vases and jeans hung next to their *Closed* signs. It's a dead man's town with living people inside.

Chidi drives to the far end of the village and pulls into a cramped nook before turning off the engine. Dusk quickly approaches and the place stinks of decomposing refuse. There's a row of back doors to what used to be shops or living quarters or both. Or still are.

When Max gets out of the car, Chidi doesn't follow.

"No way." He folds his arms in the driver's seat and pouts. Max slams the passenger door and heads for the door which Chidi has pointed out to him. He knocks, once, twice.

"Wanda?" A voice asks from inside in Hausa.

Max doesn't respond. The door pulls back, and the buyer's marked face peers out. He studies Max for a second, then frowns and steps out in a flurry of robes. Max's eyes don't miss the dagger underneath.

"Me ya sa ka 'a nan?"

"We need the goods back," Max says, pulling out the money from his pockets. "See, I have your money. Two sixty. I added ten on top, for the wahala." He hands it out to the man, but the man doesn't even look at it. His face is set, focused on Max.

"Ba mayarwa," he says.

Of course, *no returns.* Rule number three of the harvesting game: Never ask for the goods back. *Ever.*

"We can't sell it anymore," Max says, pushing his luck. "We need to use it for something else."

The man's eyes rest on Max, then flit behind him to Chidi at the steering. He finally gives one short nod, and retreats into his quarters. There's an antsy wait where Chidi smokes two cigarettes in huge drags and Max hops from foot to foot and sweats in his palms.

Finally, the man re-emerges with the familiar lunch bag and hands it to Max. Max tries to give him the money again, but he isn't even looking at it. He's looking at Chidi.

"Ba kudi." He points to Chidi. "Ina son wannan."

Chidi spooks immediately he notices the man's finger, and starts to get out of the car. Max is about to tell him to calm down, that he'll take care of this, but it happens so fast.

They appear out of nowhere. Five or six men, robed as the buyer himself, with daggers jutting from underneath their robes. They pounce on Chidi, clamp his mouth and constrain his arms without any effort. One of them whips out his curved dagger and holds it to his face.

"Wait wait!" Max says, suddenly confused. "What do you want, what?"

The buyer cocks his head, stares at Max.

"I say, we no want money," he says in broken English. "We want,"—he points to Chidi, grappling between the men—"man."

"No, no," Max says, tightening his fists. "You can't just...take him. For what na?"

"We no take am," the buyer says. "Only goods." He points to his body parts as he says them. "Yatsun, hakora, da kunnuwa."

Chidi's eyes widen in understanding as the men clamp down harder. One of them pulls out his curved dagger and steps on Chidi's ankle to hold his sandaled foot down.

"Stop!" Max screams, clenches his fists and charges for them. The men back away and circle the nook, dragging Chidi along. Chidi's whimpers echo off the walls. A shutter opens somewhere in response.

"I'll kill you if you touch him," Max says, following them. "I'll kill you, I swear."

They keep their daggers pointed at Max until they reach the buyer where he stands. The buyer rolls them in his palm as he steps out to meet Max.

"We stop," the buyer says, "if you bring goods." He shows his hands. "Dukiya," he says, weighing one hand. "Mutum." He weighs the other.

Goods. Man.

I'll make you fucking goods right now, Max thinks, head pounding and vision blurred. But truth is, for breaking a harvesting rule, the buyer is well within his rights to ask for whatever he likes from them.

Chidi might be a bastard, but he's Max's bastard. Yes, he'll even admit it now: Chidi is his vent, his release. Saving Chidi is the one thing that keeps the pressing guilt of leaving Mazi to die from smothering Max in his sleep.

Oh.

Max stops and unfurls his fists. The haze in front of his eyes wipes away.

You still have something that keeps bringing it back, Nwanso said, *that you need to destroy.*

She wasn't talking about the body parts.

"Wait," Max says suddenly. "What if I bring you goods *and* man?"

The buyer cocks his head.

"Leave him," Max says. "I'll bring what you need."

The buyer shrugs, then taps on the back of his wrist, universal sign for get-the-fuck-moving.

◆ ◆ ◆

The thing feels heavier than before when he pulls it from under the shelves, but Max doesn't care. All he can think of is Chidi with one of those curved daggers paused just above his fingers, his teeth, his toes. Max quickens the pace, murmurs a made-up mantra to himself. Yes, he *is* exchanging—replacing—a dead thing with a living one. Yes, he *is* doing a Good Thing.

He dumps the body into the wagon and bumps the boot, gets in and flies back to the Ketu-Oworonshoki expressway, practicing his negotiations. *Take everything,* he'll say. *Just take it. I'm done.*

Mazi used to say knowledge is power, and the lack of it, danger. But Max thinks it's a blessing sometimes. Like now, when he'll sleep better not knowing what they do with it. How he'll sleep better knowing it's never coming back.

Chidi is freezing by the time Max gets back to him, shivering after being left out in the post-drizzle cold. Max places his own dry shirt over the whimpering man and lays him down in the back seat.

Max gets in the hearse and turns the rear-view mirror away as he eases out of the nook. He does not look back at the men who, under the pale light of yellow bulbs, circle around the thing that was Mazi and confer in hushed tones. He does not look as the buyer pulls out his curved blade and putters about the body. He does not look as the rest follow his lead, synchronous, making dead again what was once extinct.

He refuses to look.

CLANFALL: DEATH OF KINGS

ODIDA NYABUNDI

PROLOGUE

Fisi Wahoo basked in the rapturous applause of the crowd. It seemed like the whole population of New Machakos had turned up for his coronation. *Fisi! Fisi! Fisi!* He could hardly believe that a few cycles ago the same crowd would have torn him and his to pieces. He glanced to his left. Fisi Twi was grinning in ecstasy, his ferrocalcific teeth gleaming in the sunlight. On his right, Fisi Tri was clearly having difficulty controlling his urge to cackle.

"Don't," he vibed over their neural connector.

Fisi Tri turned to look at Wahoo with his one good eye. The other had been ripped out by the *ua* claw of a Simba warrior. It was covered by a black plasteel patch. He grinned his acquiescence. Satisfied, Wahoo turned back to the crowd. Everyone was there. Everyone! Even the proud Ndovus and the recalcitrant Kobes. They loved him...or at least feared him, which was even better. He wanted this moment to last forever. In this charged atmosphere, he could almost forget how he had gotten to where he was. Almost.

The Plasteel wall of the meeting hall melted like hot butter under the sustained plasma fire from Wahoo's main canon. Suddenly the whole edifice went up in a whoosh, purple sparks winking in the soft gloaming as superheated ions escaped. Inside the hut the Simba Cubs squealed as their immature carapaces caught fire in the hellish heat. One of them tried to bolt but Tri's clawed foot lashed out and booted it back into the inferno. Their dams were already on fire, their screams adding to the cacophony of the Fisi clan's mad cackling. The Simba Clan warriors who had tried to defend this last refuge lay dead in front of the burning hall, many of them in pieces. Wahoo looked around. Perhaps they had been a tad enthusiastic in their attack against this last bastion of the ruling clan. But the job was done. A sudden gust of cold wind made him shiver in his night-black armour. Something made him look up and there in the sky, was a speck. His ocular implant immediately zoomed in and suddenly he was looking at a Mark 2 reconnaissance Ndege. Shit! He brought his main canon online and activated his targeting software, but it was too late: the Ndege was gone.

ONE

Harsh panting and darkness. That's what she wakes up to. It takes her a while to realize she is the one doing the panting. She doesn't know who she is. She doesn't know where she is. She doesn't know anything. Except that it's very hot, very dark and she is in a lot of pain. She tries to moan and fails. Is she alive? Who is she? Where is she from? Desperately she tries to move a body she isn't even sure she has. Pain, like an unlovely flower blooms within her and awareness goes away for a while.

When she next awakes, it's still dark and she still hurts, a lot. But it's not hot anymore. In fact, it's damn cold. And her teeth are chattering. Teeth! She has teeth! Where there are teeth there is often a head. And where there is a head, eyes are sure to reside. She opens her eyes and sees...nothing. "I am blind!" she screams silently. Suddenly...a memory rises in the stygian depths of her mind like a star in the darkness. Her name.... Shibuor. And she remembers more. She is a warrior. *There was a battle and...* "No, please no," she whispers between frozen lips. And then like a lanced boil her memories return in a thick spurt.Her only escape is back into the comforting darkness.

Agony in her leg, sharp as a Mbwehas combat claw. Shibuor jerks back into the world of the living. Her whole existence is pain, but the one in her leg screams louder than the rest. Her eyes fly open and the sunlight stabs her retinas. Quickly, she snaps them shut.

Again, the stabbing pain in her leg.

Frantically now, she opens her eyes again, slitting them against the bright sunlight. Slowly the world swims into focus. She is lying on her back in the sand. It is hellishly hot. Her mouth tastes foul. Her whole body aches. Her throat is dry and inflamed. And just to further complicate matters, there is an Achuth hacking a chunk out of her leg with a vibrasaw.

Fuck!

She jerks her leg away. Startled, the Achuth turns its wickedly beaked and horribly bald head to regard her. Warrior Instinct clicks in and her *ua* combat implant scythes out and impales the Achutch punching through its thin synthweave armour and bursting out of the unfortunate scavengers back in a welter of blood, gore and hydraulic fluid. The Achutch squawks once and dies. But the action fills Shibuor's whole body with hot tendrils of pain. She almost blacks out again, but as the world fades around her, she makes out more Achutch, silhouetted in the sun.

Many more.

Shit!

Achutch are lightly armed and armoured and not overly burdened with intelligence. But a gang of them can be dangerous. Especially in her weakened state.

She runs a quick diagnostic.

Autocooler unit: offline.

6cm Main canon: offline.

2cm arm canon: offline.

Shit shit shit!

The Achutch gang is approaching. They are too light to mount canon but they have 9mm repeaters and those vibrasaws...

Ua combat implant: online.

That's better but it may not be enough against the gang.

Armour: 25%.

Fuck me.

Mobility: 45%.

Not bad.

But it won't be enough to escape the Chutes. They only tackle the dead and dying. That they are advancing on her doesn't bode well for her condition.

50 calibre repeaters: offline.

Dorsal jahanamu missile tube: offline.

Just as well; antimatter missiles would have been overkill for these fucking vultures anyway.

Half-centimeter wrist canon: online.

Yes!

Targeting software: offline.

Oh crap.

Ah well, she will have to wing it. She sits up in a tangle of pain. The sun overhead is relentless. The Achutch are upon her.

The half centimeter canon is embedded in her left wrist. She brings it up and aims at them. The lead vulture opens up with his 9mm repeater and the rest join in. Shells ping off her abused armour. One penetrates a weak spot and tears a bloody hole in her gut.

That does it.

Shibour roars in pain and rage. She leaps to her feet and extends the *ua* implant to its full five-foot length. Forgetting the wrist canon, she wades into the gang. Death made real. Few things are as graceful, as fluid and as lethal as a Simba Mk 4 warrior in the grip of *Zimu* Rage. And Shibuor is one of the best. Deep in her battle trance she carves a bloody path through the Achutch. When her dance is over, 19 lie dead. Seven are horribly maimed and three survivors have taken to the air, squawking in indignation. She watches them flee.

If I let them go, they will be back in force.

Back for their dead. And for her. She aims her wrist canon at them. Her arms are wavering. Her vision blurs. She blinks rapidly, but it is no use. Even the *zimu* rage has left her. She is empty. Done. Her head swims and the desert floor slaps her hard in the face. And again, the darkness takes her.

Kaka Sungura is bored. He squints across the blasted landscape and sighs. His ears twitch with a faint whine of servomotors. He turns back to Mzee Kobe.

"Ok, let's try another one. Riddle me this: what is it that falls but makes no noise?"

Kobe thinks for a while.

The sun rages. The wind blows, flies buzz sleepily in the searing heat. Kaka waits eagerly for Kobe to fail. But he is disappointed.

"The night," Kobe finally answers, his voice like boulders mating.

Kaka Sungura sighs, his long ears drooping. "Dammit, is there a riddle you don't know?"

Mzee Kobe looks placidly at Sungura. "No."

Kaka Sungura mutters darkly to himself, "I'll get you yet, you big bastard, see if I don't."

The sun hammers relentlessly down on them, creating green tinted shimmers in the irradiated sands of the desert. Kaka Sungura turns up his autocooler a fraction. It coughs a little before settling down with a slightly louder hum.

Fucking sand, it got in everywhere.

He eyes the desert balefully. It stretches into the distance, straight and smooth as far as the eye can see. Probably all the way to New Machakos. They have been patrolling this, the furthest reaches of the territory, for over a month. And they have seen nothing. No bandits, no invaders, not even a bloody scavenging Achutch. Just sand. And they have ten more days to patrol before they can go back to town to report.

Ten days! Fuck me!

Kaka has just about had it with this place.

"Look Mzee, we have been here twenty-nine days and we have seen nothing but sand and bloody flies. We are wasting our time. Why don't we dash back to New Machakos? Make a race of it, y'know. Get some R&R, sip a little whiskey, maybe get our rods lubricated..."

Mzee Kobe regards Kaka for a long moment. "No," he grinds out.

The sand, the heat, the flies, the monotony, the uncongenial company. Suddenly it's too much for Kaka.

"Oh, for the sake of Holy Man above! Why not, you pea brained, inbred, stupid piece of..."

Alarm bells jangle inside Kaka Sungura's cybernetically enhanced brain. He stops like a thing strangled.

"I mean," he licks his lips. "I meant..." his voice is a cracked whisper. A cold sweat envelops him. "I meant no offense, Mzee." His voice trails off. Ice crawls down his spine. "I beg your *msamaha.*"

For a long moment, Mzee Kobe stares down at him from his 9-foot height, dorsal canon locked, combat blades fully unsheathed from his massive forearms.

Sungura sweats.

Then the canon whirrs back to the safe position and the blades retract smoothly and Kobe hunches back into safe mode.

"Ok," he says placidly and goes back to scanning the empty landscape.

Sungura breathes again. *Fuck! That was close.* You had to be so careful around these Kobes.

Especially this one.

The damn things were so touchy about their honour. Sungura wipes his damp forehead, wrinkling his nose at the acrid stink of fear that clings to him like a shroud.

If I have to spend another ten days with this mad, hulking, rusting piece of crap, I may just have to strangle myself with my own entrails.

His thoughts stray to the town of New Machakos. An oasis in the midst of a poisonous desert. Fresh cool springs. Hot women. Cold beer. The best gambling in the Cracked Realm. In New Machakos, he is not just a gun for hire: he is Kaka Sungura, trickster, shyster, ladies' man and the sharpest mind across the sundered realm.

His ears droop as he broods. This job had seemed so easy. Patrol the desert for mutants, bandits or invaders. Kill them on sight and come back. Granted, not his usual thing, but the governor had offered a generous retainer plus 500 shillings per head of any bounty he closed. Easy money.

"Oh and take Mzee Kobe with you," the governor had added smoothly. "He is getting bored. We don't want him to uh, prematurely retire any overly boisterous customers now, do we?" Reluctantly Kaka Sungura had agreed. Mzee Kobe was the oldest Kobe in town. And by far the most dangerous. Not a bad sort to have around in case things went south in the desert. But nothing had gone on in the desert. It had been irritatingly peaceful. And now he was stuck with a dangerous war machine who might or might not be clinically insane. That, and the sun.

Shit.

Kaka spits in the sand. *Can't believe I let the governor saddle me with the demented...*

"There's something out there," Kobe's grave voice interrupts his dark thoughts.

"Huh? What? Where? I don't see anything."

Mzee Kobe points. "Use your optic magnifiers."

Sungura snorts. Senile old fart is probably hallucinating, he thinks, uncharitably.

But obediently he clicks his magnifiers on.

He draws a sharp breath.

"Shit. Is that what I think it is?"

His only answer is a shower of sand as Mzee Kobe lights out, leaving Sungura standing there, spitting grit out of his mouth.

Shit. That old bugger can really move when he wants to.

Kaka Sungura brings his bounders online.

But then again so can I. Especially when there's a princess to save and lots of murdering to be done!

Bounders at full power

He lets out a wild whoop.

Game on.

The Nyati's head smashes through the wall in an avalanche of bricks, dust and blood. The rest of his body remains in the room, jigging and jiving like a *nyatiti* dancer. Chui5 doesn't have time to admire the Nyati's newfound dancing prowess. He ducks under a hastily flung sonic spear and smashes the second guard across his breastplate pulverizing his internal organs. He flops over like a broken doll. The last guard reacts quickly and targets him with a wide pattern flamer. *Too close to avoid.* Chui5 activates his burrow and disappears.

"What the fu..."

The words end in a gurgle as Chui5 unburrows behind the guard and chops his vibrio through the Nyati's thick armoured neck. A whining hum. A burst of blood. And the guard's head with its domed boss of wickedly curved horns thuds to the floor in a vermillion puddle. The decapitated body blunders about as if in search of its missing head before collapsing onto an intricately carved Meru oak table, smashing it matchsticks beneath its two-ton weight. It shudders a bit and is still. Chui5 cleans his vibrio on the guard's tunic before stowing it in the dorsal harness it shares with his war hammer. He scans the room. Dead Nyati guards litter the airy space. There is smashed furniture everywhere. Blood covers the plush carpeting. In great glistening gouts. A huge viewer hangs drunkenly from the wall, its cracked screen flickering like a giant winking eye. Chui5 sighs.

Such a mess. Father will be most displeased.

But that's nothing new. Father is always displeased with Chui5. Too tall, too bulky and almost as heavy as a Simba, Chui5 is a far cry from the lithe, silent, graceful, bringer of death that should be his birthright. Instead he is big, blunt, brutal and frighteningly strong. A brute. A throwback. An animal. Chui5 has been called many things. The names bounce off him like stones off armour. He doesn't care. His closure rate is the highest of the five princes in his father's kingdom. Five brothers. And he is the fifth and youngest. Still, he always gets the job done and done quickly, if a tad bit messily. Behind him, the view screen crashes to the floor in a shower of sparks. Chui5 sighs again and turns to the task at hand.

His contract is sitting bolt upright on a richly embossed throne, emitting a palpable odour of fear.

President Panya is as afraid as he has ever been in his life. The apparition before him has smashed through his elite guards in less time than it takes to draw four breathes. Nothing in the Cracked Realm could do that except.... *But it can't be.* He swallows. Burrowers are a myth, a bedtime story to scare unweaned pups. *Surely they don't exist.*

Whether they exist or not is now an academic question. A burrower is now on his throne room, and it's gliding towards him. Black, fluid death. Time to go. President Panya activates one of the bolt holes scattered throughout his throne room. Or at least he tries to. Nothing happens. He activates the autocanons hidden amongst the filigreed cupolas high above his throne. Nothing. His jaw drops. *Impossible!* Somehow this creature has managed to bypass his internal security network and killed his AI. Without it he can't access his systems. Any of them. Even his exoskeleton is useless. Just so much metal and ceramic circuitry. He is trapped. He licks his lips which have suddenly gone dry. *Pull yourself together. Everyone has a price. Even this... thing. Do what you do best, what you were born to do. Make a deal with him.*

"Wait," he winces at the quaver in his voice.

A dry swallow.

"Wait," he says again, his voice firming up. Now he sounds like what he is. The president of one of the Cracked Realms' biggest and richest corporations.

"Look friend, let's not be too hasty, ok? Tell me what you want, what your heart desires. Whatever it is, you shall have it."

The apparition continues its inexorable advance.

"Whatever they have paid you, I will double it."

Chui5 draws a long thin blade, black as midnight. President Panya can't take his eyes off its oily surface. "I'll triple it!" he shrieks. But the apparition continues advancing.

"Ok! Ok! Ok! You can have it all! All of it!" President Panya's voice is shrill as a songbird's. "Take it all! I will give you my personal access code! You can be rich. Rich beyond your wildest dreams." Spittle flecks his thin lips.

The apparition stops. "All of it?" Its voice is a muffled growl.

I knew I could reason with him. "Yes, yes, all of it. You will be the richest being in the Cracked Realm."

Chui5 appears to think for a moment. "Hmmm, tempting. But I think not. "

He moves. Fast. Faster than his bulk will have you believe. Faster than President Panya would have thought possible for anyone to move. He is still marvelling at just how damn fast the thing is, when the carbonium blade punches through his exoskeleton's armour and in a bright, burst of blood, snatches his life away.

Chui5 looks at the Panya's corpse. Blood, hydraulic fluid and coolant are leaking from the exoskeleton. Both man and machine are dead.

"Now, now '5. Mummy always said don't play with your prey."

Chui5 chuckles as he withdraws the compkiller software that he had insinuated into the recently deceased President Panya's AI. The room's internal security net sputters back into life. But by then he has activated his burrow and is gone like he had never existed.

◆ ◆ ◆

There is blood and fire everywhere. A hot wetness splashes across her eyes. Screams of dying cubs. Butchers everywhere. Someone thrusts a raw piece of meat at her face. Disgusted, she recoils. Smoke tickles the back of her throat. She bends over, coughing violently. Her air recyclers are offline. She is choking.

I am going to die.

Suddenly, she is in her father's arms. She looks up at his fierce face. "Baba," her voice is a whisper.

"Shhh, be still, blood of my blood." He looks down at her, his gentle expression sitting oddly on his cruel warrior's face. "You are now the future, kitten. You are clan Simba. "

"No, baba... I can't...I "

'YOU CAN AND YOU WILL! PROMISE ME! PROMISE ME!"

◆ ◆ ◆

Shibuor wakes up with a start, her face wet with tears. "Baba!" she struggles to remember, but the dream slithers out of her subconscious like a coy snake and retreats into the ether.

Slowly, she becomes aware of her surroundings. She is lying on the baking sand surrounded by dead and dying Achutch. The sun is still high in the sky and the thirst is barbed wire in her throat. But she has bigger problems than that. A dark cloud approaches in the distance. But this is no raincloud: it is made up of flesh and blood and bone and death. The Achutch are back. And Shibuor knows her life is over. She has nowhere to run. Nowhere to hide. And no strength left to fight. She drags herself to her feet. Her body is a cacophony of pain. But she ignores it. She is a warrior and she will die standing up straight. The Achuth are closer now. A few have already started firing their repeaters. They are not close enough for any sort of accuracy.

But that will change soon enough.

Visions flash before her eyes. Her father, stern of face but with love in his eyes. Her mother, petite, always smiling, but deadly. Shimba, her brother, huge, gentle and clumsy. Her sister and namesake, deadlier and faster than even their mother.

Their youngest brother, Sibuor, still unenhanced, just a playful little cub.

All of them dead.

She shakes her head and extends her *ua* combat claws one last time. The Achutch are almost on top of her now. Rounds are pinging off her abused armour.

One last dance then.

She roars her defiance at the approaching horde and prepares to sell her life dearly.

An actinic light flashes so close to Shibuor that she smells burning ozone and singed hair. The front row of Achutch simply ceases to exist. Another flash lances into the cloud and the Achutch burst apart in a noisome rain of ash, boiled blood and severed limbs. The cloud recoils, the Achutch squawking madly. They are no longer attacking but trying to get away. Another flash, more dead Achutchs. The offbeat metallic buzz of a twin mounted autocanon and the remaining scavengers are blown apart. A lucky few would be marauders flap off into the lowering sun, squawking indignantly at their thwarted revenge. Shibuor can't understand what's going on. Blackness nibbles at the edge of her vision.

Oh no, not again. I am getting really fucking tired of fainting.

She wills herself to stay awake. She can feel blood dripping warm and wet somewhere beneath her armour. Slowly, carefully she turns around and there before her like an unlikely pair of guardian angels are a Mk 5 Sungura and what looks like a Mk 1 Kobe of all things.

I didn't even know there were any of those left.

"Hey there princess," the Sungura's voice is sardonic, "you don't look so hot. How about you put away that steak knife there and let us help you?" He gestures at her arm.

Shibuor looks down at her combat claw. It seems really far away. Slowly she sheaths it. And that action seems to drain her of the last of her strength. She sinks to the desert floor. The hot sand is warm and comforting. She snuggles into it.

So, this is what death feels like.

And then, somehow, she is in the Sungura's arms and he is dribbling cool delicious water into her sandpaper mouth. "There we go, a little water, some stitches, a hot meal and you'll soon be murdering your enemies and glorying in the wails of their children again." He grins. "I am Kaka Sungura. Maybe you've heard of me?"

A huge shadow blocks out the sun and the venerable Kobe looms over her. His brutal features are almost prehistoric in their bluntness.

"Oh yeah, this here is Mzee Kobe. He is a bit err... eccentric but he is good people." The Kobe regards her impassively, and then in a whine of ancient servomotors withdraws.

"Mad as a snake that one," Kaka whispers and he winks at her.

Shibuor tries to say something. She isn't sure what. But her mouth is gummy. "Shhh , I am sure you have quite a tale to tell us, princess, but that can wait till we get back to New Machakos.

New Machakos! Noooooo!

The memories flood back like a tide of blood. Suddenly she knows everything. She knows everything. She struggles to speak, but the words turn to mud in her mouth. All she can manage is a guttural moan.

"Sshhh, sleep now." A small sting on her shoulder. Too late she sees the hypo in his hands. Her thoughts turn to cotton wool. Her vision wavers.

"Sweet dreams, princess." The last thing she sees is Kaka's grin.

For almost twenty centuries, the ancient walled fortress of Chui Clan has stood atop the summit of the mountain that was once known as Kenya. Its dull grey walls rise from the flank of the mountain and thrust 200 meters into the sky like a giant metal spear. Nobody knows who constructed it or why. In its entire known history, the fortress has never fallen to an enemy force. To attack it, one will have to first climb the mountain, which in itself is no mean feat. Once this is accomplished, one will then have to somehow gain entrance into the edifice itself, an impossible task.

The fortress walls are impervious to shells, lasers, plasma weapons and even antimatter missiles, as many a clan has discovered to their cost. There are no windows or doors. The walls are sheer and smooth, and no claw, grapple, magnet or suction device can gain purchase on its featureless surface. The metal that forms its walls is unlike any known substance. Deep scanning it reveals nothing. It is not observable on radar, infrared or lidar. Yet Clan chui members somehow enter and exit the massive building. No one knows how.

There are legends of course, stories stretching back to the mythical time of Man. Stories that claim the fortress was a defensive outpost of a great empire that once stretched across the continent from E'gipt in the north to Azania in the south. Others say that it was part of a chain of super weapons capable of harnessing the very power of the sun and roasting the entire planet to a cinder. Nobody knows whether there is any truth to these stories. The fortress is a mystery within a conundrum within a cypher. No one but members of the Chui clan has ever been inside. And naturally they are saying nothing—not even under torture or mental deep scanning.

The histories are unclear on how the Chui clan came to take possession of the fortress in the first place. Legend has it that the clan's Primarch, Chuil and the Clan Simba Primarch, Sibuor Mager, had a fierce rivalry that had lasted their entire lifetime. It is said that on one cold storm-swept night, Sibuor had dared Chuil to a race to see who could climb the mountain the fastest. They started on opposite sides, unarmoured and unclothed, their weapon implants disabled. And then completely at the mercy of nature, they swarmed up the mountainside, past freezing meadows, treacherous bogs, frigid forests filled with all manner of mutant creatures, giant glaciers and unceasing rain. They both came close to death half a dozen times, but eventually it was Chui1 who got to the top first. Frozen and half dead, he crawled to the top of the mountain and discovered the fortress. With his dying breath he beseeched the massive structure to grant him access and it heard his desperate plea and took him into itself, leaving Sibuor to batter himself to death in a rage against its impassive walls. And thereafter it had remained permanently closed to anyone not of Chui1's genetic lineage.

Other stories, however, say that Chui1, with the stealth and cunning of his kind, had taken the fortress by deception and slaughtered its original inhabitants, taking it for his own. Some religious fanatics in their ecstatic trances had even been heard to say that the Chui clan had been given stewardship of the fortress by Man to safeguard until His triumphant return.

Of course, no one can verify the truth of any of these legends. What is not in doubt is that the Chui clan has ruled the fortress unchallenged for almost twenty thousand years. And in all that time, no other clan has set foot in the mountain fastness.

Within the fortress, Chui1, the supreme patriarch and head of Clan Chui, sits on his raised throne brooding at a large view screen set into the featureless wall before him. The throne is soft and padded with a grey material of unknown origin. It is set into the floor before a curved bank of massive viewscreens. Chui1's ebony face is impassive. Still, it is clear that what he is watching on the screen troubles him. He sighs, snaps off the view screen and rises to his feet, the throne harness automatically retreating. He has no idea why a throne needs a harness; but then again even after twenty thousand years, there is so much about the fortress that is inexplicable to Clan Chui.

Silently he pads down to the stairs and stands before the northern wall of his throne room. A mental command, and the wall ghosts into transparency, revealing the barren windswept mountain outside. He studies the view, revelling in the sheer cold power of the snowstorm raging on the mountaintop below. Immense, frigid, relentless, like the power that lies coiled within him. The muted pop of an unburrowing announces the arrival of his youngest son. Chui1, like millions of disappointed fathers before him, purses his lips.

"Rise," he says without turning. Behind him Chui5 gets off his knee and stands at ease.

"It is done father."

"In your usual messy way, no doubt?"

"Well, perhaps they'll think an army of angry Achutch's done it."

The silence stretches and grows frigid. Chui5 winces; his father is not a humorous man. He opens his mouth to speak, then closes it again.

I will just wait patiently.

He has been trained since birth. He can stand at ease without making a sound for days on end. Unlike the rest of his clan, it doesn't come easily to him though. Sweat trickles silently down his back. His armour chafes and itches. He studies his father's back. Physically, Chui1 is not large or imposing. But an air of menace shrouds him like a cloak. One does not become the patriarch of one of the most powerful clans in the Cracked Realm by being weak. Finally, Chui1 turns to face his huge son.

"Simba clan has fallen."

Chui5 is rocked by the news. *Simba clan fallen? How? Why? At who's claws?* None of this shows on his face.

Chui1 is pleased at his son's self-control. He continues in his sparse voice. "Fisi Clan, after being faithful vassals for over a thousand years, has turned on the Simbas. The Simba clan patriarch is dead. His wives are dead. All his children are dead. His warriors are broken and declawed. Simba Rock has been burned to the ground. Simba clan is finished."

Chui5's thoughts are whirling. Simba clan had been Supreme Clan for over 5000 years. Even Chui Clan paid them fealty, nominal though it was at best. The Simbas had produced some good kings, some bad kings and some truly disastrous kings. But in the minds of the beings of the Cracked Realm, they had always been kings. Magere, the current clan head, always strikes Chui5 as fairly astute in addition to being a mighty warrior. How had the Fisis laid him low? Surely they couldn't have done it without help. He looks suspiciously at his father.

"I had nothing to do with it," Chui1 says evenly. "But I did see it coming and made certain...preparations. In any case, Fisi Wahoo is now supreme lord over the Cracked Realm. His coronation is tomorrow in New Machakos. All clan heads have been invited to attend."

In all the five centuries which Simba Clan had ruled, not once had Chui clan sent a Patriarch to the coronation. They always sent a proxy. Over the years, some had inevitably come to sticky ends. The ruling clan had never given up on cracking the secret to the Fortress. Chui5 sees with horrible clarity where this conversation is going.

"You want me to be your proxy don't you?"

"Why would I choose you?" Chui1 asks conversationally.

Chui5 doesn't hesitate. "Because I am expendable, because it will give you an excuse to get rid of an enduring source of embarrassment." His father's expression doesn't change, but Chui5 senses his disappointment like a cold wind against his face.

"Stop thinking like a petulant child. I am not going to send you to New Machakos. I am sending your brother."

Chui5 is rocked with surprise. "Which of my brothers?" he blurts, then at once goes on his knees. "I am sorry my liege. It is not my place to question you."

Chui1 snorts in annoyance. "Get off your knees and use your brain for once. What does the fall of Simba Clan mean to us?"

Chui5's mind races, searching for an answer. *What web is the old spider spinning?*

With the fall of Simba clan there would be instability. Fisi Wahoo's grubby hands would not be secure on the golden stool of power yet. He would be consolidating, wooing allies, cementing his claim to the throne. Where would Chui Clan stand? Traditionally they had stayed out of clan politics, offering their lethal services to whoever could afford their exorbitant rates. But it had been centuries since a clan had been overthrown. Not since the mad rule of the Kobe's had a ruling clan fallen. The aftermath of that particular disaster had been terrible. The Kobe clan's gene seed was ripped from their Matriarch and destroyed and the Kobes were obliterated as a clan. They never recovered from that catastrophe, which was why, centuries later, they still lived on the fringes, close to extinction.

Chui5's cybernetically enhanced mind freezes. *The gene seed!*

"Father, did Fisi Wahoo recover the Simba clan gene seed?"

His father smiles thinly. "You do have a brain after all. No he didn't."

Chui1 gestures at the view screen and it winks into life. The picture is grainy, characteristic of an mk2 reconnaissance Ndege's night vision recording. There is a building on fire. With a start, Chui5 realises that it's Simba rock. The image zooms in. There are armoured Fisis slaughtering Simba cubs. Chui5 recognises Fisi Wahoo from his night black armour. The Ndege accelerates and turns sharply and the picture blurs. When the picture steadies again, Chui5 can see Sibuor Mager, Patriarch of Simba clan and supreme king of the Cracked Realm. He is on the balcony of the highest tower of Simba rock. The door behind him appears to be barricaded. There is a gray mass the size and shape of a coconut in his hand. And before him there is young Simba lying on a couch, apparently unconscious

His daughter?

Sibuor Mager studies the gene seed in his hand for a minute and then implants it into the chest cavity of the Simba. He finishes and rouses her. She appears groggy but is quickly on her feet. They embrace. Just then the door behind them bursts open in a blinding flash of actinic light. The Simbas turn in unison to face it, *ua* claws at their full extent. Three Fisis emerge onto the balcony. Three more Fisis join them and then three more. Chui5 can't hear what they are saying because the recording has no audio, but their body language implies a conversation.

Then, without warning, the Fisis open up with their main canons. The action is swift and brutal. The Simbas fight well but there are just too many Fisis. The sheer energy pouring from the firefight temporarily blinds the camera. When the picture clears, the Fisis are all dead.

Sibuor appears badly wounded and so does his daughter. She is having an argument with her father. He pushes her towards the edge of the balcony. She resists but he pushes her again, much harder this time, before collapsing. She stumbles against the railing. Just then, Fisi Wahoo, Fisi Twi and Fisi Tri appear on the balcony.

They are always three.

Sibuor screams at his daughter as the Fisis bring their canons online and aim them at the Simbas. She hesitates and then resolution shows in the set of her shoulders as she turns to face the yawning chasm beyond the railing. Then she jumps. The Fisis run towards the edge, but she is gone. Her body tumbles into the Mara River 700 feet below and disappears. The Fisis turn towards the wounded Sibuor. They retract their canons and extrude their combat fangs instead. As they advance on Sibuor, the recording goes dark.

Chui5 is silent for a long moment. The recording has left him shaken. His father studies him with shrewd eyes. Finally, Chui5 speaks.

"You want me to find her."

Chui1 walks back to the window and studies the storm outside. "My son, you are without grace, finesse or precision. And you are no good at finding things. I have already located our young princess. She is currently in the Cursed Desert in the company of an untrustworthy Sungura and an insane Kobe."

Chui5 is now thoroughly confused.

"What I *do* want you to do," his father says in his ever-even voice, "is to befriend her, protect her and keep her safe and away from here until I summon you."

Chui5 blinks. "And her companions?"

Chui1 turns to face his son. His eyes are as cold as the storm outside. "I thought that would be obvious. Kill them both."

EPILOGUE

"So what are we going to do with our little princess here?" Sungura gestures at Shibuor who is bobbing gently on the antigrav disc Mzee Kobe is towing behind him.

Kobe turns his massive head to regard Sungura. "We will protect her."

"Protect her? From what? Those Achutch? I doubt they will be back after that drubbing we just gave them. Besides, she is in stasis now. All we need to do is to deliver her to her father, pick up a well-deserved reward and...oh oh oh wait a minute." Kaka Sungura stops so suddenly that Kobe almost runs into him.

"Mzee," Sungura continues, slowly. "What is a Simba princess doing out in the Cursed Desert, alone and wounded to boot? Why would the Achutch dare attack a royal princess? Where are her bodyguards? Her clan mates? Simbas never walk alone." Sungura's mind races. "Unless..."

"Unless clan Simba has fallen," A voice said behind them. Sungura turns in an instant, Mzee Kobe half a second later. The speaker has appeared suddenly and inexplicably behind them. He is covered in chameoweave armour, which makes him look as if he is winking in and out of existence. Crossed on his back are a war hammer and a vibrAx. Death drips from him in oily black droplets.

"Fuck me sideways! Is that...," Sungura swallows hard. "Is that a *Burrower?*

Kobe is already in combat mode, his main canon centred on the figure before them, carpal blades unsheathed.

"Now, now gentlemen I am only here for the princess. There is no need for you two to die here today." The figure's voice is oddly muffled, as if coming through wads of cloth. Sungura glances nervously at Kobe. "Mzee should we…"

"We fight." Kobe says implacably.

"I was afraid you would say that," the figure says.

Sungura is sweating despite his autocooler.

Chui5 unlimbers his war hammer. "I have never killed a Kobe before. And I really don't want this to be the day that I start. Won't you gentlemen reconsider?"

The hum of Kobe's main canon charging is his only reply.

"Ah well, you can't say I didn't try." He draws his vibrAx

"Shit Kobe, how the hell did you get us into this mess?" Sungura asks wearily. But even as he speaks, he is activating a long dormant subroutine in his neural matrix. The subroutine activates a Psi force gland deep in his bounders and they begin to vibrate slowly at first but then faster and faster. Chui 5 steps towards them.

"Sorry *Burrower* but today isn't the day you kill a Kobe," Sungura grins. "Not even a mad, bad one like Mzee. Hold on Kobe."

At exactly 5700 vibrations a second, the Psi gland drips a tiny bit of antimatter into his bounders. Instead of exploding, the unstable compound tears a rift in the time space continuum. There is an almighty bang and Chui5 is thrown back ten feet. He lands painfully on his kneepads. He slowly gets to his feet, small pebbles from the explosion pinging off his armour as he stares at the slagged circle of sand that had moment before contained three living beings. But Sungura, Kobe and the unconscious Shibour are just… gone. Chui5 sighs and stows his weapons.

Father would be *most* displeased.

THE SATELLITE CHARMER

MAME BOUGOUMA DIENE

"Can you see it?!"

Abdou was an idiot. Of course Ibrahima could see it. Everybody within five hundred kilometers could see it: a beam of blood red violence crashing from the sky, grinding into the soil with the force of a finger crushing an ant. Ibrahima had been told that ants were the strongest creatures in the world, capable of carrying a hundred times their weight, yet his pinky could kill them easily.

Standing on the cliffs overlooking the old natural preserve of Niokolokoba, looking down at the expanse of lush grasslands spurred by the summer rains, Ibrahima could see the dust left behind by the stampeding animals eager for shelter before the darkened clouds unleashed a torrent. He could taste the dampness in the air, his eyes watering with the wind. He could hear the rumble in the clouds; but above all, he could *feel* the beam.

The static in the winds changed when it broke through the clouds, carrying it forward with the hungry anticipation of a carrion bird. Every muscle in his body contracted, and somewhere, deep in his mind, something opened up. It always does. Ibrahima had wanted to ask others if they felt the same, but for some reason he had never voiced it. Perhaps he didn't want to sound like Abdou, pointing at the obvious if everybody felt it too. Perhaps he feared the questions he would be asked if no one else felt it as he did.

The beam was death: he knew that; but to him it was life, in a way he couldn't quite understand. His senses heightened when it dropped, turning the clouds a deep red, every action anticipated by just a fraction. The future was not so much ahead of him, but already waiting for him to reach out and touch, if only he could break out of his body. Sometimes it almost felt like he could; that if he took a step forward and over the cliff to certain death he wouldn't fall. His body would stay behind while he floated ahead, a spirit on the charged air, in oneness with his ancestors. In oneness with the world. An infinity of possibilities. But he didn't dare. Instead he said:

"Yeah."

"Beautiful, isn't it?"

It was hard not to punch Abdou most of the time. The boy had no sense. He could stand in front of a charging lion and admire the beast's run, commenting on the richness of its mane. He could walk into a swarm of mosquitoes without a thought for malaria, drawn excitedly to the buzzing of the mosquitoes. He wasn't exactly stupid, but he was an idiot.

"Sure," Ibrahima responded. "Until you're standing right under it."

Abdou shrugged. "That's not gonna happen. I asked my dad about it. The Caliph only allows ChinaCorp to mine the Faso Subdivision, and the Caliphate gets paid for it. A lot."

Ibrahima looked at him, and then away, back at the beam. Perhaps the Caliphate did get paid in return; perhaps the Caliph was sitting on velvet cushions drinking water teased from honey and dew. But just as the tingling in his veins made him feel like he owned the world, he knew something more sinister was at play.

"Your dad is a wise man, Abdou. But we're citizens of the Massina Sokoto Caliphate too. Have you seen any of that money here? I haven't."

Abdou leaned back, drew in a thick gob of spit, and threw his body forward, launching it over the cliff and into the valley below.

"You know what your problem is, Ibrahima?"

"I have way more than one."

"You always think you know better."

"I don't see how that's a problem."

"See? Right there. That's what I'm talking about."

"You talk too much, Abdou. Maybe you should try thinking more."

"To hell with you," Abdou retorted, glaring at Ibrahima. "I'm heading home."

Ibrahima looked at him. For an instant he saw his friend standing in front of him, wearing different clothes, terror in his eyes, his body disintegrating into shreds of skin and bone, trying to scream for help. And then it was gone.

Abdou noticed Ibrahima's drift. "What? Wanna say something smart ass?"

Ibrahima shook his head. "No man, no. Get home safe, ok? I'll see you tomorrow."

"Right..." Abdou murmured, walking away.

Ibrahima turned back to the beam and saw the powerful force snapping shut with the thump of a bass line, pulling back into the sky and tearing out a little bit of his soul with it. For a moment he saw space. He saw stars. He saw an expanse so wide it swallowed him whole. Then the sky was dark again. Twilight vanished over the horizon.

✦ ✦ ✦

The hut was damp and dark. The threads on the sheet had long lost their softness, but it didn't matter. Her skin held all the softness in the worlds, rustling with sweat that tasted of sugar cane around her neck.

He had laughed when his friends described love. The oneness of bodies. All the empty poetry of minds too limp to truly flow. But he saw it now: the eye of the storm, where chaos and immortality met.

When he came to, it was night again. The day lost—except it wasn't...

Holy shit! Ibrahima thought, bolting out of bed. *I'm late!*

"Where do you think you're going?" Seynabou asked, rolling herself into the blankets.

The band was waiting for him. They had a performance soon. He should have been ready for rehearsal an hour ago.

"The guys are waiting."

She yawned. "Can't they wait longer?"

"They sure could," he said, pulling up his pants. "They could also find another bass player."

"You're the only reason they're any good." She stretched her arms, the sheet sliding off her shoulders. "And where would they find another bass player anyway?"

"Go ask them that." He walked towards the door. "I'll see you later."

"Eyo! Ibrahima Ndiaye! There you are!" Mame Fatou exclaimed as he entered their small hut, her orange and green dress wrapped around straight old shoulders, a skip in her step unexpected for a ninety-six-year-old.

"Not for long, grandma!" he answered, reaching for his worn out bass and tiny amplifier.

"Tsk" she said, her tongue slapping against her pallet like a whip on a water buffalo. "One day you're going to have to do something for yourself. That band won't last forever."

Of course it wouldn't. But who cared? He had as much the right to dream as anybody else.

His parents' picture hung from a wall in an old frame. His bed was in a corner opposite his grandmother's, sticks of incense blowing thin strings of coconut into the walls, permeating the hut with a smell that would linger long after they had burned out and he was sent to the market for more.

"Well..." he started.

"Yes, I know," she interrupted him, rubbing his cheek with her wrinkled hand. "Go ahead and have your fun, but be here before nightfall, you hear? Or you'll go to bed without super."

It won't be the first time, he thought. But he said, "Of course grandma."

And he walked out of the hut.

✦ ✦ ✦

Ibrahima twisted in his dreams, his hungry stomach feeling every absent morsel of his grandmother's promise.

He tried to open his eyes but could not. It wasn't a dream. It was the beam.

Somewhere it bore through the earth, mining out minerals from space, and whispering to him in a deep ululation. "You're mine Ibrahima. You have always been mine." It reverberated sensually, caressing him in his sleep. At times it sounded like his grandmother's loving admonitions; at other times it sounded like Seynabou's lustful whispers.

Leave me alone, he tried to say, but he had no lips, no body. He looked down and saw himself standing, an empty shell looking up at the sky, standing in a valley of sand and slowly turning to glass.

"You're not *alone*," the beam answered his unasked question. "You are *nothing*."

The beam appeared in full focus, crashing down on him, warmer, and warmer, and...

"Ibou!" his grandmother screamed, shaking him awake. "Wake up!"

He looked up to see her eyes filled with tears. "I'm ok, grandma. Sorry I scared you."

She sighed and sat down beside him on his bed and offered him a plate of cold rice and fish with vegetables and a glass of water. Her eyes were kind as she contemplated him.

"Eat. It will keep the dreams away."

He ate and drank the glass of water, and then fell back asleep. The hunger pangs left his stomach, but it didn't keep the dreams away.

Nabu let go of his hand, running ahead of him into the shade of a baobab. The tree was one of the oldest in the region, with a trunk wide enough to host a family inside, serpentine branches large and thick, near enough to the ground for people to pull themselves up and walk along them.

For as long as he could remember, the tree had been a place to rest in the shade from the heat of monsoon. A landmark for the weary traveler. A place of palaver for the elders. A not so secret rendezvous where lovers met in the quiet of its branches.

He was not old enough to palaver. Neither of them was. But they were old enough for tryst.

"Are you gonna join me or day-dream?" Nabu's chiming voice called at him.

"Can't be alone without me, can you?"

"No, but I'm just worried the heat will get to you, weak as you are."

Ibrahima laughed and strolled over to her, her grimace showing how frustrated she was at him.

How long had they known each other? They had been babies together, just a couple of years apart. They had wrestled and played together when he was six and she was four. They had always been inseparable. When had their play changed into something else, into love? He had no idea. Perhaps the love had always been there, only changing its form with the changing seasons of their lives.

He sat and rested his head on her lap. Her dress was dusty from the walk and smelled of churai and the indefinable scent that was her.

He almost fell asleep, but she wouldn't let him.

"Don't fall asleep on me, deh!" she snapped, a peevish lilt in her laughter. "Let me guess. You're having your dreams again?"

He pulled himself up. "Yup."

"They're just silly dreams. Really weird dreams, granted; but they're just dreams. You're not the only one who is scared of the mining operations, you know. They get at me too, sometimes."

He hadn't told her of the pull he felt whenever he saw the beam. He hadn't told her of the desire. He hadn't told her that his dreams occurred only when ChinaCorp conducted operations. She would think he was crazy. She already thought so, but in the excusing way of lovers she still thought of him as a daredevil young boy. He didn't want to nail his own coffin by appearing to step across the thin line to raving lunacy. He simply said, "Do they?" and looked into the maze of branches. "Sometimes it feels like I'm the only one who cares."

"You're not the only one, Ibou. The others just don't want to admit it. Life isn't easy for anybody, and sometimes it's easier to ignore what you can't control and deal with what you can."

"We can't control anything Nabu. I'm not sure we ever could. I mean look at us: our rivers are polluted, our coasts are covered in junk from both the Empire and the Republic. We scrap what we can and survive on it."

She chuckled. "You mean junk like that bass of yours?"

He glanced at her sideways.

"Yeah, exactly. It's like we're children, Nabu. We play with the toys we make out of scrap, light our homes and cook our food with them. We treat the leftovers as if they were gifts, but they're not. They're trash, and they're not even ours. And what does the Caliphate do? Give up even more, allow them to tear our wealth out of the ground. And what do we get in return? Empty promises and more junk. Have you seen what is left behind when the beam is done mining the soil?"

She nodded. They all had seen it. Entire swathes of the continent seared and bleeding with lava, like open arteries on a suicidal forearm. Soil ripped of every mineral and plant, cracked and fissured and void of life, leaking fluids like burned flesh. Earthquakes and death lingering long after the mining satellites had had their fill. Floods of displaced people fleeing the operations into the already overcrowded areas and cities.

"We will find a way," she said, rubbing his thigh. "We always have."

"That'll be new. We're no more than a playground for Han Industries and ChinaCorp to fuel their war machines. You saw what the Empire did to the Azawad Reaches? Sucked all the water out of the ground until the Imazighen were all gone, and the uranium became theirs. What do you think will happen next?"

"Han Industries doesn't have the technology ChinaCorp has, Ibou."

"For how long? How long until they bribe someone and duplicate it? What then? More one-sided contracts? We should have stood our ground, not as the Massina Sokoto Caliphate. Not as the Yoruba Heartland. Not as the Congolese Brotherhood or the South African Confederacy. As Africa."

She sighed. "You and your moods...Tell me more about your dreams. Maybe that will help you find sleep sometimes."

He nodded.

"Maybe it will, but... I don't know what else to say. I've told you everything. It's like I can see the beam, and it is talking to me, looking for me. I know it's crazy, but it's always the same dream. The beam drops from the sky and warns me that my days are numbered, that somehow it will find me. It's silly really..."

"You think you're special," she said, shoving him gently. "Are you always alone? Do you ever see your parents in those dreams? I heard that orphans often find meaning in other things to help them with the loss."

He shook his head.

"No. I never dream of them. I can't really remember them. They are the people in the picture over Mame Fatou's bed, but they're not real to me anymore. Sometimes I do wish I had a family like yours, but I don't dream of it, or of them. I don't think it's one of those."

"Then what is it?"

"A tug. Something pulling at the very core of me, Nabu. Something trying to rip me apart, to tear me from me, if that makes any sense."

She laughed again. "It makes no sense at all."

It was his turn to laugh. She was right: it made no sense. He was overthinking things, letting his creative mind run wild with the elements. And maybe he did think he was special—who wouldn't want to be, faced with the prospect of no prospects at all?

She was right about one thing. It did feel good to talk, even if he couldn't tell her everything.

She landed a kiss on his cheek and it felt like the very first time she had put her lips to his face. He remembered that day clearly. They had been playing in the sand and an older boy had come and shoved her to the ground. He punched him in the jaw and broke his tooth and earned a small scar between his knuckles. He held his hand out to lift her up. She kissed his cheek and ran away.

She got up and held out her hand. He caught it and pulled himself up.

"It's getting late," she said, "Let's go home."

Ibou's fingers slapped on the chords like gum-rubber mallets on a balafon.

The old instrument had been his first love; hitting the keys with the delusion of grandeur of the apprentice, he hoped to recreate his favorite hits from the radio on the handmade device of wood and calabashes.

That was until he had seen a music video of a musician from the Congolese Brotherhood. He couldn't remember her name or even the tune; all he remembered was the impression of the bass on him, the roundness of the sound, its sheer groove.

His father had found a broken old thing for him, more hull than instrument. But he had worked on it, acquired strings, learned to tune it himself, and purchased a modest amplifier. He was getting good, but still he chased that sound he'd heard years ago on the radio.

"Abdou! How many times do we have to do this? You're off key! Again!"

Ibrahima stopped playing and watched Mansour berate Abdou for the fifth time that day. Abdou was not a singer by any stretch of the imagination, but he was improving with every rehearsal, and that was something to respect.

"Easy Mansour," Ibrahima said. 'Don't think you could hit those notes either. None of us can. Let's just change the key and drop a few tones. It might even sound better."

Mansour rolled his eyes and put down his guitar.

"Look," he said. "You wrote the song, so you can do whatever you want with it, but we can't keep adjusting to Abdou. It's not professional."

"Hey!" Abdou said.

Ibrahima laughed.

"You know how many times I had to adjust to you Mansour? Anyway, the only steady member of this band is Balla, and everyone knows how to beat a djembe." He winked at Balla.

"True!" Balla said. "But two djembes at once? Not that many."

Every rehearsal went the same way. They would play, they would argue, and sometimes they would fight; but they kept coming together. The truth was that none of them had anything else. However, Ibou liked to think there was something more to the band, and he liked to think the others thought the same too.

They would probably never record anything meaningful, but he was content playing with his friends, way into their middle age and beyond, performing locally, reminding people that behind the poverty and the pain they still had a soul, a culture, something ineffably and irrevocably theirs.

"Alright!" Ibrahima said. "Let's take it from the top. One, two, three..." Hair rose on the back of his neck. He almost dropped the bass.

"Guys!" Saliou, one of the younger boys, barged in screaming.

"What!" Mansour said, holding his guitar like a baseball bat aimed at the kid's head. "This better be important…"

Saliou lifted a hand, panting, and bent over at the waist. "It is…super important… please…you gotta come see this…It's the Han Industries…"

Ibrahima put down his bass, quickly followed by his band mates and they followed the kid outside.

Ibrahima ran into a stream of villagers moving diligently towards Pape Camara's restaurant and the communal television. He had never herded; that was something the Fula still did, sticking to the old ways. Standing outside the divide, not playing a part in either the Empire or the Republic's sick games. Maybe they were suicidal and wanted to be the next to go. Unattached meant being vulnerable. Maybe they were too proud. Allah knew they always had been. Whatever their reason, Ibrahima was sure the Fulani dreamed of such orderly cattle.

What is happening?

It was rare to see so many villagers gathered together. A funeral maybe. A wedding or a baptism. The small things that keep humanity from exploding, but otherwise…

Ibrahima approached Pape's restaurant, shoving his way through the silent crowd. He couldn't quite see the screen yet, but the silence of his community and the buzzing from the television spoke louder than thunder.

He pushed the last person in front of him out of the way.

What you are seeing should be a mistake. It should only be a mistake. Mistakes happen. We are all only humans after all; but this isn't a mistake. This is Ouagadougou. This is real…

He dismissed the carefully manicured mandarin voice of the AfriTV host.

Ouagadougou, a city of three million. Peaceful and kind the people of Burkinabese had always been. Now thousands were no more. Parts of the city of bicycles and small buildings slowly evaporated into a red halo. People and houses were indistinguishable from each other: limbs stretched into thin threads until they disappeared, buildings seemed to crumble upwards, melting faces blended into each other, and voices were lost in the ravenous ululation of the beam.

This is murder pure and simple, ChinaCorp CEO Malika Fahrani-Yakudo said, her face appearing in a small box in the corner of the screen. *This is Han Industries' work. This is what we all who stand for reason are up against: this cruel and inhuman savagery on behalf of the Western Chinese Empire. They have perverted our satellite mining technology. We warned our African partners and begged them to head our advice. But what are warnings in the face of such barbarity? From Dublin to Dubai, to Beijing and Sydney, the Eastern Chinese Republic mourns the dead in Ouagadougou.*

Ibrahima trembled. *I knew it.* He thought. *I knew it.*

Is there something the ECR will do about this, CEO? The AfriTV investigator asked.

The CEO looked at her and shook his head. *What will you have us do? While this despicable, nigh genocidal act by Han Industries is clearly aimed at ChinaCorp, the Republic was not the target. This is for our African partners to consult and determine for themselves. If you'll please excuse me, our managing board will be meeting soon to discuss the significance of this event for our citizens. May the souls of Ouagadougou find peace in the afterlife.*

That is all from ChinaCorp, the investigator said. *While we don't know how this has happ...We now have Han Industries CEO Ednilson Aardhal on the line from their headquarters in Rio de Janeiro. CEO, how do you justify this?*

Justify? Ibrahima thought, his veins popping on his forearms.

This is an accident, the Hans CEO said. *This is a horrible and tragic mistake. The Western Chinese Empire had never wanted this and begs the forgiveness of our African brothers and sisters. ChinaCorp's accusations are baseless. Their contracts and rural mining operations are no different from this. How many people have they killed over the past decade? Our satellite misfired, but we are prepared to compensate the people of the Massina Sokoto Caliphate in any way we can. We know that nothing will make up for the loss incurred. We are human just as you. But we will work together. We will send our best and brightest to draw up plans, and free labor to rebuild. We are in a position to offer better contracts than ChinaCorp. We will...*

Do you mean that you will now both be competing over mining rights on the continent?

Haven't we always?

What if we refuse? You had no contracts signed. You should never have been here.

Refuse? Please, do not be hasty in your conclusions. This is an accident. A horrible mistake, yes, but nonetheless. There have been oil spills in the past, mining accidents are inevitable. Africa still has a lot to gain in this partnership we...

Ibrahima backed into the crowd. The beam ripped through the air and into the city, playing on a loop on the screen while the voices of the press and commercial greed drowned the voices of the departed.

"Ibou!" Seynabu's voice rang in his ear behind him. "You're on my foot!"

He turned and hugged her, weeping on her shoulder.

"Ibou. Ibou calm down. It's gonna be OK. I'm here Ibou," she whispered.

But everything wouldn't be alright. It never would again. He wasn't crying for the dead. He wasn't weeping for what may or may not happen in the future. He was weeping in shame.

Amidst all the sadness and chaos, the CEO's callous, empty comments and barely veiled threats, he longed for the beam.

✦ ✦ ✦

"Mame Fatou!" Ibrahima called, walking into the hut. "Grandma, are you there?"

The hut was dark and smelled of burned tallow and incense. Mame Fatou sat in the corner in a reclining chair by her bed, asleep in a blue dress, her head wrapped, and a small prayer book at her feet, her arm hanging over the armrest. Her breathing was gentle.

Mame Fatou was a pillar, in spite of her waning frame. She was the one solid and steady thing in his life.

He picked up the prayer book and placed it on her bed before warming water for tea.

He waited until the water had boiled and poured some into a cup before waking her gently.

"Grandma," he whispered, shaking her shoulder as the eyelids of her dark blue eyes fluttered open like the wings of a butterfly.

"Ibou?" she asked, her eyes adjusting to the candlelight in the hut. "Is that you?"

"Yes grandma, it's me," he answered, proffering the cup. "You fell asleep in your chair again. Here, have some tea."

"Good boy," she said, accepting the cup and taking a slow sip. "It's late. Where have you been?"

"I was at Camara's restaurant with the rest of the village. Haven't you heard?"

"Heard what? You know I don't go there anymore."

It was hard to believe how frail she had become. She had aged so slowly that he never truly noticed. While his parents were human shaped holes in his memory, his grandmother was still a tree. But today he saw that the trunk had withered to a willow which bent to the storm and defied all odds—but a wispy willow, nonetheless.

Looking back now, he realized that it had been months since she made it any further than the market, halfway to Pape's restaurant and back. Only a couple of times a week, maybe three sometimes. She used to walk to the cliffs to get him when he was a boy, and sometimes she would sit next to him, their legs dangling together over the edge while she told him old Jollof folktales, of the spirits of the Lebou fishermen, and tease him about girls.

How long ago had that been? He couldn't tell if they were memories or dreams.

"It's all over the news," he said, rousing from his reflection. "Han Industries found a way to mimic ChinaCorp's satellite mining technology. They claim it's a mistake, but..."

She sighed. "You don't believe them?" she asked, putting the cup down.

"That's not it grandma, it's..." he hesitated again. He hadn't been able to tell Seynabu and he definitely would never tell his friends, but she knew him, and he knew that no matter what he told her she would listen, and wouldn't mock or betray him. He knew that she would find the words he needed to hear, whatever they were.

"...It's me, grandma. Something in me is...wrong..."

He told her everything. How he felt drawn to the beam in spite of all it was. How he felt the beam even in his sleep if it was close enough – that is half the caliphate away. He told her how the beam split him in half, drawing him out of the shell of his body, making him feel alive, how it felt like something more than himself, more than human, a power he feared but relished all the same. He told her how ashamed he felt, how anxious and anticipating.

"I don't know grandma," he concluded. "I don't want this. I don't want to want this, but...One day I...I..."

He dropped to his knees beside her.

"My boy," she said, rubbing his head "My special little boy."

"What is wrong with me, grandma?"

"Nothing is wrong with you, boy. Nothing at all." She took another deep breath and finished her tea. She wiped her lips and placed her cup on the small table by her chair. "Nothing is wrong with you. Do you remember what happened to you, about twelve years ago? After your parents left to work in Gao, a few weeks before they died in the bus accident?"

He looked up and shook his head. "What are you talking about?"

She closed her eyes for an instant, breathed in, and opened them again.

"I'm so tired today," she said, yawning. "I haven't been this tired in a while... Anyway, you can't remember that, of course. You were young and considering... Well. Your parents had left you with me. That was a long time ago. You were so small, hanging to my dress all the time, asking where your parents were, when they would come back, and why they hadn't taken you with them and if they still loved you. They did love you Ibrahima, they just had to go. They thought things would be better...do you mind getting me some water? I'm still parched."

He got up, dusted his hands and went to the blue plastic bucket in the corner, removed the lid protecting the water from mosquitoes, reached for the ladle floating inside, filled it and poured some of the tepid water into a metal cup and handed it to Mame Fatou, who took a deep swig.

"Ahh. That's better. Where was I? Yes... it was before the rainy season, and we'd been having lightning showers for weeks. A few cattle had been killed, so nobody let their children out for days, but it was so hard keeping a rein on you. Ha! You were a handful, let me tell you. You were already glued to that girl Seynabu...I think I aged thirty years in the last twelve because of you."

She took another sip.

"Tried all I could but I couldn't keep you from running out of this hut. That hasn't changed much, has it?" She said laughing "You bolted out like a goat on Eid trying to dodge the knife. The lightning fascinated you. You sat there, your eyes glued to the sky, your hand opening and closing, trying to hold the lightning. Well, you did boy. That you did."

Ibrahima raised an eyebrow.

"The wind picked up something fierce. I called out the window, but you didn't move, so I started walking out and then a thunderclap sounded so loud the ground shook, and almost at the same time, a single bolt of lightning like Allah's spear came down on you, hitting you on the head..."

"What?!" Ibrahima exclaimed, jumping up.

"Right on the head. I froze and closed my eyes and starting praying. You didn't make a sound. I thought you were dead. I thought if I stopped praying and opened my eyes I would find you lying there, a small burned body that I had failed. But instead you glowed. The shine of the bolt, moving down from the crown of your bald little head down your neck and shoulders and your back, into your waist, your little legs and tiny feet, and into the ground."

"I can't...remember..." Ibrahima started.

"Of course you cannot," she said. "It must have done something to your brain. But I swear that I saw something surrounding you. Can't tell what. It had the shape of you in a halo of light, but much larger. It tried to pull itself out of you, but it snapped back and you came to, giggling as if nothing had happened."

She took some more water.

"I ran to pick you up, but I couldn't get closer than a few feet. So much heat was blowing away from you, and I could feel the electricity pricking my skin. I prayed. I prayed and thanked Allah so hard. You just sat there giggling. You said: 'Grandma! Grandma! I am flying! I can see you! I can see me! I can see everything!' I asked you what everything meant. You just kept saying: 'everything! Everything grandma! Everything!' You were so excited. I had always thought you were a special boy, but what grandmother doesn't? But then I knew. There was something truly special in you. 'Everything! Everything grandma! The world! The sky! The stars! Everything! They are mine grandma! All of it! Everything! They are mine!' I'll never forget that day for as long as I breathe. When the heat finally stopped billowing from you, I picked you up and kissed you all over. I told you, I told you...Yes, I said: 'Yes, they are, little boy, all of them; one day, they will all be yours'..."

She paused and yawned.

"So you see? There's nothing wrong with you. You are one with the universe, my boy. You always have been. That's all. I feel really tired now. I think I'll sleep in the chair. Leave me alone." She finished with a smile and fell asleep.

Ibrahima pried the cup gently from her hand and finished it, unconsciously feeling the top of his skull for a scar.

He stepped out into the night sky and looked up at the clouds hoping for lightning to strike twice. But maybe it already had. He could have been alone, but instead he had two amazing women in his life, one that loved him unconditionally, and the other whom he would strive to love forever. He had friends and a community. He was different but not alone. Blessed by lightning. Blessed by life.

He walked back into the hut, feeling lighter and calmer than he had ever been. He pulled his grandmother's sheets off her bed and wrapped her shoulders in them, tucking the sides in between her arms and the chair. Then he went to grab his own wrapper, and rolled himself on the floor by her feet and slept soundlessly.

He woke up the following morning and looked up at Mame Fatou. She was dead.

"Ibou!" Seynabu's voice rang from the window of the hut, followed by the wailing of their son, shrill but demanding and full of strength.

He turned off his plasma cutter and lifted his welding helmet and wiped his forehead. Things had changed in the three years since Mame Fatou passed away.

Her body had been buried in the cemetery they shared with the neighboring villages, by the empty tombs that had been dug symbolically for his parents. The men who carried her bier were followed by almost all the residents of the community.

She had been his grandmother, but in many ways, she was also the grandmother of the community. Everyone had known her in some way or another, had been raised by her in some way or another. She was Mame, an elder, and with her it wasn't just a person who passed but the memories of the village, harkening back to a time before the Caliphate took over the entire region from Chad to Senegal. She knew the Sahelian War and survived it. She had been a little girl too, hard as it was to believe; she was once a beautiful young woman in love, was a strict but caring parent, and she was to him most of all a mother, a father, a sister, a friend.

She was a hole in his heart and mind. Now that she was gone, some things would forever be lost to him. It was true with every generation: history is in the mouth of the elders. It is not perfect; time and experience and pain and healing color things in different shades. It is not perfect, but it is human, and in the end, when all else fails, when the power cuts, when the circuits fall silent, it's all that's left. It's the storyteller that binds the people together, that tells you where the truth lies, regardless of what is written.

"I'll be right there!" he hollered back. "You hear that, Demba?!" And to his son he said, "Daddy's right there for you!"

As usual the crying stopped at the sound of his voice.

He would finish building the door tomorrow. There was no point in rushing things; he'd discovered himself a new skill, one that never outran its usefulness. The small hut he'd shared with Mame Fatou and now share with his own family barely looked the same anymore. The roof was laced with a layer of protective metal under the straw. He'd smashed down half the wall to enlarge it and build a small room for his son when he'd be old enough to want his own, which seemed closer every day. One layer of rock, one layer of metal and another layer of rock. It was the sturdiest hut in the village. It was expensive work, and as he was no carpenter, the furniture came at an extra cost, but his welding jobs paid for it easily.

"When are you going to get to my room?" Nabu asked as he walked in. "Here, hold the boy for a moment, I'm starting to tire."

He took their child from her hands, lifting him up in the air to a giggle, as Nabu turned to their small cooking unit. The smell of rice, chicken and peanut sauce drifted out of the hut through the ventilating unit he'd built for her.

"Soon enough, shape of my heart," he said. "Are you getting tired of being so close to me?"

She turned her head from the stove and smiled at him. "Sometimes," she said. "But who doesn't? We all need a piece of our own. Let's have dinner and talk, ok?"

He nodded. "Of course, but let me put Demba to bed first."

He carried his son to bed and put him in the cradle by their bed.

Demba favored his grandfather's weight judging by the picture of his grandfather but he had Ibrahima's mother's eyes and Seynabu's mother's face, as she loved to point out. He would be a beautiful boy, tall and strong, taking after Nabu's Bambara roots; yet, dark and handsome, he would remain a Wolof from the Senegalese province of the caliphate.

Looking at Demba asleep, Ibrahima remembered his childhood and felt the child awaken within him, free of the burdens that made him who he was; he felt a lightness in his bones that he had left behind without a thought, eager to grow, to live, to love and to learn. Now he had so much to unlearn.

He sat on the floor just as Seynabu put down the bowl of mafé.

"Are your hands clean?" she asked.

He looked at his dusty fingers, licked one clean and grinned at her.

She shook her head.

"You take after your son more and more every day," she said, "Go clean those rusty fingers before you poison us all."

He laughed. "My fingers are poison and magic wrapped in one."

She smiled but said nothing. That had been their reality of late. The youthful lustfulness was still there but where it had then been an end in itself, it didn't now suffice to hold them together anymore. He knew what she would say, but she listened for it all the same.

He sat across from her, legs crossed on the floor. With her fingers she cut the chicken sitting in the middle of the rice in the bowl and dropped some pieces of white breast on his side.

"Thank you," he said, anticipating her reply.

"Let's leave, Ibrahima."

It felt like the hundredth time she'd said this. It was probably the thousandth time, but each time the longing in her voice was the same, an ounce of hunger sprinkled with fear and passion. That had always been her, always on the verge of something and ready to do it regardless of what may come.

"I thought you wanted me to finish your room."

"They're not mutually exclusive," she said, shrugging and putting a handful of rice, sauce and chicken into her mouth. "I mean it Ibou. Maybe not now..."

While Demba is young, he heard himself saying in his mind.

"...while Demba is young, but we can't stay here forever. You've got to want better for him than we had."

"He already has. He has both of us."

She smiled at him and grabbed his clean hand in hers, rubbing it gently. "I know, and we will never fail him, but the two of us are not enough. He needs to go to school and to find himself a job working for the caliphate. He is a bright child; you would know if you didn't spend so much time working."

This was a first.

"You think I'm a bad father?"

"No," she said, shaking her head. "You're a great father. You love that kid more than you love your own self, but we owe him more."

"It wasn't so long we were stealing kisses from each other by the baobab. It seemed enough at the time."

"A lot of things were enough back then. We were young; we still are, but it's no longer all about us, Ibou. There's nothing here, not even for you. But if we left, I could find a teaching job."

He looked at his bass and small amplifier, discarded in a corner of the room.

He hadn't played since his son was born. It was no fault of the child, but things just happened that way. Balla had left without a word or trace. Abdou had moved to St. Louis, claiming the ocean air would make him immortal. The others were around, but somehow, they kept pushing back rehearsals and shows. Tomorrow. Next week. Next month. It was going on that way for two years now.

It had taken a thousand and one times but perhaps Nabu was right. Their child needed more. Nabu deserved more. He had to stop daydreaming. It was time to move on.

He held her hand tightly in his grip. The taste of her food carried a little of the sweat she had put into making it.

"We're getting out of here, love. I promise."

And with that Demba started crying.

He had become better at hiding his dreams from her.

It was easier now that in the wake of Ouagadougou the Republic and the Empire had discontinued all their mining operations, and were instead scrambling to rebuild trust and contracts with the African states. He didn't feel the tugging—his soul continuously pulled apart and reconstructed, his self-thinning to bare atoms—but in many ways it was worse.

Now there was a hole, an abyss into which he stared every night, keeping him on the fringes of consciousness that opened before his falling asleep. He would feel

Nabu's warmth and breath, hear his son's light breathing in the cradle by their bed; and yet he was alone, looking down into a crater stretching through strata of rock to the world's heart, and there he would see eyes, eerily like his own, staring back at him before exploding in magma. The ultra-heated rock climbed up the hole as he struggled to move, the heat slowly turning his flesh to tallow, the ashes of his body covering his home and family in a dusty grey. He found himself in the bottom of the hole, and heard them choke to death, looking up into a world he had just destroyed.

Ibrahima held Demba's hand as he stood on a mailbox, the tide of passersby and demonstrators flowing through the streets of downtown IKapa, the white buildings bright with sunlight and glowing with a life that had amazed him at first but now seemed mundane.

Anywhere else, the crowds would turn into riotous gathering. But here, the waves of UDC supporters in yellow and green, dancing behind painted trucks of the same colors and laden with loud speakers blasting melodious and rhythmic Zulu songs, opened up to make way for the smaller crowds of Ubuntu protestors who also sang their own songs, stomping their feet to a different beat. The overwhelming yellow and green were broken by white and red blotches that dissolved into yet another crowd.

It was hard to keep Demba quiet; he kept jumping up and down on the mailbox, eager to join the demonstrators, ignorant of the politics but drawn to the liveliness of their humanity, still too foolish to know danger of what he yearned for.

"Calm down boy," Ibrahima said. "Or you'll fall and get trampled upon."

"But daddy!"

"No," Ibrahima answered firmly. "Believe me, if I had my way, I would have gotten rid of you a long time ago, but your mother would never forgive me. So better be careful."

Demba looked at his father slyly. Ibou would have to keep an eye on him. Demba had all his mother's mischiefs and if Ibou let go of his hand, the little puppy would dash and bolt away and make his life miserable.

It was hard to believe that he was almost seven. It was three years since they had left the Caliphate for the Southern African Confederacy. It took him four years to finally show Nabu that he was a man of his word. He saved scrap after scrap until he found a job and a modest place for them to stay.

They could have continued staying in the Caliphate or moved to Bamako or Jos or any of the coastal cities and find work there, but why they move to live the same life they had lived in the village? Seynabu had wanted more for Demba, and she had gotten it.

"Do we have the same thing back home?" his son asked.

Ibou nodded. He would have to bring him back to the village soon.

"Yes, of course," he said. "Taking to the streets and complaining is the most human thing there is, along with finding an excuse not to go to work."

Demba laughed. The boy was smart and kind and strong, another thing he inherited from his mother. He was already much bigger than the other children in his class and looked like he was twelve and would look down on his father any day now.

"It's getting late, boy; your mother will be home soon."

"Why did she have to work and not you?"

Smart and observant too.

"Because your father is lazy, because your mother is not, and the world is unforgiving to teachers while it is kind on construction workers."

And, of course, working for ChinaCorp had its benefits. The corporation supported the demonstrations, trying to get the government to give in to its demands and allow mining to resume in earnest. Han Industries had already signed contracts with the Congolese Brotherhood, although authorities in Kigali had not let them test their satellites yet. It was only a matter of time, but in the meantime, there were weekly demonstrations and ChinaCorp paid its employees double not to work.

That wasn't true for government employees. Nabu would remind him of that. She reminded him of a lot of things these days. That he had to move up in the world. That she couldn't carry the three of them forever. That he wasn't a boy anymore. That he was not the man he used to be... And in those moments, he missed his village, he missed Mame Fatou's comforting arms, he missed his friends, he missed his band, but more than anything else, he missed how carefree Nabu used to be.

"Jump off!" he told the kid, opening his arms to catch him.

Demba shook his head and climbed down the mailbox himself.

Ibrahima smiled.

Any day now, he thought, *any day*.

✦ ✦ ✦

"Do you think we were right to leave him home alone?"

"He's twelve," she said, picking up her glass of wine, her full lips wrapping the glass gently, leaving a faint imprint along the edge when she put it down. "He's gonna have to learn to handle the house. Plus, how much damage can he do?" she finished with a smirk.

"Are you serious?" he asked, waving at the waiter. "A lot, that's how much. A lot."

"You gotta give him more credit than that."

"You give him too much."

She laughed.

"Is that what our life has come down to? Bickering over a preteen? You're starting to sound like Mame Fatou..."

"What?!"

Nabu laughed harder. It was that laugh that kept his heart open through the years; the glimmer in her eyes hadn't changed either, though there was so much mischief there, so much wit and intelligence, and something hard and tough, like steel wrapped in silk. And all for show.

What had happened to them? They used to be so good together.

In the corner of the dining room, the band played the rhythms of the Congolese Brotherhood. He couldn't speak Lingala but the music spoke for itself, of good times and cheerful evenings, interrupted by the sirens outside.

"A dust storm is moving through IKapa," an androgynous voice boomed through the loudspeakers. "I repeat, a dust storm is moving through IKapa. All customers are requested to remain indoors. This is a minor storm. ETA in fifteen minutes. Estimated duration: twenty minutes. Expect some disruptions in the electric system."

Ibrahima sighed.

"Aren't you glad we moved?" he asked sarcastically.

Nabu raised an eyebrow.

"Why do you have to be cynical? We would have had to move anyway; they're mining everywhere in the Caliphate nowadays." She paused to dip some lobster into the butter by her plate, and continued with her mouth full. "You are co-director of a construction company you started working for five years ago—where else would that have happened? Where else would we have found as good a school for Demba? I'm the Dean at my high school. It's all worth a little dirt."

Ibrahima didn't answer. She was right of course. At least the Confederacy only allowed limited operations. The dust storms were a byproduct but nowhere near as bad here as in other parts of the continent.

He looked out the window as the blinds lowered against the incoming storm.

He hadn't felt the calling of the beam in years. He barely felt anything at all anymore. He should have been happy, but he felt empty, like the husk of a beetle eaten from the inside by hundreds of ants, tearing little parts of himself out, morsel by morsel. So he'd sought other thrills.

The lights started to flicker. Nabu put her glass down with a frown.

"Who is she Ibou?" she asked flatly, looking him straight in the eye, all the mirth gone from her voice.

There it is.

"What?" he asked.

"Don't be coy with me. Of all the things you can do, don't insult me more than you already have."

He should have known she would find out. She had always been too smart for him. How long had she known and said nothing?

He didn't answer but continued staring into his glass of wine. There had been more than one over the years, more of them as Nabu and he grew further apart.

"Does it matter who she is?" He asked.

Nabu paused to think.

"No. No, I suppose it doesn't."

"Look," he started, reaching for a hand that she pulled away, his fingers landing on the tablecloth as hers slipped passed.

"Nabu," he tried desperately. The building rattled with the strength of the flash storm. "She doesn't matter to me, I...."

Nabu smiled.

"Hmmm," she said, shaking her head. "I should have asked who this one was."

He stopped.

"Years Ibou. Years. First, I tried to ignore it. Then I decided it was just a phase. That you would come clean and we could move on. Years. But it's too late now. It never stopped. It never will."

"Nabu..." but she cut him short again, her voice shaking.

"We have a child Ibou. We had a good life. Not a great life but a good one. How could you do this?"

How could he tell her? What could he say that would make any sense? That he felt hollow? That he had some bizarre connection to ChinaCorp's technology that even he couldn't explain? That Mame Fatou told him he was special? That he hadn't felt close to her in years? That he missed his home, doing everything she wanted while all he wanted was a simple life in a village now destroyed by mining operations in the Caliphate? *That I just won't grow up?* There was nothing to say, but he tried anyway.

"I'm sorry."

She waved a hand dismissively and downed the last gulp in her glass just as the androgynous voice announced the storm had passed and the metallic blinds were slowly raised.

"Save it," she said, standing up. "I've lost my appetite. Time to go home."

Ibrahima lay on the bed next to Seynabu, shivering in the cool breeze blowing from the sea into the room through the window. Shivering at his own shame.

He breathed in deeply and let himself fall asleep, to wake up in what felt a few minutes later but could have really been hours. He was standing in the middle of a desert, the ground shaking beneath his feet. The sunny sky was a dusty beige under a cloud of dust and the soul-rattling vibration of the beam poured from the clouds like a waterfall of blood from a wounded giant, boring relentlessly into the ground.

"Where..." he started.

A million voices cut him off.

"Silence, young one. You know where you are."

Ibou looked around at the lacerated ground around him.

This wasn't a desert. It was now but jutting from the ground, crusted with dirt and rock. He recognized the towers of what used to be IKapa; he recognized the dome of the courthouse. He recognized the blasted anvil of what had once been called the Table Mountain looming in the distance. But gone were the green of gardens, the scent of iodine blowing from the bay, and the chatter of seagulls.

He looked up at the beam towering over him, at the ochre brown vortex of death and dust swirling around them, enveloping him and the ray.

"Do not rest yet," the beam said in its legion of voices. "We are not done with you yet." With every syllable the voices gained clarity, spinning around him with the storm, faces flashing in the vortex.

Ibrahima breathed in deep despite the grit burning his throat and lungs and slowly turning his insides to sand.

"Who are you?" he screamed. His voice sounded torn and he exhaled dirt back into the air.

"*We are the bedrock,*" the voices answered, now only a few.

"*We are the buried.*" Now only two voices, the beam closing down only a few feet away from him, the radiating heat burning the flesh from his body and blowing it into the storm.

"*We are the bones,*" the last voice concluded, the spinning sands shifting, slowly taking form in swirling static, and growing into a face. Ibrahima knew that last voice all too well. His eyes were running, liquefied along his flayed cheeks, stinging what was left of his nerves. He couldn't see the face but knew the look its eyes would hold.

The last of his flesh peeled off, leaving a statue of sand, eaten away by the beam. The beam that sounded like Mame Fatou.

✦ ✦ ✦

Ibrahima woke up hours later. Turning around to wrap Nabu to himself, he found his bed empty. He stepped out of his room and down the hall to Demba's room, his heart collapsing, the house void of morning scents. Demba's room was empty as well.

✦ ✦ ✦

The sun dropped behind the mountains, biting its dark teeth into the sky, the last ray of sunlight pulling back from the tiny tornadoes of sand drifting across the hundred square mile plain which the South African Confederacy had authorized ChinaCorp to mine.

Ibrahima stared outside the window of the small sheebeen connecting three workers' camps, his phone glued to his ear, looking at what had been a month's work. A month's work of mowing and cutting down trees, rounding up animals and shipping them off to preserves, and digging out remains from traditional burial grounds. Displacing villagers—that was always the hardest part; no one wanted to leave, despite whatever they were offered. They were proud. They would resist. They would die.

A month of work and death to make way for more destruction.

"Pick up, pick up, pick up..." Ibrahima whispered into the phone. It was his third call. No one had picked up yet.

"Hey Westaf!" Felicien, a dark and large man from Bujumbura, bellowed at him. "You done with the phone yet?"

"I'll trade you a drink for it," Ibou slurred back at him, walking towards the bar and dropping the phone in Feli's lap.

Feli picked it up, scrubbed it with his shirt, and shook his head.

"You need a drink like a diabetic needs a soda transfusion. You can't keep doing this to yourself every day, man. Let me tell you what, Caliphate boy. I'll drive you back into the city tomorrow, but you've got to get some rest. You don't want to sleep through the mining tomorrow. You won't wake up if you do."

"...I'll go...when they...pick up!" He screamed at Feli. Feli rolled his eyes, shook his head again and walked away.

"Hey love!" Ibrahima screamed into the phone. "We're done here. I'll be home soon..."

Ibrahima dropped on a stool and rested his head in his arms on the bar.

"Another shot?" asked the bartender, a young Xhosa girl named Philasande.

No! He thought, but murmured, "Yes," anyway.

Here, the ChinaCorp employees were called Satellite Hounds or China Rats, neither of which was preferable. They were probably called by different names in other parts of the continent. They were doing the Republic's dirty work against their own land, their own people. Felicien was lucky he had a wife who was probably selling herself at another sheebeen at another site somewhere. But such was this world, this tiny, filthy excuse for a community.

You came here to forget where you came from. Then you started drinking to forget you came here. Neither of them worked.

"Neither of them work!" he yelled, slamming his fist against the bar between three empty shot glasses.

Three more? he thought.

Felicien walked back to the table.

"Jesus, Ibou! What has the world done to you?"

"Just hand me the phone, Feli," Ibou answered, snatching it out of Felicien's hands and walking back to the window where he stood to dial the number.

"Pick up, pick up, pick up..." he whispered as the dial tone started ringing.

"Hello?" a male teenage voice answered.

"Demba!" Ibrahima screamed.

"Dad?!" the voice responded "Dad? Is that you?"

"Son! It's me! I..."

"Fuck you dad! Who the hell do you think you are calling here!"

"Demba look..."

"It's been three years. Three years since you bothered to call."

"You both left me!"

"And? What did you think was gonna happen? Mom told me everything. How could you do that to her? How could you do that to us? You're a piece of shit dad."

"Don't talk to me like that! I'm still your father!"

"Demba! Demba who is that?" Ibrahima heard Nabu's voice on the other end of the line, every sensual memory of her plunging into the liquor in his stomach, building to a pressure point and lurching out of the window. "It's dad!" he heard his son answer, a slimmer of excitement in his voice in spite of everything. "Hang up!" he heard Nabu yelling "Hang up now!"

And the line went dead.

"Let me go!" Ibrahima screamed, trying to pull himself free of Felicien's gargantuan grip, and failing miserably.

He had slept only a couple of hours, on the floor of the sheebeen, his legs lying in his vomit, his shirt crusty with it, his breath drifting into his nose in redolent bursts of guts and bile. He wouldn't have touched himself. He wouldn't even have looked at himself if he'd walked past himself on the street. Yet Feli seemed intent on saving his smelly life, probably because his bible told him to do so.

Felicien yelled back at him. "No matter how bad things are, you...will live... caliphate boy!"

Ibrahima could feel Feli's grip weaken; perhaps Feli had realized that not all wretches could be saved.

"There is a place for you Ibrahima!" Feli continued. "God says..."

I knew it, Ibrahima thought. He screamed aloud: "Fuck your God!" He spit in Felicien's eyes, kicking him in the stomach, and falling back to the ground as Feli released his grip on him. "Fuck! Your! God!"

Feli looked down at him, seeing him in all his filth for the first time, and he turned and spit on the ground. "To hell with you, caliphate boy!" he said. "You want to die here?! Then die! You'll find out too late what the afterlife has for you!"

He picked up his bag and stomped out of the sheebeen, hopping into the last taxicab waiting for the last workers to flee the area before ChinaCorp blasted the area with radiation.

Ibrahima heard the engine start, and the faint smell of gasoline seeped through the open door and into his nose, covering his own stench for a blissful second.

He pushed himself up, hesitating to chase after the car. Nabu popped in his mind. Naked and sweating in the arms of another man. Demba... He couldn't even picture his son now. He remembered him as a child, as a teenager; but he didn't know the man he was becoming. Most of all, he felt his anger surge amidst his desperation. His son's cursing. Nabu's eagerness at hanging up on him.

Where was their forgiveness? After all he had done for them? Had his dreams ever mattered? His pain?

He pushed himself off the ground and stood on his legs and wobbled towards the bar for some hair of the dog.

He found a half-empty bottle of Castle Beer. Sitting warm and flat behind the counter, he drained it in a few gulps. His stomach lurched again, struggling against the punishment it was taking. Ibrahima rested a hand on it.

"Don't worry," he said out loud, "it's almost over."

He had loved her so much. He had never stopped loving her, even when with other women; he still loved only her. Even now. He'd just... Her and their son. He would be a foot taller than his father now. The little boy who loved to dance and pull pranks on his parents and neighbors. In his experience, it was always the more troublesome ones who became the best adults.

The beer bottle dropped to the ground with a clunk and rolled away as his skin covered with goosebumps and the hair on his arms rose with the change of static in the air.

You're coming, he thought, pushing the door of the sheebeen open onto the barren waste left behind for ChinaCorp.

He looked up. The cloudy sky should have been grey with rain clouds. Instead, deep in the cycling mass, a red glow laced the sky, mingling with the charcoal clouds, layers upon layers high in the altitude, slowly making way for the one thing that he could rely on, the one feeling that connected his waning soul with his body and the world around him.

The beam.

The wind began to rise around him, the tiny maelstroms of dust spinning and merging into each other. The air went damp. Then dry. Then damp again, until his skin raged to crawl off his bones, rippling with the wind and the electric charges, the clouds growing bloodier, the smell of the air thickening, his tongue growing pasty and numb.

Somewhere deep in the clouds there was a thump, as if a thousand elephants pounded the ground with one foot all at once. And then silence.

It was but a second of silence; yet in the shifting elements it seemed to last a lifetime. It lasted long enough for him to want to run, and stay, and change his mind again a dozen times until the silence cracked with the deep rumble of bass. The clouds burst open, and the beam crashed down with the anger of an avalanche of rocks and glass, his ear drums exploding with the pressure in the air, the influx of pain searing through his brain as he screamed but couldn't hear himself, and never would again.

The earth shook beneath his feet, rising and settling in waves, trying desperately to resist the onslaught of energy pouring down from space to rape it over and again.

He was a shell drifting at sea, a shredded bird blown senseless by the gales. And yet, through the blood leaking from his ears, through the air searing his lungs with grit, he felt whole. Whole and waiting to die.

Would his wife and son care? Would they even know what he had passed? There wouldn't be anything left of him, not even a shadow imprinted on a rock. Nothing. They would never know and never find out.

Somehow the thought comforted him. They would never have to grieve. They would go on with their lives thinking he had given up on them. They would never have to question leaving him, or feel any remorse for pushing him over the edge. It was easier to work through hatred than through pain, he knew that now.

He thought back to that morning. The house, empty. His heart, empty.

He had gone back to bed. Numb yet cold. So cold. He had curled up in the sheets that smelled of Nabu's sweat and churai, and fallen asleep, waking up shaking, a fever running through his blood, cold sweat dampening the sheets and his forehead burning.

He screamed for them. He dreamt of them in the midst of the furnace that was his skull, each succeeding dream worse than the previous. He saw Nabu crying while he was away on one of his trysts. He saw Demba consoling his mother, too young though he was to understand and not knowing which words to use to comfort her.

He should have seen it all. He should have seen the relief in Demba's eyes when he walked through the door, covered in cologne to conceal his current mistress's perfume. He should have seen Nabu's eyes avoiding his for only the slightest instant before putting on a mask of strength that she wore for so long he didn't know the mask from his wife anymore. He had convinced himself that she didn't know of his trysts, that their marriage was healthy, that his family was alright.

The sky over him glowed red from horizon to horizon, and also the air around him; the swirling sand burned red, grating relentlessly against his exposed flesh, his threadbare clothes caked with vomit and sweat slowly torn off his body.

The beam was out there, closing in on him, finally coming to claim him and take him out of his misery, his own, Ibrahima-made misery. Mame Fatou would have laughed, not mockingly but in her delicate and light-hearted way.

And he heard her now, like a whisper in the wind. He shouldn't be able to hear her. He couldn't hear the wind or the storm, yet riding ahead of the beam, surfing waves of immense heat battering his now naked body, were voices. A carillon of millions of voices, trillions of them, drawing back to the edge of time when the first voice rang alone in the void and cried at its own loneliness, when love and longing were born, when fear and emptiness were so real there was no room for hate, only room for desire, only room for life.

Ibrahima felt at one with the voices, at one with their finite eternity and for a moment, he felt peace. For the tiniest fraction of a moment, all his pains were alleviated, and he was the voices too, the laughter of his ancestors.

We are the bedrock.

We are the buried.

We are the bones.

His dreams finally made sense. The void that had reflected itself upon his soul was an all-embracing light, welcoming him, calling him with the softness of his grandmother's loving tones.

Sirius exploded at your birth, Mame Fatou's voice whispered softly in his mind. *The Bandiagara cliffs collapsed into powder that day. An earthquake buried the pyramids. Space itself will be YOURS.* The voices joined Mame Fatou's whisper.

The beam was on him, drowning him in radiation, cracking open his cells and remolding them, his inner organs boiling to stew, pulling at his mind, trying to make Ibou one with it, or to become one with him.

But it couldn't.

Somehow, where the ground had burned, where thousands had died, he still stood. Blind and deaf, his eyeballs melted down his cheeks, but he stood.

There were other voices in the beam, voices he understood but couldn't recognize. The cry of animals were caught up in the beam and strongest among them, a mandrill more self-aware than man. It was an old mandrill, probably the leader of his clan, powerful enough to retain his consciousness, his knowledge of self where millions could not.

There was a will in the voices: a will to dominate the beam, to own it, to bite and tear it limb to limb in revenge.

And in the midst of the soothing ancestors was rage, single and purely focused. And the rage fed into his rage, read his pain and knew his heart. The Mandrill's eyes opened onto the universe, folded it into the shape of Ibou's heart and took a bite. In that bite the Madrill tasted love and tasted anger; and the anger matched his anger, its longing matched his longing —two faces that awoke the pain inside him.

Nabu his wife.

Demba his son.

In the onslaught of the beam the Mandrill's face appeared, a powerful jaw and all too human eyes, looking at him in suffering, wanting to help him the only way it knew how...

The spell lost its hold on Ibou as the beam moved away from him, leaving him a shivering burnt and purulent mass of brown and red-welted flesh. The beam turned south, moving with the slowness of a distant tidal wave towards IKapa.

Light.

The universe is light.

It seems dark as night, but it's an illusion.

The universe is light.
It seems empty as a pit, but it's an illusion.
The universe is a web.
The universe is light.

✦ ✦ ✦

The hunt continues for the conspirators who commandeered the gruesome attack on IKapa three years ago.

The city remains empty, a broken ossuary, where millions were buried and burnt in a flash of light.

The billions of yuan poured and still pouring out of Beijing make no difference, and how can they? You can always rebuild buildings; stone and steel are always plentiful. But what about soul? What do you do when that is gone?

What soul wants to live in this city, built on embers and blood, staring into the split carcass of Table Mountain cracked open to the clamor of millions?

ChinaCorp and Han Industries are not without their detractors, not with the shadow of Ouagadougou still stretching over their every move, but the data is unanimous. Someone somehow managed to divert the beam.

Suspicion first pointed at Han Industries, but this is not the misguided act of a competitor but the murderous game of the coward, the callousness of wanton politicized violence. This is an act of terror.

As three years close on the destruction of IKapa, the search continues, and will not stop until the cowards are brought to justice.

On the anniversary of the tragedy that struck IKapa, we remember the buried.
Masha Villiers for the *eThekwini Gazette*.

✦ ✦ ✦

Soul.
The universe is soul.
It seems cold as a shallow grave, but it's an illusion.
The universe is soul.
It seems dead as a rotting corpse, but it's an illusion.
The universe is life.
The universe is soul.

✦ ✦ ✦

IKapa is far from empty. There is always someone to hear the fall of the tree in the forest. There is always someone to pick the pockets of the dead.

"This place stinks, girl."

"You mean you can smell something beyond that breath of yours?"

"Remember that time I banged your mom? Close enough."

"We have the same mother...Of course it stinks, Greekson. It's a fucking graveyard. They don't call it Pompeii Black for no reason."

It was wrong to say that IKapa had been destroyed. Abandoned yes, but the beam had not destroyed the city. It had only sliced through the Hottentot mountain chain like an industrial saw through unlucky fingers. The mountains split open, bursting tons of rock and ash into the atmosphere, some of it swallowed by the beam while the rest settled around it, covering neighborhoods in thick dust and debris, trapping hundreds of thousands in homes running out of air, trapping others on the top floors of buildings as they watched their neighbors die while waiting their turn.

Instead, the abandonment of IKapa created an opportunity for all kinds of scavengers. Some were people left behind at the expansion of the Confederacy. Some were farmers from the old homelands who had never seen a city. Some were rebel groups from the old nations of the Republic and the Empire, hoping to weaponize debris against the corporations. Some were religious fanatics of different bigotry. There was a fortune in valuables, materials and anything that could be salvaged.

And radiation.

Most scavengers had left after a year. The city was baked in decomposing bodies. The money wasn't worth the price of scavenging in IKapa: the hair and nails of the scavengers would fall out in clumps, and anything out of IKapa was a tough sale, for very few would touch it. Except Greekson and Charity who, through some luck in the gene pool, were less affected than the others. At least early on.

"You can't smell anymore," Greek snapped back at Charity. "You think I can't tell, but I've been letting them rip for months and you never complained. You always complained, ever since we were kids."

Charity shrugged. "Doing what we do, I call that a blessing."

"Yeah, but we can't do this forever," he said, coughing a few speckles of blood into his fist. "And no more tasting food for you either."

Charity was getting used to that. She had never been a big eater anyway. She said, "I can handle that. A few more months and we should be able to pay off Big Caffer and get gandma her meds and our asses to the Republic."

"You said that a few months ago," he said.

"Can't help it if water prices keep going up." She handed Greek a dusty handkerchief with brown traces of dried blood. "Here, wipe that off your hand."

Clean water was easy enough to come by if you had the yuan. The shantytowns surrounding IKapa had developed an economy of their own, reliant on water Wallas, and a host of bottom feeders with more courage than scruples.

It was a beautiful day. It happens in disaster zones too. Already, flowers and vines made their way through the dust and the cracked concrete, up the sides of the houses and buildings, wrapping old buses in cocoons of giant green thorns. Beautiful, fairy tale things, all of them deadly.

"We're heading into the crater."

Greekson spit out the little water in his mouth. "What!?" he yelled. "Are you out of your mind?"

"There hasn't been a flare up in months," she said, looking towards the vaporized bay and the giant hole known as the crater, full of broken buildings and who knew what. "Plus, I have a feeling about that place. I think that's where the guys who stuck it to ChinaCorp are hiding."

Greek shook his head. He loved his sister. She was the only reason he was still alive and prospering beyond all beliefs, but sometimes...

"Are. You. Out. Of. Your. MIND?!" he yelled again. "That's where the radiation is the strongest. That's why there are the flare-ups. We've been lucky so far, but...damn it you've lost your sense of smell already sis! There's nothing there but radioactive slag!"

Charity shook her head.

"Think about it," she said, spinning around and grabbing him by the shoulders. "There has to be something there. What is with the flare-ups? It makes perfect sense when you think about it. Something is controlling the satellite and it's always stopping there. Right there Greek. We don't even have to catch them, just confirm that they're hiding there."

"Who're they?"

"The hell if I know. But what do we have to lose?"

"Our lives!"

"Come on. In and out. A quick recon mission. If we find something we'll be rich. I mean Republic rich. We won't have to work another day. Ever. And if we don't find anybody...well, we're back to the daily grind."

Greek wanted to argue but knew it was pointless. Once Charity had made up her mind, that was it. It had always been so. She'd been getting him in trouble since they were toddlers, including their current predicament with Big Cafer.

"Ok," he said. "Ok. But no more than an hour. In and out like you said."

Love.
The universe is love.
It seems heartless as a snake, but it's an illusion.
The universe is love.
It seems lonely as an owl's song, but it's an illusion.
The universe is everyone.
The universe is love.

What was left of Ibrahima's shell sat on the floor of an old building, buried deep inside what people called the crater.

On the stone were stuck bits of his skin which peeled off him when he moved, leaving pus filled holes in his flesh. Most of the skin on his eyeless face and skull were gone, exposing the nerves and bones beneath. His right arm had fallen off years ago, the bones lying discarded in a corner of the den. The wound had never healed and occasionally leaked fluids onto the floor. The legs folded under him looked closer to chicken wings than a man's legs; but then he didn't need them, for he never crawled further from his seat of meditation than the small crack in the ceiling that dripped rainwater when the skies were clement. Every inch of his body was covered in bubbling sores, bursting open and closing whimsically.

No one would have recognized him. Not even himself.

Inside his mind, Ibrahima could see the universe unfold, travelling far into space where wormholes bloomed and faded out of existence in a blink. He could see the explosion of distant stars showering the galaxy with gamma rays, destroying life on one planet and creating life on another.

Sometimes his thoughts would surf on a comet until it crashed into a moon and shattered it into orbital rings.

All of it. All of life. In its nigh infinity. They were right within his grasp, yet utterly out of his reach.

And somewhere in that void Demba and Nabu danced with the stars, their shapes elusive, oft times whole, and oft times just a string of elements scattered on the immortal canvas.

When the beam had released him, a blind and quivering wreck seared to perfection, he had screamed after it. In his mind. His vocal cords had been shredded by the air and radiation. He didn't know that he was mute. He didn't know that he was blind. He didn't know that he was deaf. Despite being erased from his body, his senses were somehow heightened. He could see clearer, hear louder, smell stronger, and suffer more intensely—infinitely more so.

Every fiber of his being yearned for his family. He had pushed himself up and desperately tried to follow the beam which, guided by the primal rage that he had shared with the force, had zeroed in on his loved ones. He screamed after it, pleaded with it, begged for it to stop, told it that the fault wasn't theirs but his. It was his own selfishness. His self-pity. Not them. But the beam ignored him and marauded further, relentlessly.

He picked up himself and repeat his appeals for days. Days after the destruction was wrought on IKapa, the city was covered in ash and the last living residents fled in a slow river of molasses, passing him by and pushing away the bleeding lumpy creature crazy enough to march into IKapa.

He heard his family scream when they died. He shared their panic at the incoming slaughter, the brief moment of disbelief when pain fades and death strikes, just a nanosecond between life and oblivion.

There had been something else there that had taken him the last two years to accomplish. Acceptance. At the very last moment they had accepted and embraced their fate: his strong and beautiful childhood friend who had become his wife, his son young yet tough enough to stare death in the face with a smile. He felt so proud of him.

Would he have had that courage? He who had taken the coward's route, tried to end it and failed? He couldn't even kill himself. All he could do was hurt others. He had wanted the beam, yearned for it since he was a child, but he had killed it, and enjoyed killing it.

And for two years he sat in this den, his body decaying as he breathed, racked by guilt and by a lifetime of emotions held at bay, never more than a heartbeat away, hammering him over and again until his soul cracked open and he couldn't take it anymore and had to let go.

Acceptance.

It flew off his bony, raw and uneven shoulders, leaving a calm breeze. Where every living thought had been a nightmare of the past, there was now nothing left between him and the universe, except him, sitting in his den, contemplating the realm of myriad possibilities but too scared to take that step.

He was running out of time. He had to act now.

"And I thought outside was bad," Greek said, holding the bloody handkerchief to his nose.

"Let me guess," Charity said. "It stinks. Am I right?"

Greek grunted and moved on ahead.

The climb down had taken more than an hour, not because they were deep, but because the crater was a mess of old rubble and torn down buildings, unlikely hallways and rooms that somehow had been preserved intact, the walls covered with the pictures of the people buried somewhere deep below.

Crawling ahead of him through a tiny hole between slabs, Charity called out to him, flashing her torchlight in his direction. "Almost there baby bro!" she yelled before throwing a raspy fit of coughing and spitting a gob of phlegm her brother knew was thick with blood.

It wasn't only the radiation getting worse: they too were.

"I don't like this sis!" Greek yelled back. "This is bad. It's been over an hour! We should go back!"

"Don't be a pussy!" she yelled back at him. "I can see something!"

The tunnel was dark and the floor uneven and he couldn't see his sister; but as he moved slowly forward, his visibility came back gradually, like the proverbial light at the end of the tunnel—a tiny red glow.

He crawled out behind her.

"I'm telling you..."

"Shhhh," she said, nodding her head, a finger to her lips.

A man sat on the floor in the middle of rubble and waste. It must have been a man, or what was left of a man. It had the general shape of a man but bits like limbs were missing, and you could see through him in some parts. Although the room was dark, they could see the wall through his stomach.

There should have been blood everywhere, but instead, the man basked in red glow, seemingly bathed in the fluids leaking from the holes in his body and from his missing limbs. There were no feces, expectedly of one without limbs and consequently without movement. The room did not, as they expected, reek of sweat, piss and shit—the musky smell of a lion's den. There was neither sound nor smell; just a man meditating, his skin bubbling and bursting pus.

"I told you..." Charity whispered.

He almost yelled in shock.

"What? This thing? He doesn't have enough fingers to wipe his own ass. There are holes on him, sis. Holes!"

There was no sign from the meditating one.

"Ok," Charity said. "Maybe it's not *the* guy." She coughed, rubbing her eyeball. "But I was right. There was something."

"He's glowing brighter, sis!"

She turned toward him, her right eye bouncing against her cheek, holding by a nerve to its socket.

✦ ✦ ✦

Me.

The universe,

Is ME.

✦ ✦ ✦

There were two intruders in his lair. A boy and a girl. Young. Foolish. Brave enough to have made their way down to him, but unbelievably foolish all the same.

He hadn't felt his body in a year, but for the first time in his life he felt his soul. He felt his soul in the tiniest of places where it connected with his body, wrapped around his tendons, bit into a neuron in his brain, buried inside his liver; it was still thinking with his body, still denying its own potential, terrified of breaking free and rising.

It was up to him, not Ibrahima Ndiaye the man, but Ibrahima the god.

He could see them, their bodies dying so slowly they could see each other falling apart. There was love between them, not lust; these two were family and there was a bond and a purpose to them. They were foolish, yes, but foolish for a reason.

He didn't want them to die, but they had made their choice. It was too late for them to turn back.

He only had little time left himself. The time was now.

He bundled the little energy left in him. His heart was empty of pain, his mind free of thought, and his body empty of soul.

He let himself float as the young boy who'd been hit by lightning had let himself go. The boy was young enough to not know fear, and fearless enough to embrace change.

"I'm sorry," he murmured to the two siblings, but only in his mind, for he had no tongue to speak.

It was time to go.

"Fuck," Greek said gesturing towards his cheek. "Your eye, it, it...oh sis..."

She reached to her cheek, holding her eyeball in the palm of her hand.

"Sis...I told you... Sis..."

She pressed her hand against his cheek, and when she removed it, it was covered in blood leaking from his ears and nose.

She shook her head, pointing to the man in the middle of the room. "I don't think it matters anymore," she whispered.

The man had not moved, and perhaps couldn't move anymore, but kept glowing brighter. The faint red light now blazed a violent crimson, radiating heat, burning hotter second after second, the skin on his bones melting off until the bones were completely bare. From his body seemed to emerge something vaguely shaped like him but translucent, as if his shadow had taken on the life he had left.

Charity's eyes fell out of her skull and Greek's eardrums exploded, but the man glowed brighter still, the red tide washing over them, the raging heat barely registering against their frayed nerves. They grabbed each other's hand, pulled each other close, their flesh melting into each other, and a voice rang in their heads: *I am sorry.*

The man glowed with the strength of a dying star and exploded in one final burst of radiation, leaving his shell intact, but taking them away with it.

Ibrahima floated in the immensity of space, struggling to keep himself together. A ball of blue and green and brown shone in the distance, and glowing all around like diamonds were hundreds of mining satellites, so small from where he swam in the void that they seemed like mere pinpoints, though each of them was deadlier than an army.

He felt himself dissolving, losing the solidity he had felt in his flesh and in his soul. There had to be something he could hold on to, something he could anchor himself to. There was yet one last thing to do, he remembered.

The mandrill. He remembered its jaw etched in energy and the primal rage of its paws. It couldn't let go of itself, not with all that rage; it was ready to bite and tear apart friend or foe alike. The beam had consumed the beast after all.

But he didn't have to.

There was a beauty in retaining part of oneself. His former self sat abandoned in the rubble, amid thirty-four million square kilometers of broken earth, of ancient knowledge, of bones buried in the bedrock. He was but an empty husk; he couldn't recognize in himself the young boy he'd been, the boy who'd been content with the simplest things.

He would have to let go of himself, but not just yet.

He called out and let himself expand, feeling himself grow thin, almost dissolving into the void. And gathered around him were the tiniest of particles, fragments of fragments of possibilities, worlds that had flirted with existence, all drawn from the very edges of his immortality.

He snapped his fingers and the pieces came together, the one last thing he still held on to. His middle finger struck a chord. A polyharmony in B minor rang from a bass of space dust, drawing an undulating ♫ on the void from a tense string.

The sun shone inside his iris, a nebula tickled his inner ear, and each satellite mining Africa from space sparkled around the blue pebble where he had abandoned his body.

He poured a planet's energy into the instrument, the sound box expanding, his fingers drumming the thick chords with the fury of a mad pianist. The satellites winked out as giant ♫♫♪♪ hammered them in waves, destroying cities across the planet. Somewhere, his body died. His fingers merged with the chords till he and the bull fiddle were one vibration, and he was everywhere at once, bouncing between satellites until the drifting debris circled the earth in a ring. He inhaled, or rather somewhere in the vastness of space a galaxy exploded. He let his fingers rest. Light years away the bass line birthed a star.

He reached out a hand and grabbed the strange world and smiled, rolling it between his fingers.

His grin lingered as he dangled the insignificant planet, tempted to crush it. Then through a black hole somewhere in infinity, something glowed, something new, and he turned his eye away from Earth forever.

THRESHER OF MEN

MICHAEL BOATMAN

Officer Greg Fitzsimmons was working up the nerve to tell the chief to kiss his hairy white ass when Black Edie attacked. Six months of modified duty with the Lincolndale P.D.'s traffic unit had nearly drained him of the will to breathe, and since no one who knew him believed he would ever make Detective, Fitzsimmons figured real estate offered him a brighter future.

He was scrolling through some listings on his iPhone when he looked up to see Black Edie's silver Mercedes Benz bearing down on him.

"Shit!"

The old tank swerved to the left and the driver's side mirror smacked Fitzsimmons's right wrist and sent his iPhone flying.

"Owww!" Fitzsimmons yelped. "Hey!"

The silver Mercedes rolled over his phone and continued along Lincoln Avenue at a stately twelve miles per hour.

Fitzsimmons jumped on his Harley and gave pursuit. He hit his lights and siren and punched the public address button on his right handlebar.

"Pull over," he roared via his helmet microphone.

The silver Benz crossed two lanes and jumped the curb in front of Mel's All American Barbershop. Fitzsimmons thought the old bat was going to plow through Mel's front window until the sedan swooped to the left and bounced back onto the street. It trundled along with its right-side wheels up on the curb, the busted exhaust pipe striking sparks. It swerved to avoid a fire hydrant and rammed into the streetlight at the corner of Lincoln and Main.

"Jeee-sus fuck," Fitzsimmons snarled, envisioning the shit-ton of paperwork he'd just inherited.

The old Mercedes had come to rest in front of the newer downtown Starbucks. A gaggle of looky-loos was already buzzing around the scene as Fitzsimmons rolled up to the intersection. He reckoned they were mostly hipsters and retirees. Who else had enough free time to buy gourmet Crap-in-a-Cup at ten o'clock on a Tuesday morning?

Fitzsimmons massaged his throbbing wrist as he dismounted.

"Lincolndale Police!" he barked. "Clear a path!"

To Fitzsimmons' savage delight, even the geeks and trannies that drank iced Senegalese butt-milk acknowledged his authority and let him through.

A jet of steam was whistling up from beneath the Benz's crumpled hood. The murdered streetlight had snapped in half, and now its shattered lamp swung like a lynched pervert, mere inches above the Benz's roof. As he shouldered his way through the crowd, Fitzsimmons mentally counted the citations:

Failure to Yield to a goddamn emergency vehicle. Destruction of goddamn City Property. Reckless frickin' goddamn Endangerment...

"Goddammit, lady! You nearly killed me!"

Black Edie was trying to restart the Benz. The old hermit kept turning the key and stomping on the gas pedal so hard she was bouncing on the driver's seat. By way of a reply, the car she'd owned since Jesus was a toddler wheezed, smoked... and died.

The look of dazed resignation on Black Edie's face infuriated Fitzsimmons even more.

Black Edie (for that was what everyone on the right side of the tracks called Lincolndale's only African-American librarian) wasn't just old; she was practically prehistoric. And as far as the Lincolndale Illinois P.D. was concerned, Edith Frazier was a royal pain in the ass. She'd harassed the chief about her asshole nephew every day since the shooting.

"*Hell,*" Chief Krieger always said after one of her daily rants. "*Maybe if she'd raised him right, the stupid son-of a bitch would still be alive.*"

That one always got a laugh out of the fellas.

Except for Driscoll, Fitzsimmons thought. For some reason, Fitzsimmons' former partner had refused to lighten up about Roosevelt Frazier. But since Danny Driscoll was the one who'd shot him, Fitzsimmons and the other guys usually just let him sulk.

Fitzsimmons wasn't laughing now, because his wrist hurt like a bastard. And why did everything smell like...

"Hey," Fitzsimmons barked, rapping on the crumpled hood with his nightstick. "What the hell's your problem?"

Black Edie squinted up at him. In the glare from the summer sun she looked as if she'd just been caught sleepwalking.

"Blood on these streets," she muttered. "Too much blood for such a small town."

Then she tried to start the car again.

Great, Fitzsimmons thought. *Probably got Alzheimer's.*

"Oh, I remember you," Black Edie said. "Master Gregory Fitzsimmons: The rambunctious one."

Fitzsimmons grimaced. He hated Edith Frazier. As far as he could remember, she was the only black who'd ever been allowed to work at the public library. Apparently, she was the only person, black *or* white, who'd ever wanted the job.

Black Edie was infamous for her collection of hideous pantsuits. Each one was like an abortion for the eyes, and they came in a variety of cornea-blasting colors. For decades, Lincolndale's kids had made naming each pantsuit a rite of passage. There were doozies from Fitzsimmons' time, like "The Booger-Green Ass-Hammock", or "The Camel Toe Express." Fitzsimmons' own nephew, Chase, had come up with last year's winner; "The Cat-piss Yellow Monkeynut Pimpstriper." The one she was wearing now.

But what really annoyed Fitzsimmons was the way Black Edie *talked*. She had this grandiose way of speaking, like she thought she was better than all the white folks in Lincolndale. She'd even had the nerve to correct his English once. And in front of Jenny Gorlick of all people.

Civilized people don't say, "ain't," Master Fitzsimmons.

Now here he was, twenty-five years later, remembering the hot flush that had raced up the back of his neck. Jenny Gorlick had treated him like he was a ree-tard for the rest of freshman year.

Bet you weren't so snooty when they scraped ol' Roosevelt's brains off the sidewalk, bitch. Bet you hollered like a regular old...

"Dan Driscoll knew my Roosevelt," Black Edie said. "All you boys played football at the high school."

"Look, lady," Fitzsimmons said. "I'm only gonna say this..."

"Ms. *Frazier*, young man," the old woman snapped, cutting him off mid-sentence. "Ms. Frazier."

Fitzsimmons itched to reach through the window and drag her scrawny ass out of the car, but then he remembered all the "citizen journalists" surrounding them, a virtual army of assholes just waiting to whip out their smartphones and push "Record."

"I heard he returned to full-time duty," Black Edie said. "My Roosevelt's been dead for two years, but Dan Driscoll gets to act like nothing ever happened."

"Take it up with the chief," Fitzsimmons snarled. "Right now we need to get this piece of shit off... ah..."

There it was again: the odor of gasoline, heavier now that he was close enough to reach for the door handle, the fumes so strong they pricked at his sinuses.

What the hell?

The smell was coming from inside the car.

Fitzsimmons saw them then: Six red five- gallon plastic containers lay in puddles on the back seats. Two overturned containers lay next to Black Edie on the soaked passenger seat. Each of the containers was open. Someone had removed the yellow safety caps.

Fitzsimmons heard a sound like the edge of a quarter scraped across the teeth of a tiny steel comb.

"It's my birthday, Gregory," Black Edie said. "I turned eighty-five today."

The inside of the car was soaked with gasoline.

"Hey now," Fitzsimmons said. "What the hell...?"

"Folks my age get lonely," Black Edie said. "Roosevelt and I were the last of the Illinois Fraziers. After he was murdered, I travelled along strange byways seeking a worthy champion. Then... I found *her*." The old woman chuckled. "On the *internet*."

"Okay, lady," Fitzsimmons said. The fumes were giving him a headache. His wrist hurt and he needed to take a piss. "Gonna need you to exit the vehicle."

"Turns out she's an old family acquaintance," Black Edie continued. "There were certain arrangements... delicate preparations... and then...last night... *she came to me.*"

"Lady," Fitzsimmons growled. "You got gas all over the place!"

"She made me an offer, Gregory. In exchange for a small token, a *leap of faith,* she promised me the answers I'd sought for so long."

Fitzsimmons heard that tiny, *metallic* sound again.

Clink.

"'Vengeance is mine, saith the Lord,'" Black Edie said. "That's from Romans, Gregory. Chapter 12 verse 19."

"Not gonna ask you again, lady," Fitzsimmons said. "Step out of the car. Now."

"Your God demands our forgiveness, yes?" Black Edie said. "I certainly wouldn't have survived this long without that."

Like a magician performing a coin trick, Black Edie opened her right hand. When Fitzsimmons saw what she was holding he grabbed for his sidearm, only to remember, too late, that he'd surrendered it during the Frazier investigation.

"*My* savior has a long memory, Gregory. Longer than King James ever dreamed. And she's strong. She doesn't *have* to forgive."

With a flick of her wrist, the librarian opened the Zippo lighter...

"Vengeance is *hers, boy. Kisazi* forgives nothing."

Then Black Edie and the old Mercedes and Officer Fitzsimmons became fire.

The goddess had lived a million lives.

As a child, she had raced Sister Sun across the endless savannahs of Home, singing songs that inspired queens for a thousand years.

Fly, sister! Dance with us across the sky!

Oh! See how she frowns!

Much later, she had travelled in the bellies of slave ships, listening to the voices of her people as they cried for her, never knowing that she rode beside them in the deepening darkness. She had watched her people sundered from their histories and wept for the beloved ripped from her million loving hearts. And at the end of every life, the parts of her that lived *in them* had also gone into that darkness.

But she always returned, nameless and ignorant, her consciousness fractured and divided across a new generation of stolen souls. For this was the goddess's doom: to watch over the journeys of her people, and to deliver her judgment upon their sins. Bound to mortal flesh, she was dragged across oceans and time, until she and her shining siblings had become little more than myths.

The shards of her divine essence, however, still lived within the souls of her dispersed people. Unable to remember herself, she'd begun instead to weigh the sins of those who had trespassed against them.

Until a willing supplicant restored her truest name.

Elliot Cream hated the burnt ones.

He'd seen a lot of gross shit during his stint as the Lincolndale Medical Examiner's morgue attendant; shotgun-suicides, car wrecks... He'd once helped autopsy a Puerto-Rican landscaper after the poor son of a bitch plunged through a sinkhole and drowned in the mayor's septic tank. Anyone who thought death by blunt force trauma was ugly had never scooped a tampon out of somebody's esophagus.

But Cream really hated the crispy critters. And the poor old biddy on the examining table definitely qualified as one of the crispiest. He'd unzipped "Frazier, Edith A.", taken one whiff and nearly puked in her body bag. It was the smell, he decided as he rinsed out his mouth at the sink; like sweet & sour pork flash-fried via high-octane shitstorm.

Still, Cream had a job (such as it was) and the dead cop the old woman had ambushed was due to arrive any second. Cream popped a mint and turned away to grab his notepad.

Behind him, the body bag on the examination table shuddered and sat up.

This time Kisazi remembered laughter.

The sound of men taking pleasure from her pain vied with the smell of whiskey and the taste of blood and dirt.

Get in there, boy! Get her face down in that mud!

She remembered light and opened one unburnt eye.

She didn't know this cold place, or the fat man who stood gawking at her like a frightened child.

Be very quiet now. Quiet as mice until I come back.

But the fat man had something she needed.

Kisazi leapt, covering the distance between them faster than he could blink, and caught him by the throat. Fingers scorched to the knucklebones plunged into the fat man's mouth, pinched the thick meat of his tongue and tore it out.

She remembered the taste, and with the blood came a flood of strength...

Dance, sister!

She is more stern than Brother Death!

...and memories of her immortal siblings. (How they shone with the flame of Creation!) She sank needle-sharp teeth into the fat man's throat and bore him down to the cold floor, riding the sacrifice the way she once rode her brother the Wind. The offering struggled in her grip, but she brushed aside its complaints, for with each bite, she remembered more and grew stronger.

She remembered youth, and her scorched skin became smooth. She remembered beauty and her melted eye regained its sight. She remembered the shrieks of children, the taste of their terror as vital to her kind as human devotion. She remembered godhood.

So she took from the sacrifice all the wonderful things she would need.

Lester Lee Carson had decided his oncologist was a lying bitch. Those cayenne pepper "nausea pills" she'd recommended gave him the burning shits. They'd also loosened his bowels so much he couldn't get off the toilet.

No way for a man to die, Lester Lee thought as he flushed for the third time. He'd lost thirty pounds and most of his hair from all the chemo and radiation. Between grunts, he lamented. If he'd known how much misery his four-pack a day habit would eventually cause, he would have jammed that first cigarette up Alice Copley's perfectly round ass.

No good feelin' sorry for yourself, he thought.

But more and more these days, it seemed, Lester Lee would catch himself rehashing old mistakes when he should have been enjoying a hero's life in the here and now.

Reckon there ain't too much "here and now" left, he thought, as another bowel-quake made him clench his knees together.

Lester Lee and the boys had been all too ready to boast back in '53, after the event they'd come to call, "The Barbecue." And why not? They'd stormed into Darky Town and burned that whole rotten mess right down to the ground.

"*We got down to it alright,*" his cousin Hal said for years afterward, usually when the fellas were too drunk to care who might hear. "*Got right down to where the pope shits in the woods!*"

Hal Corliss had spent his last three years shitting in an adult diaper. Frankie Foreman had suffered slow dismemberment from diabetes and Corny Driscoll got so drunk at his daughter's wedding he blew his own goddamn head off. Dave Whitlock was seventy-five when he got run over by a bunch of Mexicans running from the deportation police.

But Lester Lee was still alive and licking numerous assholes just to keep a roof over his head.

What the hell happened to the American Dream?

They were getting drunk on cheap whiskey out behind Davey's old barn when Hal said what had been scratching at all their minds during that hot summer of '53.

"They're makin' us look like a bunch o' shitheads."

"Who's that?" Lester Lee asked.

"Goddamn *Colored Business District*," Hal spat. "Oughtta be a goddamn law."

"Damn right," Lester Lee proclaimed. "We're American citizens, ain't we? Supposed to have a say about how this town runs."

"Oh, we're *gonna* have our say," Hal snarled. Then he stood up and threw down the whiskey bottle. "Let's go."

"Hey!" Corny whined. "That one's still got..."

"Shut the fuck up, Corny!" Hal barked.

They'd rounded up forty or fifty like-minded ol' boys, advising them to bring heat in case they met armed resistance. They stopped over at the Driscoll's filling station and paid for the extra gasoline. Then they crossed the railroad tracks and headed into the neighborhood they called Darky Town.

They started with the barbershop.

It was well after midnight, so all the shops were shuttered. The two-mile stretch of Lincoln Avenue that cut through the center of Darky Town was deserted (although anybody unlucky enough to have spotted them never had the courage to come out and admit it later). They'd filled the night air with the crash of shattered glass and the smell of burning leather before Clarence Dozier showed up.

The black barber had brought along five of the other "colored businessmen," all of them carrying shotguns. Since Hal Corliss was the sheriff at the time and everybody looked to him to set the tone, he simply raised his shotgun and blew ol' Clarence's head off.

After that, the boys opened up on Darky Town's most prominent citizens for a total of fifteen seconds. During the brief gunplay, Jasper Douglas, the Grand Wizard of their Klan chapter, took a shotgun blast in the shoulder. He lost his right arm to infection six days later. The other side hadn't fared nearly so well.

The boys had fanned out, up and down Lincoln Avenue, rousting the residents as they roved and whooped from house to house. They'd given the suckers the business alright, burning and beating and killing as they went. Most of Darky Town was in flames and the residents scattered to the four winds or dead by the time they broke into the First Shiloh Missionary Baptist Church.

They caught the girl hiding in the upstairs toilet.

Somebody suggested having a little fun with her before they burned the church, so Lester Lee pistol whipped her to shut her up. Then he and Corny dragged her out to the field behind the old church while Hal, Frankie and Davey lit the fires.

In the wicked glare of that burning, Hal and the others had returned to find Lester Lee with his pants down, grinding away at the bloody, half-conscious girl, while Corny cheered him on.

"Get in there, boy!" Corny cried. "Get her face down in that mud!"

Hal and the others took their turns, then Corny shot the girl. After that, they'd headed over to Copley's Diner to celebrate. *That* was where Lester Lee met Alice and her perfect ass. Old man Copley was Alice's daddy and Alice waited tables there on alternate Saturdays. She also smoked Chesterfields like a man.

Lester Lee had felt so relaxed that he'd immediately asked Alice out. She'd offered him a cigarette, and he accepted, mostly on account of how cool Bill Holden looked in *Stalag 17*, Lester Lee's favorite movie that summer. They'd gotten married the following Spring.

Fifty years later, Alice and the boys were dead.

Most of Darky Town's residents had been chased off, never to return. The powers-that-be had rebuilt Lincoln Avenue and welcomed a whole generation of decent *American* small businesses to invest in the town's future.

But as for the patriots who'd gotten Lincolndale's renaissance rolling? Well, here sat Lester Lee, shitting his life away and reminiscing about the good old days.

"Was it a good day for Edith Frazier?"

"Ah hell," Lester Lee growled. (He'd been talking to himself a lot since Alice died.) "Don't start that crap again."

For that was the colored girl's name, *Edith Anne Frazier*. She was the daughter of Ben Frazier, the only colored dentist in town. Lester Lee had shot the uppity son of a bitch on that very same special night; tagged him right through the left lens of his prissy little eyeglasses.

"That was a long time ago," Lester Lee whined. "That girl... all that stuff is ancient history."

"She lived," the voice said. "Others died."

"How the hell was I supposed to know about them," Lester Lee cried. "That wasn't my fault!"

"You laughed while they burned."

"Nobody told me," Lester Lee shot back. "What the hell were they *doin'* down there in the first place?"

"Seeking sanctuary."

Lester Lee froze. He'd just remembered where he was.

"Nineteen children, Lester Carson," the voice continued. "Hiding in the church basement."

"Wait..." Lester Lee said. Something was wrong.

"Hiding from you."

The voice in his head...

"Trapped by the flames."

At first Lester Lee thought he'd imagined it, like so many times before.

What do y'all want? Please... we don't want any trouble!

But now the voice from his nightmares was here.

In his house.

Lester Lee stood up and was immediately rewarded with a blast of red -hot agony. The chemical fire in his rectum commanded him to take a seat.

"Oowww!" he wailed. "Oh... you cocksuckin' son of a whore!"

The bathroom door clicked open.

"*Hey!*" Lester Lee roared. "Who the fuck is that?"

The door slowly swung open, and Lester Lee saw who it was.

The girl from the colored church stood in the doorway. She was covered in something that looked like a hospital gown stained black with dried blood. And she looked exactly as she had that night, fifty years ago.

"Corny..." Lester Lee stammered. "Corny *shot* you!"

The girl let the bloody hospital gown slip from her shoulders, revealing the puckered, pinkish brown knots of scar tissue where her left breast should have been.

"Thief."

The floor lurched beneath Lester Lee and bucked him off to the toilet. He sprawled, with his pants down around his ankles, at the nude girl's bloody brown feet.

"Wait," Lester Lee commanded. "You just wait one *goddamn minute!*"

Agony stabbed the sole of his right foot. Galvanized by the new pain, Lester Lee looked behind him.

"What... *what the fuck is that?!?*"

Something had him by the foot. Before he could make sense of what he saw, a geyser of dark red water blasted out of the toilet-bowl and smashed the seat into the ceiling. The porcelain tank cracked open, and in an instant, Lester Lee was soaked.

The dark thing rose up out of the toilet bowl.

Black, sinuous and dripping with muck, the thing thickened as it emerged. The main trunk split into two separate stalks, only to re-braid itself and repeat the same multiplication, each stalk splitting and re-braiding, until a horde of writhing tendrils whipped and swiped swathes of filth across the walls and ceiling. It was one of the smaller tendrils that had gripped Lester Lee's foot.

"Oh..." Lester Lee said, as the rising shadow of the black stalk fell across his face. "My... *God!*"

"A god of thieves," the nude girl said. "Now... I'm God."

A long black tendril separated from the central stalk and whipped itself around Lester Lee's right ankle. Lester Lee's howls were drowned out by the crackle of scorching meat; the tentacle *burned.*

"It wasn't me," Lester Lee shrieked. "Hal! It was Hal and Davey!"

Then the burning tentacle snapped his right ankle.

Lester Lee whooped in a great gasp to scream as a warm red mist obscured his vision. Another appendage whipped out of the toilet and wrapped around his left calf, searing into his flesh. Lester Lee scrabbled at the floor, fighting to resist the thing from the shitter.

"Burns," he hollered. "You dirty bitch... that *buuurns*!"

Another hissing limb reached up between his legs and wrapped around his left thigh. His skin smoked as the tentacle melted flesh and sank into muscle, seeking his bones. More appendages grabbed his wrists, and now Lester Lee saw what held him.

The tentacles were made of *hair*: weaving stalks whipped and snapped at the air around Lester Lee as limbs made of hair, clots of blood and every stinking foulness seared his flesh like battery acid.

"I'm... *dying*!" he gasped at the figure obscured by the blood mist. "I got... cancer...!"

The tentacles dragged Lester Lee up onto the toilet until he lay with his head and shoulders across the ruptured bowl. Then one of the tendrils yanked his right arm, dislocating it with a meaty snap.

"Fuck you!" Lester Lee howled. "Fuck every single one of you!"

Then his right shoulder *dislocated,* and he was pulled headfirst into the toilet bowl. Another limb snapped his left arm at the elbow, bent it double and then yanked it from its socket. Black tendrils wrapped around his left leg and pulled until it separated at the hip, then at the knee. Then the whole lower leg unhinged, and Lester Lee kicked himself in the nuts.

The searing black tentacles *digested* Lester Lee. Lester Lee screamed and choked and dissolved, until his spine snapped.

Kisazi threw back her head and accepted the tribute. The warm red mist flowed into her nostrils and pooled in her eyes, filled up her open mouth. It covered every inch of brown skin and smoothed the thick rings of puckered scar tissue across her chest until only flawless skin remained.

Then she was gone.

◆ ◆ ◆

As she walked along Lincoln Avenue, Kisazi recalled the lives of her lost worshippers (for indeed, she had lived them), and she considered her judgment. Then, as Brother Dawn once stretched his fingers over the mountains of Home, the goddess raised her voice and began to sing.

The power of her convocation wound through the dark streets as her *fingers* extended, serpentine shadows as black and prickly as a plague of spiders. They wound past the library and the downtown Starbucks: passing the All-American Barbershop. They crept along the sleeping streets of Lincolndale at her command: For she was *Kisazi*, the Thresher of Men, *She Who Separates* lovers from beloved, only to reunite them at the journey's end. She was the Protector of travelers, the Taker of tolls: The Goddess of Memory and Vengeance.

And centuries of rightful tribute had been stolen.

The children of Lincolndale emerged from the shadows.

Beguiled by sacred songs, one hundred fresh offerings clamored to touch the singer. Every eye adored her as she stooped to caress each pink cheek. As she'd instructed, they'd brought their sharpest toys, and now a hundred blades flickered in the light from Uncle Moon.

She walked and the children followed, leaping and feinting like lion cubs, but slashing only at phantoms, for she would waste no tribute this night.

They reached the outskirts of the town and entered the abandoned cemetery. Kisazi could hear them now: the mortal souls who had once partaken of her blessings, even as she had partaken of their curse.

Some of the very oldest welcomed her with ancient hymns. Others roared. Freed from fear by Brother Death, they condemned her.

"You abandoned us!"

"We prayed to you!

"Waited for you!"

And why and why and why...

Soon, my people she promised. *An answer. Very soon.*

The goddess arrayed the offerings around the graves until the tiny cemetery was encircled. One hundred pale fists raised their blades. One hundred young bodies turned, giggling, to their neighbors, or pressed sharp steel to their own flesh.

Then she commanded them.

"Dance, my darlings."

As one, their blades fell and rose again, fell and sank deep as the offerings slashed and hacked. With every plunge of a knife, every slice of a scalpel or thrust of a screwdriver, the blood mist thickened and spread across the cemetery, and within that swirling cloud the offerings laughed and danced and killed. Only when the soil of the old cemetery had been soaked did the ancient souls reply.

They rose quickly, as spirits sometimes will, and consumed the sacrifice. Soon, each spirit was strong enough to command his or her new body to stand. With new eyes they watched the Thresher of Men kneel, and press her brow against the bloody earth.

"Precious ones," she whispered. "I was lost to myself, and to you. I beg your forgiveness."

The oldest souls wondered then, to see one of the Old Gods abase herself before slaves.

"Enough," they cried. "She has released us from her brother Death!"

"Yes," Kisazi said. "And ordained a new journey for you. Listen."

With new ears they listened, and heard a great wailing; a roar of grief so deep it filled the night with mourning. Even the ancient dead cried out to hear such suffering.

"The soil of this world was sown with their grief," the goddess said. "This nation was built upon the broken backs and shattered hearts of your children, and even their children's children."

"Yes," the spirits cried. "Where's their share of the harvest?"

"I have weighed the cost of their passage," the goddess said. "I will redeem their suffering."

"We've been deceived by false gods before," the younger spirits warned. "How may we trust another?"

So Kisazi sang of a new world, a land of warm blood and soft flesh, and of *life* unending for a thousand generations. And as she sang, she retrieved a scalpel from the red soil, raised her chin, and pressed the blade against her throat.

"My blood will strengthen you," she said. "My blessing will increase your numbers, and together, you will reclaim your destinies."

With divine strength, she sliced the blade across her jugular vein.

When they understood the benedictions the goddess offered, even the youngest spirits drank from her, and they honored her and offered their forgiveness.

Dying again, the goddess laughed at the sounds of her children as they faded into the night, and she remembered dancing in the rain with her siblings, their silver eyes glinting, every shining face upturned as sharp teeth parted to drink the storm.

Dance, little one! Your trial has not yet come. Dance!

So stern! Harsher even than Brother Death!

How they'd danced, those immortal spirits, golden hearts and shadow-limbs pulsing with every drumbeat from Uncle Thunder.

"Tell them all," she whispered. "They're free."

This time, she remembered joy.

Officer Danny Driscoll had just locked his front door when his wife tapped him on the shoulder. Driscoll spun around with his Glock 19 gripped in his right fist.

"Dammit, Tiffany!" he hissed. "Never sneak up on an armed man in the dark!"

Tiffany Driscoll waved away his admonitions. Her eyes were wide in the blue glow from her smartphone.

"What's happening?"

"Quiet," Driscoll snarled. "You turn out all the lights like I said?"

"Danny... what's going on out there?"

Driscoll shuddered. "It's all over the radio. Kids... damn crazy..."

"What do you mean *kids*?"

"They're going crazy! Killing people... all over town!"

Tiffany's face turned even paler in the blue-white glow. "*Killing* people...?"

"I responded to a domestic disturbance at Brad Krieger's place," Driscoll said. "When I got there... *oh Jesus!*"

"Danny, you're freaking me out!"

Driscoll forced himself to speak slowly. He had to keep it together for Tiffany, and for Jessica, their twelve-year-old daughter.

"The Chief's kids... They were covered in blood and...and there were these... *things*!"

"What "things?""

"The kids were on top of them... *naked*... And the... black *things*... Jesus, Tiff... they were crawling everywhere... hissing like snakes! *And... the kids were feeding pieces of Brad and Dottie to those things!*"

Upstairs, something roared with a million throats.

"What was that?" Tiffany said. "Danny... *what was that?*"

"No," Driscoll moaned. "Jessie?"

"Daddy."

Black blessings slithered up the stairs leading up to the second floor. Blood-red veins pulsed beneath the plaster of the ceiling and the walls at the top of the stairs. A pale figure stood on the landing, shrouded in writhing shadows.

"He was scared, daddy," it whispered. "He remembered you and you denied him. So he ran."

The shape stepped into the wobbly blue illumination.

When Tiffany Driscoll saw what the blessings had made of her daughter, laughter burst like horror from her lips. Roaring obscenities, she fell to her knees and clawed her own eyes from their sockets.

"Never laughed," Danny Driscoll cried. "I... *nevernevernevernever laughed*!"

Then he bit down on the barrel of his gun and blew his brains out.

"Mommy."

This time, the goddess remembered *judgement;* the taste of bitter tears sour as spoiled mother's milk. She opened her arms to embrace the shrieking blind woman, bright blades glistening in her infinite hands.

"*We're so hungry.*"

She remembered everything.

And she would never forgive.

IFE-IYOKU, THE TALE OF IMADEYUNUAGBON

EKPEKI OGHENECHOVWE DONALD

The hunting party waited quietly at *Igbo Igboya*, the forest of fears. Morako oversaw the hunt; he was a *lero* or feeler. The rest waited to move on his signal. But for now, he lay waiting, careful not to alert the beast lest the intended prey became the hunter. Here, the roles of the prey and the hunter could switch in a flash, leaving the hunter to scurry for survival. But he knew that the father Obatala himself had chosen them and imbued them with sacred gifts which, though not making them immune, offered them a measure of protection.

The Nlaagama slithered forward. At almost twelve feet tall, the enormous, lizard-like beast towered over banana trees. Its forked tongue, about eight inches, swung pendulously and tasted the air. It bent on the bait left by the Umzingeli hunters, a horse-like antelope with thick, strong legs and a horn like the mythical creatures of the old world. The Nlaagama ripped into the antelope with the savagery that made Morako swallow.

With the beast distracted, Morako gave the signal. The Umzingeli, four coal black forms, detached themselves from the trees around. The beast stirred only momentarily before resuming its feeding. The Umzingeli merged with the environment, activating the power of *anjayiyan-okan*, the chameleon mind, and becoming part of the environment to remain hidden and undetectable until they detached themselves.

The beast would sense them soon. Morako signalled them again and they ran towards the beast with their spears extended. It stood still, trying to detect them, sensing that something was wrong.

Morako shot a spike of placidity at the beast. It struggled to cast off the artificial lethargy. The warriors were closing on it. They needed to be close enough to access the gaps between its scales. Without their skill of merging, the beast would detect them before they got close enough to use their weapons. This was the tricky part: attacking while maintaining the chameleon mind, the delicate merger that allowed them to move silently and remain invisible.

This was not a static merging which shielded them completely from detection. It was a minute merger of their feet with the ground and the leaves and twigs and droplets of water as they ran. It was activated as they stepped, but deactivated when their feet left the ground, so that they had to consciously reactivate with each step. It was more difficult and required a delicate touch and a continuous synchronization with the environment. It was a skill that only the best of the Umzingeli could use. Properly timed, it enabled them to mask their movement as when they used static merger in complete stillness.

They were within striking distance of the beast when it reared suddenly and howled, shaking its neck violently and throwing something off from its back. The last hunter materialised some yards away and Morako noticed the broken half of the spear protruding from the back of the beast. It was wounded but far from defeated. He stared at it. The hunter pulled out another spear and twirled it, preparing to attack. The beast pawed the earth and roared, belching liquid flames at the hunter. From his vantage, Morako saw the hunter roll out of the path of the lava like substance the monster spat and vanish, re-merging and blending into the environment. The beast howled again as a spear found its way into one of the gaps between its scales. The beast bathed the clearing with lava, turning to search if the burnt body of a hunter would appear. None did.

But it seems to Morako that the beast could perceive the hunter, though it could not see him. It screeched and two large wings unfurled from its body. With its enormous wings, the beast fanned the air. In a swift movement, it lifted itself off the ground.

Morako nudged the Climbers. It was time for their role. As the beast soared upwards, the Climbers dropped a net from the trees and entangled its wings, dropping it to the ground. Flames cackled around, and the climbers, armed with clubs and spears, attacked it. The beast snapped at most of their attacks as it ripped the net with its claws and fangs. Morako knew the reinforcements would be in trouble if the beast managed to free itself. He signalled the remaining hunter who materialised as from thin air and buried his spear in the neck of the beast. As the hunter yanked his spear out, hot sizzling blood spurted from the wound, scalding the climbers as they scurried away. The hunter backed off to join the other hunters where they had been knocked off. The beast belched liquid fire amidst its dying throes, panting but refusing to die.

A figure walked in, dragging a tree trunk. It was Oni, the elephant man. The climbers and hunters made way for him. He hefted the trunk and walloped the dying beast in the head. He didn't need to do it twice.

WEAVER

Morako arrived just in time to catch the concluding part of the story which his mother, Ologbon, was weaving for the children. She was old but firm, a consecrated Weaver of Stories, who spun tales that fascinated both the children and the adults. But today's story, Morako knew, was no ordinary tales to fascinate but history to instruct. He felt a sense of loss and longing whenever he heard the story told, and he often turned away to hide the tears budding in his eyes.

It was night in Ife-Iyoku and everywhere was alive with merriment. Elders gulped down their Amala and Ewedu with palm wine and *ogogoro* which flowed freely. Some children danced and laughed at the pursuit of masquerades; others ran around playing games of *Ite* and *Suwe*. Another group of children gathered in front Ologbon, the Weaver, as she enraptured them with tales.

Tonight, the Weaver spun the history of Ife-Iyoku to her attentive audience.

"This is how the people of Ife-Iyoku came to be," she said, pausing until she was sure all of them listened rapturously for her story. "Long before you were born, the world was not like this. It was much bigger and encompassed different countries and cultures. Then there was a war, and all was lost. The contenders attempted the destruction of one another and ended up almost destroying us too. It was a fight between two elephants in which the ground suffers.

"Once we were a vast group of people in Afrika, peoples of special and diverse cultures and breeding. They lived in peace and unity before the war of the nations around them. These nations had developed nuclear weapons but entered into a pact not to use them against one another.

"But the pact was broken, and everyone launched their warheads. The disaster did not come immediately, until America joined in the war. America was the greatest nation in the war at the time and had prepared very well for it. She had missile defence systems in place. She also had systems to seize the missiles in the air and redirect them back to the sender. She had the power to quash the missiles. But she did not do those things. Instead, she wanted to show her power. She wanted to punish the enemies; Middle-Easterners from a faraway continent called Asia who they felt had been causing trouble for everyone. That was how the seed of destruction that is fully grown today was sown. America directed hundreds of nuclear warheads to the enemies, but unknown to America and her partners, the enemies had obtained some of the missile redirecting technology from their allies, China and Russia.

"The enemies had the technology but did not know how to use it properly. Their control of the technology was not strong enough to allow them to send the weapons all the way back to those who sent it to them. Their range was small, and they had friends and allies around them. So, they redirected the weapons to Afrika, the closest place where their friends would not suffer them.

"Nearly all of Afrika was destroyed by the missiles of the combatants. Nothing would have been left of Afrika if not that we are a special people. Our land, Ife, is a sacred ground where all life originated. We were saved because of our connection with the gods, and with the heaven and the earth. We called on Obatala and he interceded on our behalf as he had done when his sister Olokun threatened the world with water in a period known as the age of global warming. He pleaded with Olorun, the sky father, to save us. Olorun urinated in a gourd and told Obatala to sprinkle the water on the affected area and all the destruction and left-over radiation would dissipate.

"The urine was not enough to sprinkle in all the affected parts of the world. Obatala could only use the urine in the healing of the land of his own people. Despite Obatala's intercession, Olorun did not care about the rest of the world. The smoke from the bombs covered the sun and temperatures dropped. Life everywhere was threatened, not just the lives in Afrika. Obatala in his infinite love and mercy decided to share the cure with rest of the world, even though they were responsible for the disaster. With the sacred urine, he was able to wash away the radiation and nuclear waste. However, what was left was insufficient to totally reverse the effect of the bombs in Afrika.

"Obatala cut himself and let some drops of his blood mix with the urine in the gourd to increase its potency. With the mixture he saved Ife. Nothing was left to save the rest of Afrika. Only this small circle around Ife is clean. We are trapped and all around us is the lingering destruction from the folly of man. The first rain that fell after the destruction affected the land and people around Ife. The sacred land rejects and repels the radiation and waste. Our blood and bodies are stronger. We adapted abilities to make up for what we lost and to enable us to survive in this new world. We became *Ndi Lana Riri*, the ones who survived. And what is more, Obatala left us a lasting gift. Each time one of us dies, our blood thickens, and the remaining ones evolve further to make up for the numbers lost with strength. His blood keeps us and strengthens us further to ensure that his people endure. It is said that in the hour of our greatest need, he will return to restore us and the whole of Afrika fully.

"Some may wonder why he saved the world. It is because despite all that happened, survival is collective. If man would survive, we must do so together, as one. We must think of all and not of individuals."

"If we don't die out before that day comes," Chief Olori said. He had been standing for a while with Morako, listening to the story.

The Weaver looked up and saw her husband, the Ooni Olori and Morako. The Ooni tied a wrapper tied around his chest in the manner of Igbo chiefs. Standing beside Morako was a young girl called Imade. She followed Morako with her eyes as he contemplated the children and smiled at them and they smiled back at him.

The Weaver rose to greet the old Chief. "Welcome, husband."

"Thank you," he said affectionately.

The children rose and squatted in greeting.

The Chief turned to his wife. "The fell beast has been slain. Imade has healed the hunters and drained their bodies of the corruption they contacted in *Igbo Igboya*. The beast lies ready for the final phase of the ceremony and I have come personally to inform you. As Chief Priestess, you must be there to consecrate the sacrifice to Obatala."

The Weaver nodded. He turned to the children to dismiss the campfire session, but she raised a finger to forestall him.

"The night's session is not done," the Weaver said. "The Chiefs' Council may be your domain, but this is mine. Obatala entrusted this sacred task on me and my successor. My time is nigh, and I must do as much of my duty as I can before it comes."

Morako watched in silence as husband and wife exchanged words. Imade caught his eye with a sly smirk on her face. He returned her smile.

"We shall give the Nlaagama in sacrifice to Obatala in this festival," the Weaver was saying to the children. "Every day before this festival, our best warriors must go to hunt these creatures which have been twisted by the corruption in *Igbo Igboya*. They are for sacrifices to Obatala. It is the only way we can show that we are strong enough to play our part in guarding and preserving the sacred life he gave us with his blood."

The Chief squatted to address the gathering. "I speak in my authority as Ooni, head Chief. Obatala may return, or he may not. Whether Obatala comes or not, we will be strong and lead ourselves to our own destinies. Ife thins every day. The corruption keeps creeping in and the creatures in Igbo Igboya grow more twisted. We have been given the sacred gifts already. We carry the power of our salvation in our blood. In our moment of near destruction, we were mutated and thus acquired resistance to things that would have killed us. Perhaps it was Obatala who had done this for us; perhaps it was not him. Whatever the cause or reason, we have become stronger than we were before. We have acquired the ability to heal and manipulate the elements. Every time one of us dies, our powers wax stronger. Let us use these gifts to counteract our possible extinction. Our powers were less when we were more. With the reduction in our population, our gifts have been strengthened. The gifts call on us to use them. We must take our destiny in our own hand, whether Obatala returns or not."

The Weaver clicked her tongue and asked: "Is this another exhortation for migration? You know that we have tried that before and many were lost. There is no way through the corruption surrounding Ife. The outside world does not even know we exist. This issue has been raised before the council and voted down."

The Chief raised a placatory hand. "This is not the council, woman. I merely informed them of what they must face someday."

He turned to the children. "Tomorrow is your first day in the house of learning. You will be tested. All who are old enough will begin training on how to use the sacred gifts you are imbued with and how to take on your sacred duty of survival so that someday you may face and take on your destiny. You are no longer children. You will be great men and women of Ife-Iyoku." He thumped his chest and all the people did the same.

He continued. "With the permission of the Weaver of tales and teacher of the sacred lore of Obatala, we go to offer the beast as sacrifice to Obatala in honour of our sacred charge to survive."

The Weaver pulled out a clay cup and beckoned to one of the children to come forward. He took the cup from her, drew in his breath and dragged with his fingers as if pulling something, his focus on the cup. There was a rushing sound. He handed the cup to the weaver and resumed his seat. She put the cup to her mouth and took a pull. Water leaked out and ran down her mouth. The Chief looked at the child and nodded in approval. The child beamed with pleasure.

The Weaver set the cup down and explained. "This is our ritual. Talking is thirsty work and Ake here keeps me hydrated. He is a puller and can pull the elements. He helps me with water after our sessions."

"That is very good, but we will need more than a cup of water to survive," the Chief muttered.

"I heard that," the Weaver said.

"Well, the festival awaits."

"One more thing," the Weaver said as she manipulated her light weaving gifts in complex patterns. A trail of light followed her fingers. The light glowed brighter until it became a full ball of light. She released it and it shot into the night. It exploded in a brilliant rainbow of colours and illuminated everywhere. The hitherto solemn children jumped up squealing and screaming in joy and wonder, running, laughing and clutching each other. The Chief shook his head in amusement as the four adults went walking after them towards the festival grounds.

The Chief turned to the Weaver and asked, "The substance that Ake pulled couldn't have conjured palm wine, could it?"

The Weaver sniffed. "You know very well that at his age, the wonder is that he could do anything at all. Besides, from what palm trees could he have pulled the moisture? He could only pull water from the moisture in the environment. It was even a bit salty, and I think there must have been some sweat mixed with it."

"What a shame," the Chief said. "If he could conjure palm wine, that would have been something."

FEELER

Later that night, Morako and Imade lay cuddled up on a mat listening to the drumming and singing from the festival and watching the stars. She ran a teasing finger up his arm, her breath warm against his cheek. He trembled at her touch, as though it drained something from within him.

She whispered in his ear, "Why does a warrior like you tremble at my simple touch?"

"You know that my skill as a feeler makes me more susceptible to your touch. I *feel* an overwhelming warmth seeping from you whenever you touch me. Yet each time I ask you to be joined to me as a full-grown woman who has passed all the rites of womanhood, you refuse. Why do you keep refusing me?"

"That is not the case, my strong one. Just that I am not sure of joining with you and bringing a child into this uncertain world."

"But it's our sacred duty to survive and that involves..."

She lifted her hand and looked at him reproachfully. "Sacred duty, is it? You're all about duty and nothing more!"

"I desire you, my love. I want more than just fulfilment of duty from you."

She drew closed and nibbled on his ear lobe and clutched him tightly. "Maybe someday when things change, we will get our desire. I assure you that my refusal is not about you but about other things. You are sufficient for me. I can desire nothing more in a mate."

"I am quite assured of your affections," he said. "But let us try not to burn down Ife-Iyoku with the fire emanating from your body."

"But you do like it, don't you? When I nudge your body and dampen your pain receptors and enhance your immune system. Like this.' She ran a finger down his belly and drew on her gift, sending a line of energy into him.

"Will you not do that!" he said, but he could not extricate himself from her. The art of healing was an art of bodily control and manipulation and he was powerless to resist her. He watched as she tinkered with him, revelling in the passion coursing through him. When her palm reached down his crotch, he said, "Do not wake the beast, unless you are ready to do battle."

"The beast was already awake," she said with a sly smile. "I am merely teasing it. And who said I am not ready for battle?"

She drew his mouth to hers and kissed him. He drew her closer, pulled her wrapper over their heads and shut out the sounds of merriment without, while within they created their own happiness.

OUTREACH

Next morning, Ooni Olori stood in front of the thatched town hall where the children of eligible age waited for their training. The children were seated cross-legged on mats before him, chattering noisily amongst themselves. The Ooni carried a supple cane which he slapped against his palm. The children fell silent and he started to speak to them in a grave voice.

He talked of their sacred duty as men and women of Ife-Iyoku. Men were designated to be hunters as they were naturally stronger and faster, while women were healers and growers and weavers. That was how nature distributed the abilities to them. Both sexes could be equally endowed as climbers, see-ers, feelers, light weavers, and pullers. They would use these abilities in service of all the survivors of Ife. They would be trained by the older and experienced heads in the community and grow their gifts and use them for the collective benefit of all the children of the sky father Olorun and small father Obatala.

"Of course, all your abilities are not for the community," the Chief continued. "You may use your ability to acquire your own personal possessions. You may exchange what you produce with others who produce other things. You may sell what you produce with your ability and receive cowries in return. But a measure of whatever you make in whatever department you are placed goes into the central silo for the collective use of everyone when the need arises."

He paused and scanned the children; their unflinching attention was on him. "Perilous times lie ahead in our battle for survival. There will come a time of drought when the rain will resist the call of the pullers. There will come a time when the land will refuse the call of the growers. There will come a time when the hunters will be hard pressed to find meat. What shall we do then?"

He waited, as if for an answer. None came. He continued. "That is why we must contribute to the general silo. Our survival is collective. We must collectively prepare against tomorrow. We must provide for those among us who are too old or sick for the touch of healers to bring reprieve. Survival is the noble task for which all must put their gifts to achieving."

The Chief motioned to the attendants who were mostly women to administer the Age test. The Age test was administered by having the children put one hand over their heads. The child whose arm could touch his or her ear was qualified. The children who could not do this were adjudged too young and were sent home to continue their baby days with their mothers until they were older.

The children who passed the Age Test were adjudged old enough to proceed to the next stage. Their development would be observed by their teachers and families to see which gifts they had aptitude for. At the end of the one year of teaching, there would be interviews to discern those whose gifts had not developed or were not obvious. Those whose gifts had sufficiently manifested would be paired with gifted teachers who would help them build their gifts until adjudged ready to pass the rite into full manhood or womanhood. Those who had no gifts or whose gifts fail to manifest would be sent with other adults to learn any general task or skill they had inclination for. In that way, everyone—the gifted and the ungifted— would be useful. They had to survive, by ordinary or extraordinary means. This was the sacred charge of Obatala and it would be carried out till the day of his return to save all Afrika in fulfilment of the prophecy.

The Ooni clapped his staff on his hand and the class dispersed. The ones who passed the Age Test were to assemble the next day in the village's eastern town hall for the commencement of their classes.

As he left the town hall, the Ooni walked to a small hut that stood between rows of trees at the outskirt of the village. He took out a key from his wrapper and opened the door to the hut and walked in. He pulled out a beautifully designed foot mat from the floor to uncover a compartment dug into the floor. From this compartment he pulled a plain looking but strong box. He unlocked the box and brought out several items from it. They included what looked like a car battery from the old world, a pair of wires, a transistor radio, satellite phone and two more items. He fiddled with the satellite phone until it came on. He connected other devices to the battery and pressed a button and a voice issued forth.

SEE-ER

Classes and other tasks were over for the day. It was late afternoon, approaching evening, and classes were over for the day. Morako who oversaw one of the classes was just dismissing his students when Imade came to pick him up. He was with a lad who stayed back after the rest had gone.

"I will be taking Ake to see one of the see-ers," Morako said, nodding towards the lad. "He appears to be a puller and has been developing an unusual amount of aptitude for one so young. I want them to do a reading to see if it is fortunate for Ife-Iyoku."

"Have you talked to Ooni Olori about it?" Imade asked.

"No, I haven't. It is my duty as head trainer to determine the aptitude of a pupil under me, not abdicate it to my father. And come to think of, I think I feel a special kinship with this one. I am curious as to what the see-ers will see in his fortune."

Imade shrugged and bent to interact with the young lad. "How are you Ake?"

"I am fine, aunty Imade," the young one replied shyly.

"Can you go home to nana while I and uncle Morako get somewhere? We will see you at tomorrow's class."

He looked to Morako who was watching with a slight frown on his face. Morako shrugged and nodded. The boy whooped and ran merrily home.

Morako said, "Do you mind telling me what this is about, why you prevented me..."

"Sacred duty," she cut in with a smile. "I know it is always sacred duty with you. But I want some time with you. I want you to accompany me somewhere." She was already leading the way and he followed.

"Where to?"

"Across the southern farms and towards the..."

"Shrine of the See-ers?" he interrupted her. She nodded.

"Then why did you..."

"I told you I want some time alone with you."

He was silent for a few seconds. She sighed and said, "You're not subtle at all,

Morako. I can feel your words dying to be said, so you might as well spill them."

"Well," he said slowly and carefully, as if sensing a trap with the invitation to talk and wary to spring it by talking. "Sometimes I feel that you challenge my authority just for the fun of it."

She raised an eyebrow but did not say anything.

"I see how you enjoy watching my mother challenge my father's authority."

She tried to look solemn but failed and broke into a grin. "Yes, I enjoy that. What about it?"

He frowned.

She turned squarely at him. "Have you ever wondered what it feels like to be a woman? For all your gifts as a *lero* and the most sensitive of men, the plight of womanhood is beyond you. You cannot understand how it feels to be handed tasks and opinions and expected to just follow suit because you are a woman."

"It is the way of things for men to lead. Only a man can be Ooni or hunter. It is how it has always been."

"Who made it so?" she queried, then added wistfully as if confessing a secret, "I have sometimes wondered what it would be like to be able to train as a hunter or to have the gift of Ooni, a leader. To do something beyond the roles assigned to me as a woman."

"Well," he said indifferently, "the blood of Obatala gives us the gifts suited to our roles. Men are hunters because they possess the strength and speed to guard the boarder from beasts that move in from the corruption. And only he who would be Ooni gets the gift of leader. Women get other gifts and have their place in the sacred order of things. On women's shoulders lies the most sacred charge of our continuity."

She sniffed.

He continued, "Truly, survival is our most sacred duty and only women may fully enable us fulfil it."

"Well, you play your part," she said wryly. "And you know, it doesn't always come in that order. Sometimes women get the gifts of men. Rarely perhaps, but it does happen. And men also get the gifts of women, like you for example." She looked up at him. His face had darkened.

Morako said, "You know that my case is different. I am a man, and the son of the Ooni. Those two things are absent in the case of the women. A man is set in how he sees things. It would be difficult for him to see things differently. Look around you," he gestured at the surroundings. They were in the Southern farms. Several women were working the soil, tilling and planting and going about other different tasks.

"Without the powers of the growers," Morako continued, "we wouldn't have enough food to feed ourselves. So, their work is important enough."

Imade looked away. "Forgive me, but I don't find anything extraordinary in the tilling of the soil."

Morako held her hand and stopped her in mid-motion. "Why do you run away from womanhood so much? I see you with children. You don't do so badly. You would do quite well with your own."

She unclasped her hand from his and resumed walking. "I just don't see myself raising children in Ife-Iyoku as it is. To what end will I raise them? To serve in fixed roles instead of doing what they wanted? To bring the children up to be content to be guards if they were men or breeders if female, for duty's sake? To bring them up merely to survive? I want more for them."

She noticed that Morako had stopped walking. He wore a hurt expression. She walked back to him and cupped his face. "I do care for you, but I just can't accept life the way it is. I want more."

She took his hand and pulled him gently. "Your father requested a see-er and a babalawo for a reading. There's a judgement for a matter set for this evening. We best hurry if we must catch up—on our duty." She said the last phrase with a smile. His mouth quirked too, and he followed.

Morako and Imade walked to one of the huts to inquire of Omenga the wise. An old woman was lying on a mat in front of the hut and another woman was fanning and tending her. They stopped to inquire what was wrong with the woman and where they could find Omenga. The woman on the mat reared up suddenly, her old wasted hand clawing at the sky. She rasped: "The boy...the one you should have come with... will destroy us all. She..." looking strangely at Imade, "will be the last...the last of us. Obatala will return..."

Her head fell back into the mat and she resumed her former position as if nothing had happened, as if she had not seen them.

Morako was alarmed, but when he looked at Imade, there was only solemnity on her face but no sign of worry over the woman's words.

Imade said, "I am a healer. Can I help her?"

"No," said the woman tending to her. "She is a see-er and is merely facing the affliction of the mind. It comes to all see-ers when they use the sight too much or peer too far into the other side. It is not a thing your healing can touch. She woke a few days ago after a dream and laid her mat here saying she had a message for you. She was greatly distraught at what she saw and kept trying to use the sight to glimpse more. She eventually fell into this state today. But before she did, she said to leave her here till you came, and she would deliver her message when you did."

Morako shifted uncomfortably. Questions lingered on his lips, but before he could ask them, the woman tending to the sick woman was talking again.

"The House of Omenga is the last house by the road behind the house next to ours. It is just as she said. Before she entered her present state, she told us that you would inquire of Omenga."

When they got to the hut of Omenga, he was sitting outside tying a wrapper on his waist, with white chalk drawn round his left eye. Several cowries hung from his hands and neck.

"I have been waiting for you Imade," the wise one said, looking at her and ignoring him. "You are the last woman."

Imade was taken aback but said nothing.

Morako sighed, and Omenga looked at him as if seeing him for the first time. "Morako, son of Olori, you were still a boy suckling at the Weaver's tits when last I saw you. That was long after she gave up her position as my apprentice."

Morako opened his mouth to ask question, to say something, but Omenga rose to his feet and said, "We best be on our way. The fate of Ife-Iyoku waits to be decided."

Morako shuffled along.

TRIAL

Imade and Morako stood in the town hall after bringing Omenga before Ooni Olori and the Ogboni, Council of Chiefs. On their way to the town hall, they had recounted what transpired at the abode of the sick old woman and Omenga received it solemnly, promising that he would get to its root after the hearing and judgement. But for now, the Ooni and the Ogboni had an official business at hand: the dispensation of justice.

Morako and Imade waited. In a short while, several families strode into the hall and waited at the end. Some sat on stools they had brought, others on their own mats. The victim and the accused walked in and stood in the middle of the semi-circle formed by the judges consisting of the Ooni and the Ogboni. This was the setting for judicial administration in Ife-Iyoku; once a determination has been made by the combined gathering of the Ooni and the Ogboni, the hunters would be entrusted with the execution of the judgment.

The victim alleged that the accused was her husband's friend and had sought for her to be tied to him while she was a maiden, but she had refused. Nonetheless, he remained in good terms with her husband, although he knew that the accused had always lusted for her. On this particular day, while her husband was away, the accused stole into her bed and violated her while she slept. She became aware of what the accused had done when she woke up and saw semen around her crotch. In addition to violating her, the intruder also took her jewels.

She found out his identity through her neighbours who had seen the accused come in and leave her chamber. She then called upon the neighbours who swore in the name of the gods that it was the accused whom they had seen enter and leave the complainant's house within the period.

The accused was called upon to state his case. He agreed that he had indeed gone to his friend's house within the period but had found his friend absent. He also agreed that he wanted his friend's wife and had always done so since she refused to be joined to him and chose his friend instead. But on this occasion, seeing her near-naked on her bed, he was so overtaken with his desire that he stood astride her and fondled himself until he emitted his semen upon her. It was his way of sating his desire for her. As for her cowries, he denied taking or even seeing it at all.

When the facts were fully set out and corroborated by the witnesses, the Ooni addressed everyone.

"This man here is facing a charge of violation and theft. It is hard for us to treat the evidence as proof of her violation, as he insists, he did not touch her. But her husband is a hunter and crime against a hunter carries weight. So, it shall be treated weightily.

"Violation of another man's woman is a grave wrong, but in times like this when our survival is hanging on a thread, violation can be tolerated if it results in the production of a child. If Okanga had violated a maiden who had not been joined to another man, it would have been a simpler matter, and we should have asked them to be joined together so that the fruit of the act may be raised properly. But this woman here has been joined with another man, a hunter and one of the honourable men of Ife-Iyoku. Okanga did not just violate this woman but also betrayed his fellow brother and hunter. And besides his act of betrayal, he also stole her cowries. An act of stealing is not just against the victim but also against the people of Ife-Iyoku and Obatala himself, for our lives and possessions are united. We must eschew greed, for greed is of Eshu the mischief maker. It is what led to the war of separation. It will not be tolerated here."

He paused and seemed to draw his breath before he asked, "Is the offended husband here?"

"No," replied one of the guards.

"How can he not be here when he is the aggrieved party?" asked one of the chiefs in annoyance. "The cowries belong to the wife, but he is her head and the one defrauded."

One of the hunters came forward and offered an explanation: "He vowed to kill Okanga should he ever set eyes on him again. In fact, he tried and had to be restrained and it took great persuasion by the elders to get him to agree to submit to the law of the Ogboni council. We had to promise him that we would see maximum justice is meted out."

Chief Elumelu muttered, "The young and hot-blooded."

"Peace, Elumelu," the Ooni said. "He is a hunter and it is in their nature to be hot-blooded. However, killing will not be condoned. All life is precious in Ife-Iyoku, even the life of an offender. In the days before the war of separation, we did not kill our own. How can we now kill our own people when we are charged with the sacred duty of survival? How can we take the life that we did not give? It is Obatala's prerogative to give and take life. But," he turned to Okanga, "you have threatened the peace of Ife-Iyoku. Your friend desires war with you, and we cannot have that here. Were he willing to forgive, it would be another matter. He has expressed his unwillingness for peace by absenting himself from this proceeding. For that, he will be called to order later. But for now, we must respect his resolve as a hunter. You both cannot coexist here if we must have peace. You must leave Ife-Iyoku. For your crimes and threatening the peace in Ife-Iyoku, I pronounce you Mbadiwe and you are henceforth exiled from Ife-Iyoku."

The guilty hunter protested that he had not stolen the cowries of the woman but was set up to be punished. She knew his actions, improper as they were, did not merit grievous punishment, so she framed him up for stealing. But the judgment had been passed and would not be recalled. Okanga was dragged away by a group of hunters appointed to execute the judgment.

Ologbon the weaver, having been summoned by Omenga, now walked in with the other chiefs of Ife-Iyoku who constituted the Ogboni. There were grave tidings to deliberate on. One of the chiefs pointed at Morako and Imade and asked, "Are they allowed here?"

"Let them be," the Ooni said. "They are part of what we want to discuss."

They broke kolanut and chewed them noisily, and beyond the noise of their chewing, there was silence. The matter before them was the gravest they had had to contend with since the War and their first attempt to emigrate from Ife-Iyoku. Besides Morako and Imade who sat apart as observers, Ologbon was the only other female in the gathering and she was there by virtue of her position as Chief priestess of Obatala.

Omenga cleared his throat and started. "The gods have made their revelations to those in commune with them. What I have seen with my eyes, my mouth is reluctant to speak. But it is not for me to say. It is for the Ooni on whom the gods have laid the burden of leadership in Ife-Iyoku."

The Ooni's voice was cleared and controlled when he spoke. "When you have a poisoned fruit to feed another, it will not grow sweeter by keeping. There is no point in stretching the revelation of the inevitable. My people, was it not for this that the head which assumes leadership must wear an iron crown?"

The gathering cheered, and the Ooni continued. "The gods lure us with the powers they have placed at our disposition. I have used my power in my attempt to find salvation for Ife-Iyoku and what I have done I did for her good."

In the brief silence that followed the Ooni's pause, everyone in the gathering stretched their necks. Then, when the Ooni seemed unwilling to continue, one of the chiefs asked, "What have you done, our Ooni?"

"I have been in contact with the outside world."

The silence that followed was of inexpressible shock.

"It is my sacred duty to find a way for my people," the Ooni continued. "We dwindle with each passing day. The evil prophecy of our extinction is never nearer its fulfilment than now. Perhaps it was meant as a warning, for us to find our way out before we die to the last man."

The implication of the Ooni's words had sunk on all present and their silence was transformed to whispers.

"I have been in contact with the outside world for a while now," the Ooni continued. "I had negotiations with them. They offered to help us evacuate our people using aircrafts."

He paused and looked around. The whispering voices had died, and all eyes were fixed on him. "Those I contacted wanted to know how many we were, how we survived and our location."

The weaver gasped. "And you divulged our secrets to them, these strangers? Who are they?"

The Ooni shook his head. "I contacted them using a universal outreach radio. Yet, the only places it could reach were nearby places. They did not at first understand me, but they got an interpreter."

"So, we do not know who they are, but they know who we are?" the weaver asked.

"We need them," the Ooni said, his voice impatient. "They cannot help us without knowing our identity."

"But you embarked on this course alone. That was wrong, my head and head of Ife-Iyoku. It is not your burden alone to decide and plan the fate of all Ife-Iyoku."

The weaver gestured at the chiefs seated around. They were like a gathering in which the news of death of the clans-head had just been announced. Not one of them said a word in support or against the Weaver's opposition of her husband. Imade and Morako observed in silence.

"In any case," continued the Weaver, "you gave away more than you got. Women have always been more adept at bargaining. Had you let others in on this course of action perhaps we would not have been short-changed for information."

"We have little of value to offer. They barely accepted what we have to give."

"And what have we to give, our Ooni?" one of the chiefs asked.

The Ooni looked down and said in a low voice. "I gave them Mbadiwe, the rejected."

"What?" the elders echoed in unison. The Weaver covered her face.

"They were unwilling to help at first," the Ooni explained. "And they were the only ones I could reach. They wanted something. When I told them of the gifts we have developed, they wanted to have some of us for testing to find out how the gifts worked. So I gave them our location and the leave to take some of the rejected. The Mbadiwe are already lost to us. They are as good as dead to Ife-Iyoku. I did not see what we have to lose by giving them to the strangers in exchange for helping to evacuate our people."

The Weaver said angrily. "In times past, we sold our people as slaves to the white men. Those ones were rejected too. But we did not stop with the selling of the rejected. It became a rampage that led the white men into carting away our people in thousands, and this set us back in development hundreds of years and made us vulnerable in the very war that led to this. Are we doomed to keep repeating the same mistakes?"

"Remember your place woman," one of the elders admonished. "The Ooni is still your husband and our leader, whatever his actions."

The Weaver looked at him with undisguised disgust.

Another of the elders said conciliatorily, "Let us focus on a way forward now. Are we to follow these strangers to a better land? Can we trust these strangers who are willing to use fellow humans in experiments?"

Omenga who had been quiet now spoke. "I looked into the future with my gift as a see-er and consulted all the spirits and ancestors on the other side. I saw visions of the future. I saw soldiers invading Ife-Iyoku. These strangers would not be satisfied with taking the rejected. They will come into Ife-Iyoku and try to take some of us. When Imade and Morako were sent to come and get me, they met Olumo who told them that she foresaw the end of our race, the death of our women and children, and our bondage by these strangers for their experiments. Is this not so?" He directed his question at Imade and Morako and beckoned them draw closer to bear witness.

"It is so," Imade said.

"I will step down as Ooni and face the judgement of the council and new Ooni after this debacle is over," the Ooni said. "This is not the time for rash actions, my people; but I acknowledge the errors of my indiscretion. For now, however, we must find how best to avert this horrible future. We can only do this if we are united."

The Ooni turned to his son Morako. "Send word to the headhunter to call the council of war. And send town criers and alert every hunter in the village to be present. We must prepare to fight for our survival."

COUNCIL

Morako met Imade outside his hut when he got back. She was pacing to and fro. She confronted him immediately, inquiring of him the events that transpired in the council. He took her hands and led her inside the hut where they both sat.

He locked the door before he spoke. "You know I am not supposed to be divulging the words of the *Aare ona kakanfo* and the other war chiefs in a war council to others who are not hunters or of the army." Seeing her slanted eyebrow and the frown on her face, he added, "I'm not supposed to be seen telling you anyway."

Imade tapped her foot impatiently and he continued.

"The Aare Ona kakanfo and the entire council have decided on a plan of attack when the invaders come."

"You mean, defence?"

"War is coming upon us, Imade. We must meet war with war."

"Should we not attempt to confront them and determine their purposes before launching into a war? It is not wise for us to start a war with those we do not know their purposes yet. It seems to me that Ife-Iyoku would be most hesitant to be embroiled in an avoidable war. And you know that we have not hunted after men since the War of separation."

Morako shook his head. "War is already in motion, Imade. The Ooni has already offered them Mbadiwe. Their coming to Ife-Iyoku is an indication of breach of faith. They can only do that if they want more. And don't forget the words of Omenga. He said that this incursion could lead to the end of Ife-Iyoku if not handled carefully. Do you doubt his words?"

Imade was lost in thought, defeated by logic she could not refute.

Morako continued. "More was said in the meeting. In fact, this aspect concerns you. The Aare ona kakanfo and the other war chiefs decided that the women and children must not be left unguarded when the war starts. Being the most vulnerable and most valuable, they will be taken and hidden in the town hall beyond the hills."

Imade shook her head and held up her finger. "I will not be part of such schemes.

You know how I feel about women being treated like little precious object that needs special protection. The women could fight instead of being hidden away. Why hide them away like sheep in what may be our most crucial fight for survival since the war of separation?"

Morako sighed. "The Aare ona kakanfo, the Ooni himself and most of the headhunters agreed that the women should be kept away for the very reason you want them to fight in the war. Our survival is crucial, and the women are the most important ingredient of that survival. Only they can carry the seed of new life. No matter how many men fall in the battle, when it is over, even just one man can populate a village. But with fewer women, this task will be all the harder. We are getting fewer every year and the boundaries of Ife-Iyoku grow smaller."

Imade frowned, but Morako continued. "This was the argument of the head chiefs and the Aare ona kakanfo. Ologbon agreed with them. I argued that some of the women may be useful in battle with their gifts, but I was overruled and told that the hunters cannot afford the distraction of looking after the women while in battle. Women if not killed outrightly can easily be overpowered and taken where a hunter or male warrior would fight to the death."

Imade listened calmly but was unmoved. "They have never entertained the idea that women can be useful. They have only thought women as liabilities from the start."

"Well," he said, "women are more valuable than men here."

"Indeed" she said her eyes glittered and her fingers tightened in his hair. "Women are so important that they cannot make their own decisions. They are so important they cannot decide their roles in life. They are so important they can only be hidden away like livestock only to be brought out for breeding."

She saw the embarrassment on Morako's face and added, "But at least you spoke up for us, my brave hunter and feeler." She climbed on his lap and ran her hand through his cheek to his hair, twirling a braid with her finger.

They sat together in silence for a moment before he said, "I must be leaving soon. The council has sent out town criers to every corner of the village with instructions for the hunters to gather and for the women and children to also gather to be taken to their hiding place. The weavers have been entrusted with the task of weaving light to render the hiding place invisible as further protection."

"Oh, we have always been invisible before now," Imade said, but her joke was lost in the seriousness of the situation. Morako stood suddenly while she was still on his lap and she almost fell before he caught her.

"You see," he said with a grin, "for all your talk you still need a man to catch you when you fall. How will you fare in battle?" He kissed her to keep her from responding. "Don't forget to join the other women at the central town hall."

She shook her head and muttered under her breath: "You made us fall in the first place."

CONTACT

The invaders came at dusk when they thought the villagers would be winding down from the day's activities and least prepared to put up resistance. Or so they imagined. But the invaders had no way of knowing that their attack was expected and prepared for. They did not know of the resources available to Ife-Iyoku.

Three helicopters draped in camouflage green and carrying soldiers landed in the center of the village and the men inside them alighted. They were garbed in protective suits that left no part of their bodies exposed. They also wore face masks and carried oxygen tanks which they breathed through. They did not trust the air in the place which the rest of the world considered a dead zone. They had come fortified to resist radiation, though there was none in the village.

Their leaders signalled them, and they fell into formations, fanning out in twos, a team of almost 30 people all wielding rifles and tranquilizer guns—the one for dispatching and ending opposition, the other for subduing without termination. They had come for a quick snatch and grab but were surprised to find not a soul to confront. Two of the teams fanned out following some coordinates that they had already been given, to later make a rendezvous at their landing point. The commander stayed back with a team at the site of the landing where the helicopter stood. He coordinated the mission through the radio in his mouthpiece.

The commander signalled his men and they froze, listening, their weapons at the ready. The air was tense with the unseen. Then suddenly, one of the soldiers screamed. He had been pierced by a dark metal which burst through his chest. The spear seemed to have materialized from thin air, accompanied by a disembodied hand which promptly vanished after the havoc had been wrought. One of the soldiers reacted swiftly by firing his rifle into the spot where the hand had appeared from. Nothing happened. He stopped shooting. The men looked around furtively. Another soldier screamed as he felt a stab at his foot and as he fell to the floor, his throat slashed through.

The soldiers started firing rapidly and the clearing became a full-fledged war zone. Ghostly men, half seen before they struck, attacked from every direction. The soldiers fired desperately at the half-seen figures, hitting a few but losing four soldiers for every one they killed. Several dark, tattooed bodies of hunters, as well as more bodies of the soldiers, littered the ground.

The hunters materialized, stalking the soldiers and taunting them. The soldiers backed away without firing, realizing that they were low on ammunition. The commander and his few remaining men were almost backed against their helicopters now. The commander looked almost about to give the command for them to leave. But he seemed to be waiting for word from his other teams. And word came at last. The sound of screaming and shooting from running men came into the clearing, the last ragtag members of the other teams. A handful of men, wounded, and carrying some of their comrades rushed for the helicopter. They were attacked by the hunters who had assumed *anjayiyan okan*, the chameleon mind.

Meanwhile, as the hunters were embroiled in their attacks on the soldiers, another helicopter had landed, and the soldiers made their way to a location where almost a hundred women and children of Ife-Iyoku were hidden. It was an abandoned town hall in a section of the town which was now in disuse. Weed had overgrown most of the properties as the people moved to the centre of Ife-Iyoku. The squad of soldiers who alighted in the location of the hall moved carefully with their guns at the ready. They had received correspondence from the other teams as to the manner of attacks they had met and with that information, they had prepared themselves. They put on thermal and infrared goggles. These, along with coordinates and surveillance correspondences, guided them to a building in the center of this abandoned town.

Two of the soldiers conversed with themselves. Their equipment told them there was something here, but their eyes and senses saw and perceived nothing. They felt their way furtively around. The feel of their hands told them there were things about, even though their eyes told them otherwise. The leader of this team told his demolitions man to set the c4 charges. Whatever was hidden would be revealed when it was brought down. His man looked him askance. After all, the mission was a snatch and grab. But the mission had changed with the slaughter of their men. And they would not return empty handed and without having exerted any retribution.

Meanwhile, several dozen women and children hid in the hall and the light-weavers maintained the cloak that covered the hall. Ologbon communicated to them nonverbally that they would have to fight their way out of their hiding, if the situation called for it. If the men set off their charges several of them would die, the light weaving spell would end. And they would be taken. She mobilized the sturdier and younger women and older children. They had to drop the light spell weaving which rendered them invisible and create a distraction that would allow them to attack the soldiers.

The soldiers were setting the c4 charges on surfaces which they could not see but could only feel. And then, in a sudden instance of revelation, the building became visible, and seemed to materialize out of thin air. The soldiers stopped setting up the charges and moved into the building with their guns held out. But before they got into the hall, a blinding white light blazed from the building. The soldiers were blinded—some momentarily and a few permanently. Several people rushed the soldiers with knives and other weapons and some gifted ones with their gifts. The creeping tendrils of vines curled around the building came alive, wrapping some of the soldiers, stifling and choking them. This was the manifestation of the growers. The Lightweavers launched their attack with illusions, distracting the soldiers while others took them down. The Pullers attacked with fire and the elements, drawn from the neighbouring space.

But the tides soon changed. It was not long before the temporarily blinded soldiers recovered their sight and assumed battle formations. They were a trained military unit, and when they began to shoot at the resisting force, it was with merciless ferocity. The leader of the team eventually signalled them stop. Not one of the women and children of Ife-Iyoku stood in resistance. The soldiers could still fulfil their original mission of capturing the people. They pulled their tranquilizer guns. Several of the resisting soldiers still trained guns on the people who cowered in the building. They shot a few of them with tranquilizers and carried them. Many soldiers kept their guns trained on the rest of the women and children of Ife-Iyoku to ensure that they did not attack in return. Those left behind, who had been unable to join in the attack, were mostly the too old and infirm, and children. As they stepped out of the building, they heard a sound and found a child standing there, fist curled into a punch, and fierce and defiant look on his face.

It was Ake and he was trying to pull. The soldiers looked at him curiously.

"Perhaps he wants to join his folks," one of the soldiers said.

Ake raise a hand towards the soldiers. One of them raised his weapon and trained it on Ake, but the commander said, "Take it easy. He is just a child."

"They are all dangerous," another soldier said.

"Perhaps. But I don't think this one has the skills of the others."

"Should we take him too?"

"No, leave him. We have enough samples."

As they prepared to leave, Ake pulled a gust of wind. The soldiers turned to him. The grenade on one of their jackets came away and the pin was off, sparking an explosion which tore through the clearing, igniting the other explosives. The chain of explosions spread and by the time it subsided, not one person in that part of the town, both soldiers and people of Ife-Iyoku, was left alive.

✦ ✦ ✦

The commander and his men stood with guns at the ready, watching the soldiers stalk them. They were ready to depart. And then they heard the booming sound and the ground trembled beneath them. The hunters looked to the direction of the explosion, where their women and children were hidden. They rushed at the remaining soldiers in a blood curdling scream, assuming the *anjayiyan okan* and vanishing before the soldiers.

The commander signalled his men to cover for him as they retreated and mounted the aircraft. The invisible hunters rushed at the retreating soldiers and the soldiers started shooting. The hunters began to spasm between visibility and invisibility. One of the hunters was caught mid-strike, in the chameleon mind, appearing with his spear against a soldier's throat, about to run him through. He seemed frozen for a second; all the other hunters seemed caught spasming mid-movement, then the hunter collapsed on the ground, into air. The hunters all dissipated, into the air. The soldiers rushed into the two copters, started the engine and rose into the air.

Before the helicopter could manoeuvre its way out, a burly figure walked calmly through the throng of dead soldiers on the ground, his gaze on the rising helicopter. He was Oni the elephant man. He walked up to the last copter on the ground, lifted it with his hands and with a scream tossed it at the retreating copters. One of them swerved out of its path, but collided with another copter. The blades of the copters tangled, and they crashed down and exploded in a blaze. The last of the copters sailed away, carrying the ragtag band of soldiers who had failed in their mission.

Morako rushed to the venue of the explosion. He was the first to arrive and a scene of death and destruction met his eyes. The abandoned town where the people of Ife-Iyoku sought refuge had been blown flat by the explosion. The bodies of women and children, with soldiers scattered amongst them, lay strewn about. He fell to his knees and retched violently. He had nothing to throw up but bile. Nevertheless, his body protested the horrid sight. He sensed someone behind him and turned. His eyes widened in disbelief as he looked upon Imade.

"How?" he struggled to mouth but the words stuck in his throat. He stared at her for a while, then picked her up and wrapped her tightly in his embrace. Tears started in his eyes, and Imade cradled his head on her shoulder.

"I left to join the battle," she said. "I didn't believe in hiding out here while the men bleed and die to keep us safe. I only started coming back as soon as I heard the explosion."

She pulled back, taking his face and looking at him. "These people need not have died. If they had stood and fought with you, some of them might have died, or been taken. But they wouldn't all have died."

Morako shook his head. "I fear it is too late for that." He pulled her back and whispered, "Truly you are the last woman now."

THE LAST

The remainder of Ife-iyoku stood in the townhall. They were only men; Imade was the only woman in their midst. The Ooni was at the concluding part of his address.

"I have broken the sacred charge laid upon me by the gods and the ancestors. I led the marauders to Ife-Iyoku. I meant well for us, but I have nevertheless failed in my sacred charge to safeguard Ife-Iyoku. I promised the council of elders I would face judgement once we had successfully repelled the attack. Having failed at that too, it is time for me to face their judgement. I have committed the most heinous crime a member of Ife-Iyoku can commit. I have threatened the existence of the people. For my crime I am willing to face the ultimate punishment, banishment. I will go on exile and join the Mbadiwe. The council may elect another as Ooni to oversee the village activities."

"Father!" Morako shouted, unclasping himself from Imade and walking towards his father, his hands held out in desperate plea. "Please don't do this."

The Ooni looked at his son and shook his head. "It is already done."

"I have already lost mother," Morako said. "To now lose you too..."

The Ooni's voice was firmer than before. "I lost her too. But you must be strong, my son. Be a man, for there is yet more to be done. The survival of Ife-Iyoku lies in your hands now." He cast his glance in Imade's direction. Morako followed his gaze and saw she was his object of reference. She noticed them both looking at her.

The Ooni tapped Morako on the shoulder. "I know you will do well." He pulled his son in an embrace and whispered in his ear, "We have to survive."

Morako nodded. The Ooni pushed Morako back. Reluctantly, Morako resumed his place with Imade. The Ooni turned to the other chiefs. They avoided his gaze.

The Ooni raised his voice and said. "I will leave now. The duty lies on the council to pick a leader and decide other matters relevant to the survival of the remnants of Ife-Iyoku."

He took off the beads on his neck and hands and other accessories, the regalia of the office of Ooni. He laid them on the ground and started to walk out. Morako made to follow him. The Ooni looked at him sternly and said, "Do not shame me, son. I will not suffer your womanly ways on this day. Let me see no tears from your eyes." With that, he turned and walked away and Morako followed his father with his eyes while his legs stayed back with the remnants of Ife-Iyoku.

With most of the general issues settled and the final and private deliberations left for the chiefs to dwell upon, Morako and Imade got up to leave. But one of the chiefs beckoned on to Morako and both of them went over to chiefs.

"We want to speak to Morako," the chief said. Imade folded her hands and kept waiting. "We want to speak with him alone. We have matters to discuss."

"Now?" she said, as though the chief had made an unspeakable suggestion. "Can this not wait, seeing all he has been through?"

"Do not think to question us, young priestess. That you are the last of the women does not mean your place has changed. If anything, you should brace up more firmly in your place."

"And what is my place?" Imade said in a rising tone.

Morako looked at her warily and she smiled at him. He smiled back, and she left with a huff at the elders and the elders shook their heads at her. They turned to Morako.

One of the chiefs addressed him. "You and the young priestess have refused to be joined since you partook of the rites of passage, despite being smitten with each other."

"It is her decision," Morako said.

"You are the man," another chief replied. "There are ways to ensure she complies with your wishes. Few women with child will refuse a joining."

"It is not my way to secure compliance by such method," Morako said with an almost indignant tone.

"Well, it is not a joining that is required now," another said.

"What is required?"

"Children. You must get her with child."

Morako's face turned red. "That choice is not mine alone to make."

"We do not have the luxury of making choices. We do what nature demands of us."

An elder pulled him closer and said, looking him in the face. "She is the last woman. There is no child left in Ife-Iyoku. We are dying. She is the only way we can grow and survive. She is the only means to fulfil our sacred charge."

Morako rolled his eyes impatiently. One of the elders noticed it and said, "You have spent too much time with her without doing the things you should. Now you have started to imbibe her disrespectful ways. Do I need to remind you that she is the only woman left and our regeneration must be through her? If you do not want to do your duty by her, then someone else will do it."

Morako was outraged, but he said nothing in reply.

"It is what your father wanted," the elder continued. "It was his last wish."

Morako was quiet for a while, then stood and walked away.

One of the chiefs started after him but another chief dissuaded him.

"We have done all we can. The fate of Ife-Iyoku rests on their actions henceforth."

"Then we are doomed."

INTERCOURSE

Imade and Morako lay on his bed and she clutched him in her arms and rocked him gently.

He whispered, "I wish I was strong enough."

"You don't have to be. You just lost your mother and watched your father leave. It is all right to feel weak."

"A man cannot be weak."

Imade sniffed.

"The chiefs..." Morako began.

But Imade cut him off. "I will rather not talk about depraved old men."

He nodded. "My gift is enhanced. I can feel more now. It happened after the explosion."

They knew that what they had heard at the townhall was true: the mass deaths of the people of Ife-Iyoku people had affected its gifted survivors, leading to a massive upsurge in their powers. That was why there had been an upsurge in the powers of the hunters when they were in the middle of their mergers and they lost control of the chameleon mind.

"That was why Oni was able to lift the copter," Morako continued as if speaking from their thoughts. "He had never lifted anything that heavy before. He felt the jump and acted on it immediately. He was quick to action and decisive, just as a man should be."

Imade made no reply.

"This upsurge is good for people like him. It just means more strength. The hunters need more time and effort to master and work with the new gifts."

Imade said in a sleepy voice. "It is too bad that nobody grew a womb from the process. At least that would have been useful."

"As my gift is sensing emotions and feelings, the death of all these people at once impacted me greatly," Morako said. "I soaked up all the grief and agonies of the living and the dying. That is why I got to the venue of the explosion before everyone else. I could sense the pain immediately it happened. It blew a hole in my chest."

Tears gathered in Imade's eyes. "I had no idea. I should have thought of that. But I didn't feel any change in my own gifts. Perhaps mine too has increased. Maybe I should try raising the dead, if they have not all been buried by now." She caught the anxiety in his face and added, "You should not have kept this from me."

"I was trying to be a man about it."

"But that does not mean keeping these things to yourself and suffering them alone. That's what I am here for, to carry the weight with you. I love you. You know that, don't you?"

"I do. I can feel that too, and I long for you."

"Never you forget that, my *feeler*."

"I will never forget," he replied.

He was quiet for some time, thinking. Then he tried to shift. She did not budge. She was sound asleep in his arms.

In the morning, Imade woke up and stretched herself. For a while she searched her mind, trying to understand which of her experiences in the night had been real and which was dream. She touched herself and her countenance contracted. A cloud came over her face as the truth came upon her. She stood up and went outside. She found Morako standing, looking far away. She called him several times to get his attention.

He turned to her and said, "I can still feel the pain from the deaths. It is like an echo reverberating in my heart. It hangs like foul air in my lungs."

She waited until he finished, then she said in a voice cooler than her temper. "Morako, did we have sex last night?"

He recovered his wandering mind and nodded in reply.

She stood looking at him with creases in her eyebrows, like one trying to remember a dream. "Did you ejaculate inside me?"

His look gave an affirmative response.

"I have always told you that I don't want you ejaculating inside me."

"But you wanted it!"

"What do you mean, I wanted it? When did I tell you I wanted it?"

"You don't have to tell me. I can feel these things without being told. After you slept off, I felt your longing for me intensify. I felt you wanted everything I had to give. So, I gave you all."

"So you felt I wanted it and poured yourself into me? Have I not always told you that I don't want it, even if I seemed to? Why could you not just respect my wishes?"

"They were your wishes," he said.

She seemed to reflect on his answer, but something else was on her mind. "The elders put you up to this, isn't it?"

He shook his head. "They asked it of me and even all but threatened to get someone else to. But that was not why I did it. I wanted it myself and I felt you wanted it too."

"I did not want it."

"It is not a big deal," he said conciliatorily. "It has happened before."

"I wanted it then," she said, unappeased.

"If you don't want a child yet, there are herbs, like you've used before."

She was quiet for a while.

He tried to go to her and hold her, but she hit him in the face.

He held a hand to his face, more hurt by her behaviour than by the slap.

"I have told you before. I won't be used by old chiefs, by Ife-Iyoku, or even by you. My body is mine, to do as I please." She gritted her teeth.

"You said you loved me."

She opened her mouth to protest.

"You don't need to say it," he said. "I can feel it. And I can feel your loathing for me now."

She did not meet his eyes. And he knew. They were both quiet for a while, then she walked away. He just stood watching her departing figure like a lost soul.

Imade went to the hut of Chief Ududo and banged at it repeatedly until it was opened. The chief was surprised at seeing her.

"What is it this early, Imade?"

She folded her arms akimbo. "I have come to warn you. Tell your chiefs and old men that I will never be used by you and the people. I will not be a vessel for childbearing to satisfy your desire to populate Ife-Iyoku."

He looked at her quietly for a few moments, then laughed. "The boy has planted his seed in your soil, has he not? Who knew the boy could do it?"

Imade was shaking visibly.

"What is it woman?"

Imade strode towards him. He was oblivious of her moves, quite consumed in his mockery of her. He only became aware of her after she had reached out to grab his wrapper and tear it down. With the wrapper, she tried to throttle him. They danced around for some time before she caught hold of his arm, activating her gifts. He fell to his knees, retching and shaking. She had a hold on his neck now. He wheezed and struggled to breathe. She held on fast.

The old man would have died but for the intervention of some passing hunters who saw the altercation and rushed in to drag her off. She considered using her power on them, but she knew they would knock her out.

The chief gasped out after a couple of breaths.

"We were forbidden from telling you this as a way of protecting you," he said to her. "You were responsible for the death of all the children and other women of Ife-Iyoku through your foolish insistence on being strong and doing the work of the hunters. Bearing children is the least you can do to atone for your deeds."

Imade cocked her head, curious in spite of herself and her loathing for him.

"The footprints you made when you left the townhall doomed the occupants of the hall. The intruders followed it to find the hiding place of our women and children. All because you simply cannot be what you were made to be, a woman. I curse you!" He spat out the last sentence and spat a wad of saliva at her. She didn't bother to dodge it. Her eyes were red with anger. She turned and started to walk away, but one of the hunters went after her.

"Let her be," the chief said. "She has done enough harm."

She was assuaged somewhat by her attempt at killing Chief Ududo. As she walked away, she heard the chief telling the hunters to leave her alone, that she was the last woman and she mused to herself. "These people will never leave me alone. They will continue to work their evil designs on me unless I leave this evil place"

Three of the chiefs walked into Morako's hut. He was sitting with an expression of loss on his face.

"Morako! Morako!!" They called repeatedly.

He snapped out of his distant mindedness, his face losing its vacant expression.

"Have you seen Imade? She attacked a chief recently."

Morako looked uncomprehendingly at the chief.

"She is acting crazy. But that is not the issue. She is missing, and some tracks were found leading out of the village, towards the path that leads to the forest of fears. What do you know about this?"

Morako seemed to comprehend them, and the alarm started on his face. He shook his head, but more in apprehension than in answer.

"She would not actually be so foolish just to spite us, would she?" one of the elders said. "I told hunter Agabo to contact me here once they were sure it was her."

They looked at Morako who was now staring into nothingness. At that moment, a hunter knocked, and they opened for him. He brought news that Imade had indeed left the village for the forest of fears.

"Ah, has she?" Morako said and muttered to himself. "Even without the radiation, that forest has creatures that will kill her a thousand times over. And the Mbadiwe lurk there."

"Assemble a team," one of the chiefs said. "We must go after her immediately, for her own good and more importantly for the good of Ife-Iyoku."

The hunter nodded and left. The chiefs all stood. One of them barked at Morako. "Do you even care about any of this?"

"The boy has lost his mind," another chief said.

"It does not matter," Morako said to himself after they had left him. His face still carried the vacant expression of one who had lost in his mind before losing physically. "She hates me."

He stood up and opened a box and brought out a new wrapper. He unfolded it and tied it into a noose.

FOREST

It was getting dark in Igbo Igboya. Imade coughed and stumbled over a vine. She was starting to think to herself that maybe coming here was not such a good idea. She had no map, did not know where she was going and sooner or later the radiation would get to her. With her gift she had managed to slow its progress and how it affected her body.

She decided to find the path that led to the village of Ife-Iyoku. It was better to return with shame to the land she knew than to remain in this place of uncertain dread. But as she turned on her homeward path, she stumbled over something. She squawked in fright when she realized it was a body.

She thought, "It must be one of the exiled, the rejected." But the body looked rather fresh, like someone just coming from civilisation and not of one who had been living in the wild. Its hair was well braided. And he had multiple stab wounds all over his body and his throat had been ripped out.

She found the path she sought and hastened along it. Some steps along the path, she found several other bodies, mangled and scattered about. They were hunters; and now she realised the first body was a hunter's too. She wondered what could have killed a group of hunters in this manner. She knew that Igbo Igboya was a dangerous place where all manner of creatures haunted and hunted, but she could not think of any creature that could kill a group of trained hunters in this manner. It seemed as though the hunters had not hunted but had been hunted right from the onset. And then it dawned on her as in a revelation that these hunters had come from the village probably in search of her, the last woman.

The guilt of this realization, and the knowledge that she was the cause of these deaths, caused her to start running. Something caught her leg and she lost her footing, sailing to land on the ground in a painful thud. She groaned, rolling about in pain.

She opened her eyes to see a pair of yellow, feral eyes looking at her. The eyes were attached to an inhuman-looking face. Coarse, rough hair grew on the face, and its teeth were yellow and jagged, serrated as if they had been filed to look like fangs.

Drool dripped from its mouth; its arms were corded and rippled with muscles; and its hands were lined with sharp and dirty claws. She got a good look of the clawed hands as they swung at her face in a full-forced slap that sent her into blackness.

When she woke, she found herself tied to a tree. She struggled vainly against the cords, then gave up struggling when she realised she was tied too tightly. She screamed for help, hoping one of the hunting parties searching for her would find her. But no one came.

After a while she noticed that there were glowing yellow lights moving around the forest. These glowing lights, she realized, were eyes and not lights. She shivered and clamped her mouth shut. Her heart started to tremble. Was this the answer to her cry for help—these unknown eyes whose owner was likelier to devour than to liberate? And then the yellow eyes strayed away. They kept dancing out of reach, never quite coming close enough to keep her dread alive. It seemed to her that something was keeping the monsters at bay, if monsters the eyes were. Or the something was the monster and eyes the redeemer keeping other predators at bay. Tied up as she was, she found it difficult to focus on anything. The pain of the ropes around her and the sheer exhaustion of the hike took its toll on her and she dozed off.

She awoke to the blazing light of a torch on her face. She squinted at the brightness of the torch. As her eyes adjusted to the light, she noticed that the figure holding the torch held a calabash in the other hand. The figure brought the mouth of the calabash to her parched lips and she drank greedily and without apprehension. The water dribbled down her mouth and she coughed. She finally focused on the figure and saw with surprise that it was the Ooni.

"Help me please," she said in relief and nodded at her bonds. She tried to stretch out her hand as if already loosened. Then, when the help did not come, she noticed the Ooni smiling slyly at her as if she was a plaything for his amusement. His eyes were yellow, and he had a somewhat rough and feral look about him.

"Things have changed Imade," he said, and even his voice sounded different. "I am no longer the Ooni you knew. I am more than that here." He made a gesture and several figures crept closer. It was the figures with yellow eyes. She stretched her jaw and winced at the pain and taste of blood she had forgotten in her struggles and bigger worries.

She knew the figures were the Mbadiwe, the outcasts of several years ago. They had not died but evolved and adapted to survive in Igbo Igboya. They were strong, powerful-looking, and half-naked with only loin cloths and ragged apparel to cover their members. Some of them were stark naked. They had fierce glowing yellow eyes, powerful claws and jagged, serrated teeth. Their hair was dirty and matted.

She turned to the one she had known to be the Ooni. "I see you have found a new group to lead."

"A new group to control, not to lead," he said. He made a gesture and the creatures twisted and writhed on the floor. As he twisted his hands, the creatures reacted similarly, like puppets responding to their strings. Imade looked with disgust at both the Ooni and the hapless creatures under his control. He looked quite mad to her. His glowing yellow eyes had a focused, abnormal intensity.

She said, "It seems the radiation in Igbo Igboya does more than twist the body and kill."

The Ooni threw back his head and let out a loud laughter.

In a sudden curiosity, Imade asked: "How do you control them and what will you do with me now?"

The Ooni stopped chuckling and said in a more intense voice: "I have plans for the village of Ife-Iyoku. After the explosion, I benefited from the upsurge in power. I gained the ability to completely control the bodies of any of the gifted. I can do more than simply switch on and off their powers. I have implicit control now. These rejected ones have evolved beyond what any of them formerly were. Those who survived the radiation are stronger and faster than the hunters. You saw the bodies of the hunters, did you not?"

"So you killed them?" she said in disgust. "Why?"

"To test the power difference between the old and the new breed of hunters. And because they are not part of the new order I am building, they were unworthy to be in it and trespassed in coming here. They failed to obey the sacred charge by Obatala to survive."

Imade looked confused at his last words. One of the rejected held the torch aloft and it cast a frightening shadow of the Ooni as he paced and gesticulated wildly, explaining his mad plans to Imade.

She asked, "What of the sacred charge? What business is our survival to you now? Did you not exile yourself? Have you not become an Mbadiwe?"

The misshapen hunters began to yap and growl. A look from the Ooni silenced them. He turned to Imade and said, "The prophecy said that we were to survive till Obatala returned. That task is now my charge as the last man."

She smiled in spite of herself. "If anyone is the last of anything, I am the one."

"No," he said. "After the destruction and in the latest upsurge, I gained the power to control. A leader must have the power to control. Look at you. You are just a woman. Women cannot wield power. Nature chose us for that and chose you for the task of breeding. The jump skipped you, did it not? Have you wondered why?"

Imade was silent. In truth, she had wondered. Her face must have given that away. The Ooni's eyes blazed in triumph.

"It is because you are unworthy. You are unruly and unwilling. That is why any significant power skipped you. No power was gifted you with which you can escape your foreordained task. The only power you were granted was the power to produce and carry on life. Like the one you carry within you."

Imade started.

"Oh, you don't know it?" he said. "You are with child. That whelp of mine must have finally done something manly for once."

Imade was numb with disbelief. "It was just yesterday," she said aloud to herself. "How do you know I am with a child anyway?"

"You forget that I have the ability to control the gifted. All the gifted, even the yet unformed. I can sense the one in your womb. I cannot control it yet, but I can sense the part of it that makes up the gifts of Obatala. And do you wonder how? Conception was recent perhaps, just yesterday you said?"

Imade was silent.

He was thoughtful for a second then said. "I see now that I was wrong. The jump did not skip you; it merely affected you in other ways. It accelerated your reproductive processes. As the last woman you evolved in ways that would ensure our survival. No wonder I was able to sense the child. This one will be strong and will grow swiftly. It will have a place in our new world order."

Imade cast him a look of pure loathing. "I curse you and your new world order and this child that I don't even want."

"Don't be like that Imade. It is our collective charge to survive and ensure our continuity. Nature has merely imbued you with that ability. Now you may conceive in a matter of weeks. And this way we may populate Ife-Iyoku in no time. Though in all honesty I had planned to tear down what you know as Ife-Iyoku and rebuild the land with a stronger tribe. I wish to repopulate the land with these ones who have survived greater ordeal. We will keep you here after we destroy the old ones. We will keep you for ourselves and build our tribe with you."

He gestured to the rejected. "Cut her loose, she is with child now. But there is no reason you may not have sport with her."

One of the rejected slashed the rope with his clawed nails. It gave way immediately. Imade might have noted how sharp the claws had to be to cut those thick ropes so easily if she had not been preoccupied with all she had just learned. The Mbadiwe pounced on her. Three of them fought over her, leaving her in the dirt. They punched and clawed each other for the right to mate with her.

The Ooni cut in. "Enough! Must you act like dogs without my guiding voice?" He pointed at one of the rejected and said, "Now, you will go first." The rest slunk away and the chosen one pounced on Imade. She tried to fight him off, but these Mbadiwe were stronger than even the regular hunters, who were themselves stronger than regular men. He picked her up and slammed her on the ground twice and she stopped moving and surrendered. He started to rip her clothes off.

Just then, one of the rejected came and communicated something to the Ooni. He signalled to the rejected who was about to mount Imade. When the rejected did not respond, the Ooni used his power on it and it fell to the ground, contorting.

"I will not be disobeyed," the Ooni said as if in afterthought. Then after the rejected stopped writhing, the Ooni added, "I have just received message that the hunters of Ife-Iyoku are amassing and preparing to come into the forest for her."

Imade crawled gently to a tree and leaned against it.

The Ooni addressed her without looking in her direction. "They want to come and fight for you as the last woman. I think they now realize your value in the continuity of their tribe."

Imade merely looked at him from where she leaned. Her eyes had begun to turn a dull yellow.

"Imade!" the Ooni called. And when she still said no words to him, he said, "We will return for you when we have destroyed the others and made them Mbadiwe. Then we will burn the village and let all who will join the new order meet us here."

As they turned to leave, Imade shouted after him, "My name is Imadeyunuagbon. I have not come into this world by mistake. I was put here for a purpose. I shall not fall into the hands of the world or to its expectations."

The Ooni chuckled. "Invoking your full name will do you no good now. They are just words. You were born for a purpose, yes; and that purpose is to ensure the continuity of life. You have already fallen into my hand. And I will make you meet and conform to my expectations. Your name is meaningless. Imadeyunuagbon!" He spat after saying her name and motioned to one of the rejected. "Secure her."

That one moved to tie her back.

"Call the others," the Ooni shouted at the rejected tying up Imade.

A moment later, dozens and dozens of the rejected lopped from the surrounding forest. The Ooni raised his hand and started to walk towards the village. All the rejected let out yaps and barks, lopping and jumping after him.

IMADEYUNUAGBON

Imade reached for the knife she had strapped to her lap. It was the dagger that Morako had given her to protect her from the world, from himself, from all who meant her harm. She could cut herself loose and run. But there was nowhere to escape to. So, she did not even bother cutting herself loose.

She held the knife to her gut. She breathed in and out several times, her eyes bulged but unseeing, her mind unfocused despite the clarity of the decision she had made. She removed the knife from her throat, held it out as if to give it to a nearby person, took a deep breath. But before she could expel the breath, she returned the knife to her gut and plunged it in. The knife fell from her fingers and her lifeblood flowed freely down her body.

Her life fled fast as the blood poured from her gut. The universe spun to her quavering eyes. This was it, she thought in a mind that reeled, a morass of images and memory. The end of the last woman, with her child. This was the end to all the steps that evolution had taken to preserve Ife-Iyoku.

This was for her the finest moment, to triumph over her life and the lives of the race of Ife-Iyoku and all those who had thought to use and triumph over her. This tremulous end was all it took, this disorderly liquidation. Her mind wobbled as her blood filled the ground.

Then her heart stopped; her head went blank and the last woman in Ife-Iyoku expired.

◆ ◆ ◆

The dead woman's eyes opened. She was in a clearing in a forest but not the forest, still tied to a tree. The place had the surreal feel of somewhere that was, but wasn't. It was like a dream, but a dream in which she knew she was dreaming. The dagger was not there; the rejected were not there; she was all alone. Then she saw a woman walking to her.

The woman had not been there before. It was Mama Inkiru. She seemed to have walked through the space behind her, as if there was a doorway, but one she could not see. Mama Inkiru walked towards her; no, Mama Inkiru did not seem to walk, though she was moving. She could not see Mama Inkiru's steps.

She felt the blowing of a chilled wind, but Mama Inkiru's wrapper did not stir in the wind. Mama Inkiru sailed slowly to her, and now she realised why everything had seemed so hazy to her, why the wind had had no effect on her, why she had cast no shadow: Mama Inkiru was dead. Her throat became dry and she could not utter the cry that had formed inside her head. She watched Mama Inkiru as she stood a few steps before her.

"You killed us Imade," Mama Inkiru said in a voice more declaratory than accusatory.

Imade recoiled from her. They appeared to reach beyond the haze that clouded her thoughts. Mama Inkiru lifted her hand and slapped Imade across the face. Imade was too shocked to react to the slap, and before she could respond, Mama Inkiru walked right into her body and disappeared.

And now she saw several figures she had not noticed all sailing towards her in the same manner as Mama Inkiru, faces bland of expression. The next that came was her friend Sade. There was no recognition on Sade's face, and she said no words as she approached Imade, gave her a slap and walked right into her as Mama Inkiru had done. Next came Mama Igbinola and did the same as Sade had done. And so continued some other figures, some known intimately to her, others casual acquaintance. But each entrant into her body left her colder, so that when the last of the figures had slapped her and vanished into her body, she was shivering.

The last in the procession was Ologbon the Weaver. As Imade raised her bowed head to look at her—for she had delayed in her approach than the rest—she trembled more at recognition than from the cold in her body. The Weaver approached her and cupped her trebling cheeks with her palms, and instantly she felt warm, not from the Weaver's palm but from within. Tears streaked from her eyes.

The Weaver looked so unlike the other women; she did not have the dull, ashen look of the dead. She smiled warmly at Imade, and when she spoke, her voice was soft but firm. "My daughter," the Weaver said.

"I killed them?" Imade asked.

"Yes," the Weaver said. "Your actions led to their death. But if you hadn't done what you did, someone else might have brought about their death as well. Still, you are responsible for what happened. Through you the intruders discovered their hiding place and dealt death on all."

Imade slumped. The Weaver caught a droplet of tear running down her eye. It sparkled on her finger before dropping to the ground and being absorbed into the substance of the place.

"I failed everyone," Imade muttered.

"I did not say so."

"But I killed them."

"You did. But you did not fail."

Imade's mouth moved wordlessly as she struggled to form the thoughts into words. The Weaver answered her unspoken questions.

"That a thing ends badly does not mean it was bad, or not the required or needed end. And that an end is favourable does not also make it the required or needed end. Things have ended as they are meant to end."

Her voice became sad and hardened. "You did what you were bound to do and lived how your spirit led you to live. It is what it is that your life is their death. Life must yield to death, till it refuses, then it is death that must bow to life. You were the harbinger, the centre. You have taken their deaths into yourself, and now you must live for them."

She opened her arms. "Step forward daughter and receive your final reward. Step through and beyond the chains of your human coil, into the spirit one and serve finally the purpose for your pain."

Imade noticed that the ropes had loosened around her and they parted as she stepped away from the tree. The Weaver clasped her in her arms and kissed her. She closed her eyes in surprise, having braced for a slap.

The Weaver became a flame and Imade, still closing her eyes, sucked the Weaver into herself. Thus the Weaver's spirit and the spirits of all the dead women of Ife-Iyoku were absorbed in her. Her eyes were still closed, but she knew she was no longer in the spirit plane where she had but lately encountered the residue of the dead of Ife-Iyoku.

Imade felt in her the spinning of the machinery of evolution. The sky opened its huge and infinite mouth and began to pour rain to the earth. And in that moment, an Orisha was born in the rain of rejuvenation. And this is how Orishas are born: in moments when the universe loses control of its measured pacing. Only then are beings of immense powers born. The phenomenon birthing each Orisha differs, and that is why all orishas are different. In this new birthing, all of evolution poured into the old being and the butterfly spread its wings, a caterpillar no more.

Imadeyunuagbon's eyes finally opened. They glowed fiercely, with power.

The battle loomed at the boundary between Ife-Iyoku and Igbo Igboya, the people of Ife-Iyoku on the one side and the Mbadiwe on the other side. The hunters of Ife-Iyoku stood with their weapons out. And on the other side of the boundary, the Mbadiwe stood yapping and eager to savage those who had rejected them, and in command was the towering form of the Ooni. The two armies confronted each other. But before they attacked, something alerted the former Ooni and caused him to look back. And as he looked back, he saw a ragged, dirty female figure staggering towards them. Her eyes were wide open, and she was stained with blood and mud and her hair was wet from the rain.

The Ooni looked with profound disbelief. He reached a hand towards her, trying to seize her with his power. But nothing happened. She only smiled at him, her lips curling into a mocking grin. His eyes narrowed in anger and he pointed at her and screamed at his creatures: "Bring her to me!"

About a dozen of the rejected began to rush at her. The hunters of Ife-Iyoku also charged forward. As both sides sought to recover her, it seemed as if all the powers of evolution and of the material universe coalesced together in her form. Obatala was indeed returned, and he was female.

She inhaled and pulled at the earth. Sharpened spikes formed of earth and debris and wood tore forth and impaled and blasted the rejected rushing at her. The earth rippled further, throwing them off their feet. The hunters of Ife-Iyoku were too far away to suffer similar fate.

Two of the rejected made it through the blast and advanced with dogged determination. They were almost on her now. Imade glanced at them and pulled again; water and fire. Water from the air, a spear of ice. The icicle took the first Mbadiwe in the chest, tearing out his heart. She kept pulling. The other Mbadiwe was almost face to face with her now. She pulled the heat from the sun, guiding it and moulding it with her fist. A ball of fire that blew outward, consuming the second Mbadiwe. It rushed past her in flames, screaming until the flames consumed it, its screams blown away with the ashes.

She took a step towards the remaining Mbadiwe. They turned and fled, running sideways from her and from the hunters of Ife-Iyoku. They vanished into the forest. The Ooni watched in anger as they departed. He shot a look of pure hatred at Imade before he joined his fleeing servants. Some of the hunters wanted to chase after them, but Imade walked to the lead hunter and signalled him to call them off.

"Nature will deal with them," she said. "Nature is a woman now. And she will not let leave loose ends."

"Would you like to return to the village now?" the lead hunter asked.

"Morako," she replied. "Take me to Morako."

MORAKO

Imade stood tremulous. This was her first cause of disquiet since her transformation. She beheld Morako hanging from the mango tree in their favourite hangout spot. It was the very mango tree under which they had made love many times. Several villagers stood behind her to witness the scene and her reaction. The headhunter was beside her and other chiefs were chattering. Words like "taboo" drifted to her ears.

She raised her hand and the lot fell silent. She pulled fire from the sun. The rope caught fire and snapped. The body crashed to the ground. She walked to it. It was cold, although it had not been long dead. She held its throat. She healed and pulled. Heat went into him. His heart began to beat. A gurgling sound came from his throat, a sound of agony, as of one dying, struggling to breathe. Some of the villagers wailed in fright, some ran from her, some moved closer. She ignored them all. She pulled more intensely, and it seemed as if the air passed through him. His windpipe repaired itself and caught the breath, his brain cells were regenerated. And his eyes opened.

Imade stood with Morako. She did not tell him what she had done. She did not tell him how she had woken him with her power. The blood on her was not hers even though it came from her. She did not tell him how she had snuffed the life of her unborn child, ripping it from her womb, the blood running down her legs as she made her way to confront the rejected. She did not tell him what she felt about any of all this. He had not told her before he put the child in her, so she did not tell him when she removed it.

She only said to him: "I did not bring you back so I would be with you. What has happened cannot be undone. I brought you back because you did not deserve death, either as punishment or reward. You will live with what you have done. That is fitting."

He nodded, looking at her eyes. He understood her and accepted her pronouncement. They walked to the village town hall where everybody was gathered. She addressed them and told them she would be leaving the village. The village of Ife-Iyoku was no place for her any longer.

When she finished talking, one of the elders asked, "What of Ife-Iyoku and our sacred charge to survive? You are our last woman."

She was silent until the silence became uncomfortable. Then she said, "Ife-Iyoku will be open to the world again. You will have a way to go out. The radiation and corruption will be dealt with. You shall meet women of other races and use them to fulfil your purposes of procreation and survival, if they so wish to be used. But I will not be used for that, anymore. I am Imadeyunuagbon. I will not fall to the expectations of the world."

She turned and walked away as the heavens opened and the deluge of change poured forth.

ABOUT THE EDITORS

JOSHUA OMENGA (Line Editor) is an editor and writer of literary fiction. He is a practicing attorney who divides his time between the legal and the literary professions. He can be contacted via the following media: Email: joshuaomenga@gmail.com; Blogs: www.joshuaomenga.wordpress.com; www.lexgius.wordpress.com; Facebook: /JoshuaOmenga; LinkedIn: / joshua-omenga.

ZELDA KNIGHT (Publisher & Editor-in-Chief) writes speculative romance (horror, science fiction, and fantasy). She's also a cryptozoologist in training. Keep in touch on social media @AuthorZKnight. Or, visit www.zeldaknight.com. You can also email zelda@zeldaknight.com.

EKPEKI OGHENECHOVWE DONALD ("Ife-Iyoku, the Tale of Imadeyunuagbon") is a Nigerian writer and editor. He has been awarded an honourable mention in the L. Ron Hubbard Writers of the Future Contest, twice. His short story "The Witching Hour," made the Tangent Online Recommended Reading List and won the Nommo award for Best Short Story by an African. He has been published in *Selene Quarterly, Strange Horizons, Tor,* and other venues, and has works forthcoming in several journals, magazines, and anthologies. He has guest edited and co-edited several publications, including *Selene Quarterly*, *Invictus Quarterly*, and the *Dominion Anthology*.

He is a member of the African Speculative Fiction Society, Codex, the Horror Writers of America, the British Science Fiction Association, and the Science Fiction and Fantasy Writers of America.

You can find him on Twitter at @penprince_NSA and on his website https://www.ekpeki.com

Twitter: @AureliaLeoCo • Facebook: /AureliaLeoCo • www.aurelialeo.com

ABOUT THE CONTRIBUTORS

TANANARIVE DUE (Foreword) is an American Book Award winner who teaches Afrofuturism and Black Horror at UCLA. Her website is at www.tananarivedue.com.

NICOLE GIVENS KURTZ ("Trickin'")'s short stories have appeared in over 30 an-thologies of science fiction, fantasy, and horror. Her novels have been finalists fo r the EPPIEs, Dream Realm, and Fresh Voices in science fiction awards. Her work has appeared in Stoker Finalist, *Sycorax's Daughters*, and in such professional anthologies as Baen's *Straight Outta Tombstone* and Onyx Path's *The Endless Ages Anthology*. Visit Nicole's other worlds online at Other Worlds Pulp, www.nicolegivenskurtz.net.

DILMAN DILA ("Red_Bati") is a writer, filmmaker, and author of a critically ac-claimed collection of short stories, *A Killing in the Sun*. His works have been listed in several prestigious prizes, including a nomination for the British Science Fiction Association (BSFA) Awards (2019), a long list for BBC International Radio Play-writing Competition (2014), and a short list for the Commonwealth Short Story Prize (2013). Dila's short fiction and non-fiction writings have appeared in several magazines and anthologies, including *Uncanny Magazine, A World of Horror, AfroSF v3*, and the *Apex Book of World SF 4*. His films have won many awards in major festi-vals on the African continent.

EUGEN BACON ("A Maji Maji Chronicle") is a computer scientist mentally re-engineered into creative writing. Her work has won, been shortlisted, longlisted or commended in national and international awards, including the Bridport Prize, Copyright Agency Prize, L. Ron Hubbard Writers of the Future Contest and Fel-lowship of Australian Writers National Literary Awards. Eugen is a recipient of the Katharine Susannah Prichard Emerging Writer-in-Residence 2020. Publications: *Claiming T-Mo*, Meerkat Press. *Writing Speculative Fiction*, Macmillan. In 2020: *A Pining*, Meerkat Press. *Black Moon*, IFWG. *Inside the Dreaming*, Newcon Press.

NUZO ONOH ("The Unclean") is a Nigerian/British writer of African Horror. She holds a Law Degree and a master's degree in Writing, both from The University of Warwick, United Kingdom. Dubbed "The Queen of African Horror" by fans and media, Nuzo has featured on multiple media platforms as well as delivered talks on African Horror at numerous venues, including Libraries, the Warwick University Law Society and the prestigious Miskatonic Institute of Horror Studies, London. To date she's the only African Horror writer to have featured in Starburst Magazine, the world's longest-running magazine of cult entertainment. Nuzo is included in the reference book, "80 Black Women in Horror" and her writing has featured in multiple anthologies. Her short story, *GUARDIANS*, which won second place in the Nosetouch Press contest and featured in THE ASTERISK ANTHOLOGY: VOLUME 2, is arguably the first African Cosmic horror story published. She lives in Coventry with her cat, Tinkerbell.

MARIAN DENISE MOORE ("Emily" & "A Mastery of German") converted a childhood love of science into a career in computing analysis. Her love of literature led her to writing both poetry and fiction. Her poems have been published in periodicals ranging from Bridges to Asimov's SF. Her fiction has appeared in the anthology "Crossroads: Tales of the Southern Literary Fantastic" and the online journal, rigorous-mag.com. While Marian did some writing while attending LSU-BR, she began to first sharpen her skills in George Alec Effinger's UNO workshop and then in NOMMO Literary Society, led by the New Orleans writer and activist Kalamu ya Salaam. Her book of poetry, *Louisiana Midrash,* was published by UNO Press/Runagate in January 2019.

DARE SEGUN FALOWO ("Convergence in Chorus Architecture") is a writer of the Nigerian Weird. His work sometimes draws on Yoruba cosmology, Nollywood and pulp fiction. He has been published in *The Magazine of Fantasy and Science Fiction, Brittle Paper, The Dark* and *Saraba Magazine.* He haunts Ibadan and tweets @oyodragonette.

RAFEEAT ALIYU ("To Say Nothing of Lost Figurines") is a writer, editor and documentary filmmaker based in Abuja, Nigeria. Her short stories have been published in *Strange Horizons, Nightmare, Expound* and *Omenana* magazines, as well as *Queer Africa 2* and the *AfroSF Anthology of African Science Fiction* anthology. Along with Chitra Nagarajan and Azeenarh Mohammed, Rafeeat edited *She Called Me Woman: Nigeria's Queer Women Speak.*

Rafeeat is a Clarion West Graduate (2018). You can learn more about her on her website rafeeataliyu.com.

SUYI DAVIES OKUNGBOWA ("Sleep Papa, Sleep) is a Nigerian author of speculative fiction inspired by his West-African origins. He is the author of the highly anticipated Nigerian godpunk debut, *David Mogo, Godhunter* (Abaddon, 2019). His shorter works have appeared internationally (or are forthcoming) in periodicals like *Tor.com, Lightspeed, Nightmare, Strange Horizons, Fireside, Podcastle, The Dark* and anthologies like *Year's Best Science Fiction and Fantasy, A World of Horror* and *People of Colour Destroy Science Fiction*. He lives between Lagos, Nigeria and Tucson, Arizona where he teaches writing while completing his MFA in Creative Writing. He tweets at @IAmSuyiDavies and is @suyidavies everywhere else. Learn more at suyidavies.com.

ODIDA NYABUNDI ("Clanfall: Death of Kings") is a reader, writer, and blogger who works as a copywriter in the advertising world. He holds a bachelor's degree in communication from Maseno University and has two blogs: Cartastrophe about his enduring passion for cars, and Freeze Frame which takes a gritty look at various snippets of life usually through a supernatural lens. Odida has also published four short stories in *Manure Fresh*, which is a local Kenyan publication that showcases up and coming writing talent on sale in Nairobi.

Odida has been writing from as long as he can remember. He has also dabbled in many things including stints as a broadcast reporter, a butcher, and a beekeeper. He loves science fiction, fantasy, and horror, and has an abiding interest in African culture and folklore.

MAME BOUGOUMA DIENE ("The Satellite Charmer") is a Franco–Senegalese American humanitarian living in Brooklyn, New York, and the US/Francophone spokesperson for the African Speculative Fiction Society (http://www.africansfs. com/). You can find his work in *Brittle Paper, Omenana, Galaxies Magazine, Edilivres, Fiyah!, Truancy Magazine, EscapePod* and *Strange Horizons,* and in anthologies such as *AfroSFv2 & V3* (Storytime), *Myriad Lands* (Guardbridge Books), *You Left Your Biscuit Behind* (Fox Spirit Books), *This Book Ain't Nuttin to Fuck Wit* (Clash Media), and *Sunspot Jungle* (Rosarium Publishing). His collection *Darks Moons Rising on a Starless Night* published last year by Clash Books, was nominated for the 2019 Splatterpunk Award.

MICHAEL BOATMAN ("Thresher of Men") stories have appeared in places like *Horror Garage,* and *Weird Tales*, and in anthologies like *Dark Delicacies III: Haunted,* and *Sick Things*. He's the author of three novels, *Revenant Road, Last God Standing,* and *"Who Wants to be the Prince of Darkness?"* By day, Michael is an actor, currently co-starring on the CBS drama, *The Good Fight*.